T4-ALE-052

DESIRE'S DESTINY

"I swore to have you the next time I found you," Holt said huskily.

Tauren lifted her chin defiantly. "And I swore to have your black heart for dinner."

Her tart remark brought a full, lusty smirk to his arrogant face. "I take my vows most seriously. . . ."

He quickly closed the distance between them. His mouth lowered to hers slowly, testing, then tempting the lush promise of its warmth.

One ineffectual push against his hard chest was all she could manage; then her hands lingered there against his mesmerizing strength. His kiss deepened and he clasped her tighter against him, molding her soft coolness to his angular heat. She was drowning, unable to breathe, incapable of thought, of anything but feeling.

Slowly, tentatively, she returned his kiss, feeling that strange wanting that had alarmed her so in recent nights. Now she allowed it, explored it.

She pressed against him, wanting, needing—something more. Suddenly the vague night longings, the hungry achings of her ripe young body became focused, sharpened, and she knew that this was what she had craved these evenings in her maiden's bed. This was what she had been waiting for. . . .

HISTORICAL ROMANCE AT ITS BEST!
by Carol Finch

MIDNIGHT FIRES   (1487, $3.75)

Danielle should have been terrified when the handsome American captain who rescued her told her they were now in the midst of war. Instead, all she could think of was how his tight breeches clung to his thighs, and the way his eyes dwelled on her full red lips!

PASSION'S VIXEN   (1402, $3.75)

Mesmerized by his sensuous smile, Melissa melted in the powerful arms of her captor—the awesome woodsman, Jack. Having teased him with her charms, she'd leave him in the morning and pray he wouldn't betray her love . . .

RAPTURE'S DREAM   (1037, $3.50)

By day Gabrielle is the insufferable waif who tests Dane Hampton's patience; by night she is the phantom lover who brings him to the heights of ecstasy!

ENDLESS PASSION   (1155, $3.50)

Brianna was a sensuous temptress who longed for the fires of everlasting love. But Seth Donovan's heart was as cold as ice . . . until her lips burned his with the flames of desire!

DAWN'S DESIRE   (1340, $3.50)

Kathryn never dreamed that the tall handsome stranger was wise to her trickery and would steal her innocence—and her heart. And when he captured her lips in one long, luscious kiss, he knew he'd make her his forever . . . in the light of DAWN'S DESIRE.

Available wherever paperbacks are sold, or order direct from the Publisher. Send cover price plus 50¢ per copy for mailing and handling to Zebra Books, Dept. 1609, 475 Park Avenue South, New York, N.Y. 10016. DO NOT SEND CASH.

PASSION'S STORM

BY BETINA M. KRAHN

ZEBRA BOOKS
KENSINGTON PUBLISHING CORP.

ZEBRA BOOKS

are published by

Kensington Publishing Corp.
475 Park Avenue South
New York, NY 10016

First printing: June 1985

Printed in the United States of America

for Dors and Regina,
who taught me to love.

Prologue

Spring 1636
Somersetshire, England

The uncloaked rider of a foam-flecked black stallion shifted in his saddle and scoured the disordered courtyard of the rough country inn. In the heavy gray mist and lowering darkness, the black-clad rider and great horse blended into a single dark phantasm to the fear-filled eyes that watched.

"'Ere, sir," a small, half-strangled voice rasped loudly, straining to be heard. "'E cannot stop 'ere. 'Tis full. Go on along now, sir . . . please."

"Show yourself!" the rider commanded in a deep voice as he shifted further on his mount to ease the strain of his aching limbs.

A ragged boy skittered out from the corner of a low stone wall and startled the rider's horse as he grabbed for the bridle and began to tug. The rider worked hard to keep the huge jet steed in check and was about to rein off angrily when the urchin turned a mute plea upward from under a dirty mop of brown hair. As the rider eased atop the great horse, the boy succeeded in leading him to the shelter of a low, pole shed in the rear of the inn's yard.

Something in the big man was stunned by the swollen, misshapen face and bloodied features of one so young. He felt a prickling up his spine, a queer, but familiar feeling that years of harsh survival had taught him was anticipation as well as dread. Furtive glances about him and over his shoulders did not ease his mind that this was not a novelty from the highwayman's bag of tricks.

The tall rider landed softly on his booted feet, his back warily toward his mount as he peered into the gloom beneath the thatched roof. He removed his stark, high-crowned black hat and followed the beckoning urchin warily.

"What's this about boy?" His voice was low and full of the threat of action.

"Ye cannot stay. 'Tis not safe 'ere now," the boy swallowed convulsively and moved to peek around the edge of the shed toward the inn. "Please, milord . . . on yer way."

"What happened to your face, boy? What goes on here?" He grabbed the lad's shoulder to keep him from fleeing like a frightened rabbit, but the lad's thin arm came up to shield his face from the blow he expected. That telling movement wrenched something in the big man's belly.

"Who's beat you, boy? Your father?" he demanded. Something in that voice caused the boy to lower his arm and stare into the stranger's piercing eyes.

"Who!" The man's grip tightened on the lad's

8

shoulder, causing him to wince. He released the boy immediately, realizing that the boy's face had taken but part of the punishment.

"K-king's men . . . or they was. They'll hurt Polly or Meg again if I tell. Go away, sir . . . afore they find ye 'ere." The boy's voice trailed off into an incoherent plea of fear and tears.

The muscles of the big man's face tightened suddenly. The scene was now all too familiar, an aftermath of wars he thought long buried and on another shore. Before his mind's eye came the images of hungry and beggarly soldiers pillaging and scavenging in the wake of their killing. But this was England . . . and there was peace. . . .

"How many are there?" He understood now the anticipation he had felt earlier. A curious tremor of relief went through him. "Six?" Receiving only a shake of the head, he continued, "Five? Four?" A nod. There were four of them.

"Why did you not go for the bailiff?"

"'E wouldn't come."

The big man's face set hard. "This is Somerset land. How dare he refuse? Tell me and be quick about it!"

The boy haltingly related that four riders had entered the court, the night before, just at dusk. They had quickly taken over the inn's taproom, demanding and consuming large quantities of rum and ale. The innkeeper had been brash enough to require money before they were shown rooms for the night . . . in payment they had begun to beat him.

"Pa jus' lay there not movin' and they kept kickin' 'im. Ma kept us all in the kitchen till they stopped, but they come an' got Polly and Meg. Ma fought 'em and

9

yelled fer me to fetch the bailiff. . . ." The boy stopped, his eyes brimming at seeing it all again. "I begged. 'E wou'n't come. I come back an' Ma was battered up an' I could hear Meg screamin' upstairs. Later Ma slipped me out an tol' me not to come back 'til they gone."

There was silence as the boy closed his eyes against the brutal memory. Before he could draw breath again, the dark stranger was moving away from him with strong, sure movements. The man strode purposefully toward the front door of the beleaguered inn, his face a fearsome mask of resolve.

The door of the taproom slammed open with shuddering force, and in the opening loomed a figure of wrath, large and terrible, come to inflict justice on those who had abused this place. The man was tall and broad-shouldered, such that he had to dip his head to enter the pall-stricken room. His strange, green-brown eyes burned with righteous anger and his dark hair shone like a raven's wing, framing the harsh strength of his wrathful face. His sword was drawn in his left hand and swept the air before him, as if to purge it of fouling influence.

Those who might have benefited from a warning of the retribution to come were not present in the taproom. A short, graying woman was the room's only occupant, and she started fearfully and huddled deeper into the recess of the corner. From beneath swollen, bruised lids, she peered at the awesome apparition that filled the entrance. The stark, black garments of the tall figure lent a brooding hardness to his sharp-featured countenance.

"Merciful Father, please," she murmured from between swollen lips, "no more. . . ." But, fixing on

10

her, the wrathful visage spoke with a human voice, demanding the whereabouts of the malefactors. It was all she could do to raise one gnarled finger upward, indicating the sleeping rooms above.

Swiftly, the avenger mounted the wooden stairs, his face set with cold determination. The first room was empty but in the second, the big man found the object of his search. The chamber was chaos; torn ticking, broken porcelain, scattered straw, and emptied wine bottles lying about. His eye traced the ugly trail to the coarse wooden bed and straw-filled ticking where two forms lay silent, awaiting his presence to bring them to life.

One was the sprawled form of a well-muscled young man, wearing boots and little else, snoring with the fatigue of dissipation and drunkenness. But it was the other figure who drew his eyes and lit cold fires of rage in them. It was a young girl, or a cruel parody of one, beaten about the face and breasts and abandoned to a deathlike sleep. Her few remaining garments hung in shreds about her waist, protecting none of her crumpled form. Ugly weals darkened her limp legs and exposed hips. The avenger was motionless as he gazed at her, a form cruelly bereft of any womanly semblance or dignity. He exploded.

The toe of the avenger's hard jackboot found its target in the crotch of the sleeping outlaw with a viciousness born of outrage. The outlaw moaned, his voice rising into a gurgling scream, as he came fully awake and grabbed his injured parts, trying to rise from the pallet.

"Filth," the avenger spat, drawing the eyes of his victim to his sword with its ominous motion. "You will pay for your murder and abuse of the wench . . . with your life." Seeing a blade that was cast on the floor with the outlaw's crumpled doublet and shirt, he kicked it to the feet of the man whose eyes bleared through a reddened haze at him. The man stared disbelievingly, at the avenger.

"Pick it up," the big man growled, "so that you may die with it in your hand."

Swallowing convulsively, the outlaw dove toward the blade and lunged upward toward the ominous, dark figure that was the source of his pain. One sleek movement of the avenger's blade, dispatched the cur to the highest court of judgment.

The dying scream of the first outlaw had alerted the less besotted of the two in the next room. When the avenger entered, they were both on their feet and fumbling with their breeches although still feeling the effects of their long debauch. The movement in the doorway galvanized the nearer one into action and he cast quickly about for his blade, filling his hand with the comfort of cold steel. As the avenger's blade struck, the outlaw barely had time to parry the thrust, and he felt a cold hand squeezing at his innards, shaking him bodily with the ferocity of this contest for death. In four strokes, with no words exchanged, the second outlaw lay on the rough planking of the floor, his life ebbing out with each pulse of his blood.

The third rogue, eyes wide from witnessing the fate of his comrade, laid to with his blade, forcing the avenger back into the narrow hallway with his harried assault. His cohort's life had bought him time and now the third criminal fought viciously in the cramped quarters, spewing curses under his breath. He would

12

never know the identity of his executioner, but he would remember through eternity the eyes before him, eyes in which burned the very fires of hell itself.

Their blades crossed at the hilts and they were face to face in uneven struggle. Sweat poured from the outlaw's face and ran torturously downward toward his rum-stained collar. The avenger's breath was hot upon his skin. When they broke apart, the outlaw sprang back only to plunge anew at his attacker, gambling all on that one thrust—and losing. The blue steel of the avenger's blade tore upward through his chest and then was gone. The cur fell back against the wall and slid down into a heap, leaving a scarlet path downward on the dingy wall to mark his passage. Even in death his face would bear his surprise.

Four, there were four . . . one yet to be found. The avenger stood in the dim passageway, his chest heaving as his mind charted his course. The blood pounding in his ears abated and cooler thought prevailed. Killing another would serve no further purpose. He pushed through the next doorway with lowered sword and eyes glittering with tamed fury. The fourth brigand stood with back against the wall, blade in hand. The outlaw's muscles tightened at the crimson dripping from the dark specter's blade. His sword came up nervously in anticipation of the avenger's rush.

"Raise your blade against me and you will join your comrades in hell," came the ragged, deadly voice. "I am through killing, though you will receive your punishment." The growl in the avenger's throat and the dangerous gleam in his eyes made resistance impossible. The outlaw's weapon clattered ignominiously on the planking of the floor.

13

"Downstairs!" After a stunned moment the outlaw hastened to comply, afraid to believe he would fare better than his companions.

In the taproom below, the battered woman hugged the boy ferociously and listened fearfully to the sounds of death above her. Shock immobilized them both as the avenger backed slowly down the stairs with the fourth of the murderers nearly skewered on the point of his blade. The avenger grabbed the neck of the murderer's shirt and pushed him before the astonished pair. He snarled and pushed the criminal down on his knees before the wondering victims.

"Beg for mercy, pig!"

The woman stared uncomprehendingly between the criminal and his judge, still stunned by the accumulation of horrors she had experienced. It was only within her power to nod dumbly as the murderer wheedled and begged pathetically, not realizing that in doing so she herself had spared the wretch's miserable life. For had she been of more vindictive mood the avenger might have recanted his resolution not to kill again.

The dark avenger dragged the wretch to his feet and raised his sword again, with a voice low and full of malice. "Your life is spared by these, your victims. But you will bear evidence of your crimes before you all the days of your life." With a swift stroke of the blade, the tip of the man's nose was severed and before he could react or withdraw, his left ear was gone completely also. The outlaw let out a gurgling scream as he bent double and clutched at the gaping holes in his face and at the side of his head. The avenger shoved his weaving wailing form toward the door and outside, where it collapsed into the dirt of the courtyard.

14

"Begone filth," the avenger spat, "and tell all you see that there is justice in Somerset again."

The man struggled to rise, a strangling, weeping sound filling the air as he ran haltingly to where some horses were tied at the end of the stable building. Grabbing the mane of one of the animals in his blood-soaked hand, he scrambled aboard and was away like the hounds of hell were upon him.

The avenger looked back at the lad and the woman in the doorway. "There are graves to dig."

That night an eerie peace had settled over the inn. The boy and his mother brought a loaf of hard bread and a flagon of dark ale to the black-clad man who sat brooding before their fire. The woman nudged her son as they stood by.

"What be yer name, milord?"

The man turned from his food and regarded the boy with something akin to sadness. "I am no lord, boy." His voice was rich and deep, now relieved of its burden of anger.

"Then ye best be leavin'. The bailiff will hear and come for ye. We thank ye for all ye done." The boy's head bobbed respectfully.

"For all ye done," his mother echoed. "Without ye come, there'd be more graves to dig. I 'ave me girls, God save 'em."

The avenger's eyes darkened at the mention of the woman's daughters. For the rest of their lives, they would bear scars of body and mind from this foretaste of hell.

"I shall stay. This is an inn and I have need of

15

lodging." He saw the exchange in their eyes and knew their concern. "You need not fear I will bring rebuke upon you because of what I did. I but meted out justice as God saw fit to allow me to do. None will question the decision of the new overlord of Somerset."

His face was flint hard again. "If by default of proper authority there is no justice, then let one man's will suffice." He stood and stared into the flames before him, speaking now to the wondering pair. "You will do me this courtesy . . . when the bailiff does come, tell him Holt Reston is the man he seeks. . . ." He turned from them and made his way upstairs quietly to fall into a deathlike sleep of exhaustion.

Mother and son exchanged looks, wondering if the man be mad or if he be an avenging angel come to aid them. What man had the power to set himself up as law and justice in the Duke of Somerset's lands? Again they thought of his skill with a blade and his concern for the welfare of this house of strangers. If there were such a being . . . it would be he.

.

.

One

October, 1640
Northumbria, England

Dove gray skies matched the gentle sadness of the autumn landscape. The soft rains that washed away the color seemed also to have washed away the hope of the people for a quick, peaceful settlement to the conflict that now caught them between opposing faiths and governments, Edinburgh and London. The people knew little of the grand designs of lords, archbishops, and ministers, of canon law or political representation. The Scots had invaded their lands, unopposed by the king's soldiers or cavaliers, and they had come to understand well the pain of occupation by the Scottish brigades. The bans, curfews, floggings, these they knew. They had watched powerlessly as the tides of tartan swept over their lands and set in turmoil their way of life, their hope dwindling as their urgent pleas to London went unanswered.

Now even nature conspired to add to their hopelessness; the harvests had been poor and the tribute had been high. Every household prepared to meet the scarcity of the barren season ahead, and the coming of winter seemed fitting to the mood and situation of England's far North Country.

But there was one for whom the drab skies and deadness of the fields were a welcome relief from the darker pall that had spread itself over her life. She had fled her home into the cool, comforting gray of the weather and was reluctantly returning now across the barren fields.

The chestnut-haired maid was wrapped in a great, hand-knit shawl that only partly protected her from the bite of the rising wind. She walked slowly up a rise and found herself overlooking the small cluster of modest stone and half-timbered buildings. Plopping unceremoniously down atop a hummock of faded grass, she pulled the shawl tighter about her and shivered as she pulled her knees up against her chest and wrapped them too. She rubbed her cold-blushed cheek against the soft woolen of her stark black gown. Watching, but only half seeing the scene below her, she thought guiltily of the incident that had sent her flying from the house.

Aunt Veldean had commented that sooner or later a new bishop would be appointed, most likely when the troubles were over, and then they would need to make other plans . . . find other lodgings. The house and stables would be needed for the church's new man. Tauren Wincanton had turned on the venerable old lady in a rage and had bitterly declared what she thought of such a church—one that made no provisions for the widows and orphans of those who had died in its service.

"Others might be pushed about like sheep and doddering old fools, but I shall not!" She had seen the old lady's spine straighten and her lips tighten at the barb and instantly knew regret over her unbridled tongue and the horrible damage it could inflict on those she held most dear. Not waiting to see the pity in her aunt's face or the rebuke and love in the old woman's ageless eyes, Tauren had grabbed her thickest shawl and fled the house, knowing all the while that she could not flee the real cause of her torment—the grief she bore inside her for her father.

A long, shuddering sigh welled up from deep within her. The Bishop of Greaves, Edward Wincanton, had been truly a man of God; righteous, loving, and strong. He had deserved to be revered and honored, not packed off to the cold exile of the north moors to serve one of the poorest of England's bishoprics. Even so, he had never complained of his lot; he had chosen it and found joy in this life of service and in his children.

"He deserved better," Tauren murmured, daring her own eyes to let another tear fall. "And he deserved a better daughter . . . one who was gentle and sweet, a comfort to him, a lass of purity and meekness—not the stubborn, willful child that was born to him." She was passion and opinion, fire and honor, unable to bear falsehood and arrogance . . . and unable to mold herself into that pale, perfect, maidenly being that might have comforted and supported a true bishop of the Church. She loved her father with a worshipful devotion and tried repeatedly to change; but there was always one injustice, one stupidity too many for her to bear, and then her passionate nature reasserted itself, twice more virulent for her attempt to deny it.

"Ah, Tauren, lass," her father would say, wiping the tears of mirth from his eyes, "there's not another to match the trueness of your heart nor your sense of justice. If only you knew how to temper your words and gentle your will with patience." He would take her in his arms and she would hear an irrepressible rumble in his chest as he assured her, "It will come, lass . . . it will come." The weight of her own conscience often had conspired to bring disappointment to his eyes and now on her windy knoll she saw that look one last time and vowed to see it never again.

He had died as he had lived, serving others. He rode the gray, damp mists of the moors, ministering to the parishes that were banned from attendance at mass by the stern Presbyterian invaders and in so doing he had contracted lung sickness.

An unruly tear slipped from Tauren's long, sable lashes, defying her will more surely than any mere mortal dared. Her father would have the daughter he deserved. If he could yet know what transpired in the mortal world, she would make him proud of her. She would gentle herself and care for her younger brother, Revan, as befitted a young woman of her station, if it killed her.

Rising and squaring her shoulders, she breathed deeply of the earthy smell of the damp grass and earth about her. Slowly she descended the hill to her home to take up her new life.

Tauren Wincanton, eighteen and now a woman fully grown, stepped into the kitchen of her home and instantly found herself shushed, brushed, and summarily ushered along toward the parlor by their cook. When she paused outside the door, the stout, formidable Laraby shot her a meaningful look and jerked her head authoritatively toward the door before them.

With a last smoothing hand on her wind-ruffled hair, she drew a deep breath and turned the creaking handle to enter the main parlor.

"Here is Tauren now," Aunt Veldean was saying crisply in a tone that clearly conveyed her annoyance.

All eyes were upon the comely form of the chestnut-haired maid who stood, wide-eyed, in the doorway. Her own eyes, like great pools of sky, stared incredulously at two Puritan-clad strangers, and a rush of angry, enchanting color swept upward across her creamy throat to the perfect skin of her heart-shaped face. Her stark black gown was drawn taut across full breasts and fit snugly about her waist before dropping provocatively over her unpadded hips. The wind had teased wisps of that sun-burnished mane from her plain chignon and they curled lovingly about her slim neck and temples. She was freshness and spirit, woman and innocence, determination and softness all at a glance.

Momentarily struck dumb by the sight of them, she could only think that the Puritan jackals had invaded her home once more, and she felt heat pouring through her veins. Her narrowing eyes took in everything about the men quickly; their solemn black doublets and breeches; their stiff, linen collars devoid of ornament; their plain, polished jackboots; and especially their bold scrutiny of her. She turned to Aunt Veldean and was confused by the woman's meaningful stare in the awkward silence.

"A lovely young maid . . . such fairness is hardly rivaled even at court." The taller of the men spoke and bowed authoritatively from the waist, still examining her openly. The shorter, stouter visitor copied the gesture.

"These gentlemen have come from the duke . . . with an authorization." Aunt Veldean labored to her writing table near the small window and produced a leather packet of documents which could be seen to bear official seals and markings.

Tauren's gaze flickered back and forth between her aunt and the tall Puritans. She recognized the old lady's well-disguised distress.

"The duke? An authorization? . . ." Tauren's melodious voice was full of puzzlement. Why did Aunt Veldean not order the scum from the house and be done with it? How could they have anything to do with her uncle, the wealthy and powerful Duke of Somerset?

The taller Puritan thumped his thigh impatiently with a pair of incongruously scarlet gloves as he approached her. "I am Belford Chester, Baron of Greers, and emissary from His Grace, the Duke of Somerset. His Grace sent me to see you and your brother southward to his estates now that you have been made his wards by the king. I am accompanied by Calder, the captain of the duke's guard."

"Wards?" Tauren breathed as the impact of his words seeped through to her. "Wards of the duke . . . my uncle?"

"You are the children of his dead brother; His Grace felt it his duty to assume guardianship—a right none could dispute. It is all settled, as I have explained to your aunt. There only remains for you to pack a few of

22

your belongings and we must be on our way at once."
His sidelong glance at Aunt Veldean hinted that he was
not yet assured of her cooperation, proof that her
legendary manner remained intact under the assault of
time.

"Surely you can find better sport than this," Tauren
scoffed bitterly, her resolve of only moments before
sorely tested in the face of this challenge. "You believe
us gullible enough to accept such a story and to
accompany two Puritan henchmen into God only
knows what?" Her eyes were suddenly flashing and her
ripe lips reddened with her cheeks.

Lord Chester's surprise turned blatantly to irritation, and he turned on Aunt Veldean. "Madam," he
demanded, "please explain the urgency of our mission
and its authenticity—of which you must have no
doubt."

"It appears in order, Tauren. And it is not totally
unexpected. These gentlemen hazarded life and limb,
appearing in this false Puritan guise, to fetch you and
Revan. They carry letters of authority, one from the
king himself. You must settle it in your mind, child, this
is to be. Your future is with your uncle, the duke."

Tauren felt a smarting at the corners of her eyes and
grappled with her unruly senses to retain some outward
semblance of calm. "We are in no immediate danger
from the Scots and Puritans now; since my father's
death they have ceased to pay us mind altogether. We
need no favors from the duke or anyone else."

"It was your father's stubbornness and poor judgment that brought you here to this godforsaken
wasteland at the start and it was his imprudence that
kept you here long after it ceased to be safe. In rejecting

23

his title and rightful duty, Edward Wincanton was derelict in his duty to you—a situation the duke must now remedy!" Lord Chester's face had taken on the hue of his lordly gloves and he barely held himself in check.

"No!" Tauren breathed, clutching her hands together as if to constrain their impulsive actions, and turning to her aunt, "Tell them we won't go. . . ."

"Tauren! You forget yourself." Aunt Veldean drew a hard breath and steadied her frail frame on the writing table. "Edward instructed me to write the duke immediately of his death and to see that you and Revan were placed in his care." She beckoned Tauren closer and took the girl's cold hands, drawing her nearer the fire and away from the visitors.

"It was a deep sorrow to him that he had no dowry to give you and he worried what might become of you. We talked of it sometimes at night after you were asleep. He made me promise to see you into his brother's hands. I honor that pledge, though the keeping of it gives me no pleasure."

Tauren raised tear-glazed eyes to the old woman who had been teacher, guide, and judge for her and her brother since she could remember.

"I can give you nothing more. Your destiny is elsewhere. I will not long remain after you have gone. I have seen the signs. . . . You and Revan must do your duty as God reveals it to you."

Tauren stared at her unbelievingly, stricken by the finality in the old woman's words.

"The duke has installed Revan as Marquess of Wells by proxy. There is no turning back. You must be with him, Tauren, as you have always been. He will be duke someday, perhaps soon."

Tauren's anger was replaced in full by astonishment. It was really happening. They had talked about it—jested about it—Revan, a duke of the realm. But it had all seemed a jest to them in their remote home on the north moors, a tale to build cloud castles from. Now it had come true; Revan was named heir to the Duchy of Somerset. She would be sister to a duke.

The door to the parlor flew open, causing the room's occupants to snap their heads about in surprise. A lanky lad of twelve years rushed in, his eyes sparkling with excitement and exertion.

"There's a real coach outside!" he exclaimed, stopping as he spied the two forbidding men in Puritan garb. His young brow furrowed beneath his unruly mop of brownish hair and his eyes sought first his aunt's and then Tauren's face.

There was no further time for deliberation—no time to prepare. Tauren felt Aunt Veldean's tired eyes looking at her expectantly, and she felt the convincing pressure of her recent vow. She swallowed hard and stretched out her hands to take Revan's.

"Revan, these men are emissaries from our uncle, the Duke of Somerset. They bear most exciting news. . . ."

25

Two

Tauren sank back against the seat of the coach and moaned, thinking that the conveyance must be padded with rocks. Her whole body throbbed and ached from three days' rough jostling and bouncing in the clumsy, unsprung coach. She arched her back as furtively as possible, feeling the gentle pressure of her brother's sleeping head against her shoulder.

"Are you tired, milady?" Calder asked, drawing a disapproving frown from the lord. "I could fetch another lap robe or change seats with you."

"Nay," she responded hastily, "I . . . am fine, thank you. You are most kind." Tired though she was, she would not let the duke's men see it, nor let them think her soft and weak. For all their godly penury, her father had taught them to be proud of their heritage and to bear discomfort with grace. Revan's head was heavy against her shoulder and his large, boyish hand gripped hers even in his sleep.

Tauren turned her eyes and thoughts to the two men before her. As their journey progressed the tall, disdainful lord grew more generous with his sly, courtly smiles and with his helping hands. Tauren felt suffocated each time his bold gaze fell on the neck of her bodice. She could not have known how heartily the imperious baron now regretted his own recent marriage to the widow of Belmargen.

A fair young virgin, he mused silently, one to warm a man's bed and blood on a cold winter's night. The duke surely would have entertained my offer for this Tauren, had I waited. Bad timing . . . the ruination of many a delectable possibility. He turned his mind to the intimate possibilities inherent in such a journey, rejecting them one by one. She was a prize worth risking for, but not worth risking all . . . no woman was worth that. It would be a true exercise of will to keep from setting hands to her, and it had been far too long since he had troubled his willpower about anything.

Tauren heard for the hundredth time Lord Chester's sharp sigh of irritation and it grated upon some hidden nerve. She roundly detested him and in spite of her vow to gentle her nature, this feeling was being transferred to the man he represented as well.

The other man, Calder, displayed few of the unpleasant affectations Lord Chester prided himself on and was shown little consideration by that exalted gentleman. Though shorter than the lord and of heavy frame, he moved with astonishing agility and seemed formidable with his weather-bronzed face and graying temples. He wore a small beard, neatly trimmed, and his brown eyes sometimes twinkled with what Tauren imagined must be some private amusement as they fell on her. But, strangely, she was not offended by it.

Calder too had feasted upon her abundant charms, though for different purposes. There would be another in the shire who had interest in the outcome of this venture and he wondered about that one's response to this maid. A lass unschooled in allurements and already mistress of them all. Innocent she be, she knows not what she does to men. No mere pert face or comely turn of ankle; she'll take a strong rein . . . and lead some man on a wild ride. He frowned, considering what report he would make to the overlord. What would the powerful overlord do if he knew the lass to be a great beauty, potentially a rich prize? The combination of passion and vulnerability in this girl appealed to Calder's protective instincts in a way none had before. Perhaps I'll keep the lass's true value to myself yet awhile, he thought, till her future is secure.

Hearing the nobleman's sharp sigh beside him, Calder smiled a slightly crooked smile in recognition of the conflict that produced it. He would see her safely through.

When their coach pulled into the yard of a roadside inn at dusk, it was inundated by a sea of scarlet, and exuberant shouts and laughter were everywhere about them. Calder bounded from the beleaguered coach and with a few terse orders delivered in a commanding tone, restored his men to order. A compliment of the duke's soldiers had awaited them at this inn and would accompany them the rest of the way to Lindengreen. Only now did Tauren fully realize, from the look of relief on Calder's face, the true danger they'd been in.

In their modest chamber that night, Revan fell

quickly asleep and Tauren watched by the light of the fire as he slept. He would have to battle his very boyish nature in the days ahead in order to become the nobleman and leader that his future would demand of him, and she mused on how valiantly he would try.

She would be there to see to his welfare, his future, as it seemed she had always been. Whatever jealousy the seven-year-old Tauren had felt for her infant brother had vanished on that distant day when she had seen the dog with the foaming muzzle and bared teeth stagger into the dusty yard of the rectory. The animal's madness-glazed eyes were fixed on the nearby basket where the infant Revan slept. She had crept to the untended basket, grabbed Revan, and run to the open door of the kitchen just ahead of the deadly, snapping jaws. And from that time forward, Revan was hers; she played with him, made rag toys for him, shared her sweet treats with him. When their mother, Arden, died a year later, it seemed natural for Tauren to take him further into her care; she taught him letters from her slate, slept with him when he cried out in the night, and kept his mischievous secrets.

Revan turned in his sleep and she reached out to stroke his lustrous brown hair. He was lanky and taller than most lads of twelve; bright and sometimes too adventuresome. Before the invasion he had ridden with his father about the parishes, observing keenly the respect and affection the bishop commanded from those he served. Those memories would have to be sufficient to see him to manhood.

Shivering and drawing the heavy quilt tighter about her, she slipped into bed and snuggled over against her brother to share his warmth. She wondered uneasily what her new role in the duke's household would be. Was it likely that the duke would be of a mind to supply her with a modest dowry? In a new place, with different connections, there might be a better chance of finding a husband suited to her education and station. This thought gave her something to cling to as she drifted off to sleep.

Ten days after their journey began, the coach carrying the young Marquess of Wells and his sister pulled through the gates of Lindengreen long after the sun had set.

"Look at those doors," Revan whispered, his voice thick with sleep, "they're huge." He gripped Tauren's hand tighter while she nudged closer to him, feeling the same wonderment.

They paused on the massive stonework of the steps leading up to the imposing brassbound oak doors. Lord Chester checked his austere Puritan garb and Tauren found herself sending a smoothing hand downward over her modest black woolen gown.

Following the baron inside, they were astonished by an array of colors so vivid and furnishings so elegant that Tauren was caught speechless, gawking like a child at county fair. They stood in a large hall, ringed above on three sides by a gallery from which a massive staircase descended. The walls were plastered and hung with rich, vibrant tapestries whose themes were echoed in the intricate moldings and friezes of the ceilings. Shades of brilliant blue, mauve, and the green of the forest mosses flowed over chairs and windows in watered silks, satin brocades, and lush velvet. Persian carpets cushioned their feet against the cold gray marble of the floors, and above them an exquisitely wrought French crystal chandelier poured forth a lavish flood of warm light. In all her life, Tauren had never imagined, much less seen, so elegant a room. Her mind stumbled to consider what visual treasures the other chambers of the great house would hold. This was a palace . . . the duke must be a fabulously wealthy man.

A small, graying woman with clear blue eyes and an air of authority appeared from nowhere and approached their weary party. Her fresh, white cap and crisp appearance belied the late hour and caused Tauren to again smooth her skirts beneath her modest cloak. Tauren noted that Lord Chester did not bow at her approach and accepted a polite nod from her. She was a servant, then.

"Good evening, Mrs. Murdock. As you see"—he gestured toward his charges—"I have fulfilled my mission. I deliver them into the hands of His Grace in all humility." Tauren choked down the urge to scoff, for his lordship's stance at that moment was pure hauteur.

"Indeed, my lord, you have done that." Her voice carried a measured respect. "His Grace is somewhat indisposed and will be unable to see you. I have orders to see to his lordship and the lady." Tauren detected a tone of mutual dislike between these two minions of the duke, and it marked Mrs. Murdock as an ally in her mind.

"Of course, your lordship is invited to stay the rest of the night; rooms have been readied. The duke did not wish to see you make the long trip back to Enderfield

31

this night."

So, Lord Chester was given to know that since his function was fulfilled, his presence was no longer required . . . or desired. The duke had dismissed him summarily, without even an audience. Tauren marked this mentally. To have risked so much and to have come so far . . . to be sent away like a common errand boy . . . what kind of man was their uncle?

"I am most grateful for His Grace's . . . thoughtfulness."

With a nod to a liveried servant, Mrs. Murdock turned to Tauren and Revan, who felt suddenly quite conspicuous in their plain woolen clothing and rumpled state. "You will come with me, I shall show you to your chambers myself."

Following her up the grand marble staircase, Tauren managed a backward glance at the hapless Lord Chester being led off in another direction by an efficient houseman. They would need allies in this place.

Mrs. Murdock showed Revan to an elegant suite of rooms done in heavy, wine-colored velvets and brocades, and introduced a dour-looking young man as his new valet. Then she proceeded far down the hallway of the east wing to a much smaller set of apartments, decorated femininely with hand-painted violets on the wallpaper and violet and gold silks.

"But it's so much smaller than mine." Revan stood in the doorway of the bedchamber scowling. Before Tauren could warn him with a look, he turned on Mrs. Murdock with an idea of trying out this new status of his. "We shall trade . . . Taurie may have the big rooms—"

"Revan!" Tauren interrupted, fearing such boyish candor might be counted against him. "It would be ungracious to amend our host's arrangements." She turned to Mrs. Murdock, managing a tight smile. "We are aware there is much to learn of our new way of life."

The sincerity in Tauren's voice and face softened something in the older woman's countenance. "You must be tired. I shall escort you back to your chambers, my lord. And I shall send Janice to you, my lady."

Revan struggled manfully with the lump in his throat and held out his hand to Tauren. Seeing the liquid forming in his eyes and the uncertainty in his chin, Tauren held out her arms to him and hugged him a long moment, not noticing or caring what the formidable woman thought.

When the door closed behind them, Tauren felt very alone. It had not occurred to her that they might be separated in this venture. She closed her sky-colored eyes and sighed heavily. She was so tired. Too many times in the past week she had constrained her temper, bitten her tongue, stopped a tart remark. The keeping of her vow to become a gentle lady required more energy and effort than she could have imagined.

She removed her cloak and collapsed into a chair near the dark fireplace, feeling ragged and uncertain. Some minutes later she was roused by the sound of the door to her bedchamber.

She turned, half expecting to see Revan. A plump, blond serving maid in a rumpled, coarse woolen dress stood against the closed door, gawking about the room, mouth drooping and eyes sparkling.

"Um-hmmm," Tauren murmured.

"Oh!" the girl jumped visibly, "Lor' ye near scared me outta me wits!" She held one hand to her half-opened drawstring bodice and breathed deeply. Then, as if something sharp pricked her, she jumped again. "Oh!" Spreading her heavy, dark skirt awkwardly, she managed a deep curtsey and looked up at Tauren from beneath a clearly anxious brow. Seeing Tauren's nod, she rose and stood a bit closer, clasping her hands tightly before her.

"Janice . . . she took ill and so I said I'd come to help ye with . . ." She was staring openly at Tauren, apparently at a loss for just what she was to help with. Her face flushed a becoming rosy color, and she lowered her eyes to her work-reddened hands and shifted her feet.

"And what is your name?"

"Oh, milady," she breathed and bobbed another half-done curtsey, "Roxie, milady. Roxie's me name."

"Well then, Roxie, suppose you lay a fire so that I don't catch my death while undressing. Then you can help me with my laces."

The girl brightened immediately and set about warming the room; here was a task she was thoroughly familiar with. When a cheering fire blazed in the grate of the stone fireplace, Tauren rose to wash.

Roxie watched every move she made with an awe that amused Tauren. The girl had the manners of a scullion and from the looks of them, the hands to match.

"My trunk, I believe, may have been brought up by now. Perhaps it is in the next room." When the girl nodded expectantly, Tauren sighed quietly and continued, "Will you get it for me?" A true lady's maid would have been insulted; but then a true lady's maid would never have to be asked.

"That will be all, Roxie, thank you." Tauren was fatigued and anxious to drown her unruly thoughts in sleep.

"But . . . yer hair, milady. I ain't done that yet."

"Hair?" Tauren was puzzled and then brushed one hand over her braided coif, feeling its disarray. "Tomorrow, perhaps . . ."

"Oh, milady, ye can't let it go . . . it'll pull the hair right out if it's not brushed proper."

The girl's face was so expectant, Tauren sat down tiredly at the vanity and handed her a boar's-bristle brush.

Roxie smiled broadly and set to work, her short, work-reddened fingers flying nimbly over Tauren's disordered coif.

"How long have you been at Lindengreen, Roxie?" This Roxie might prove a source of information, Tauren mused.

"Three months, milady." The maid paused over a strand of lustrous dark hair kissed with fiery streaks of red-gold. "Afore this I was at 'Lisbeth Townings' house in Keenings. . . ." Seeing Tauren's brow crinkle, she explained, "She's the dressmaker in the town nearby. I were there for a year, but she sent me here to work in the kitchens. She never liked me, but me mum made me come—said I'd learn here." She laughed impishly, "I learned, a'right. O'course she couldn'ta known about Miz Townings' precious baby boy or that skinny lord of hers."

Tauren frowned again, feeling she'd prefer her own

thoughts just now, but Roxie sallied forth again.

"She taught me to do hair. I stayed up at night and practiced on Jenny, the parlormaid. I got good at it; she said so. Then her boy come home and ruint it all." She lowered her voice conspiratorially. "She said I lured 'im upstairs. Huh. Randy as a goat, he was—I had naught to say about it." She got a naughty twinkle in her eye. "Can't say I didn't enjoy it though . . . he was good . . . lot's better than her man . . . that lord somebody. He was my first an' not much fun. Too tall and skinny and right snooty after, givin' me a silverpiece like some tart an' tellin' me to keep me mouth shut to the mistress. Like he thought I'd be so thrilled, I'd shout to the housetops!" She turned her perky little nose up in distaste; then she became thoughtful. "Miz Townings never knew about 'im—so I guess it's fair enough all 'round."

Tauren stared unbelievingly ahead, trying to maintain some semblance of calm at the girl's tale. She had heard whisperings of such things, but her sheltered home and family had prevented her from contact with people who used servant girls and expected them to like it. This Roxie seemed to think it all a part of the way things were . . . and maybe they were!

"Roxie, the duke . . . has he ever tried to? . . ." She couldn't finish. What was she saying?

Roxie was the one amused now. "'As 'e ever tossed the serving girls?" She laughed ruefully. "Nah, not 'im. There ain't much o' that in this house, I can tell ye. That Mrs. Murdock keeps a hawk eye on the girls. Won't let us near the foot rooms or stables. I doubt the old boy 'as it in him . . . from the looks of 'im!" Her laugh died in a gurgle in her throat as she realized to whom she spoke.

"Oh, pardon, milady, I didn't mean no offense!"

Tauren drew herself up straight and tried to act more the lady than she had been able to heretofore. "It shall be forgotten, Roxie. That's good enough for now," she declared, rising.

In a haze of fatigue, she allowed Roxie to pull her dress from her. She doused the bedside candles herself and then crawled up into the middle of the beckoning bed to surrender to exhaustion.

Three

Holt Reston strode into the private study of the Duke of Somerset, his strange, green-brown eyes blazing with scarcely reined fury. His breath came fast and hard from the strenuous ride that had brought him from the nearby town of Keenings. Close on his heels was Mrs. Murdock, wearing a worried frown and clasping and unclasping her slender hands.

"I am sorry, Your Grace, I could not stop him," she sputtered. "I told him you were receiving no one, but—"

One thin hand was raised from the chair by the fire and the woman stopped midsentence. A tall, gaunt man rose slowly from the chair, his dark eyes fixed pointedly, emotionlessly on the younger man. The Duke of Somerset was regally garbed in somber brown velvet embroidered richly in a darker hue, and complemented by a white satin waistcoat and velvet breeches.

"That will do, Mrs. Murdock," the duke said quietly, dismissing the woman. She glanced from one man to the other and withdrew, closing the massive carved door behind her. The duke moved slowly, haltingly to the fire, giving the younger man his back and clasping his thin hands behind him. This audience was granted on suffrage and the duke's manner bore witness to the fact.

"Why did you not tell me about the boy?" Reston demanded, his deep voice reverberating about the cold walls of Lindengreen.

The duke glanced over his shoulder, then back toward the flames before him. "I do not think you were unaware of the boy's existence."

At his sides Reston's fists clenched and then opened as he strove to master the anger inside him. "That was not my meaning. Why did you not inform me of your intention to bring him here and install him as the next duke!"

The clear brilliance in the duke's eyes as he turned to the overlord defied attachment to any single emotion. His silver hair and thick brows gave his hollow face a haughty cast that would have instilled proper caution in any other adversary. The duke's piercing brown gaze scoured Reston's tall, muscular form, and he prolonged the silence as he pursued his own private thoughts awhile longer, giving the younger man tutorage in the respect due to rank.

"My heir and his accession are naught of your concern."

"All that happens in this shire is my concern." Reston challenged him openly.

"Then again, you overstep yourself," the duke said evenly, deliberately, matching Reston's heated look with his own. "You have nothing to say in the matter. I have decided and it is done. Revan Wincanton, my brother's son, will be Duke of Somerset when I am gone and all will give him their loyalty."

It was a command Reston could not help but refute. "My loyalty is not yours to command, nor is it inspired by titles or promise of influence. The whelp has no right—"

"Right! If we speak of rights, then let us first ask by what right you place yourself in judgment over me. You have assumed power and rights in the shire second only to my own—and by what authority?"

A hard, unflinching gleam in Reston's eyes answered the duke's burning glare. "By authority of my sword and arms, and by the risking of my life. I have earned the power I have here. It is dearly bought . . . from the whores you squandered it on when you sought relief from the troublesome, mundane world of men. It is my shire because the lord did not want it and I took it!"

The sting of the retort hit a tender spot and the duke stiffened with a jolt. "Then what is yours is yours . . . the power. Or do you covet the title as well to crown your noble efforts here? Would you petition the king himself to set aside the lawful successor and settle the honor upon a bastard?" The duke turned away, trembling with anger, and leaned heavily upon the back of the nearby chair.

That last taunt carried a barb evil enough to pierce pride's stoutest armor. Reston winced inwardly as his hot gaze followed the proud old nobleman's movements. The triumph of a moment ago vanished completely.

"Well enough you know my parentage." Reston's voice was low and once more controlled. "It has long been my only recommendation to you. But want of a true name makes a man no less than what he is. I was meant to rule here."

"Then you pretend to a title you shall never have." It was the duke's turn to find a private pain in the turn of this confrontation, but he would show none of it. He turned to Reston once more and squared his aging shoulders, meeting the other man's heated gaze.

"You have all the inheritance you shall have from me. The shire itself is yours, that is true enough." The duke's laugh was guttural, bitter. "You have made it yours by force and persuasion, even charm. But still one thing is beyond your reach—and you will never have all of Somerset." The old man's face was stony as he pointedly sought the comfort of his chair by the fire.

"Content yourself with what you have." The old man raised the book that had occupied him before this unsettling interruption, seeming oblivious to all else.

Reston stood a moment, experiencing the finality of the old man's conclusion, and rage roiled anew inside him. He wheeled and slammed open the door to the library, storming through the still trembling portal in a red haze of fury.

Geoffrey Eldred Charles Wincanton, seventh duke of Somerset, sat a moment as though he heard nothing. As the noise of Reston's departure through the front hall wafted back to him, he lowered the book to his lap and his head dropped back against the chair. His tired eyes closed tightly.

Two days . . . Tauren's foot impatiently tapped the cold marble floor of the solar where they waited. Two

41

long, nerve-tangling days. Standing, pacing, gazing out the windows that overlooked the entry court—there was little enough to do and more than enough to worry about.

The day had dawned unseasonably balmy and for the second day she and Revan had been ushered into the upper solar to await the duke's call. The only break in the tedium of waiting came that morning when Revan was whisked away to read for a tutor.

"I won't have to do it every day, will I?" he had asked later.

"I suspect so, Revan. You've much to learn before you'll be a proper duke."

"But he's a stick. Can't I have somebody like Ted Nabors? If I'm the future duke, I should be able to have anyone I want."

"Revan . . ." Tauren had stopped. He was a boy, in spite of his size. How could she make him understand that things are not ever so simple as just getting what you want . . . even for a future duke?

Now the sun stood directly overhead, heating the cold stone floor and the coals of Tauren's suppressed anger.

Revan wrestled about and finally sprang up from his chair. "I'd give anything for a set of bowls or a game of quoits."

Smiling sympathetically, Tauren mused that her wants were simpler; a length of stout rope and access to an aging neck. "There must be some reason for the delay. If we don't see the duke soon, I'll find Mrs. Murdock myself."

For her fifteenth change of scenery, Tauren took the window seat on the side of the room that overlooked the court and gazed longingly down into the entry below, wishing to be out in that rare bright sunlight. She wanted to believe there was a good reason for this delay, but her more pragmatic sense warned her that the old man could be keeping them waiting to demonstrate his power over them. This thought caused an unwelcome heat in her veins and a stubborn urge to do battle with the arrogant old aristocrat.

A movement in the courtyard below caught her eye and she followed it . . . a man, moving quickly away from the great doors to the main hall. The way he moved and the length of his stride seemed to indicate concentration on something—purpose or strong emotion. Tauren watched as he had a word with the footman who was off in an instant at a dead run.

In the moment the footman took to bring around the huge, black stallion, the man—a young man he seemed—threw his long black cloak over his shoulders and jerked on his leather gloves. His highly polished jackboots paced the cobblestone paving impatiently. Tauren had little time to notice his clothing, but it was not the scarlet of the cavaliers; she would have noticed. No, it was more somber—dark, mostly. He wore no hat, but from her angle there was no ready view of his face.

Just as he had mounted the great beast, a scarlet-clad figure she instantly recognized approached him from the side of the court and lay hands on the reins. Calder talked with the man for a moment, seeming to restrain him, and the man gestured broadly, angrily. They might have been shouting but Tauren could hear none of it from her perch high above in the great house. The man seemed to calm and paused, leaning one arm

43

heavily on the saddle and glancing up toward the house in the very direction of Tauren's window.

She drew back instinctively, realizing only later that he could not possibly have seen her because of the window hangings. She stared at his face, and all time seemed to stop. Whether for seconds or whole minutes, she could not later tell, but in that time his raven hair and angular face were burned into her mind—an image somewhat indistinct and yet lovingly embroidered by her imaginative longings into a perfect face: strong, handsome, intriguing.

The man returned his gaze to Calder, unaware of his impact on the hidden viewer, and his manner seemed less intense. After a few words, he jerked the reins hard and rode out of the court like the hounds of hell were upon him.

Tauren watched, unable to tear her eyes away, as Calder waited until the man disappeared from view and shrugged slightly before returning to the great house. Somehow she felt comforted to know Calder was near, although she felt unsettled at the effect the stranger had had upon her. A chill passed through her even in the sun-warmed room, and she put it down to her loneliness and her fears for their futures.

The strange episode was an intriguing break in the tedium of waiting, and Tauren's mind kept returning to it, even as she attempted to entertain Revan. Who was that man? Calder knew, but she could never ask the identity of a strange man who had so obviously quarreled with him. What did they argue about? Did Calder order him from the duke's land?

Stop it! she ordered herself. There was enough to

concern her in her own situation.

It was well into the afternoon when the summons came and the wait had been sufficiently long to bring Tauren's pride to a boil. In the private study of the duke, the tall, thin man sat behind a large writing desk and her first impression was that the old man seemed tired, whether from years or from his memories she would have cause to ponder in the days ahead. He looked up as they entered and placed the quill back in the inkpot on the desk before him.

The boy and his sister stood side by side, contesting for his eye, so striking a pair they made. But the boy, his heir, captured his attention.

"Come forward, boy." The duke scrutinized the mop of brown curls and the keen gray eyes that duplicated those of his younger brother, then cleared his throat.

"You are Revan Wincanton, now Marquess of Wells." The duke ordered him to turn about with an authoritative swirl of his hand and after a surreptitious glance at Tauren, the lad complied, turning slowly about to let the old man view him.

The duke studied the straightness of the boy's limbs, the set of his jaw and the widening spread of his young shoulders. "There is no mistaking it, you are Edward's true enough. Have you a tongue, boy?"

"Yes, sir, Your Grace."

The duke leaned backward in his seat propping his chin on his thin hand and allowing silence to reign. "Your rooms are satisfactory?"

"Quite" and "Yes, Your Grace," they answered at one time, causing him to cast a fleeting glance at Tauren before returning to the boy.

45

"You may wonder what is planned for you, boy. The tutor tells me that you read quite well and cipher also. This pleases me. I should have expected as much from Edward. You will need a keen mind for the days ahead. I have made plans to continue your education in other areas as well. Soon you will go to foster in the house of Strafford."

If he said more, it went unnoticed by both. His words dealt a near physical blow to Tauren. Foster? Send Revan away to live and grow in another house?

"No." The word escaped Tauren's lips before she could stop it. She held her breath as the old man turned slowly to look at her, incredulity on his face.

"Surely you would not send Revan away. It is . . . a relic of the past. . . ."

The duke paused to regard the lass before him, taking in her cheeks, glowing with angry color, her sky-blue eyes that seemed filled with sparks, her shining chestnut hair. . . . She made a fetching sight, one worthy of Calder's praise and an unexpected asset, until this annoying outburst. Still, he might have expected some resistance. They would not be worth much to accept the will of a total stranger and without a whimper go meekly to their fate.

"It is still commonly done among the nobility, girl. You would do well to remember that your isolated and common upbringings have ill prepared you for life in gentle society. Had your father not clung to such religious fanaticism, you would this day be well set in society, enjoying the best England has to offer, instead of depending upon the mercy of highly placed relations."

How dare he! "And you, Your Grace, had you one whit of humanness, love, or compassion in you, you might this day have a son of your own to heir instead of resorting to stealing your brother's children before he lies cold in the grave!" Two long weeks of uncertainty and frustration burst out virulently, leaving her aghast at her own words. Tauren's eyes widened and then, realizing that words spoken could not be recalled, she lifted her chin to brace for the worst, taking Revan's hand in hers and drawing him back to her side.

The duke's sallow cheeks flamed at the impertinence of this mere woman-child. Her remark bore more of the sting of truth than she knew. He suppressed the desire to strike back and reasoned with himself in the shocked silence that she had but inherited her father's spirit and strong sense of loyalty. It was a regrettable combination in a woman; the one characteristic being most abhorrent in a female and the other the most desirable.

"Your tongue, girl, is too sharp. You may be cured of it in time, but not at my expense, nor at your leisure." The duke's response was made through tight lips, but in a markedly restrained manner, for he noted that the lad watched them uneasily.

"I do not wish to live anywhere else, Your Grace," Revan stepped a bit foward. "I would not leave my sister alone. I shall study whatever Your Grace requires, diligently, but I shan't leave Tauren."

Even Tauren was surprised by his refusal. She had not considered that her attitude, adopted by him, might be seen as disobedience or disrespect, and dealt with accordingly. Why had she not checked her own

47

reactions more closely? What had happened to the gentle lady she had promised for her father?

"My lord Marquess, your tutor awaits," the old duke commanded. "Leave us to our discussion."

"But . . ." Revan stopped at a warning frown from Tauren and looked from the duke to his sister and back. His face reddened and his resentment at being treated as a child showed clearly in his gray eyes. He turned to the doors with a manly grace Tauren had not known he possessed.

"Young woman"—the voice was hard and cold now, drawing Tauren's gaze back to the silver hair and imperious brow—"your brother is my heir and my concern. Your wishes, however adamantly expressed, will have no impact upon his future. He will foster in the finest house in England. The distinguished future planned for him will not only be important for him, but for England itself." The old man's voice had risen and cracked at the end. His face was flushed as he leaned across the desk toward her. "A duke that clings to his sister's skirts is not worthy of the title."

Something in the old man's words brought the enormity of the loss of her former life crashing down upon her . . . and the finality of this impending separation—this inexorable destiny. She was never one to be bested easily, she reminded herself. She clamped a hard grip on her temper and tried again.

"Can you not see? Revan is a bright, headstrong boy, greatly grieved by our father's loss. He needs the comfort of his remaining family about him for a time yet. He can be taught here quite adequately until he is ready to go."

The duke's brown eyes gleamed with ire, though the rest of his manner gave little evidence of it. She had not repudiated his right to the lad again, only claimed her share of him. She could be brought to his will.

"It seems you are the one in need of comforting, miss. That is why you would keep your brother near you at the expense of his future and welfare."

"That's not true!" Tauren declared, realizing that she had mistaken the easing of the old man's manner for an easing of his determination. She now realized that it had but heralded his anticipation of victory, and she began to see everything in shades of red.

"If he were to stay here, you would still see little of him. You will be married and bedded as quickly as is humanly possible." He waited a moment for his words to bear fruit and then continued, breaking into a strange parody of a smile. "You will put this mourning business behind you immediately and prepare yourself to meet your suitors. I trust you know how to comport yourself on such occasions as to bring no disgrace upon your brother and this house. I shall have the matter settled within the month."

"No," Tauren breathed, feeling the killing thrust had been delivered—the one that would separate her from Revan forever. "You cannot do this . . . it isn't decent or godly. I still mourn my father and I must do as my conscience dictates."

"Few here knew or remember your father. Folk will not think it strange that your mourning ends soon, for they have no knowledge of it." Had he sought the world of language through, he could not have found words with a keener, more painful edge to them. She felt a fortnight's stifled tears pricking the backs of her eyes and she lashed out.

"I shall refuse to marry! You cannot force me or the marriage will not stand!"

The piercing brown eyes studied her a moment with deceptive casualness. "How naïve you are. Should you choose to be so stupidly stubborn, I shall send you away . . . to a nunnery in France. I should think marriage into an English family with a good dowry would be preferable to that. I have entertained offers from two nobles on your behalf already, but have not yet decided whom you shall marry."

"You have not yet decided!" she scoffed, realizing belatedly that he held out a bribe for her cooperation.

He straightened sharply, his ploy refused. "I see now I have erred. Indeed, I have just now settled upon your future husband, girl. You may marry this man I have chosen, or prepare yourself for a nunnery this very week!" His eyes were aflame as they met hers. Liquid prisms framed her big eyes and defied nature to stay in place. God, she was a beauty, he tallied her coolly. Flushed with anger, soft, proud, womanly. Sappington would be glad to get her, he mused, and would make an alliance for the young duke later on.

She met his gaze and saw there the weariness of a lifetime turned inward into hardness and contempt for all the vagaries of the mortal heart. He would have his will in this, and no argument in heaven or earth would move his calcified heart. No longer ashamed of her outburst, she straightened proudly and surrendered her fate to this merciless old man who had forsaken all of the tender qualities of the heart.

"You may have my fate, old man, but you shall never

have more. Marry me off, it changes nothing. Revan is still Edward's boy. He will never be yours." The old duke's eyes hardened with the impact of her bitter words, and she moved toward the door before she could bring more calamities upon her head with her unbridled tongue. As the latch clicked behind her, Tauren gathered up her skirts and ran.

Four

Tauren held her long black skirts up with tightly balled fists. Her stride was long and angry as she muttered dire and florid pronouncements about the old duke and his suffocating household. She looked up from her feet and found herself approaching the stables. A groom had saddled a fine, dark gelding for exercising and was just bringing him out of the large graystone stable. He left the horse standing a moment while he closed the door, and in a moment, Tauren had seized the reins and drawn herself up into the saddle before he realized she was near.

"Hey!" he shouted at her back, "come back. Ye can't take that horse! Come back 'ere!"

But she had hooked her knee about the pommel and was off across the paddock and through an open gate, onto the road—free. She had no destination, no plan, no thought but to ride until this heat and anger in her blood subsided.

The horse sensed her will and stretched out his legs joyfully beneath her, covering untold distance in this unknown land—unmindful of the time. The cool wind on her face drew the heat from her anger, and the strong, graceful movement of the animal soothed her ravaged temper.

She slowed her mount as she entered a stand of trees, skirting in and out of them, giving the nameless horse below her a chance for wind. Some of the leaves of the past summer were still clinging to the dark boughs tenaciously. The lowering sun streamed through the bare branches, dancing on her hair and moist skin, setting her eyes aglow with its precious light. She had not felt such release for a year.

Then, less welcome thoughts intruded on her peace, among them an angry silver brow, sentencing her to a loveless marriage and separation from her vulnerable young brother. Her future was secured, cleverly masterminded by the selfish old man who hoped to make himself remembered through the manipulation of an innocent boy.

"Tauren, girl, you may have to marry some stupid, mincing noble, but there are ways to see the duke pays for the privilege of holding your future in his hands."

She crested a hill, pulling her mount to a halt and surveying the little valley below. Her senses were returning to her, and she recognized the ache of her limbs and the dry heaviness of her breathing as the warnings they were. She rode down the slope and into a copse of trees near a stream.

She dismounted, finding her legs weak beneath her, and pulled some dried grasses to wipe the glistening sweat from the horse's flanks. Climbing up onto a massive boulder that jutted out into the sun over the water, she stretched her aching muscles luxuriantly on the sun-warmed surface of the rock, arching her back and neck. The scrape of a hairpin against her skin signaled that her hair was torn irreparably from its ladylike coif. To hasten its descent, she yanked vehemently at the remaining pins and sent her fingers up through the glorious chestnut mass. She willed all thought away and sank back to lie on the rock.

Later, she could not say just how long she had been there, for she drifted from consciousness into more peaceful realms. Something warm and soft pressed against her lips, drawing her back from that netherland found just the far side of full consciousness. Her dissembled wit had difficulty making it out; it was a strange sensation, familiar and yet not pleasant . . . disturbing.

Then, unhappily, it was gone and a long moment passed before she thought to open her eyes. Just above her face was the image of another . . . the face of the man from the early afternoon's encounter at Lindengreen. She smiled as she realized it was slightly different than she remembered; even more handsome; angular, with a square jaw and generous lips. His eyes were the dappled green-brown of the forest and they glowed intriguingly above the deep bronze of his high cheekbones. Again, she closed her eyes, concentrating on the image and feeling lazily guilty about it. Daydreaming about a face—and likely that of a scoundrel who was tossed out of Lindengreen!

Then the feeling came again, stronger, and her arms came up quickly only to encounter an obstacle—a body! Her eyes flew open. She was not dreaming, she was being kissed . . . and by that man!

As if sensing the change in her, the lips against hers

withdrew and the glowing eyes seemed to darken a shade as they stared mockingly into her own.

"I have stolen a kiss." The deep, rich voice near her ear reverberated through her body. She felt the warmth of his breath against her temple, her cheek, her ear. What was happening to her? She could neither move nor speak with him so tantalizingly, frighteningly near.

"But I am no thief," the voice continued, the rolling tones pouring over her like caressing hands. "I shall give it back." Again his lips found hers and poured over them slowly, mesmerizing her further with their warmth and sweetness, hardness and softness. Her hands against his chest related to her the heat and strength of his hard chest, and the powerful thudding of his heart. She tried experimentally to move her head to one side, but only succeeded in producing another heavenly sensation against her mouth. So this was kissing, she thought distractedly, feeling an uneasiness growing inside her.

The warm tip of his tongue tantalized her lips and they gradually parted with an instinct of their own. His mouth tasted faintly of wild mint as she allowed his tongue to explore hers, vaguely aware of the rush of her blood in her head and the unnerving staccato of her own heart. There was a slight change of pressure from those marvelous lips and a scraping sound of something on the rock beside her; then suddenly she felt a weight upon her belly, thighs, and breasts. Her eyes flew open in surprise and stared into a piercing hot gaze from eyes now black and quite unlike those of only a minute before. These eyes held the promise of . . . she knew not what, but they frightened her. All too late she realized this was no phantom lover and that he covered her body with his own.

His mouth was not as gentle as before, but demanding, hard against her lips, pulling something from her that frightened her, an unnamed something she did not wish to surrender.

She pushed hard against his chest, surprising him and forcing him up a bit from her. Her mind finally answered the call of her outraged moral sense and now registered the full impact of what was happening to her. She was alone, isolated, with this strange, powerful man.

"No!" she uttered hoarsely, her eyes wide with the belated knowledge of where his actions were leading.

He laughed, a deep guttural sound from within his big chest. "Your lover won't mind if I take his place—and neither, my little love, do you." His eyes glittered ominously as he again lowered his mouth to hers.

"No. You cannot do this! Let me go!" She found her tongue at last, not caring that her words carried the edge of her fear. His large hand found one ripe, eager breast and explored it above the woolen of her gown, oblivious to her gasp of outrage and to her hand as it tried futilely to check his progress.

"Don't worry." He chuckled arrogantly. "We won't be disturbed here. And if your lover appears, I'll simply have his head."

"I have no lover!" she shouted breathlessly. "Let me go! I order you to release me!" A guttural grunt of dismissal answered her demand, raising her fear to fever pitch. She could feel his tension and excitement along the length of her as he pressed himself against her, moaning softly at the effect of her soft, curved

56

body beneath his.

Instinctively she understood what he intended, and the awareness fueled her panic. She struggled furiously, pushing against his iron-hard chest and writhing desperately beneath his huge, muscular weight. She jerked her face away as he sought her mouth once more, and he found the slim column of her neck instead, applying his lips like scorching brands that would mark his possession of her.

"Stop . . . please . . ." she pleaded, then felt an angry spur to her pride at such wheedling and demanded, "Let me go or I'll have your head. I swear it!" A strange animallike laugh was his answer as he shifted his weight more fully upon her and caught her flailing arm and pinned it above her head with ludicrous ease.

"And what will you have my head with? Still, it might be worth it afterward, with a wench like you." He buried his face against her breasts and nuzzled them and kissed them passionately, forcing the fabric of her gown down with his chin. In spite of her anger, she was aware of a curious warmth spreading through her as he neared the hidden nipples of her breasts, now tingling strangely. Combating her own traitorous impulses, she wriggled determinedly, finding to her horror, that these movements seemed to add to his pleasure. His knee parted her thighs and she felt her skirts drawn slowly upward.

"You blackhearted bastard . . . scurrilous wretch . . . you filth—" He stopped the flow with his mouth on hers, searing her lips and seeming to draw the breath from her. But she sank her teeth into his lower lip viciously and he drew back with a yelp.

"You little bitch," he blazed, his face red-hot with

lust and anger. "I don't know your game, but you've met your master, wench. I'll have you now or die trying!"

Her satisfaction at the crimson oozing from the corner of his lip was short-lived as she again felt the punishment of his lips against her neck, devouring her, and felt her skirts now up about her waist, leaving her thighs and buttocks bare. She realized through her angry red haze that he fumbled with the buttons of his breeches.

"No! God, no!" she begged, anguished, then angry again. "The duke will have your head for this—if you leave me alive. I swear it!"

He paused, grappling with her squirming form to scoff maliciously, "The duke has no ear for the complaints of a woman. Your only hope now is to please me!" His breath came in ragged spurts as he pulled at his obstinate clothing, staring hotly at her elegantly rounded thighs and delicately tapered calves and trim ankles.

"He may not, but the Marquess of Wells will avenge me. And if my brother fails, I'll take a knife to your black heart myself, I swear to God I will!" But again his full weight pressed down upon her and she felt the alarming heat of his chest against her bared breasts. A sob congealed in her throat with a strangling scream, and she felt paralyzed, knowing his superior strength would succeed and in a matter of moments she would be conquered—raped. Then, as if a hidden stinger in her last threat finally reached him, he was up on his elbows and knees above her thrashing form, scouring her reddened, mutinous face.

"You're an imaginative wench, I'll give you that.

What makes you think I give a damn what the duke or his milksop of a nephew want? They have no power in this shire. I rule here! My word is its law and my arm is its protection!" His words were ground out from between clenched teeth and he shifted his position above her, causing her to wince as if expecting a blow. The shudder of her delectable young body somehow shocked him back to a saner frame of mind. His posture straightened so that he was on his hands and knees above her, astride her. She lay still beneath him, wondering at his abrupt withdrawal and feeling the first glimmerings of hope.

He knelt above her, staring with leering appraisal at her openly displayed assets; her lithe legs, rounded hips and half-bared breasts. She blushed furiously at his leisurely perusal of her but feared to try to cover herself lest she prompt him to renew his assault. If she were still . . . perhaps if she talked . . .

To her amazement, he was bounding up and away from her with a rugged display of his powerful muscles. There was an angry, sardonic twist to his sensuous mouth as he began to adjust his clothing, still ravaging her with his eyes. "Sorry to disappoint you wench, but I prefer more willing partners—and less treacherous ones." He put one hand to his bloodied lip and touched it experimentally, inspecting the small stain on his fingertips. "Save it for your lover, he will need the lives of a cat to make love to you."

"I have no lover, you jackdaw," she muttered hatefully, instantly realizing that he might yet punish such a challenge. She sat up angrily, pushing down her skirts, and tossed her wildly disheveled hair back over her shoulders. She tried to ignore the screams of her aching muscles and wrists, her scraped skin and bruised lips. As he towered above her on the rock, looming dark and powerful, her only thought was to get to her horse to escape him. She trembled as she smoothed her bodice and wondered what he would do next.

He watched her intently as she adjusted her clothing and started to slip from the rock. In an instant he was on the ground before her with his hands on her waist, lifting her down as though she were mere fluff. Her head barely reached his shoulder but her hand came up instinctively, aimed at the broad hardness of his cheek. He caught it easily in a viselike grip before it found its generous target.

"Nay." His eyes glittered dangerously. "You'll not punish me for denying you what you so clearly asked for."

"Asked for!" She was aghast and glared furiously up at him. "You bumbling ass . . . I never asked you to attack me and—"

"Are you afraid your lover might find out that you made love with a real man?"

Again he made that accusation!

"I've never had a lover!" She clamped her mouth shut in horror. What was she saying? "Let me go!"

He held her for one minute longer, searching her sweet, heart-shaped face, its full lips reddened by his intense attention to them, her eyes like great sky pools, littered with early stars that sparkled. Swiftly and without warning he pulled her to him and planted a quick, rough kiss upon her warm mouth, releasing her so suddenly that she staggered.

Catching her balance and staring at him in surprise,

60

she gathered up her skirts and fled to where her horse was tethered, her heart pounding in her chest at the realization of what had almost happened to her.

It was growing dark now and she hadn't a clue as to where she was—except trapped in an isolated wood with a lecherous brigand and an acknowledged enemy of the duke.

Her fingers seemed made of wood as they struggled with the reins and she heard the crunch of footfalls in the dry leaves behind her as she made to mount the animal. An instant of terror gripped her as she felt his hands on her waist; but to her amazement, she was lifted up and onto the saddle, and she felt her skirt being pulled down over her shapely calf.

Only then did Tauren dare a downward glance, holding her breath for fear he might yet drag her back to him. He stood beside her, his hand resting insolently upon her thigh, and a mocking half-grin on his outrageously smug and handsome face. His eyes were full of derision as they touched her body freely. It was then she noticed . . . he wore black—plain, defiant black.

She snarled at him and whipped the horse sharply with the reins, startling her mount into action and knocking the rogue back a pace.

It was several minutes before she slowed her breakneck pace across the darkening countryside that grew ominously colder as the last of the sunlight faded. Her hair whipped about her, and she pulled a strand from across her face as her eyes scoured the land for a familiar tree or hill or outcropping of rock. A breeze had come up and she felt the late October chill it carried in her very bones. She paused on a ridge, choking back angry tears, wondering where she was and how she might find her way back to the duke's mansion. No! She pounded her thigh with a tight fist; she'd not whine and dissolve into a mass of tears. She'd find her way!

She rose up in the saddle to better survey the shadowy landscape and her breath caught in her throat. Behind her on a high knoll sat a dark figure on a huge dark horse, watching her. She felt a shiver of recognition run through her, and she cast her eyes about frantically, finally lighting on a darkened ribbon in the bright moonlight that might prove to be a road. She struck out for it, furious that he should follow her after what he had done and had tried to do. She'd see him hanging from a gibbet, she vowed, grinding her teeth as his mocking grin appeared before her mind's eye.

She had ridden some time in the cold, closing darkness, seeing no sign of life until she spotted what appeared to be a signpost and a fork in the road. She murmured a prayer of thanks for the great round moon that was her only source of comfort. In the worn lettering of the faded post she recognized the word "Keenings." She shuddered; it was worth a try. Roxie had said something about the town being near Lindengreen.

"Lady Tauren!" The familiar voice called to her across the meadow to her right and her heart leaped nearly out of her chest at the sight of the jaunty white plumes and moon-brightened cloaks that she knew to be scarlet in the light of day. She pulled her tired mount to a halt and waited as they raced toward her. It took a grip of steel upon her will to prevent her from throwing herself into Calder's arms by the time he reached her.

"Lady Tauren," Calder grabbed the reins of her horse, trying to decide whether to treat her like a lady and express his relief at her safe return, or to treat her like a stubborn, willful child and give her a stern lecture. "Good God, woman, where 'ave you been? We've been out scouring the hillsides for hours! The house is frantic."

"I simply went for a ride," she demurred guiltily, "and I'm afraid I lost my way." She flashed a disarming smile at him, like the smiles she had used to melt the bishop's staunch heart.

"But," she ventured in a small voice, drawing his alarmed gaze back to her delicate face, "I am fairly frozen now. I left my cloak behind." As if to authenticate her statement, a small shiver ran through her. In an instant, all three men had doffed their cloaks, two only to put them back on at a scowl from Calder, who leaned across his saddle to place his own warm, woolen garment about her chilling shoulders.

On the mercifully short ride back to Lindengreen, she had time to dread her reception there. What could Revan be thinking? And what would Mrs. Murdock say? The duke?

No, she determined, remembering the early resolve of her ride, she would not let them see weakness in her; she must strike first and let her pride carry it off.

Thus, when she stepped through the great doors of Lindengreen, she seemed outwardly as calm as though she had just stepped in from a stroll in her own garden.

"Sorry to have troubled you, Mrs. Murdock. I was a trifle late with my ride. I'll go to Revan at once."

63

"He has been quite concerned, my lady." A million questions sparked by the lady's impetuosity and disheveled state were smothered by the housekeeper, but she could not help staring.

Tauren wondered if there were much damage to her appearance. Not knowing, it would be awkward to return Calder's cloak. "Please send Roxie to me Mrs. Murdock, and see that hot water is readied for a bath. I am positively chilled through."

"Roxie, my lady?" Murdock stuttered, "b-but she's—"

"Yes, I am quite aware of what she is, Mrs. Murdock. She will make an excellent lady's maid with proper training and there seems no better time than the present to begin." Her level gaze, aimed at the woman's surprised face, was most convincing.

The housekeeper stiffly nodded acquiescence and withdrew to fetch the scullery maid.

"I fear I may be more chilled if I return your cloak now, sir." Tauren extended her slender hand to Calder and he accepted it gallantly.

"Of course, my lady," he rumbled, reddening slightly at the blatant charm bestowed upon him. "Keep it altogether if ye like."

"Nay." She laughed throatily. "It suits you far better than me. I am grateful for your concern and efforts on my behalf. I shall not be so thoughtless in the future, you may depend on it."

"As ye say, milady." He returned her hand to her reluctantly.

Revan was alone, already prepared for bed in his

princely apartments. He bounded up from his seat by the fire and pounced upon her in his eagerness to see her. His eyes shone luminously, a liquid indictment of her foolishness clinging in their corners. She held him tightly.

"But where did you go, Taurie? I was so worried when you didn't come back for supper."

"After the duke and I . . . talked, I had to be alone and think. I . . . went for a ride. Can you understand?"

"I . . . guess so. I was just scared something happened to you. Don't do that again, Taurie," he admonished in a very adult tone.

"I can take care of myself, Revan, you know that."

He hugged her with rib-crushing completeness and allowed her to tuck him into his grand, polished bed. "We'll find a way, Taurie."

As she gave his hair one last stroke, the duke's harsh words came back to her. But now was not the time or place to tell Revan what their uncle had planned for her.

Roxie had taken charge of her own rooms when she arrived and was ordering two sullen-looking scullery maids about with the aplomb of a lifelong bluenose. When they departed and Roxie helped her off with the heavy cloak, she heard the girl whistle softly.

"Where 'ave ye been?"

Tauren cast a sidelong glance into the looking glass beside the tall French armoire, then turned a sour look upon Roxie. The girl fell silent, but kept an impudent grin on her face all the same. When she turned back to the glass, Tauren didn't know whether to laugh or to cry at the reflection of her tousled self, unquestionably disheveled and disreputable-looking. Her face flamed as she wondered if that were what the rogue took her to be—a joy-woman.

But something about her seemed different. Some small, inexplicable change eluded classification—but made itself known all the same. She knew it had to do with the evening's encounter and silently condemned the Puritan hypocrite who had caused this unnamed but loathsome change within her.

Five

Later that same night, Holt Reston sat before the dying fire in his modest house in the village of Keenings, easing the strain of his body with a tankard of hot, mulled wine. In the glow of the cooling embers, he saw the glowing anger of a woman's eyes and quickly downed another gulp of the strong brew, wondering why it failed to deaden the annoying pain in his damaged lip and the sharper one in his loins. His imagination went on to other parts of that same woman, softer, more comforting parts; but remembering them only served to heighten his discomfort and to drive him steadily downward toward the bottom of the pewter tankard.

The door to the small parlor banged open forcefully, but Holt didn't have to look up to know the owner of those hard-heeled boots and jangling spurs.

"Mulled wine!" Calder barked good-naturedly at the young houseboy who had admitted him and who now received his gloves and cloak but not his rakishly tilted hat. "I need ease of mind and body this eve . . . and I can think of no better comfort, or at least none to be taken here!" His eyes sparkled with good humor and the lad caught his contagious smile and returned it. The visitor came to stand by the fire in front of Holt, measuring his host's mood by his slumped posture and the way his long, booted legs sprawled carelessly out before him.

"Sit down, Calder," Holt said and, without raising his head, flopped one arm over the edge of his chair in the direction of the other massive chair nearest the center of warmth.

"Thanks for yer hospitality, my friend," Calder remarked dryly, noting from his speech that Holt had a head start on the wine. He judged the younger man to be the better part of drunken, an abnormal state for the strictly disciplined overlord of the shire. "But no thanks. I've rid me arse off this eve o'er half the countryside." He rubbed his posterior gingerly. "If it's all the same to ye, I'll wait 'til the first of these makes itself felt." He accepted a tankard from the houseboy and raised it in an exaggerated salute.

Still Holt stared moodily into the coals, uncharacteristically silent and unreadable. Calder studied his friend and wondered at this unusual temper. In the four years of their friendship, they had ridden, wenched, and fought together; but he had yet to see this precise mood upon his friend. Holt's usual mode was to have out whatever gnawed at him and then it was past, but clearly that was not to be this night.

"What's the matter with ye, man? Ye act as if ye been struck by lightning!" He reached out one spurred jackboot and gave Holt's foot a prodding.

Holt jarred back to reality and looked up at his

friend who leaned one shoulder against the mantelpiece, that cock's pride of a plume still in place on his elegant high crowned hat. Holt lifted one side of his mouth in a lazy grin as he recalled the sight of that plume and two similar ones intercepting a lone rider on a desolate road just after dusk. Involuntarily, his thoughts were drawn back to that curvaceous little spitfire who had aroused his strongest passions and then turned on him like a she-lion. It had to have been Calder and his men on the road . . . and now he had part confirmation of the identity of his provocative little vixen. His head dropped back against his chair as his face sobered.

"The duke and I argued this afternoon . . . is that not enough?" His eyes were far away and his words were tinged with bitterness.

"Ah," Calder responded, waiting for further comment. Why hadn't he considered that? Of course the old duke was responsible for his friend's strange mood. Calder felt a guilty sense of relief, from what he was not sure.

"But when do we not argue? Damn him! He uses me to run the shire and still he denies me!" Holt's eyes narrowed slightly as if a secret vision passed before them. "But I shall have my time . . . he will not live forever. When he is dead, the shire and all in it will be mine." He glanced at Calder, half expecting some challenge. They had spent their anger on this very topic before and Holt was surprised that the battle was not rejoined at his blatant claim.

In the deepening silence, Holt's face relaxed and his eyes half closed so that he regarded Calder surreptitiously.

"When I left you at Lindengreen this afternoon, I went straight to Peg Mead's, but I didn't stay. I rode about the countryside awhile." He rubbed his black-clad thigh absently, giving the impression of deep preoccupation, or wine-dulled thoughts.

Calder smiled at his friend encouragingly. "She has a healing gift, that woman. Relief to a man's wearied soul, I say." Then he buried his nose in the fast-dwindling tankard.

Holt smiled lazily, letting his mind drift back across the nights Peg Mead had healed his wearied soul and wearied his strong body with her tantalizing ministrations.

"I didn't stay. I rode out by the old tenant's cottage by Craven's Bend and spent some time there thinking." He shot a quick glance at Calder as he continued. "It was there I met her. . . ."

"Her?" Calder seemed to have some difficulty in swallowing his brew.

"Aye. A witch or a wench . . . a bit of both, I vow. She lay on one of the great rocks, tantalizing me with her movements until she sent the blood pounding through my veins. I nearly took her, but her kisses held promises she was reluctant to keep. . . ." He fingered his damaged lip conspicuously, knowing Calder watched. "By God, I'll have her yet, I swear it! She's put an ache in my loins I can't drown with a barrel of this." He raised his tankard and tossed down the rest of the brew. When he lowered it, he dropped his head once more, watching Calder from beneath heavily lidded eyes as he continued.

"She was a vixen, this one. Dressed in black—but no Puritan, to be sure. Her hair was loose and hanging down like a fiery waterfall and her lips were the color of ripe peaches. They tasted just as sweet. Full, ripe breasts . . . and her legs—"

"Stop it!" Calder choked nervously. "Ye have me fair to burstin' me britches now, man!" He tried to show enthusiasm like that due a comrade on any campaign, but his intensity slipped though. "Who is she?"

Holt watched Calder's face grow more serious and he smirked, having now the full confirmation he sought. "I do not know her name," Holt declared truthfully. "We had little time for talk. But I'll find her again, and when I do I'll have her on the spot. I shan't rest a night until I do."

Calder laughed nervously. "Sure lad, I'm surprised she could resist yer silky tongue and elegant manners. Or did she now?"

"For now," Holt grinned, repaying Calder in kind for not telling him the truth about the boy's sister. He could see now why Calder had not told him about the girl's beauty and it angered him. "Twenty-seven and a spinster true," the dutiful captain had reported, and "quiet little brown mouse." What did Calder think he might do to her . . . storm the mansion to attack her under the duke's nose? He smirked drunkenly again. By withholding the truth about her he had nearly insured that very happening. So, he mused as he studied the captain, the old fox was now given to protecting the young chicks that he once swallowed for dinner himself!

"I'll find her." Holt's eyes gleamed with such anticipation that Calder straightened visibly, ceasing the pretense of a smile altogether. "And when I do, she'll learn to treat her betters . . . and treat them well."

71

He laughed raucously at the consternation on Calder's face, raising his empty tankard in salute to his friend.

Calder joined him after a long minute, wondering about the events just past and authenticating parts of Holt's story with bits of his own memory. Holt left no doubt in his mind as to the identity of the girl who had marked him with her passion. The conclusion brought Calder much unease.

The dawn of the new day found Tauren tossing fitfully in her postered, heavily draped bed, and finally wakening to the dull throbbing of her back and limbs. In the morning mist of memory, she again saw a pair of green-brown eyes, darkening dangerously as they hovered above her. Her heart quickened as she fastened her mind's eye on the full lips beneath that rapacious gaze—full, gracefully formed, and mockingly curved upward. As she lay in her maiden's bed, she felt the startling return of those delicious sensations she had experienced yesterday, a warmth under her skin and a hungerlike pang in her stomach and below. What was happening to her?

Her humiliation at her body's abject mutiny was heightened by its determined repetition of those same feelings now. Part of her was deeply shamed that she could be so marked by a backsliding Puritan rogue that even the recall of his features summoned forth a wanting within her. And yet, another part of her reveled in this newfound sense of womanliness, instinctively rejoicing in the natural yearnings of her lithe, young body. It was all so confusing, this part of her she had not dreamed existed—a part she both longed and feared to explore.

72

Perhaps the duke's plan to marry her off was not so unwise as she had first thought, for in marriage she would be safely beyond such temptation, as her father had often preached. Yes, perhaps this idea of the marriage was not so bad a happening after all.

Roxie burst in to throw back the heavy tapestries at the windows and the bed hangings, and to bring the news that Mrs. Murdock had ordered a coach for the morning. Today Tauren would begin the laborious process of being dressed for her station . . . and prepared for marriage. Apparently, her misadventure of the night before would not be held against her; the fittings would go on as planned.

Roxie was a stream of unbroken chatter about the goings-on in the kitchen and about the estate, gossip which both irritated and mercifully distracted Tauren from her aching body and the arduous day ahead. But she forgave all when Roxie worked unexpected magic with her hair, giving her a sweetly sophisticated coif worthy of any lady of the court. Dressed once more in her stark black and standing before the long, silvered glass, she sighed that it might be the last time she would wear the gown, for today her mourning had ended, by the duke's callous decree.

Adjusting and smoothing her bodice, she turned to Roxie and tilted her chin up with mock hauteur.

"Aye, yer lovely today milady. He done ye good."

"He? What are you prattling about?" Tauren demanded, her brow darkening.

"Yer lov—er, fella. The one ye met last eve. Ye did meet someone, didn't ye." Roxie, unschooled in the subtlety required in serving the nobility, especially in

73

tender matters, gazed at her mistress expectantly, as if awaiting an answer.

Unused to dismissing personal inquiries as impertinence, Tauren answered in the manner of a true lady without realizing it. "Don't be absurd. Whatever put such an idea into your head?"

"Well"—Roxie put one little red hand upon her rounded hip, and grinned slyly—"there's a look about a woman who's been with a man. Yer hair all toused an' hanging' free—and 'alf the forest floor clingin' to yer skirts. 'Twould be daft to think other."

Tauren's eyes narrowed briefly as she swallowed hard and turned back to the looking glass, trying to sound collected and controlled as she smoothed the soft folds of her skirt. "Well, you're wrong. The duke and I crossed words and I went for a ride to collect my thoughts. I lost my way—"

"Ye needn't worry. I won't tell nobody." Roxie shrugged, feeling that she had just offended her lady. "A woman's entitled to a romp an' some fun afore she's wedded off like some prize mare."

"There's naught to tell, Roxie," Tauren declared heatedly.

"Aye, milady." Roxie dipped respectfully, an annoying grin upon her pert, round face. "As you say, not a word."

Tauren lifted her skirts and, with a pointedly disgusted look at her maid, made her way to breakfast in the morning room, taming her screaming muscles and managing a modicum of grace in her painful descent of the main staircase.

*   *   *

"In the last fortnight, I've raided the finest of London's shops and silk merchants." Elizabeth Townings took Tauren's hand and lifted her arm, turning her slightly to view her elegantly curved shape. "How lovely . . . I have even enlisted the help of an exquisite French seamstress to see to the small clothing. Nothing will be left to chance, your ladyship."

She led Tauren from the front parlor of her modest house into a room cluttered with crates and trunks stuffed with bolts of rich velvet, shimmering brocade, heavy silk, and tissue-thin lawn. A table strewn with sketches and the tools of the seamstress' trade stood ready.

Tauren was forthwith divested of her modest black gown and measured, moved, prodded, posed, and draped until she ached with fatigue and longed to scream for relief. Her head throbbed and her shoulders drooped, her eyes itched from the lint of the fabrics and her nose burned from the smell of the exotic dyes. There were so many decisions to make; dazzling rich fabrics and furs to be selected, elegant sketches of gowns to be chosen as well as embarrassingly meager underthings that were apparently in vogue for ladies of rank and fashion.

As she paused over a particularly costly weave that embodied tiny gold wires in the pattern and started to dismiss it on account of extravagance, she remembered her resolve to make the duke pay for his control of her future. She caught Mrs. Murdock's amused smile upon her and blushed annoyingly, wondering if the woman could read her mind. But Murdock only turned to the dressmaker and remarked, "The duke will be pleased to have naught but the best for his niece; it will be Lady

75

Tauren's wedding gift from him. You will see to appropriate nightclothes for such a purpose?"

Tauren watched, stunned by the topic and by Murdock's casual handling of it. Nightclothes for her marriage bed? The very words sent a shiver through her body as she recalled vividly the shocking feeling of a man's hands upon her. Her enthusiasm for this gift waned measurably and was snuffed entirely as the dressmaker produced a sketch that she identified as a perfect wedding gown.

"This will do splendidly," Murdock declared, "a heavy ivory satin, trimmed in ermine, I think. Perhaps lower the bodice a bit to take advantage of the lady's perfect skin. Do you not agree?"

Tauren felt a rising irritation toward this vexingly efficient minion of the duke. If she objected, Murdock would most likely invoke the duke's authority and have the dratted gown produced anyway.

Irritably, Tauren snatched up a sketch on the floor that had caught her eye. "What's this?"

"It is . . . a jest." Elizabeth Townings colored and glanced nervously at Mrs. Murdock. "The little Frenchwoman's idea. A Puritan dress but made in such a way that no Puritan man could resist. It is made to not lace fully in the front. . . ."

Tauren caught Murdock's stiff bearing and laughed delightedly. Taking the sketch near the tiny window to catch the light, she stared at a dark gown with a great, white collar that was smartly edged with dark cording, after the proper Puritan fashion. But the neckline was most decidedly anything but Puritan, plunging precariously downward, not permitting the lacings that ran upward from the waist to meet.

"Scandalous! I must have this one as well," she commanded, feeling no remorse when Murdock's lips tightened. She chose a delicious black brocade shot through with silver threads for its completion. It was a small revenge, a ladylike balancing of the scales. And what a marvelous jest on that piously overbearing sect that had troubled her family, just to own it.

While Murdock remained in the fitting room to discuss times for future fittings, Tauren sat in the parlor of the shop sipping a mug of cider served with a pinch of costly cinnamon. Her head throbbed. They were making plans for her wedding night and bedding when she had yet to learn the identity of the man who would claim her.

Outside the small window at the front of the shop, movement caught her eye—a quick rush of forms about the far side of the small square. They were two male figures; one a man who chased the other, a boy or a small youth . . . perhaps Revan's age. The tall, darkly clad man soon caught the lad as he ran toward the side of the square where the shop stood and they grappled in an uneven contest clearly visible from Tauren's window. Something in the scene caused her heart to beat faster and she was suddenly unable to take her eyes from it. It was *him*! The blackguard who had assaulted her only last night in that isolated wood!

None of the men who watched made to intervene and those who passed by gave wide berth to the venting of the big Puritan's wrath. Tauren was stunned as she watched him threaten the young boy. Her mouth was dry and she felt her heart beating in her throat. She wanted to call out but seemed paralyzed.

Their words were withheld by the distance, but she

knew from the scarlet of the big Puritan's face that his anger and his words were white hot. Light glinting from metal reached her and she realized that he had drawn his short sword in a single, unnoticed movement and now held its point to the lad's throat, his mouth twisting cruelly.

Tauren's horror was full-blown, equal to that the lad must have been feeling in that steely grip. How could she stop this outrage?

But as quickly as it had begun, it was over. The lad seemed to wrench away from his tormentor and before he could be grasped again, his lithe form had ducked out of reach and was darting down the nearest alley. The Puritan rogue stood, tensed, watching the retreating form of the boy, making no attempt to follow, though with his long legs he might have easily overtaken the lad. Slowly he replaced the cold, blue steel in its sheath and strode off across the square in the opposite direction.

Tauren was horrified, staring out the window into the empty square as the scene replayed itself in her mind's eye. She shuddered as the lad's face became Revan's and as the rogue's violence ran full tilt. Why did no one attempt to stop him? Could it be there was some truth to his words of last night? He was a local tough none dared cross? He had boasted that not even the duke himself held dread for him.

Moments later, her conscience pressed her hard, reminding her of the night-spawned thoughts of him that had obsessed her and of the more loathsome whisperings of delight that tainted her very soul.

"Lady Tauren, we shall have two day dresses completed this afternoon." Elizabeth Townings entered the small parlor, startling her and bringing a flood of crimson to her cheekbones. "I do not think another fitting will be necessary for some of the gowns. We shall have them stitched and sent to you at Lindengreen. Mrs. Murdock has said you will need a ball gown for Lord Eddys' gala. I think the sea-green brocade with the ivory satin underskirt . . . yes?"

"Gala? Wha— Ask Mrs. Murdock. She seems to know more about it than I," Tauren was furious. No one had seen fit to tell her she would be attending a ball. Then a shot of welcome defiance went up her spine.

"Oh . . . Mistress Townings, please see that several lengths of serviceable wools and muslins and a satin or two are included in the things we take today. My new maid, Roxie, is lacking in suitable apparel."

Six

Lindengreen's kitchens steamed with the heavy aromas of baking breads and savory meat pies; the pungent spiciness of wild onion, ground sage, and basil; and the tang of pot cheese and of curds being pressed. A pig had been butchered and the resulting extra work had sent the cookhouse servants into a flurry, drawing water, cutting, washing, and curing.

Revan peered around the corner of the great stone cookhouse, watching the bustle with boyish fascination, but his eyes fixed on a tray of raisin and custard tarts that sat cooling on a baker's board near the open door. By a rare stroke of luck he had escaped his tutor for the afternoon, and since the staunch housekeeper was off in Keenings with his sister, he was free to explore this marvelous place, unsupervised and unfettered.

A massive hand came down upon his young shoulder, jolting three inches from his future height and sending him gasping through the door beside him.

"Why so skittish, lad?" Calder swept the everpresent

hat from his head and placed a friendly hand on Revan's shoulder.

"I . . . I thought you might be my tutor," Revan replied truthfully, knowing his conscience bore more.

"Escaped, have ye? Well I'll not tell on ye for chosing me favorite place in all Lindengreen to dodge yer master." Seeing that some of the servants had paused in their labors, Calder gestured to them and offered, "I'd have ye meet some of me friends, here."

"This sweet thing is Cassie." Calder kissed the hand of a handsome, dark-haired woman who was in the midst of kneading dough.

She pulled her floury hand back and gave Calder a doubtful nod. "Don't be plyin' me with your roving charm, Captain. Ye be settin' a poor example for a young lad."

Calder sighed heavily and set one hand to his dapper chest. "She be a hard woman, lad . . . hard, but not impossible, me thinks." He winked at her and steered Revan on to where two young women were plucking hens. "Clara and Annie. They be twins and the finest hearth tenders about anywhere." Then he drew Revan up before a stout, stern-faced woman whose eyes twinkled at the dashing captain and came to rest keenly on the visitor. "This is our head cook, Mrs. Whitelaw. Now ye want to stay on her good side, lad. She'd be a powerful good friend for a lad with an eye for raisin tarts."

Revan's face reddened with embarrassment, but he heeded Calder's advice. Copying the captain's manner with the young woman, he reached for the cook's sturdy, work-reddened hand and placed a genteel kiss on it. "I am purely delighted, Mrs. Whitelaw."

The sturdy, sensible woman was momentarily surprised and drew her hand back to hold it gingerly in her other one, resting both on her ample stomach. "Sir," she nodded in return.

"Now, this young man is my friend, Mrs. Whitelaw, a very good friend." Calder put his hand on Revan's shoulder again. "You'll be wantin' to fatten him up a bit, eh? Maybe slip him an extra tart or dumpling from time to time? Ye must treat 'im right, Master Revan, for someday he could grow up to be an important man about 'ere." Revan caught Calder's wink and returned it.

No one had to ask who the well-formed and pleasant lad was, or why he deserved Calder's, and their, special treatment. His genuine smile and respectful manner endeared him to the kitchen folk immediately. Soon, he was on his way, stuffing his mouth with a raisin custard tart.

Clad simply in a plain shirt and dark woolen breeches, Revan made his way from the cookhouse to the stableyard, munching thoughtfully. His mind was set on the boyishly wayward pleasures of the harness room and loft.

Holt Reston dismounted from the great bay horse at the edge of the side court and walked the mount toward the stableyard. Usually a groom would have his horse by now and he would be on his way. Agitated and casting his eyes about him, Holt spied a lad about to enter the stable. "Boy!" he barked, halting Revan in his tracks.

Revan spun about, sure it was not the voice of his

tutor and, thus, no great cause for alarm. But the tall, scowling man in Puritan dress gave him cause to think again.

"Take my horse, boy," Holt ordered, holding out the reins of the huge animal, "and see he gets a good rub."

Revan, drawn by the natural authority of the man himself as by his own curiosity, swallowed the last of the sweet treat and wiped his sticky hands on his breeches.

"Step lively, or I'll have the stablemaster on you," Holt threatened, his mind occupied elsewhere.

"Sir," Revan drew himself up before the forbidding countenance and screwed up all his courage. "I am not a groom, but I shall take your mount and see it well tended."

Holt was unexpectedly jarred back to the present and found himself staring down into cool gray eyes, hauntingly familiar, under a brownish thatch of hair. It was a moment before he could absorb the un-deniable—this was the lad, the chosen one. It had to be; he had the same eyes; the same fiery cast of hair that had marauded through his dreams just the night before.

"Don't be impudent, boy," Holt glowered, irritated and surprised at just happening upon the usurper of all he had come to think of as his own. He had pictured the lad as smaller and whining, or as older and calculating. The boy before him, with a straightforward gaze and an easy, erect carriage to his broadening shoulders, bore no resemblance to either imagining. "Groom or no, you'll learn respect and do as you are told."

Revan stiffened and took the reins from Holt, weighing his response to this authoritative stranger. In

83

three short days he had learned that his new status provoked an interesting effect in those he encountered, and he pondered the wisdom of trying it here. "Sir, I do not mean to appear insolent. I am Revan Wincanton, nephew of the duke; I would have you know that before you say more."

Holt's eyes narrowed briefly and his tone was curt. "I have come to see Calder." Seeing the lad pull on the reins and start for the stable, Holt was annoyed and unable to pin this reaction to any rational motive. "I've need of his farrier. My best stallion was hurt . . . injured by a damned-fool boy!" he said with betraying vehemence. "I don't want to put him down unless I must."

Revan saw the tightness and strain on the big man's face as they entered the warmth and pungent smells of the graystone stable. "What did you do to him?" Revan asked, pausing in the alley between rows of straw-littered stalls to stare at the big Puritan intently.

"I staunched the blood as best I could—" Holt stopped, aware he was accompanying the lad and roundly irritated.

"I mean to the boy. What did you do to the boy who hurt your horse?" Revan was leading the bay into a generous box stall, "Jeremy!"

"I haven't decided yet," Holt scowled. "What would you do to a worthless boy whose stupidity and cruelty ruined a valuable mount's legs?"

Revan shoved his thumbs into his pockets and joined Holt in the alley, frowning thoughtfully and wondering what a good ruler would do. "I suppose the punishment should suit the misdeed. I'd . . . make him work . . . care for the horse as it mended . . . and work in the

84

stables, unless he'd done such before. That'd be another matter."

"Yes, milord?" Jeremy came running up, breathless and covered with straw, nodding at them both.

"There's a big bay needs tending," Revan pointed over his shoulder.

"Aye," the boy grinned up at the overlord, "that be Atlas, I guess. I'll see to 'im good."

Revan watched Holt's look soften slightly as he accepted the boy's respect, then return sternly to him.

"Who are you, sir? Are you a neighbor of Lindengreen?" He had to move quickly to keep up with Holt's long legs.

Holt stopped suddenly and gazed coolly down at the lad. "I am not your uncle's neighbor." Holt clipped his words. "I am Holt Reston . . . an . . . official here in Somersetshire."

"Which office do you hold? Magistrate? Bailiff? Sheriff?"

"All of them," Holt said tersely, watching the lad handle his less than friendly declaration.

"It is good we meet, then. I need to know the men who serve my uncle."

Holt felt the innocent slap of the boy's words and his face cracked into a sardonic smile. It hadn't occurred to him that the lad might know nothing of the strange distribution of power within the shire. Holt rapped his muscular thigh with his gloves impatiently. "I must find Calder."

"He's likely in the cookhouse. I've just left him there. It's this way." Revan headed quickly down the alley toward the harness room, Holt trailing reluctantly in his wake.

"Ned, you have a visitor," Revan called to the harnessman and smith, Ned Wright. Ned stepped out from behind the posts draped with harness and saddles and his face brightened at the sight of Revan and Holt.

"Master Holt." He wiped his hand on his soft leather apron before extending it to Holt who accepted it warmly.

"Ned, you do not change." Holt observed his broad girth and pleasant, fleshy, red face, smiling tightly.

"Only now I have a better class of pupil." He winked, nodding in Revan's direction. He noted that Holt did not smile at his little jest.

"Pupil?" Holt looked at Revan critically. "Is this not a vulgar pursuit for one of your rank?" The words came out more bitterly than he realized and caught both the boy and his old friend by surprise. "Are you not the heir to Somerset, a Marquess in your own right?"

Revan was puzzled at the rapid change in his new acquaintance and the cutting-sharp edge of his words. He summoned every shred of dignity he could muster, staring straight up at Holt.

"A man who is to rule wisely must know both his people and their work. There is much to learn here."

The response brought a piercing glare from Holt. Was there inside that boyish skin a grizzled old veteran? Had the duke himself found a way to reenter the world of youth? He muttered something unintelligible and wheeled, striding angrily through the open door.

Revan and Ned Wright watched him go; one unable to fathom his response and the other reading it all too clearly.

"You know Master Reston well?" Revan asked,

following Ned back to his workbench and settling himself nearby on a half-finished saddle.

"Yes, I knew him years ago as a lad. He used to come here, like you." Ned cast a guarded glance at the young lord before picking up a punch and mallet in his brawny hands to pierce a harness strap.

Revan saw the look and hazarded a guess. "He's a powerful man in the shire, isn't he?"

"Yes," Ned struck a tap and repositioned the punch before striking again. "He has . . . power."

"Then you must tell me about him—all about him."

Something in the lad's voice caused Ned to look at him. He was surprised by the determination in the striking gray eyes and the command in the tilt of the chin. As he began his story, he remembered the same look in a darker face, the same intensity and natural authority in a pair of green-brown eyes.

Seven

"Miz Townings' gowns for all the ladies were just as low, milady. Naught but a red-blooded man would take notice . . . and yer not likely to meet up wi' one about here." Roxie's impudent look brought a laugh to Tauren's lips.

"Roxie, you've got to be brought under rein." Gazing at the pier glass, she pulled futilely at the top of her low, rounded neckline. "The duke will join us for supper this eve . . . I'll not give him cause for disparagement again." She tried to rearrange, then jerked the padded farthingale that encircled her hips. "I detest these things. It's like wading about in a barrel. They're intolerable!"

"They be all the fashion, milady. Not a lady goes about without one."

"Naught but an empty-headed 'lady' would," Tauren mused tartly, throwing up her skirts and jerking the irritating roll from her hips.

Trying to walk, she still felt weighed down by the

lace-bedecked royal blue sateen. In the days since her first fitting, she had tried to accustom herself to the rich, heavy fabrics, the tiers of silk petticoats, and the round wadding of the farthingale. But just walking in the restrictive opulence was a chore. Compared to her plain, but supple, woolen gowns and lambsoft linen petticoats, these stiff corsets and voluminous sleeves and skirts were atrocities to live in.

She left her chambers and wandered about the second floor of the mansion, past the old duke's apartments and into the west wing. Here the plastered walls and ornate ceilings gave way to expanses of bare stone and the hallways narrowed. The light dimmed, for the windows were smaller and more infrequent, making it difficult to appreciate the time-dulled tapestries and the heavily carved furnishings.

Here was the original hall of Lindengreen, Tauren mused, once a fortified hall that lent protection from viking attacks and from avaricious neighboring lords. But even these sturdy walls were no protection from the merciless onslaught of her future.

Finding herself in a large bedchamber, she plopped down unceremoniously onto the woven ropes of a great wooden box of a bed. Her seat reminded her that in a few weeks, she too would furnish some nobleman's hall, bearing his weight at night.

A husband. She shivered involuntarily, sending her arms up across her fashionably bare chest and shoulders. Her narrow escape in the glade had taught her part of what a husband would soon demand of her. Alarmingly, her breath quickened and her stomach and below felt suddenly empty, almost . . . hungry.

Dark angular features rose unbidden to her mind's eye and again her lips seemed warmed by some phantom presence.

"Stop it!" she commanded her unruly senses. "He's an unprincipled rogue. Count yourself fortunate indeed to have escaped him." But she could not stop herself from wondering if she would feel the same startling pleasure with a husband.

"Will he be fair or dark . . . handsome or ill favored?" She frowned and sighed heavily. Other things mattered more. What would be his feelings toward Revan? Could he be convinced to bring the lad home once the old duke was gone? Would he see to her brother's affairs honestly and rightly until Revan might manage on his own? Her thoughts turned inward. Would he be good to the children she might bear him . . . or would he tear them from her at a tender age to pack them off to foster, because it was the fashion of nobles?

Her winsome face fell at the irony. The circumstance of poverty had saved her from the ravages of an early marriage, only to see her disposed of now as a minor family asset. She bounded up from her seat to staunch the flow of hurt with action.

She rounded the corner of the hallway leading past the duke's apartments, near the great hall. Something arrested her in midstep and she froze, not realizing at first what had so instantly paralyzed her.

She listened tensely to a hauntingly familiar voice that drew closer by the second. She fled to the safety of the corner she had just turned and there pressed herself against the wall, feeling her heart pounding. She knew beyond all doubt; the voice and deep laugh she had just heard belonged to the one man in the world she despised and prayed never to set eyes on again.

Impulse belying her resolve, she turned and peeked about the corner to catch the appearance of two figures, one in familiar scarlet and the other in stark black and white. It was *him*—and wearing that cursed hypocrite's garb. It was just like a Puritan wretch to sing psalms on the Sabbath and then assault an unprotected girl two days later. She drew back, wondering furiously at Calder's seeming acceptance of the duke's enemy. They were exiting the old duke's private study.

"He'll come 'round sooner or later. There are some things he cannot wish away."

"He's a stubborn old goat, ye must give 'im that." Calder's response contained a seriousness that made Tauren swallow hard.

The door closed and she could not resist one last peek. She caught sight of *his* face as he turned an arrogant smile on Calder and it was clear from the way his eyes lit that he had seen her as well.

"I'll see my way out through the old hall," the rogue drawled, sending angry confusion boiling up inside her.

"Suit yerself," came Calder's retreating voice.

Gasping, Tauren lifted her heavy skirts and forced herself to run on tiptoe back down the cold hallway she had just taversed. She turned a corner and ducked hurriedly into the same large bedchamber she had left moments before, eying it wildly for some means of concealment.

His heavy footfalls seemed almost leisurely as they drew unerringly closer. But nothing in the room could be found to offer her protection.

The arched doorway filled suddenly with a powerful dark frame, and Tauren swallowed against a choking in her throat to whirl and meet his handsome, mocking stare with all the angry poise she could summon. Anticipation sent annoying little trills racing along her arms, tingling her fingertips and reddening her bosoms.

"You!" she spat huskily, noting that he leaned his broad shoulder against the doorframe and relished his control of the chamber's only exit.

"And you," he returned, visually touching every part of her from across the distance. His sensual mouth curled upward at one end as he let his eyes have their fill of her. "I swore to have you the next time I found you."

Tauren's face drained of some of its heightened color, but she lifted her chin defiantly. "And I swore to have your black heart for dinner."

Her tart remark brought a full, lusty smirk to his arrogant face. "I take my vows most seriously . . . still, I might be persuaded to recant." He sent one finger up to stroke the strong curve of his chin.

"In that case I might be content with a simple hanging." Her eyes danced becomingly with ire. "Do you know with whom you speak, swine?"

"A hot young wench with highly placed relations."

"Cur!" she hissed. "I know not your name, but I know what you are . . . a bully, a low-minded molester of women, an abuser of the small and weak—"

"Then I can hardly lower your opinion of me by taking my pleasures after all." He moved stealthily toward her, eyes hardening and unrelenting.

She backed away slowly, not wanting him to see the

fear blooming within her and silently cursing her own watery knees. "I'll scream," she threatened.

"Scream then, wench, call whomever you will."

But before she could open her mouth he pounced upon her and hoisted her up and against him, imprisoning her arms at her sides and catching one of her calves between his knees. Her other leg flailed ineffectually in midair as she sputtered and pleaded incoherently, demanding release and promising dire punishment if he failed to do so.

"Make good your threats while you can, you vile, skulking brute," she gritted out, bracing for his worst.

But the tension about his mouth subsided when no scream split the air and his arms about her eased, allowing her rigid body to shift lower and rest against him more intimately.

Shamed to the roots of her hair at the ignominy of her posture, she slowed her struggles and had time to wonder at this pause, looking upward into his guarded gaze.

"I am not so vile nor are you so innocent that we could not find pleasure in each other. 'It is most blessed to both give and receive.'"

"You blaspheme!" she breathed hatefully.

He dropped her unceremoniously, barely landing her on her feet, as his laughter boomed. She stood, mouth agape, looking at him in astonishment, forgetting for a moment her peril and possible escape. As the ring of his laughter died in the room, an impudent grin spread across his fascinating mouth, revealing a dimple in the smooth, hard plane of his cheek. Tauren's eyes fastened helplessly upon that feature, and she felt a confusing warmth coursing through her. An unstoppable tide of crimson invaded her bosom and face and betrayed her wayward impulse.

Before she could master her feelings, Holt had closed the distance between them. She felt paralyzed, panicky, and jittery inside as his hand reached toward her. Then her head was spiraling upward, reeling out of control. His mouth lowered to hers slowly, testing, then tempting with the lush promise of its warmth.

One final, ineffective push against his hard chest was all she could manage, and having failed, her hands lingered there against his mesmerizing strength. His kiss deepened and he clasped her tighter against him, molding her soft coolness to his angular heat. She was drowning, unable to breathe, incapable of thought, of anything but feeling. Slowly, tentatively, she returned his kiss, feeling that strange wanting in her loins that had alarmed her so in recent nights. Now she allowed it, explored it; and it sent a startling flush of excitement up under her exposed skin, setting the nipples of her breasts atingle.

With a small noise of distress, she surrendered to the double assault of his overpowering maleness and her own body's vibrant demands. Her slender arms slipped about his lean waist and she pressed fully against him, feeling him tighten all along her in response.

His arms crushed the breath from her as he lifted her breasts against him and caught her dangling legs with one muscular arm. He placed her gently on the unfurled straw ticking of the venerable old bed and removed his short sword and doublet to lower himself beside her. Her eyes glazed with wonderment and passion as his strong, work-hardened fingers traced tenderly the glowing heart of her face. She felt the weight of his bent knee across her thighs and turned her winsome face to him.

The naked hunger in his forest-flecked eyes stopped her heart, then set it hammering wildly. Again he pressed her lips, sending one big hand down the smooth marble of her throat and to her half-revealed breasts. The stiff sateen yielded eagerly to his questing touch and Tauren jumped as his lips followed.

The heat of his face rubbed the cool mounds of her breasts, and he lavished attention on their sensitive rosy tips. Waves of breathtaking sensation engulfed her, sending a curious drawing tingling through her loins, as if the two were tied by some invisible cord within her.

She pressed against him, wanting, needing . . . something more. Suddenly the vague night longings, the hungry achings of her ripe young body became focused, sharpened, and she knew that this was what she had craved these nights in her maiden's bed without knowing what she needed.

She moaned softly and his mouth returned to hers with a comforting possession. Her skirts were drawn slowly up over her legs and his hard weight bore down against her, parting her silken thighs.

The breath stopped in her throat as she felt the press of his full manhood against her moist flesh. Her eyes flew open and she tensed suddenly with a vague, slow-rising alarm.

He felt the change in her and touched her face. "Tauren . . . my love . . ." he uttered hoarsely, claiming her mouth again.

The sound of her name snapped some restraining band of her consciousness, and through the bright haze of her passion, Tauren struggled toward sanity.

A jagged flash of stinging pain seared upward through her, jolting her with the horror of what had transpired. Her arms jerked back from their caressing embrace and she began to push against his chest with all her strength. The pleasurable fullness in her loins suddenly horrified her. She began to writhe frantically beneath him.

"No . . . dear God . . . *no*!"

He was suddenly up on his elbows above her, scouring her terrified face with eyes full of dark, unsated desire. "Tauren"—he stroked her shoulder— "I won't hurt you just be—"

"No-o-o," she wailed frantically, panting for breath against the choking in her throat. "Stop! You can't . . . do this . . ." With a sickening sense of shame, she realized it was too late. Wildly, she pushed with all her strength against him and he withdrew abruptly.

Her hands covered her face as he moved over and beside her. He lay watching her, his dark face taut with angry confusion.

"Dammit!" he grabbed her wrists and pulled them to him, revealing the great tears burning trails from her troubled, luminous eyes back toward her hair.

"Please . . . no more . . ." she murmured brokenly, squeezing her eyes tightly shut.

Now more bewildered than angered, he searched down the bare satiny skin of her hip to her rumpled white petticoats and was arrested by stark scarlet stains that bore silent testimony of virtue surrendered.

His jaw slacked and he drew back his chin sharply, gentling his hard grip on her wrists and finally freeing them. Tauren lay motionless, biting her lip, misery blotting out the all but shattering reality of what had happened to her.

"You were a maid, then," his full, deep voice penetrated her enshrouded senses. He moved beside her and she heard the scrape of his jackboots on the bare wooden floor. She sounded the depths of her despair only to rise to slowly mounting fury.

Her eyes flew open as he pulled her up against him, cradling her in one muscular arm and turning her streaked face up to his.

"I didn't know. . . . But then it wouldn't have changed anything . . . hardly anything."

The curl of amusement about his mouth ignited a blaze of anger in her, and she jerked away from him, twisting out of his grasping attempt to retrieve her. She was on her feet, fists whitened at her sides.

"You . . . you still would have forced yourself on me. You loathsome . . . evil—"

"Forced?" Holt Reston rose with a sardonic tilt of his head. "Nay, you cannot play that virgin's game with me. It always hurts the first time, but it will get better. I can promise it. And you've seen how seriously I take a vow."

His words slapped her, taking her breath. His vow . . . his damnable vow! What madness had seized her—forced her—to comply with his cynical lust? Her future was destroyed to fulfill his debauched, carnal vow . . . and the rakehell smirked about the next—

"Get better?" she gritted out nastily, just then realizing that his gaze fell below her own. Mortified to find one rosy crescent peeping over the twisted blue sateen of her bodice, she jerked the fabric up savagely, her face more crimson with rage than shame.

97

"Only, the next time," his mouth twisted into a cocky smirk, "you'll allow me to finish what I've started."

"Finish?" she raged, failing to grasp his meaning. "It is finished now! You've despoiled me."

"Pleasured you!" he insisted, edging closer. "And I will again."

She backed away, unconquered fear flitting briefly across her face before she contained it. "I'll see you rot in hell first. . . ." She stopped, immobilized by this final horror. She did not even know his name! Her face blanched of all color.

"Dear God," her knees suddenly weakened, "I might even now bear a nameless bastard's bastard."

Holt blinked, then threw back his head and laughed resoundingly, destroying the last of her pride with his mockery. Her hand went to her mouth to shield it, and tears gathered to pour out her humiliation.

Suddenly she was running through the doorway and he jolted after her . . . too late. In the hallway he watched the billow of her skirts as she disappeared about the corner. A sharp pang of fresh desire pierced him, and as it passed, a sardonic grin took its place.

"Oh, I'll have you again, Tauren Wincanton. You're mine."

Safely in her rooms, Tauren locked her door, alternately raging and pacing as she wrapped her arms about her small waist.

That nameless evil rogue had taken her virtue—then laughed at her! And she had not even resisted!

She bit her lip and found it tender. Her fingertips explored its passion-bruised fullness, and she was swept from weakened knees to tingling breasts with a tide of sensuous warmth. Even the ache between her legs seemed to mute into a pleasurable throb. She could not blot out his spell even now, in her deepest fears! How she despised that rutting cur . . . and herself for succumbing to him.

Flinging herself on the padded bench at the foot of her bed, she swiped away a tear with her palm and clasped her shaking hands together tightly. The duke would dine with them in a few hours . . . she *must* collect herself. She drew a deep jerky breath, forcing her mind to work.

He hadn't known she was a virgin until after . . . perhaps a man couldn't always tell. A faint whisper of hope tantalized her. It wasn't her idea to marry in the first place. Perhaps her husband would be a dry, crusty old curmugeon, unused to women, or a fat, indolent squire more interested in his hounds than in bedding a wife.

Slowly, her devastated spirit reassembled to bolster her flagging courage. Whatever befell, she had no one to turn to but herself. And she would have to meet the future squarely, for Revan's sake . . . and her own.

Tauren knew the moment she entered the dining hall that evening on Revan's arm that the extra effort given to her appearance was not wasted. This supper would be one of the most difficult of her life. She sent one trembling hand to smooth her elegant coif, wondering if some lingering evidence of that afternoon's shame might be detectable. The duke's calculating gaze searched every inch of the twosome and she was strangely relieved by his slow smirk of approval.

"You are a beauty, my girl. The coin was well laid."
His hand and voice were cold. Tauren noted lines in his
face she had not seen at their first meeting.

"And you, Marquess, a fine figure in your new attire.
The tutor reports that your studies go well. This pleases
me. You seem a young man of your word, for you
indicated a willingness to study and apply yourself. No
doubt Strafford will be pleased with the progress of his
new ward come the new year." He waved them to their
places at his right and left hand, never having bothered
to rise from his seat at the head of the long table.

The little conversation managed was stilted and gave
her to know that the duke was indeed informed of their
every move. No mention was made of her indiscreet
little ride, but she was sure Murdock must have given
him a full account. When the last platters were cleared
away, an auguring rumble came from the duke's
throat.

"Lady Tauren, in two days I shall escort you to a gala
at the Earl of Rentings. I have no stomach for the rich
food of a noisy banquet. We shall arrive late . . . and
return to Lindengreen the same night." He arched one
brow as his eyes drank in the effect of her well-
displayed assets. "You will meet your new husband
there. You needs make a good impression."

Tauren's jaw dropped at this untimely announcement. "My . . . hus-husband?" Revan stared at her
across the massive walnut table.

"Your husband. He insists upon meeting you at the
Eddys' gala, though I assured him no such formalities
were necessary."

"Formalities?" Her wits were scattered for an

instant; she could only echo him blankly. "Surely it would not be done otherwise." Deep within her cold dread stirred.

"It is already agreed, you will marry," the duke leaned forward as if to emphasize his point. "Sappington has some notion of making your acquaintance before the banns are read. I have agreed to allow him to validate your worth firsthand."

"My worth?"

"Tauren," Revan interjected, "what is this about a marriage?"

"Revan"—horror filled her—"I meant to tell you. . . ."

"You're getting married?" he choked, "really married? Going away?" His eyes were glazed with moisture and Tauren drew a breath of pure misery for him.

Conscious of the old duke's critical eye, she chose her words carefully, her eyes pleading with her brother for understanding. "I would have told you, but there seemed no good time. The duke has commanded it—and chosen the man. I didn't want to worry you."

In a long moment she saw the moisture fade from his true gray eyes and he seemed to grow inches as he straightened his shoulders manfully and frowned his fiercest at her. Her astonishment at the abrupt change in him was exceeded only by her bewilderment at his next words.

"Tauren, someday I shall have the worry of the whole shire and perhaps a part of England's future in my care. I am a full twelve years now. If I am to bear such burdens at twenty, I must learn to shoulder some now. I am not a child!"

"Why was I not consulted on the matter of my sister's

marriage?" he turned on the duke.

The old man's eyes narrowed slightly at this challenge, but he tilted his head to one side as if studying the lad's reaction. "Arranging a match involves things of which you cannot yet have understanding. I have chosen for her, as was my right. I am her guardian."

Revan's chin jutted out stubbornly. "And it is my right as her brother to see to her happiness."

"Happiness and duty are seldom satisfied in the same decision; this is a lesson you must learn quickly, young lord. Your sister is near nineteen and must fulfill her duty in this marriage. It will be an alliance for you in the coming years."

"If it were an alliance meant to benefit me, then why was I not told? It appears to me there are many things to learn here, Your Grace. I do not think it wise that I be sent away to learn courtly manners and unwholesome diversions while I could be learning of my people and their needs, gaining their loyalty."

Tauren was stunned. First they discussed her and her future as if she were not present and now Revan waxed eloquent in his own defense, showing cleverness and sound logic in the development of his arguments, which was more than she had been able to do in his behalf.

The duke managed a crinkling of the corners of his mouth. "What you say has merit, but the decision has been made with many things in mind. You will abide by it as will your sister."

"What, pray, is the estimable gentleman's name— this man you have chosen as my punishment?" Tauren choked.

Ignoring her ire, the duke sipped from his silver goblet and savored the wine along with his response. "Sappington, the young Earl of Sappington. An old title . . . His estates are the closest to Lindengreen of any nobleman of suitable rank." His gaze tallied her worth openly. "You will do poorly in that household, girl, if you cannot learn to bridle your tongue."

Her cheeks flaming at his censure, she rose without his leave. "Then I shall leave my future in your hands, gentlemen, for it is clear that I have no part in its making. Please let me know when you wish me to begin packing; I would not wish to delay your plans by remaining in your care a moment longer than necessary."

Revan stood and made to follow her, but the duke's thin hand restrained him. "She will accept it, in time. We have things to discuss, you and I . . . things your sister would not understand." Seeing Revan's mistrust openly displayed, he chuckled, a rusty, odd sound that might have seemed a cough but for the slight smile upon his face. "How like Edward you are. . . ."

Eight

The ballroom of the Earl of Rentings' elegant home was ablaze with the lights from crystal chandeliers and heavy with the smell of beeswax tapers, rich wine, and the warm, perfumed bodies of the sporting nobility. Heavy brocades rustled and silk petticoats swished, ivory and silk fans fluttered, and diamonds winked from coiffures, cravats, and fingers. The creamy luminescence of pearls vied for the eye with the smooth, warm marble of young girls' skin.

Tauren stood by her uncle, awaiting introduction and dreading the next few steps that would propel her into a new life. The duke leaned heavily upon his golden-headed walking stick, his face lined with irritation at these formalities and with what Tauren read all too clearly as pain. She had never seen him standing before this eve, when he appeared in the great hall of Lindengreen. It had not struck her as odd; she had assumed that his rank and arrogance put such civility beneath him.

Her thoughts were interrupted by the abrupt

approach of Lord Cedric Eddys, their host, who now bowed before the duke with great exaggeration.

"Your Grace"—his words tumbled over themselves in their eagerness to be out—"my true delight in having you here is only slightly less abundant than the grace you do this house in accepting our invitation."

Tauren saw the duke's eyes narrow slightly, but then the trace of annoyance was gone, his regal poise again covering whatever lay beneath that cold exterior. "Good to see you, Cedric." He turned his head stiffly toward Tauren. "My niece, the Lady Tauren Wincanton, my brother, Edward's, child."

The ruddy-faced earl's eyes widened appreciably as they flew lightly over Tauren's person, noting casually the ripe swell of her lightly imprisoned breasts, her tiny waist, her flawless skin and sparkling sapphire eyes. Her gown was composed of the fashionable double-tiered skirt dropped over a farthingale; a rich green satin brocade, the color of sea foam, overlayering a skirt of ivory satin. The low, rounded bodice was also of green brocade, banded in emerald green velvet and made to show the lady's full bosom and slender arms to proper advantage.

"My dear, Lady Tauren," Lord Cedric continued his effusive welcome, "you are the most exquisite blossom in all of nature's garden. You embarrass the fairest of the white roses of the field into blushing pink for shame of losing by comparison." He placed her slender hand upon his full sleeve and drew her along after the duke.

The noise and reedy music, the smells and greedy eyes of the revelers pressed in upon Tauren almost physically, forcing her to draw upon every shred of composure she could muster. A growing wave of whisperings flowed about the room, seeming to follow them along.

Lady Charlotte Eddys greeted them warmly, coaxing from the old duke a rare and curious expression that on any other would have been named pleasure.

"So this is your lovely niece," Lady Charlotte observed pleasantly. "Young Sappington has been champing at the bit to see you. Now, 'tis clear to me why."

Tauren blushed with confusion, wondering if all those gawking at them knew the reason for this exceptional appearance of the Duke of Somerset; to allow her new master to "determine her worth" firsthand and seal a bargain.

Suddenly before her was a fair young man of medium height and slender build, garbed in an opulent forest-green doublet and breeches, the doublet trimmed with scarlet satin and sporting the slashed sleeves popular with the dandies of court. His slender legs were encased in fine scarlet stockings that matched the trim of his garments, and large red satin bows topped his glossy leather pumps. His coal-gray eyes flitted over her appealingly displayed form, and one corner of his thin lips lifted in a languorous approval of what he beheld.

"Your Grace," he addressed the duke, "she is indeed the maid you spoke of in all respects, and much more. But how difficult it would have been to distill the sweet essence of such charm, such beauty in mere words. Lady Tauren," he kissed her hand with a courtly flourish.

"I am pleased to meet you, my lord Earl." She felt a sinking in her chest and her tongue played traitor to her desire to play the lady's role. "I hope we may find time this eve to keep company. If we find naught to speak of now, we shall have long years of silence ahead."

Roger Stillwell, Earl of Sappington, threw back his fair, blond head and laughed resoundingly. "Little lady," he smirked confidently, "you needn't fear I shall require conversation of you . . . for your charming person bodes of other sweet communion, as meaningful and infinitely more pleasurable."

His voice lowered at the last, and he gazed directly into her eyes while the nattily garbed young bloods about him chortled their agreement and made unintelligible but discomforting remarks among themselves.

"Be assured, Lady Tauren, you have my entire attention for the evening." He glared meaningfully at the other young nobles, drawing another round of hoots and comments Tauren was all too sorry to have understood this time.

True to his word, Sappington claimed every dance with Tauren, scowling forbiddingly whenever another male approached and thereby eliminating all competition for her favors. Those who had not yet heard or deduced the reason for Sappington's proprietary behavior were quite unwilling to test his temper. He was known to be deadly with a sword and had left two bodies already upon the field of honor. Now, Tauren Wincanton had been declared the exclusive property of the hot-blooded young earl who would brook no interference with that which he deemed his own.

The steps of the dance were new to Tauren, but Sappington's close attention to her, the warmth of his hands about her waist, drew her mind from her inexperience at the dance and back to the shattering experience of three days ago. Roger's cool bearing warmed when he was near her and his eyes glowed with a light Tauren recognized all too clearly. She shivered inexplicably and forced her thoughts back to present matters.

Breaking from the other dancers, Roger steered her away from the crowd. "You were raised in a cleric's home in the North Country, I believe." Something in his tone or in the haughty tilt of his handsome chin caused her stomach to tighten defensively. "I suppose the transition from a country rectory to the duke's great Lindengreen must be difficult for you." His eyes were coolly amused as he virtually divested her of her bodice.

She clasped her hands in front of her, suddenly noting where they were, on a bench tucked away at the side of the staircase in the outer hall of the Rentings' elegant mansion. How could she respond—to the remark and this visual ravishment?

"Your common upbringing"—he lifted her chin to catch her averted eyes with his—"the duke warned me about it. But I think it shall not prove an impediment to our union. You have made acceptable progress. You may compensate me in other ways for whatever you lack in the graces. It may please me to have you presented at court after a bit. You have the appearance of a lady already."

"But of course, my lord"—she smiled caustically, feeling a warning surge in her chest—"arrogance and avarice are man's natural state. The transition from common to noble would no doubt prove more difficult in the reverse."

It was a moment before he felt the sting of her remark and grabbed her mutinous face harshly in one hand, digging his fingertips cruelly into her jaw. Her shock at his violence seemed to check the flow of wrath in him and his touch became gentler, though the flame in his dark gray eyes still burned.

"Perhaps, lady, I shall have to judge you fairly by your conversation after all." His tone left no doubt of the threat intended, and Tauren dropped her gaze in confusion and horror at this ominous twist of events. Dearest heaven, what sort of man was this intended husband of hers?

He stood abruptly and took her hand, drawing her up after him. When she looked up, his face was a carefully drawn mask of civility and attention. "We shall join the others. I would have you meet my neighbors—and let them see why soon they shall envy me even more than they do now."

Holt Reston peeled his sodden cloak from his shoulders and then snatched the cloth from the hands of the footman who wiped at the mud and grime on his spurred jackboots. Waving the man away, he wiped the mud himself and dropped the cloth onto the smooth black and white marble of the floor. The house was ablaze with lights and he was little noticed in the noise and revelry of the full-blown gala underway.

He straightened his doublet and ran an impatient hand through his thick raven hair, careless of how its dampness curled about his sinewy hand. In a few moments, the footman reappeared and led him up the stairs, past the ballroom, to the private study of the

Earl of Rentings.

When the overlord of Somerset entered, all talk ceased; a few men stood up defensively while others chose the activity of refilling their goblets to mask their discomfort. There was not a man in the room who had not been challenged by Holt Reston at some time or other, and who had not lost to him. Resentment ran deep in a few, but none could deny that he ran the shire productively. Had he been of noble birth, not one would have abstained from following him. But there was the rub—this man who had bettered them was not their equal.

"You have news?" the duke spoke, drawing the tension of the room upon himself.

"Yes," Holt turned to address them all, having bowed to none. "This news bears hearing by you all. Indeed, you will do well to think hard upon the tidings I bring; your fortunes may depend on it."

Quick to settle on the side with the advantage, Cedric Eddys poured Holt a goblet of heated wine and presented it to him, waving him to his own vacant seat by the duke.

"I was halfway to London when a courier from my friends in the government overtook me. The Earl of Strafford was arrested and taken to the tower two days ago—charged with treason. He will go to public trial." He paused as the sense of his words caused a delayed intake of breath about the room, followed by a stunned murmur. "Charles sent men to take charge of the tower, but Sir William Balfour closed the gates against him. Warrants may be issued against some in his house for conspiracy."

"This is an outrage!" The duke nearly strangled. His

voice was joined by the others in a general outcry against the "Parliamentary swine who in this act have struck out at the king himself."

Reston sat back and propped one great booted leg upon a nearby stool, resting his goblet upon his knee. He watched dispassionately the ravings of the nobles about him, recognizing all too clearly the fear underlying their anger.

The duke raised one hand for silence. "There is more?" he demanded. "What more has the king done? Surely the council or Charles himself can override . . . surely. What evidence can they have had? Come, Reston, what do you know?"

"Letters have been produced . . . advocating the use of Irish and even French forces to invade England and drive out the Scots . . . and perhaps to control Parliament."

"Invade England? An invitation to invade the country from the king himself!" a short round noble exploded. "Preposterous . . . lies!"

"You are certain"—the duke placed one thin hand on Reston's arm—"you can trust your source? . . ." The old man's face was grim, seeing the demise of his long-cherished plans now a certainty.

"Send a courier to Parliament itself if you must verify the report. Half of London was in the streets in celebration." There was a curious nonchalance to his manner and the duke searched the younger man's face relentlessly.

"It is as you say, then. I do not doubt your word. . . . In this instance any falsehood would sound sweeter."

"There is more. The Archbishop Laud is also arrested and most of the privy council has quit the city;

111

some, like Secretary Windebanke, the country itself. There is talk the king may leave London to rally support in the provinces. It is beyond dissolving Parliament now; they'll have a taste of blood before they are satisfied."

"Well, I for one have no love for Charles's archbishop," Lord Cedric announced. "Cropping ears for not attending church—abominable. Reston here was right to defy the decree. But Strafford . . . that is another matter. The man is the king's most trusted minister, one to whom Charles has given his personal guarantee. I heard him speak in the Lords'; eloquent he was, some said brilliant . . . the backbone of Charles's body of policy."

There were mutterings of agreement and slanting looks at Reston, whose nonchalant posture in truth revealed his small measure of concern. It was, after all, more a threat to the entrenched nobility than to a man of acquired power such as himself.

When none but the duke and Reston remained in the room, the old man turned to him, searching him. "You take the news well," he observed caustically.

"It amuses me to see my 'betters' reduced to a cockfight, knowing they're bred spurless. Whatever the outcome in this test of wills, 'tis the folk who will suffer most, not the pampered, fat nobles. If I dread this, it is for the people only."

"You berate that which is denied you. In truth you envy every man here his titles and lands."

"And they envy me the power to take it from them should I so choose."

The duke dropped his tired eyes from Reston's acknowledging that bitter truth.

112

Annoyingly sober in spite of the rich wine, Holt drained his goblet and his feet hit the floor loudly. He turned to the old duke who watched him and smiled irritatingly. "Now you cannot send your heir to Strafford."

The duke's head jerked up, surprised that Holt had read his thoughts so plainly. "I cannot."

"What will you do with him?"

"I shall find another foster."

"Can you see the future to know which side to favor with your heir—and with your holdings? If you choose unwisely, his life is forfeit. Indeed, do send the whelp away. I'll be pleased to care for the estates—and might even return them to him . . . provided he returns to claim them."

"'Tis none of your affair!" the old man barked hoarsely, as irritated by his allowing the overlord to taunt him as by the predicament spread before him. "I shall wait a month or two and see what course Charles will take before deciding anon."

"And the girl?" Reston's eyes glinted strangely over the rim of his cup when the duke's head snapped up to search his face.

"For her nothing is changed, she will be married off. Naught will change that." The duke stared at him appraisingly, wondering why he asked about the girl, and was piqued anew at the powerful young man's intimate knowledge of everything and everyone in his shire.

Holt shrugged and went to lean his shoulder against the mantelpiece, warming himself. A lingering trace of amusement in his finely chiseled features taunted the duke.

A page slipped through the door and glanced anxiously about before seeing Reston's begrimed boots and settling before him by the fire. Holt raised his powerful leg and rested his boot upon the stool the lad placed before him.

Lord Cedric reappeared and clasped one of the overlord's shoulders, "Reston, you must stay and take your ease with us. I will not have you leave my house without tasting of its hospitality." Seeing Holt's hesitant look, he pressed, "Charlotte will be devastated if you do not stay; you'll force me out of favor with her for weeks to come. And perhaps you can pry His Grace's niece away from Sappington long enough for the rest of us to claim a dance with her."

"Then I accept your invitation. I'll pay respects to your lady as soon as the lad finishes my boots."

The effusive lord seemed momentarily discomforted, deserted by his customary flood of verbiage. "I . . . would have you know, Reston . . . your company . . . will always be appreciated in my house."

Holt stared intently and lifted one corner of his mouth into a lazy smile of acceptance. "My pleasure, my lord."

Tauren's back ached, her head throbbed, and the nerves in her legs were screaming with tension. Soon Roger would return to the little sitting room where he had left her and she knew by his hot looks and suggestive remarks he meant to sample her pleasures when he returned.

All that kept her from bolting for the door was the vengeful duke's will. She shuddered, clenching her teeth and fists to bolster her flagging determination. She could play the fawning maid, the outraged innocent; perhaps then he would be satisfied with some small token against full payment on their wedding night.

The dull clink of a goblet on the table behind alerted her to Roger's return and she held her pose and breath as she felt rather than heard his leisurely approach. She did not turn, but waited quietly, expectantly. She felt his press against her skirts and stopped her breath, wondering at his silence.

Then he touched her small satin-laced waist with his warm hands and she shivered as she felt herself drawn backward against his warmth. He held her for a time, her spine rigid and her tension evident in the tautness of her cheek and her shallow, rapid breathing. Something in this torturous slowness was harder to bear than an assault. She closed her eyes and bit her lower lip, feeling one hand leave her waist and touch with the gentleness of a butterfly the smooth skin of her exposed shoulder. Excitement budded within her at this unexpected gentleness; vexing and unwelcome sensations arose in her stomach and moved upward into her chest.

Her intended's lips brushed her hair near her temples, moving it gently, his breath warm and sweet. He dropped light kisses down the left side of her neck tickling and caressing her in such a manner that she began to respond in her very loins.

She dropped her head back against his chest, shoving the warnings of her better sense aside with an appeasement of newfound sensitivity. She was encircled in the tender strength of his arms and for a long moment he held her, allowing her to melt slowly against him.

Her shoulder trilled beneath his warm lips as they began to explore that splendid curve, and he smiled knowingly at the change in her skin. He nibbled her ear, sending waves of limb-weakening delight through her and striking down the last of her moral protests against him. From his vantage point above her he had an unrestricted view of her creamy breasts as they met in an alluring line that plunged beneath her bodice. She offered him the slim column of her neck, feeling the strong thudding of his heart against her back and feeling the beat of her own slow into a sensual synchrony.

Holt Reston dipped his head to one side to gaze upon the fair evenness of the features he had recalled only too often in dreams. Her long, sable lashes rested against the soft blush of her cheeks, pulling forth something excruciatingly sweet from the depths of him.

He turned her slowly in his arms and she tilted her chin up to him expectantly. The warm, moist flesh of his lips met hers with an restrained urgency, pouring over and against hers with delectable ardor. Her dangling arms came up to his sleeves, his shoulders, testing the strange hardness of his body uncertainly as he drew her breasts closer against him.

Her lips pulled heat from him and in return she melted in his hungry embrace and returned fully the heady sensations of this assault on her innermost being. Her arms wound themselves about his big frame and her slender hands caressed his back tentatively.

Holt drank deeply of the womanly essence of her, pulling her fiercely against his battle-hardened frame, agonizing at the feel of her full, eager breasts and cool, young body pressed tightly against him. He moaned softly at the torturous ache now pounding through him.

What it was, Tauren could not later say, but some sensation, some feeling was too closely remembered and her eyes fluttered open. Far above her, too far to be Roger's, was a dark angular masterpiece of a face, framed by hair of jet. She was jarred physically by the recognition of her partner in passion.

Feeling the change in her, Holt opened his eyes to stare into hers, never ceasing his attention to that pouting, rosebud of a mouth that had ruined his love-making ever since he had first tasted its rare confection.

Her first muffled moan and attempt to gain freedom went ignored by his searing mouth and iron-thewed arms. But she twisted away from his kiss and succeeded at last in putting an inch or two between them.

"How dare you! Release me at once!"

"As my lady says," Holt chuckled huskily, noting well that her own fiery responses were the true cause of her horror. His hand traveled possessively downward and seductively around her waist as he released her. "But I doubt that is what my lady truly desires."

"I thought you were—" Tauren pushed mightily, effecting her freedom but swaying unexpectedly due to the peculiar weakness of her limbs. He had done it again!

"Which of these rich young bloods were you expecting? Or does it matter?" His eyes glowed with lurid suggestion.

"Vile, foul-minded jackal." She backed away, grabbing handfuls of the sea-green satin of her skirt to still her trembling hands.

117

"I could offer my services," he continued mockingly, "but you'll have to talk sweeter to me than that."

"O-o-oh," she groaned with impotent fury. "Touch me again and you'll pay with your blood, I swear it!" she threatened, seeing his stealthy movements bringing him inexorably closer. "You've had what you wanted . . . you've ruined me! Why can't you leave me alone?"

"Ruined you?" he grinned crookedly and leaned back on one powerful leg. "A first taste of loving with me ruined you . . . for another man? You flatter me, my lady."

"Ruined me . . . for marriage," she blurted out, finding a prickling in her eyes that soon filled them with liquid humiliation. Oh, why couldn't she just flare and rage at him in honest battle? She turned her face away.

"Ah, marriage," he tucked his arms across his chest and studied her boldly. "That could prove a problem. A husband is likely to notice a thing like a missing maidenhead."

His taunt brought her shocked face round in angry disbelief. He laughed at her still. She darted for the door, finding his nimbleness the equal of his strength when he sprang to block her way. She jerked to a halt then tried another direction, also blocked by him. Wherever she turned, he was there, always with that same vile amusement.

Her shoulders rounded slightly and tears collected in her eyes again. "Please"—the hateful words stuck in her throat—"please, just let me be."

When his hands took hold of her shoulders she offered token resistance, then stood still. His lean fingers fluttered lightly over her shoulder then his knuckles traced the flushed cream of her chest down toward that alluring midline. His touch was molten silver along her skin.

"Any man who would reject you because of your passion . . . is a damn fool." His voice was husky and warm.

Inescapably, her eyes were drawn upward where, once engaged, they yielded up the most secret of her womanly longings. No supreme guile or romantic art of woman could have so completely snared his roving heart as did the fully vulnerable openness of her newly wakened passion. No touch, no embrace could have equaled the intimacy they shared in that moment.

Tauren was suddenly dizzy, swirling hopelessly in the light-dappled forest of his intriguing eyes. How did he do this to her? What unholy power did he use to command her reason to cease and her desire to spring forth?

The hapless wonderment of her sweet, dazed face quickened Holt's breath and crowded his chest with a surge of new, unnerving feeling. Suddenly he wanted to drown his disturbing thoughts in the soft fragrance of her parted lips. His mouth lowered slowly to hers, savoring the anticipation as much as the delectable conclusion. The touch was brief but painfully sweet, then gone. For a long moment they stood, not touching but very near.

"You! Reston . . ." came a harsh male voice from near the door. Holt's head jerked up, his eyes glittering brightly at the challenge flagrant in the address.

Roger Stillwell, Earl of Sappington, stood just inside the arched doorway, his hands clenched and his face menacing as he confronted his intended bride and the one man in the whole of England's south who had dared interfere with members of his family and survived to speak of it. His eyes burned brightly as they roamed the pair before them accusingly.

Tauren's heart stopped along with her breath. She knew how it must appear to Roger and instinctively dreaded his response. Perhaps he had arrived too late to witness that last kiss. She lowered her eyes and started to move away from Holt, but a big warm hand on her arm held her to the spot. She looked up, surprised, but Holt smiled smugly and leaned back on one powerful leg.

"Sappington." Holt acknowledged him without reference to his rank, an insult he knew would not go unredressed with any other man.

"You've a gift for appearing where you're not needed nor wanted," Sappington managed. "My bride and I have no need of your 'services.' You may leave us now."

Holt released Tauren's arm more slowly than was prudent, glancing from Sappington to Tauren who stood speechless beside him. She did not deny it. Then it was Sappington she expected just now.

"Indeed"—Holt's voice sharpened—"felicitations, then. When was the happy event?"

"The banns are to be read this Sabbath and the vows are a fortnight hence. No doubt you will hear of it." Sappington's face was bloated with restrained rage and Tauren shivered unexplainably as she noted how his fingers clenched slowly over and over.

"Then permit me to give you a wedding gift now," Holt said, his voice brittle beneath the cold sham of civility. Before she could react, Holt had her by the shoulders and delivered an insultingly lusty and lavish kiss full upon her mouth.

120

Fear galvanized her into action, and she thrust him away from her sputtering, "How dare you? You insult me!" But the anger in her face was for the callous way he used her to bait Roger openly, not caring about—indeed relishing—the trouble he might cause her in so doing.

Roger stepped forward angrily. "Reston! . . ."

But Holt was already near the door and striding purposefully. He wanted no blows with Sappington, yet. He paused just outside the door and bowed ostentatiously, a sneer on his handsome lips.

"For now she is yours, Sappington. I hope you are a lucky man."

Tauren's heart was in her throat as Holt disappeared from the portal. Roger turned upon her, vengeance in his eyes and grabbed her, his fingers biting into her arms as he snarled just above her.

"Bitch!" he growled, "I'll not be cuckolded, ever!" He shook her mercilessly as he savaged these words into her horrified mind. "I'll not have my wife mewling about in heat, spreading herself for Reston or any other rutting stud. I'll have you chained up like the bitch you are before that! Do you understand?"

Tears of pain and confusion brimmed in her mute blue eyes as he ceased to shake her. Her lips were reddened from Holt's last kiss and they trembled uncontrollably. Roger's anger burned anew, and his mouth swooped down upon hers as he crushed her to him harshly, heedless of the pain he caused her.

She forced herself to remain still in his cruel embrace, enduring his hot, wet mouth upon hers and praying that she could bear the suffocating possessiveness and savagery of this punishment.

He released her moments later and shoved her away from him suddenly. Her hand came up to shield her bruised lips and she straightened slowly under his scathing glare, feeling degraded and abused.

He adjusted his doublet and fluffed the lace at his wrists as if he had been engaged in mere polite conversation. "Make yourself presentable," he ordered. "And smile . . . brides must always be happy."

Nine

"It is my delight to welcome you, Lady Charlotte," Tauren's smile was genuine for the hostess of her recent debut in the shire.

"I've always thought of Lindengreen as a step away from Heaven's gate," the Lady of Rentings sighed longingly as Tauren greeted her in the great hall. "But we've not been invited in years . . . the duke never entertains."

"You will have time to stay, take some refreshment with me?"

Charlotte smiled with impish contagion. "There's naught I'd like more. I was just to Elizabeth Townings' shop and I couldn't resist stopping by to see you, it being so close. We had little chance to become acquainted the other night at my gala."

"I can offer you mulled cider or . . . tea?"

"Oh, tea!" Charlotte's lush smile again blossomed. "I cannot seem to get enough of the stuff. Cedric pampers me and raids the shops to bring me some whenever he is in London."

Tauren smiled slightly, nodding at the young houseman, Ransom, adding, "And some of Mrs. Whitelaw's delicious oat-currant cakes."

In a short while they were seated in the large salon amidst the fashionable curves of the carved French furnishings and the rich colors of tapestries and plush carpets.

"Marvelous . . ." Charlotte breathed, gawking unabashedly. "It is so elegant! The duke has such splendid taste. He planned much of it himself and constantly oversaw the builders and masons. He sent all over the world for the furnishings and fabrics and carpets . . . but you know all of that." Before Tauren could protest, she thought better of it, there seemed much she did not know about this house and her strange uncle.

Charlotte passed a respectful hand over the heavy brocade of the settee beside her. "It seems a pity . . . well . . . to share it with so few."

"I agree"—Tauren measured her words carefully— "but my uncle is a man who treasures his privacy and solitude. The betrothal is this Sabbath, day after tomorrow . . . you will come?"

"But of course, I wouldn't miss it."

Just then tall, slender Ransom returned with a large silver tray, laden with tea and sweets. Tauren jumped up to direct him to bring a small table nearby and did not again settle across from her guest until the houseman had withdrawn.

In the interval, the Lady of Rentings gazed intently at the lovely sensation of her recent gala, assessing her hostess sympathetically. The girl was new to the nobility and doubtless under strain, though she bore it well. Charlotte's perceptive brown eyes had noted well the girl's harried state at the gala, though she was sure the lateness and the wealth of spirits prevented most of the guests from such close observation. She had resolved to take the young thing under her wing and call on her at the earliest excuse. There would be little chance for such amenities after her marriage, if the man's reputation proved true.

"I am glad to have companionship for a while." Tauren busied herself pouring the steaming tea into finely painted china cups. "For all its splendor, Lindengreen can be very . . . quiet. Lady Charlotte, perhaps you can tell me a bit of the local folk and customs. Have you lived in Somersetshire long?"

Charlotte sipped the pungent tea and sighed with satisfaction, her brown eyes twinkling with delight. "Ah, since my marriage to Cedric, some seventeen years ago. My family held a small barony on the northeast coast. I was the only daughter and well dowered."

"You have children?"

"But of course," Charlotte laughed, "five at last count, four boys and a darling little girl. Cedric says he'll be content with that number so as to not overdivide the estate. But if he means what I think he means, I shan't be content at all. So we're merrily working away at number six."

Tauren's mouth dropped open and she stared unbelievingly at the woman briefly before she could think to hide her surprise at Charlotte's candor.

Charlotte chuckled at the girl's unchecked reaction. "It's perfectly all right. I have no trouble with the birthings and I am young yet." Then she thought of another possible reason for her hostess's discomforture. "I am sorry, my dear. I forget your youth and your . . . background."

Tauren found herself smiling at this lovely, rounded matron whose lively face and sharp wit had made her a favorite in local society. Charlotte was attractive and vivacious as a hostess or guest, and never failed to speak her mind in plain terms, with apologies to no one.

They drifted into talk of social matters, and Charlotte roundly and humorously roasted most of the local nobles, including the duke himself, whom she labeled a sour old hermit.

"His young wife died near thirty years ago while they toured," she explained. "They had only been married six months or so and he straightaway locked himself up behind these walls. Hardly been seen since—distracted by grief and soured upon the whole mortal race." She turned up her pert nose in disgust. "A lot of damned waste and foolishness, I say. No doubt he's regretted it aplenty over the years."

"No doubt," Tauren mused thoughtfully, her mind turning elsewhere—to questions she pondered the safety of asking. "Charlotte, who was the tall, dark man in black that you danced with so frequently?"

"Tall . . . dark? Oh-h!" Charlotte crooned with delight. "You can only mean Holt Reston. Now there is a man worthy of the name," she breathed with clear reverence. Tauren avoided her perceptive gaze.

"Lest you think me a hoyden for asking, I must tell you that we met that eve . . . and he . . . well . . . he took certain liberties."

Charlotte's delighted giggle brought Tauren's shocked face up quickly. "My dear, he always does. I should have been more shocked to hear that he had ignored your irresistible little person."

Tauren could not believe that unprincipled rogue found such complete favor with a lady of Charlotte's station. "Who is he then? Is he not an enemy of the duke? How came he among your guests so freely?"

Charlotte grinned slyly, shrugging. "An enemy of the duke? Who can say? The duke is old. . . . He had not controlled the shire for years before Holt Reston came. Holt is overlord here; bailiff, magistrate, even pontiff. He controls and husbands the shire as if it were his own . . . and nearly everything and everyone in it. He has since he entered the shire over four years ago. Peraps the old duke has not the will to fight him. There's talk, and that's all it is, mind you, that he has something on the duke—extorts power from him. But the duke has been a celibate and a recluse for so long it is hard to imagine what Holt might use against him."

"Um-m-m," Tauren mused, her finger toying with a crumb of cake. "I have seen it before. Such is the way of the treacherous Puritans."

Charlotte choked on a mouthful of tea and then recovered, looked into Tauren's puzzled gaze and laughed heartily.

"Puritan? My dear I assure you he is not. He has a string of romantic conquests astonishing in range and depth of field. Puritan!" She chuckled again, "that is too rich. Your wit equals your beauty, Tauren."

"But his garments—" she persisted.

"Bah!" Charlotte interrupted with a peremptory wave of the hand. "Chosen purposely to call attention to his handsome frame." Charlotte mentally noted how successful that gambit was for Tauren to have singled him out from the hoard of stylish and elegantly dressed nobles present. Perhaps the girl was not the innocent she appeared to be. She certainly had womanly taste in men. But then, Holt was an exceptional bit of manhood.

"It is also possible he wears them to infuriate the local nobles, rather rubs them raw, if I may be so blunt. The overlord is a vastly powerful man in the shire and his influence is felt beyond Somersetshire's borders— perhaps even in London. Most of the noblemen tolerate him as a necessary evil, but their wives and daughters have a far warmer regard for his manly qualities. Still and all, he's a bit of a rakehell and the men resent his attentions to ladies of quality." She smiled slyly. "It keeps them on their guard and attentive to have so handsome and powerful and so . . . willing . . . a man about. He has no rank to admit him to proper society fully, but he plies his usual methods; he takes whatever he wants."

Tauren flushed slightly. No rank. She had not even thought of rank in regard to him. Was it because she was so new to the nobility—or because she, like the other women of the shire, knew instinctively that he carried his own power and authority regardless of name or title?

"But you danced with him, Charlotte."

"But of course," Charlotte smiled smugly. "When you're of greater years and more experience, my dear, you'll learn as most sensible women do, that the measure of a man is not his name, but his frame! I know my Cedric might not seem the great stallion, what with all his flouncing about and endless words, but I can promise you, my girl, he's got plenty of what it takes to keep a wife warm and satisfied in a cold bed." Seeing Tauren's face pale and her eyes widen, she grabbed her hand anxiously. "Good God, you're not going to swoon on me are you?"

Tauren blushed furiously and dropped her eyes. "Of course not. It's just that . . ." She could not finish. Charlotte deduced intuitively what had discomforted her little hostess.

"Ah, you've never had a man, then. I suppose it is a bit shocking at first, and you raised a bishop's daughter as well."

Tauren started to protest but clamped her mouth shut, knowing her face reddened betrayingly and hoping that would be taken as maidenly modesty. The tormenting thought of what awaited her after her vows—at young Sappington's pleasure . . . and displeasure—chilled her.

"Then that explains Sappington's ill humor," Charlotte mused. "I wondered if there were something amiss between you. But hearing Holt was at you, that's understandable. They hate each other."

"They do?"

"Oh, yes," Charlotte bubbled, eager to retell a favorite piece of gossip made stale by the locals' familiarity with it. "Holt Reston is said to have maimed and ruined Sappington's cousin upon entering Somerset over four years ago. Sappington is not a man to forget such insults to his family easily. He has hot blood and a temper to match."

"I met my lord Sappington that night at your gala; I know little of him. But I saw him angered twice that eve." A small shiver ran through Tauren at the recalling. She hoped Charlotte's discerning eye missed

129

it, but the lady's next comment gave Tauren to know that it had not.

"Every girl is nervous and a bit afraid of her upcoming marriage. It is only natural." She reached out one hand to touch Tauren's reassuringly. And all the more understandable with Sappington as groom, she mused silently.

Tauren's mind drew back to the origin of this rambling conversation. "Maiming, menacing . . . lechery. The man should be stopped."

"Who . . . Holt?' Charlotte was incredulous. "If he did as they say, you can be sure he had cause. A touch of lechery, perhaps—it's what makes him so exciting."

"Then, dear Charlotte, you may champion his cause, but let us differ amicably. I find the man arrogant and his debauchery and violence disgusting. He might well have cost me my future husband's good opinion. He'll find my memory on that score the equal of my lord, the Earl of Sappington's."

When she turned from refilling her cup to seal her statement with a righteous nod, she stopped halfway through it. Charlotte sat staring at her with bemusement, a knowing glint in her lively eyes. Tauren had not managed to fool this woman of the world any more than she had Holt Reston. They both were keenly aware of the real reason for her harsh condemnation of him.

Ten

The next day the weather was foul again and Tauren felt her spirits washed to melancholy gray by the cold drizzle of South England's wet autumn.

"Ouch!"

She sat in her chambers trying to punch a needle through a tangle of threads above a newly begun tapestry. "It's useless," she complained flinging it down on the neighboring chair. Her thoughts kept returning stubbornly to the night of the gala; to Holt Reston's shockingly effective assault upon her feelings and to Roger's pronouncement of the fate of a cuckolding bride.

"The lout! Grabbing and pawing me . . . slavering over me as if he thinks it his right. He has ruined my marriage before it is begun!" Roger's patrician face, distorted by explosive anger, rose before her. She shuddered, reliving the pain of his grip on her and the horror of his brutal kiss. She had been stunned into inaction, unable to defend herself or rebut the conclusion he drew from Reston's insulting use of her.

A quiver of dread went through her. How could she face Roger in their marriage bed—a man whose temper and violence had flown at her upon their first meeting?

Tauren swept into the great dining hall two hours later, flushed and rosy-cheeked from hurrying. Roxie had come late to help her with her dress, but bearing news that the duke would join them for supper. Her violet velvet gown was rimmed in silk laces of dark purple, and these were even sewn into the rivulets of her long, puffed sleeves. A belt of smooth dark purple leather trimmed with golden leaf and hung with tiny golden bells rested at her waist where the shirring of her layered skirt began. Her hair shone with dancing lights and her skin beckoned one to touch it.

"I hope I have not kept you waiting, Your Grace."

"You have, but it matters little," came the terse response, softened slightly by an odd twinkle in the piercing brown eyes.

Revan stepped around the duke's chair to offer Tauren his hand in escort to her place.

"You are lovely, this evening, Taurie."

"The boy has a gift for understatement," came a deep male voice from the great fireplace to the side. Tauren stopped midstride and turned slightly, bringing herself eye to eye with Holt Reston. He stood, leaning one muscular shoulder against the massive marble mantelpiece and sipping a silver goblet of Lindengreen's finest red wine. His eyes roamed boldly over her and a crooked half-smile appeared. Lifting his goblet in salute, he toasted her. "To honor such beauty, we would wait out the night."

Tauren felt her face turning scarlet and realized that

she had been immobilized briefly by the sight of him. Her usually glib tongue deserted her completely and she responded with only a stiff, shake of her head.

The food was brought and Tauren was made acutely aware of the distance between the improbable three-some and herself. Hearing their conversation was difficult, especially when Holt lowered his voice to make comments that were followed by glances in her direction. Her face flamed at the insolence in his gaze and the appraising way he let his eyes linger as if stroking her.

She picked at her food, toying with the small, sharp knife that was the only service. Picking it up, she jabbed a piece of roast fowl, wishing secretly it were a livelier target. Her temporary status in this household was constantly reinforced, but never so humiliatingly as now. Her food became as straw in her mouth, nearly impossible to swallow. She drank liberally to force down the few bites she managed, her eyes darkening angrily as she observed surreptitiously the cause of her discomfort.

His thick, raven hair was shoulder length and given to a slight wave that provided a sinuous contrast to the lean, hard angles of his cheekbones and straight, finely arched nose. The muscles of his jaws flexed as he chewed, and his full lips seemed to glisten in the candlelight after he drew from his goblet. Each detail burned its way into Tauren's secret recesses, paining her with inescapable attraction. She tore her eyes from him and fastened them angrily upon the plate before her.

Then it dawned on her that no one had even bothered to introduce the braggart to her and that

Revan seemed to accept his presence without question. This was unbearable!

". . . My niece will be married in a fortnight," the duke intoned a bit louder than necessary, gesturing toward her with his knife. Tauren's head snapped up, eyes flashing with ire; they were discussing her.

"Indeed . . ." Holt murmured, turning an amused look upon her. "When Lady Tauren is married I shall attend. I have already given her a wedding gift I am sure she treasures." His eyes glowed mockingly into her reddening face.

Tauren drew breath for a hot reply, but seeing the old duke's inquiring scowl, she reined her anger and instead rose brashly. Suddenly all eyes were on her scarlet cheeks and heaving bosom.

"I seem to have no taste for what is served here this night," she announced, unable to keep the heat from her tone. "Pray do not allow me to spoil your delightful repartee." Grabbing up her swishing skirts, she spun and was gone.

"Sorry, milady." Roxie rushed in, breathless with the run from the hall of the old part of the house where the servants took their meals. "I tho't ye'd be yet awhile at dinner—what with a guest an' all." Her knowing smile faded quickly when she took in Tauren's harried state. "What's 'appened?"

Tauren adopted an unconvincing posture with hands on forehead and stomach. "I . . . don't feel well, that is all. Help me undress."

Roxie looked puzzled and somewhat skeptical, but shrugged her compliance and set about her tasks. "Was

134

it somethin' ye ate?" she pried. "Cook's been 'ard at it all day for a special feed."

"No!" Immediately she checked her reaction. "The food was superb. I simply did not feel well."

"More's the pity," Roxie continued casually, pulling at her mistress' laces, "with Master Holt there to look at. He's enough to whet a girl's appetite without touchin' the food."

Tauren's ears burned for more at the mention of his name, some bit of information to convict him utterly and, in so doing, defeat the hold his very presence in a room seemed to exert upon her. Here in her own room was an unimpeachable source of just such information.

"Master Holt? You know that man?" She tried to sound shocked.

"Everyone in the shire knows Holt Reston," Roxie drew off Tauren's bodice and added it to the pile of skirt and petticoats across the bed, wrapping her mistress in a heavy dressing gown graced with ermine trim at sleeves and neck. "He's every lass's dream, so big an' handsome an' . . . good." She giggled naughtily, "Tho I can't say firsthand."

"He's insufferable and crude," Tauren declared, irritated that Roxie should sing the stud's praises when she needed the opposite. "I can't imagine why the duke allowed him to dine here. He has no couth or decency about him. He is a bully and a lecher."

Roxie stared, open-mouthed, at her usually sweet mistress' tirade, unable to fathom what might have caused her virulence against the man.

"Afore ye came, Master Holt come weekly for dinner with the duke, and 'e eats in the kitchen regular with the captain. The surprise be ye ain't seen him afore this."

As soon as the words were out, they began a chain of linkages in Roxie's fertile mind that soon produced a knowing smile behind her mistress' back. "Or maybe ye seen him in a foul temper . . . 'e's not a man to cross."

"Tonight he was quite jov—" She clamped her mouth shut and resorted to her last line of "noble" defense. "I am shocked that the duke would allow such intimacy to a power-hungry commoner."

Roxie pushed her down gently upon the stool and began to remove the pins from her hair. "Well, the old man's got a right to see his son, I guess, freeman or no."

"Son?" The word first echoed, then began to rampage through Tauren, shaking her forcibly. "Son?" she repeated dumbly, "whose son?"

Roxie rested one hand on her round little hip, watching her lady. "The duke's, o' course. He's the duke's bastard."

"Bastard?" Tauren could only parrot her words unbelievingly. "Are you sure?"

"Right enough. I overheard Mrs. Murdock and Cook talking once . . . secret about it they was. I had to listen real hard. They both been 'ere since he was born. Sent away, he was, to live up in the North Country; then he come back an' near took the shire away from the old man."

Tauren was stunned; her heart was sinking into her stomach. This was the worst she could have imagined! Holt Reston already in control of the shire . . . and the duke's bastard son to boot! She submitted numbly to Roxie's ministrations and when she was safely in bed, she allowed herself the full range of her fears.

"Small wonder he disdains the duke's wishes—and those of a mere boy named heir. He wants the title

136

himself! And he has the power to take it! Oh, Revan . . ." She trembled thinking of Holt Reston's awesome strength and of the angry snarl on his lips as he announced his contempt for the duke at that fateful first meeting. She remembered Charlotte's comment from yesterday that he knew and used something against the duke. And now she had that well-kept secret as well, the one piece of knowledge that could galvanize her strength against his power and . . . yes, his overwhelming attraction.

He wanted the title and he was used to taking whatever he wanted. When the duke died, only Revan would stand between him and the title and fortune of Lindengreen. Her mind reeled. Whatever fears she had of Sappington were insignificant beside the threat now posed against Revan's future. No doubt the duke had chosen him to provide Revan an ally. And she must do her best to subdue her nature and to abet that alliance; she must become Sappington's bride at any cost and must see that he aid Revan against the duke's bastard.

As Tauren lay tossing fitfully above them, the duke and Holt Reston were in the main salon, discussing the country's affairs and Somerset's part in them.

"Charles needs money badly. I would have you know I shall send him funds . . . not what he'll want, but meaningful enough to appease him. He is not above bleeding Somerset dry to pay for his follies. I shall not let that happen." The duke's brown-black eyes snapped with determination and he straightened in his chair.

"When the king's men come in a fortnight, they shall

take back a fat purse of coin and the promise of more, but no men of Somerset or arms will be wasted to right his foolish policies. He will not be pleased." He turned to scour Holt's thoughtful face and saw it break into a wry grin of approval. In it the duke saw something else . . . something that gave him pain, and his own smile faded instantly.

Holt Reston had seen that same shift of expression many times before, and he knew what followed it— coolness and a retreat into nobility. Something about Holt triggered that reaction, some resemblance to the one woman the duke had ever loved, and it never failed to raise his wrath.

"The king cannot move against you as long as you support him, even modestly. But he will feel the insult. When you are gone, what will stop him?"

The duke shifted uncomfortably in his chair, avoiding Holt's perceptive stare, then rose with some difficulty. He did not like to hear the questions that plagued him put so plainly by another.

"Strafford could have stopped him—would have." The duke paced stiffly, pausing at last in front of the darkness of the window, staring out as if searching the darkness for some trace of the future. "The boy must have strong alliances to support him. It rides my thoughts constantly."

"And so you give the girl to Sappington." Holt's face turned dark at this thought.

"Yes." The duke studied his face.

"Why?" Holt had waged a battle with his rising emotions and lost. He checked his reactions too late; they had already been noted and he felt that somehow gave the old man an advantage.

"Sappington is a black-hearted boor of a man who has wasted his substance to clothe his strutting frame. He inflicts his debauched pleasures on those unfortunate enough to serve him! His debauchery has weakened him and emptied his hall completely."

The duke arched one brow and regarded him keenly. "And why should you care where he takes his pleasure or to whom I marry off my ward? You overreach yourself to question me in this!" His face threatened a storm.

"The Earl of Sappington is a bastard's bastard," Holt growled.

"So, for that matter, are you!" The duke pronounced the words in a cold, clipped fashion, smiling sardonically.

The remark took Holt back a moment, and he reconsidered his stance, pursuing another tactic. "You give him powerful influence over your 'heir' by this marriage. He is unworthy—"

"His influence will be abated by the fosterage."

"When you find one," Holt taunted him, "if you find one."

"The girl will have a better title than she could have aspired to . . . with her common background."

"Aye, a title—that is all she will have," Holt sneered bitterly.

Holt's words lay burning on the air as the old nobleman studied him and his telling remark.

"So, that is it. I thought your concern for my heir a bit suspicious. 'Tis the girl you want."

The declaration hit Holt like a pail of icy water and stunned him momentarily. He didn't want to be so transparent to this old man, but his stubborn honesty

139

would not let him deny it.

"Give her to me."

The duke's laughter was sardonic. "And I thought you had no mortal weakness in you." Seeing Holt stiffen, he grew fond of his game and stared tauntingly at the overlord. "Well, take her if you want her"—he leveled a mirthless smile at Holt—"but she will marry whom I choose . . . and it will be Sappington." His tired brown eyes blackened with determination.

"A man that cannot hold what he has deserves to lose it," Holt declared ominously.

"So you say."

"You will not give me an inch, will you?"

"Nay, not an inch." Then the old man's voice lowered in the pause. "You do not seem to need it." The Duke of Somerset turned slowly, painfully, and made a show of straightening the lace at his cuffs. Without another glance at Holt he left the room.

Holt stood for a moment, alone in the great room, pondering that last remark—and the challenge in it. His anger bloomed anew, and he wheeled about to seek the cool sanity of the night air.

Eleven

Tauren found her hands captive in the hard grip of her husband-to-be the moment she entered the salon. The score of guests already present joined voice in a collective "ah" for the beautiful young woman gowned in virginal white satin and a tiered overskirt of the palest blue. Rich embroidery of darker blue cascaded down the close-fitting sleeves and lapped lovingly up and about the low, rounded bodice. Tauren's chestnut hair shone violet in the warm light, and winked with pearls interwoven with ribbons the color of robins' eggs. Not a heart was left untouched as she lowered her sky-blue eyes in confusion, embarrassed by the acclaim and by the scrutiny inflicted upon her by the man who held her future as tightly as he held her hands.

"Is she not the most delicious little maid in the whole south of England?" Sappington crowed, his breath sending Tauren a strong whiff of spirits and bringing her scarlet cheeks up quickly. He gazed at her intently. "Am I not to be envied by all men for wedding such a beauty?"

Tauren heard no more, for the look on Roger's face, in his eyes, drove all rational thought from her mind. It was not the lust, the wanting, though that was present; it was another hungry look that seemed to devour and consume her.

To all looking on they were a pair of young lovers lost in each other's gaze. And her response was so unexpectedly honest as to draw chuckles and guffaws from the entire room.

"Upon my word, sir, you take my breath away." Her flushed cheeks were a fair counterfeit of virginal delight. She had spoken the truth and not even Roger detected the distress that prompted it.

"My little bride, soon I shall take the rest of you." And before she could blink, his lips were upon hers, hard and demanding. It was a short kiss, but one in Tauren's mind that branded her crudely and indelibly as his possession.

"S-s-sir!" she sputtered, spreading her fan near her lowered eyes and plying it vigorously. She felt herself dying a bit inside at this flaunting of his position over her.

"Roger, you're scandalous!" Charlotte Eddys chided him charmingly as she drew Tauren from him to press the girl's flaming cheek in an affectionate hug. "If we were not already called here for the banns, I daresay you would have them enforced upon you at sunrise for such behavior." Charlotte was laughing, and Roger, showing more humor than anyone anticipated, threw back his head in spirit-spawned mirth.

Charlotte drew Tauren about the room, first to the duke and her brother, who were seated side by side on a settee at the center of the grand chamber. Then Roger

142

could not resist joining them to present her to the gentlemen and ladies present, most of whom had some official capacity in this event. The Bishop of Wellston; an official of the court named Sir Howard Saunderston; Lord Murchis Arrington and his rotund lady, Neldeen; and Lord Belford Chester and his wife, Lady Glynis; and on. Not one of the guests bore relation to the young earl.

"Is there none of your family here, my lord?" Tauren asked as they finished introductions and were apart from the others briefly.

Charlotte stiffened beside her and Sappington's face became instantly hard. "I have no family."

Tauren dropped her eyes in confusion. Was she never to say anything that pleased him? "I only thought to—"

"It is no matter," he said tersely, lowering his voice. "We shall set about making our own family soon enough."

Soon the bishop called them, and in an astonishingly brief time, the banns were read and the agreements signed. The duke, with Calder's discreet help, placed Tauren's hand in Roger's and resumed his seat. It was done and Tauren searched her betrothed's face for signs of her future, finding things that only served to unnerve her. In exactly a fortnight, she would be the Lady Sappington and would face this unpredictable man over a soiled marriage bed.

Flagons were brought and toasts were raised, first by Calder, on behalf of the duke and then by Revan and then, in turn, by nearly every man present. Tauren drank sparingly, noting that Sappington drained every cup raised to his union and with every round his hands

143

roved more freely and his grasp on her arm or hand or waist became tighter. The talk grew loud and noisy and she desperately sought some excuse to separate herself from its hollow merriment.

Charlotte rescued her. "Roger, you'll not command her all night as you did at my gala. Shamefully selfish of you. You'll have a lifetime with her . . . let us have her now." She pried Tauren from Roger's hold on her and drew her along to where the group of ladies present had gathered about the fire.

"Dear, Charlotte"—Tauren found her chance—"I must see to the dinner, there must be something amiss, we are quite late. I shall return shortly."

There was one in the room who had noted Tauren's growing distress and was certain the reddened cheeks and tightness about her lovely mouth to be more than maidenly modesty. Revan had read from experience the truth of her reaction to Sappington, and it disturbed him greatly. He had been prepared to accept this match because of the duke's assurances that she would be well placed and near to Lindengreen. But Taurie was a good judge of people, and something about her intended husband made Tauren want to appear brave and composed.

She did not like him! Tauren was marrying a man she did not like; the thought impaled Revan and his eyes widened with the insight as he regarded his striking future brother-in-law. He watched the man's freeness with the spirits and saw with newly matured eyes his hardness so precariously concealed beneath flowery speech and fashionable vanity accustomed to the outrageous indulgence of court morality. Only moments before he could not have put into words what bothered him about the man, the marriage. But he saw it all too clearly now, as his sister fled the salon, and silently he cursed his uncle.

Tauren nodded graciously to the guests near the doors as she sailed out into the saner, cooler atmosphere of the great hall. She walked steadily toward the side hall leading to the cookhouse. Breathing deeply, she tried to calm the hammering of her heart. When she turned the corner of the hallway, safely out of sight of the salon and hall, she slumped against the wall weakly, crossing her eyes and biting her lower lip.

"Tauren, my little wife, I have you to myself for a moment." The words and hands assaulted her in the same instant, bringing her upright and her eyes open with shock. Roger now pressed her to the wall with his body and ran his hands up and down her sides. "God, you are a beauty . . . I cannot wait to have you." His hard lips descended on hers demandingly. She struggled briefly, then, hearing his growl of amusement, she ceased, horrified at his actions and at her instinctive rejection of him. She was to make a marriage with this man?

His hot tongue raked her mouth and his hands came up to squeeze her breasts while she hung between fear and revulsion, backed against the wall. His strong smells of sweat, spirits, and perfumed waters overwhelmed her as he invaded her mouth and ground against her with his pelvis, parting her legs with his hard knee.

When he'd had his fill, realizing that it could go no further, he broke off the assault, holding her pinned to the wall, legs still spread, while he peered into her dazed

145

face. "I'll wager you'll be a hot one once you learn what it's all about. And I'll have the pleasure of opening you up myself . . . teaching you special little tricks to please me." He ran his hand over her fashionably revealed breast and drew her eyes to the action with his own. Feeling her stiffen at the sight, he laughed harshly. "You'll get used to it, lovey. And soon you'll be begging for it." His face cracked into a malicious smile.

"There's no need to torture ourselves waiting for the vows, I'll come to your rooms tonight and we can begin the marriage early. I may even arrange to stay a few extra days on some pretext or other. . . ."

"My lord Roger," she began, fear shining unmistakably in her eyes, but found her protest cut off by another kiss, less punishing than the last, but wet and revolting.

His eyes were dark and shining when he moved away from her, adjusting his doublet and then the lace of his embroidered cuffs. She dropped her gaze and smoothed her hair and skirts, inwardly wild for something to say in protest of his dishonorable plan.

"Please, Roger . . . I have had many changes in so short a time . . . I know little of you . . . can you not? . . ."

His striking face was twisted into a smile of absolution as he pulled her into his arms and tilted her chin upward to meet him. "You need not worry that your inexperience will displease me. By the time you carry my child in that sweet little belly of yours, you'll know me well enough." His hand came up to squeeze her breast possessively and his eyes darkened further.

"God, I can hardly keep myself from throwing you down and pumping into you here and now."

Some flicker of dread or fear must have crossed her face for he laughed. "No, tonight is soon enough."

"I came to see about the dinner . . . it is far too late. . . ." she murmured, her heart in agony and her desire to escape uppermost in her mind.

He regarded her smugly. "We'll have the romp soon enough. We have important guests to attend. See to the dinner; then come to me." Abruptly, he was gone.

Knees like water, she made her way to the kitchens and through the cool night air into the cookhouse. Smoke greeted her and with alarm she scoured the bustling forms for the slim, gray figure of the housekeeper.

Murdock was hurrying from table to table and checking the fireplaces where the giant irons and pots warmed. Hearing her name, she hurried to Tauren's side.

"Oh, my lady, we've had a fire in the stack and some fell into the hearth. I know 'tis late, but we've saved the dinner and can commence serving soon."

"No one was hurt?"

"Nay, only a few charred pieces of meat. There has been smoke mostly."

"Thank heaven for that," Tauren breathed.

"Go back, my lady, or you'll ruin your lovely gown. I'll send Ransom in to announce dinner shortly."

Tauren left the cookhouse to return to her betrothed with all the enthusiasm the condemned must feel for the hangman. Soon, she moaned silently, it would be over. Every fiber of her being cried out demanding she fight this impending calamity. But how could she protect herself and still honor her duty to Revan and his future?

Tauren entered the great hall, straightening her bodice and fortifying herself with a deep breath. When she reached the center hall, she noted a servant at the door admitting a late comer who seemed engrossed in conversation with . . . Calder. The servant took the guest's cloak and high-crowned black hat with a silver plume. She gasped as Holt Reston turned and, seeing her, bowed deeply, his sardonic gaze never leaving her paling face. Their eyes met and she felt rooted to the spot, shaking and suddenly hot all over.

Tearing her eyes away, she forced herself to walk jerkily into the salon. With composure she barely maintained, she hastened to Roger's side and put one hand on his elegant sleeve. An eerie foreboding came over her as she smiled into the patrician features of the face of her intended. What in heaven's name was *he* doing here?

The silence was deafening when, having been announced, Holt Reston, accompanied by Calder, entered the salon. He paused in the extended archway to survey the gathering while Calder proceeded to his former place beside the duke.

Holt leaned back on one elegantly attired leg to absorb the attention turned upon him. His customary Puritanlike raiment was so in color only, for his garments were of lush, black velvet, exquisitely tailored to the lines of his big, muscular body. The square collar of his shirt was aglitter with gold cording and sewn pearls, and his cuffs were appliquéd with gold cording that circled his wrists in sinuous, elegant curls. His bloused breeches fit snugly across the hip and ended over the tops of white silk stockings. He had forsaken his prized jackboots for soft leather shoes finished in shining gold buckles. He was stunning—and the satisfied smirk on his bronzed face said clearly that he knew it. Ire coursed through Tauren at the jackanape's arrogance.

Charlotte Eddys was the one to break the silence.

"Master Reston, how good to see you." Her words seemed to signal the start of a heavy murmur that ran through the assembly. Admiration filled some eyes, indignation or hatred others.

"Lady Charlotte," he said in low, musical tones, "a delight to eye and ear, as always." Every eye was on them as he took her hand.

Unexpectedly, the duke spoke up. "Good of you to join us, Reston. Our dinner is delayed or you would have missed it entirely."

Holt approached the old man without a hint of a bow or even a nod of deference and put his hands on his hips jauntily as he stared down at him. "I would not have missed these festivities for the world. Your lordship." He addressed Revan with a formal nod. It was more than he had shown the duke and all present recognized the slight.

Amidst whispers, uncomfortable encounters of the eye, and stiff nods of recognition, Holt made his way to where Tauren stood by Sappington, gripping his arm tightly. She knew fully the reason for her dread, and it had to do with the way Holt bowed deeply before her and boldly caught her gaze, heedless of the anger rising quickly in the man beside her. The mocking light in his eyes was unmistakable as he spoke to her, and she refused him her hand.

"Lady Tauren, I present my best wishes to you on this . . . joyous . . . occasion . . . and of course, to your

149

groom." The sarcasm in his voice was suffocating as he pointedly ignored Sappington. There was a general intake of breath about the room as Roger's face went from pink to scarlet and his eyes narrowed.

Tauren was speechless with horror and she tore her eyes from Holt to plead sanity with Roger. Her hand clutched his arm from beneath, frantically, as if to restrain him and he turned his hostile glare from Holt upon her, sending shivers up her spine.

"Dinner is served," Ransom's deep voice announced from the archway of the salon and Tauren seized the opportunity as a drowning man would a rope.

"At last," she said a bit too loudly, cracking the excitement and strain that precariously approached the flash-point of open hostility.

The duke, having watched the encounter keenly, rose heavily and announced, "Let us go in."

Tauren and Roger were first out behind the duke and it was not until they were at the doorway to the great dining hall that she dared look at her betrothed. He looked at her coldly, his face hard and dull red with anger. Could he blame her for Holt's audacious behavior? How she hated Reston for the wreckage he was making of her life!

The great dining hall was ablaze with light from candelabra and chandeliers. The massive walnut table finally was used to its full potential, laden with platters of succulent food and gleaming dishes and silver goblets. Ropes of fragrant pine and holly garlanded the center of the spread. She tried to smile at Roger, mostly to assure herself, but seeing his thin-lipped response, she berated herself for even making the effort.

The duke sat in his usual place at the head of the long

board, indicating Revan's place beside him and Tauren's place next, beside Revan. Sappington took the seat at the duke's right hand, and she tried to engage his good graces one last time with what she hoped would pass for an adoring smile.

But Roger's face was turning stormy as he stared toward her across the table. It was a moment before she realized that he looked not at her, but past her. Turning quickly, she saw Holt Reston commandeering the chair beside hers from Lord Chester. His huge, dark presence settled about her like a pall, and she felt her stomach lurch downward with dread.

Desperate to give Roger no cause for affront, she turned in her seat, giving Reston her back. Roger's eyes followed her tactic and his intensity eased a bit.

Sipping daintily from her goblet, she cast a fetching smile at Roger and sought to play the willing bride to pacify his proud spirit. "Lady Charlotte has told me of the beautiful lakes in the south of Somerset. One is near your home, is it not?"

"Yes, my dear," he replied coolly. "In fact, there are two lakes on my lands."

"I have always loved the water. Do you keep a barge for outings?"

When he opened his mouth to reply, another's words came forth first.

"Barging is an expensive hobby. Those with modest incomes would do well to apply their funds more frugally." It seemed the whole table listened, for there was not another sound.

Roger leveled his reddening gaze at Tauren, plainly barbed by the comment and its insinuation. "We have two handsome crafts, which I personally pilot. I sometimes sleep aboard the larger one. You might find that very enjoyable in the warm summer."

"Whatever pleases you, my lord, I would be pleased to try."

"Humph," came the low comment from her left and she bristled, relaxing only when she realized that Roger had not heard it.

"You, my young lord"—Roger gestured to Revan with his eating knife—"when do you leave?"

Holt's head came up sharply, searching the impassive face of the old duke.

"Soon, I think, sir, soon after my sister's marriage."

"I hope you will join us for visits from time to time. I would see your family ties maintained and an alliance built between our houses. Consider my doors open to you always."

"Indeed." Revan glanced at Tauren from the corner of his eye. "Your invitation will be a boon to me in the days ahead. Tell me of your estates. Have you a large stable?"

A deep voice from beside Tauren rumbled forth once more. "Is a stable a stable without horses or stock? I wonder, Your Grace, what do you think?"

All activity and conversation was again silenced, and battling her own morbid expectations, Tauren seized her trembling wrath with an iron will.

"You turn the query into a riddle, sir, then you must answer it yourself." She would not look at him, but felt his arrogant smile upon her all the same.

"Very well. I think it is not." Holt's gaze leveled to Sappington's flaming face, and the table braced, anticipating the worst. Holt was deliberately provoking Sappington whose irascible nature was well known.

152

It was the inevitability of flint against steel.

"You are a guest here, Reston," Roger growled, eyes smoldering. "In deference to His Grace and the occasion, I will only bid you keep your philosophy to yourself and find a pleasanter topic—or better yet, none at all."

Holt's face was a mask of sardonic amusement. The Earl of Sappington troubled himself about appearances this night and held his explosive temper in check, albeit by a thread. Holt returned to his food, and Tauren breathed once more, draining her goblet and hoping the strong wine would be doubly felt.

The meal proceeded with sparse conversation, mostly whispered, about the table. The duke quietly surveyed the guests before him, and in his usual, inscrutable manner, said nothing. Revan asked Roger a few harmless questions about the hunting on his lands, and each time, Tauren held her breath for fear the confrontation would be renewed. Miserably, she noted that Roger continued to drink heavily and ate sparingly; when he came to her that night, his drunken state would not dispose him to be lenient or tender with her.

Huge platters of succulent roast duck glazed with honey and seasoned with eastern spices were brought in and carried about the table for serving. When the servants stopped by her chair she had to turn slightly toward Holt to choose from the tray. She paused to smoothe her skirt after the braised vegetables and sumptuous duck were served her, and felt something grab her hand.

The man was mad! She quickly quelled her first impulse to jerk her hand away, realizing that the slightest movement would give them away. She twisted her hand back and forth, panic rising within her as she realized that his hand moved with hers; he meant to keep it!

Mercifully, Roger had just turned to the servant to order more drink and Tauren tossed a white-hot glare at Holt Reston, whose insolent grin stoked her anger to blazing proportions. Once pale, her face now flamed in spite of her efforts to remain cool and give her husband no further cause for anger.

Her last valiant effort at retrieving her hand was observed keenly by the offense's true target. Roger's chair scraped the cold marble of the floor harshly as he jumped up. Tauren's scarlet face met his burning stare, which moved quickly to fasten accusingly upon her hand as Holt forced it up and onto the table, still captive in his own.

"Unhand her, Reston!" Sappington growled. The table chorused gasps of astonishment, chairs rumbling back as the men jumped to their feet. Lord Chester moved quickly to Sappington's side, his anger imperial.

Holt broke the charged silence with a low chuckle and rose slowly, drawing Tauren up with him. "I will release the lady," he uttered casually, "only if she tells me of her own free will that she chooses you over me." There was a sardonic hint in his voice as he turned to her mortified face. "She must proclaim to all that your hands on her skin fire her more than mine and that she goes willingly to your name and bed because of it."

Tauren's blue eyes were huge, and her jaw dropped as she looked up into Holt's determined face. "No," she whispered, shaking her head unbelievingly, immobilized by the awful impact of his words.

"You filth!" Roger raged, barely restrained on one arm by Lord Chester. The huskiness of his voice proved the effect of the wines as did the dull glare of hatred aimed at both Holt and Tauren. "You dare claim the girl is yours?"

Holt's calmness and continued holding of Tauren to him fueled Sappington's quicksilver temper.

"No man needs claim that which he already has."

"No!" Tauren burst forth, trying to wrench away from Holt's tightening grip. "What are you saying? You lie . . . you insult me!"

Holt released her hand only to grab her by the arms and to drag her to him. "Nay, the truth could never be an insult to you, for you have never been but kind and loving toward me. Such kindness as no other man may claim."

Not even the village idiot could have mistaken the intent of his remarks. Sappington nearly climbed the table to be at Holt, scattering dishes and sending silver clattering. Lord Chester struggled to hold him fast by one arm, but with the other, he grabbed his goblet and tossed the contents full in Holt's unflinching face.

"Whoreson!" the earl spat. "You'll pay for this sport with your blood!"

Holt's face broke into a smile of satisfaction as the ruby liquid dripped downward over his sharp features and onto his snowy collar. Tauren could not repress a shudder as the realization swept through her; this was what he had come for.

"No-o-o!" she groaned, still caught in Holt's possessive grasp. Pandemonium was breaking loose about them and her rising wail was lost in the noise.

Holt pulled her tight against him and bent to kiss her lightly on the forehead before releasing her. He saw her shock and anger, but heeded it little as she sputtered and then brought the full palm of her hand smashing into his rock-hard cheek. The slap dazed him slightly, so that all he saw were the huge tears in her immense, sky-filled eyes.

"Tomorrow at dawn." Holt turned to Sappington, who was now restrained by Calder as well. "The willows by Harden's Spring." With a satisfied smirk and a stinging cheek, he bowed stiffly to the duke and again to Revan who stood defiantly in the duke's unrelenting grasp. He bowed elegantly to Tauren and strode confidently out, but not before he had seen the glint in the old duke's eyes.

Twelve

The door to Holt Reston's modest parlor slammed back against the wall, shaking the entire room with his entering wrath.

"Have ye taken leave of your senses?" Calder roared, blowing with gale force into the room. "Good God, whatever possessed ye to this insanity?"

Holt smiled saltily. "Welcome, friend—do come in." He sat before the dying embers of the fire, sipping a steaming mug of negus.

"Here ye sit like ye had not a care in the world! I've a mind to call my men and keep ye in chains till past noon tomorrow." Calder towered above him, jamming one fist tensely into the other, then turned and paced the length of the room and back. The look on Holt's face stopped him. "Good God! You look quite pleased with yerself."

"On the whole"—Holt paused to draw from his mug—"I thought it went quite well."

Calder blinked at him unbelievingly. "You be mad! You know Sappington's repute with a blade. Do you think after tonight he'd be content with a paltry badge of honor? Man, he'll kill ye for what ye've done—or die tryin'."

"Calder"—Holt looked at him patiently—"you're such an old woman sometimes, it worries me."

"Worries—" Calder choked back a virulent curse and stared at Holt, slowly comprehending the deadly calm that sat squarely on the younger man's spirit. He made a stumbling step backward and sat down heavily in the other big chair before the fire. He realized that Holt had planned it all, and just this way.

"Why?" Calder breathed, fearing he already knew. It was no secret that Holt Reston considered the shire his own; his authority and influence were felt in every remote burrow and burg. Now he meant to take the rest, the girl and the lad, be damned. Calder felt his ire rising against Holt's amused silence.

"Damnation!" Calder errupted anew, coming to the edge of his chair. "I could have killed ye myself for what ye said about the little lady." His hard boots thumped the floor as he pushed up angrily out of the chair. "Is it true?" he demanded. "Did ye have her that night?"

"Ah, now, 'tis out," Holt sat up, depositing his mug on the low table near his chair. He faced his old friend squarely. "Do you admit that you lied to me, 'friend'? A truth for a truth, an even bargain." The glitter of the younger man's eyes made Calder nod stiffly, his face tight with expectation.

"'Tis true, I lied—but in a good cause and I'd do it again, come the same," Calder growled.

Holt's eyes narrowed slightly. "You old fox, did you think I'd storm the bloody walls to ravage a mere girl . . . and a parson's daughter at that? She's got you

158

dotty about her!"

Seeing Calder's fists forming and his face puffing with anger, Holt continued, "Nay, at least I told the truth—she did get away that first time." Holt's voice thickened. "But I vowed to have her . . . and I did. She's mine and now all know it. Sappington's hall sits empty, because of his profligate tastes and cock's-comb vanity. I hate him and all the stupidity and idleness he stands for. He'll never have Lindengreen, or her. Somerset is mine and after tomorrow none will ever doubt it again."

"That's what this is about . . . a nice little game between boys, with the estates and her as the prize! You've taken her . . . ruined her name. God, I should kill ye for that!" He stopped and forced himself to pace and divert the energy of his anger into action. "What's to become of her after you've disposed of Sappington, assuming he doesn't finish you first?"

"Then she's mine. . . . I'll have her." Before Holt realized what was happening, Calder was upon him, thrusting a heavy, battle-thewed arm under his chin, forcing his head back hard against the chair while he rammed a knee into Holt's midsection to pin him there.

"Dirty bastard!" Calder snarled. "I'll run ye through meself afore I'll let ye make a whore out of that sweet lass!"

Holt's face reddened dangerously under Calder's expertly applied pressure. Even so he might have laughed at the pathos in the older man's face had he not glimpsed something deeper, something unknown to him in his friend before.

"No one could call the wife of Holt Reston a whore and live," he rasped.

The words seeped through Calder's fierceness and he eased his grip and backed away. His boiling anger of a moment before was replaced in full by incredulity. "Ye plan to *wed* Lady Tauren?"

Holt eyed him warily, straightening his elegant, but much-abused doublet. "I'll have her, but not without the vows. I'll have her wedded to me, then none may dispute my claims. It has been my plan since first we met." His handsome mouth curled lazily upward as in his mind's eye the image of her, hair unbound and stretched sensuously upon a rock appeared. "Well, almost the first."

Calder couldn't believe his ears. "Ruined or no, do you truly believe she'd have ye after tonight? Man, she hates your very guts . . . and I'm perilously close to it meself!"

Holt was the image of insouciance. "I count it auspicious that you have not yet declared me unfit to wed a woman of her exalted standing. But with or without your approval, I'll wed her." Seeing the disbelieving shake of Calder's head, he continued. "Women love being fought over . . . to the victor goes the spoils." He nodded smugly. "She'll come 'round. I have it all worked out."

Calder began to jerk his heavy gloves on, gazing in wonderment at a side of Holt Reston he had never before witnessed.

"I thought ye a clever man, Holt Reston, but when it comes to that woman, you're a jackass—a wet-eared, stumble-footed jackass. This is one duel I'll enjoy arranging!" With a furl of his cloak and another room-jarring slam of the door, he was gone.

Holt smiled as he reached for his mug. He had

worried more about Calder than the rest.

Blue-gray steel glinted ominously in the cold, mist-shrouded light of dawn. Two figures in shirt sleeves attended the cold metal, wiping its keening edges with soft chamois and olive oil—anointing it for bloody service. The combatants eyed each other openly while conferring with their seconds, each seeking to plant that single reservation in the other's mind that might cause an instantaneous faltering, thereby ceding the match to the more confident blade.

"Gentlemen." Lord Cedric Eddys called them to the task, commanding their approach. When they stood face to face, all present were struck by the contrast between them. Holt was taller by several inches, broader of shoulder and dark, while Sappington was lithe and fair of hair and skin. Holt's face was a bronzed mask of purpose, while Roger's flamed with anger and impatience.

". . . at first blood, weapons will be withdrawn," Lord Cedric finished and looked to each man for agreement. "Take your stance." The judge held aloft before him a blade and waited while each man placed the tip of his steel upon it. With one deft, upward slash of the neutral blade, both weapons were set in motion to be stilled only by blood.

Sappington charged full out, slicing the air furiously and meeting only the blue steel of Holt's blade at every turn. Holt retreated, parrying effectively against Sappington's onslaught, but giving ground and sending a murmur through the handful of men who would bear witness to the outcome and the honor satisfied.

161

Calder frowned with concern at the seeming early turn of favor and squinted hard in the morning mist to discern Holt's state of mind. At first Holt's angular face seemed disturbingly impassive, but as the minutes dragged on, Calder detected the hint of a smile about his hard-set mouth. For all his size, Holt danced adroitly through the athletic maneuvers of his opponent, barely winded by the exertion, while Sappington's scarlet face was wet with the only product of his intensity.

A slow, menacing smile spread across Holt's face, and his green-brown eyes began to gleam with what onlookers could only have named pleasure. Then, as Sappington's flickering gaze betrayed his inner uncertainty at this change, Holt came to life.

The feel of the naked blade in his hand, the eager straining of his muscles, and the sensual pounding of his blood in his head—it was as Holt remembered. Brushing by death, whipping and slashing, steel clanging on steel and ringing in his ears; he had learned the trade to keep him alive in the wars of Europe and, now in the rush of excitement he felt it all in place, as though he'd never left it. It was this way with a good opponent and Sappington was a worthy adversary. But Holt knew he would take the man and coolly considered where best to make his mark—an arm . . . shoulder . . . thigh?

Sappington's face was fury unreined and he slashed wildly in an arc that Holt had only to dodge. And in that one vulnerable moment Holt's blade darted in and claimed its prize in Sappington's arm. Holt drew back immediately, sweeping his blade down to his side and gazing over his left shoulder toward Lord Cedric.

162

"First blood," the Earl of Rentings intoned with obvious relief. Holt nodded and pivoted on his heels to the murmur of the gentlemen observing the duel.

"*No!*" Sappington shouted raggedly, his eyes glazed with pain and bloodlust. "You cuckolding bastard— you'll not get away!"

Holt spun just in time to meet and parry the savage thrust as a volley of naked excitement ran through the watchers. Sappington had attacked the victor's back, and now there was no doubt as to the outcome of this ritual battle.

Roger thrust and panted and slashed furiously, cursing Holt for his own dishonorable acts while Holt marshaled every ounce of his stamina and skill against the fanatical attack.

"Damn you, Holt! I'll see you in hell this day! And your whore as well! Think on that as I kill you!"

Holt's split-second hesitation was what Sappington needed to find an opening. The twist of Holt's torso was half an instant too slow and the cold blade sliced into his left upper arm, sending a shrill pain through his shoulder and down his arm. Loud murmurings and exclamations could be heard over the field, except by the combatants who, locked in savage combat, heard nothing but the clang of steel and the sound of their own blood in their ears.

Each had drawn the other's blood and bright scarlet stains grew upon the snowy linen of their shirts. Neither slackened the pace nor yielded significant advantage to the other. Neither saw the tree root that felled Sappington, but Holt sensed it as his enemy fell and reined his blade. Sappington seized the oportunity to lunge straight upward at Holt as he righted himself, and the tip of his blade gashed Holt's thigh as the taller man swayed out of reach instinctively.

Holt knew now there was no waiting, no wearing him down to spare his life. The man was rogued of mind and incapable of stopping, now or later. The slight change in Holt's awesomely fluid style was barely perceptible, but its effect was readily seen.

The end came quickly as Holt bore down upon Roger with the coldness of death in his eyes. Sappington slashed savagely twice—three times—always finding air where his big target had been an instant before.

Holt seemed to dip or stumble and broke Sappington's concentration while his blade tore its way upward into the earl's chest. The young nobleman's sword dropped from his outstretched hand, and his last look was one of surprise as Holt pulled the blade out again.

Holt stood, chest heaving, staring at the body of his opponent, and felt only distaste—revulsion—magnified by a hundred other kills in battle. Always it was the same—the exhilaration of the battle and the horror of the carnage and the needless waste afterward.

He turned to find Calder behind him, draping his shoulders with his cloak. He was nearly to his horses when he sank to his knees.

"Mark me word, milady, only one'll come back."

Roxie's maudlin prediction did little to lighten the gray weight of the winter dawn that reached into Tauren's very soul. She jumped up from the window seat to resume pacing in the unheated solar overlooking the entry court, rubbing her hands together to warm them.

"I could lay a fire," Roxie offered, shivering and drawing her coarsely knitted shawl tighter about her.

"Nay, it cannot be much longer. The sun must be full up . . . if it could be seen." She retraced her steps to the window and balefully searched the lane before the entry court for signs of riders, stuffing her hands up into the fur-lined sleeves of her dressing gown to keep them warm. She dreaded the outcome, whatever it might be, but the waiting was just as hard. She leaned one knee upon the velvet-covered cushions of the seat and leaned her head against the leaded pane. Her breath made little clouds upon the cold glass, and she rubbed them idly with her fingertips, tracing little patterns and, in irritation, rubbing them away with one sweep of the heel of her palm. She sighed dolefully and sank back to sit on her feet.

Roxie watched her mistress and squirmed, rearranging her bottom gingerly upon the hard bench. How the nobility did it was beyond her . . . they seemed to have stamina for this sort of thing, suffering nobly. Now since she was in service to a true lady, she must be expected to learn to do it too.

"Master Holt's a fair man wi' a blade, I heard." She glanced at her mistress sympathetically, reading her reaction in the irritable toss of her head.

"The earl is my betrothed husband," Tauren declared a bit too loudly. "I pray for his safe return . . . so that the wrong that insufferable cur has inflicted upon us may be set to rights. Treating me like a common doxy, proclaiming me his mistress! I hate that lying, low-minded wretch. The earl will have right on his side."

165

But she knew even as she spoke that if Sappington were victorious, Holt Reston had seen to it that the marriage would have little chance of taking place. Her shoulders sagged with fatigue and an overwhelming sense of abandonment.

"They're just alike," she mumbled.

"Milady? What?" Roxie's nodding head jerked up, and she bleared at her mistress through hazy eyes.

"I hate them both," Tauren continued in a determined whisper, ignoring her faithful servant, who promptly resumed dozing. "Reston took my virtue—but I am not his whore. And Roger's rutting, drunken arrogance . . . Where is the difference between them?"

Two horses pounded through the gates of the long drive and Tauren raced for the door, mindless of her dressing gown and unbound hair. With Roxie close behind, she flew around the gallery and down the great stairs to greet the news, not knowing what it was she wanted to hear.

The morning's heavy moisture still clung to Calder's clothes and boots as he stepped inside the great hall. He had come straight to the duke with the news while his men saw Holt safely to the overlord's house in the town. Tauren was running across the great hall and caught him at the arched doorway of the salon, clutching his arm anxiously.

"What's happened?" she demanded, strain and sleeplessness apparent in her young face.

"Come," was all he said and he drew her with him into the salon where an odd collection of people awaited the outcome; the duke, Revan, Lady Charlotte, and Murdock. Forcing Tauren down onto a chair by her shoulders, Calder turned to the duke who sat

166

forward eagerly, the pain of uncertainty clear on his face.

"Your Grace, I bear grievous news. The Earl of Sappington is dead." Pausing a moment for the impact of his words to be felt, he went on. "Blood was drawn first by Holt, then the earl charged anew, demanding his death." He shifted an uneasy look at Tauren who had blanched white and was numbly surrendering her trembling hand to Revan.

To the duke and Murdock, who had moved closer to hear the report, he lowered his voice and head to continue. "It was savage, Your Grace. The earl was like a man crazed . . . attacked Holt's back after he withdrew. There was no stopping it." Calder's expression was grim and prepared the duke for the rest. "Holt is taken to his house and with your permission, I go to see to 'im now. He was wounded arm and thigh, me thinks not serious, but he's lost blood."

The duke's terse nod carried an odd tenor and the tension of his drawn face eased. Calder was dismissed and dropped a bow to them generally before turning on his heel to be gone.

Tauren found herself the object of all eyes in the room. But, mercifully, a veil of liquid blurred her vision, and she felt Charlotte's and Revan's comforting arms about her, lifting her up and pulling her along toward the door. The tears streaming down her face and choking her throat were more for the horror she felt at her own reaction, a detached sorrow and worse—pure relief that she had been spared Roger's plan to consummate their vows early.

They led her upstairs where Roxie quickly built up a fire in her bedchamber and ran to fetch hot wine.

Revan deposited her in a chair by the fire, kneeling by her chair.

"Taurie, you bear no fault in this. You heard what Calder said? Sappington would not be satisfied, attacked after honor was satisfied." He drew her eyes to his. "Perhaps it was . . . for the best."

Tauren again saw Sappington's eyes, blazing naked fury and full of contempt, as they turned upon her in the dining hall after Reston swaggered out. He believed all that Reston said! She had pleaded with him, denounced Reston as a rogue and a liar; then she had turned to the duke and seen his abasing sneer. The realization slammed through her as she looked about the room and saw the same dull look of disdain on the others' faces; the overlord's word was accepted—even against her virtue—so complete was his power here. She had fled the room. And now because of her weakness a man lay dead, her reputation was in tatters, her future was gone.

Charlotte sat beside her and held her while her sobs diminished. There was more to this . . . Charlotte was sure of it. But naught would convince the world, nor the maid, that Reston had meant his words in any manner other than that in which they had been taken. And there was Holt himself . . . ambitious, powerful, self-righteous. What was the charming rogue capable of? Charlotte thought back to her own tender years; the girl had good reason for her anger. Reston in one fell swoop had divested her of the two most important things a woman could have: a well-placed husband and a virtuous reputation.

"Come, my dear," Charlotte urged her up and into the pan-warmed comforters of the big bed. "Try to sleep awhile. You were awake most of the night; your eyes betray you. Cedric and I shall stay with you another day or two."

Tauren obeyed wordlessly, grateful for Charlotte's commanding presence and her restraint on the subject that she was sure must even now be spreading amongst the gossipmongers of the shire—Tauren's relationship to Holt Reston.

Thirteen

Two days later Lord Cedric and Lady Charlotte departed, sending Lindengreen deeper into its somber mood. Tauren had not seen the duke since that awful morning when Calder had come to announce that her husband-to-be was dead. The old man had stared at her with a dull contempt, and Tauren dreaded her next meeting with him, knowing that he believed Reston's words to be true and feeling his blame for the tragedy that befell them.

The evening of the fourth day Revan persuaded her to dress and take supper in the dining hall again. "You'll see, Taurie, it will all work out somehow. I'll see you're cared for . . . it's my responsibility now to find a place for you."

Tauren tried to smile but found her face frozen by her attempt not to cry again. "Of course," was all she could manage to respond.

The duke sat at the end of the long dining table, his narrowed eyes studying the pair as they approached.

"You have at last seen fit to grace us with your

170

presence." Referring to the dark midnight blue of her elegant gown, he nodded with a smirk, "Do you intend to lead us all into mourning for the late earl? Too little, too late does not become a lady."

"It is neither late nor insincere to regret the needless slaughter of another human." Tauren stiffened.

"Slaughter?" came a deep, resonant voice from the doorway behind them. "Nay, it was not slaughter that brought the earl to his untimely end, but a test of honor—in which he was completely lacking."

Revan and Tauren whirled around to face the victor of the contest. He stood, arm in sling, in the doorway, leaning jauntily against the frame. Tauren was tossed wildly by conflicting emotions at the sight of him, but it was her indignant wrath that won the right of expression.

"What are you doing here?"

"I am here for the same purpose as you, lady, to take nourishment in this congenial company." He pushed off from the doorframe and came slowly toward them as Tauren bit back a stinging retort and whirled on the duke, her face flaming and anger flashing in her eyes.

"Do you permit this—this murderer in your house, at your table?"

The duke regarded her with something cooler than amusement in his depthless eyes and said nothing. She turned on Holt, eyes flashing, determined to do something herself.

"You are not welcome at this table, sir, for reasons so obvious that I shall not recount them. Leave immediately and be good enough to spare us your presence entirely in the future."

"Such a sharp tongue." Holt studied her patiently. "I

had almost forgotten it. But it is easy to forget details when gazing upon such beauty."

"How dare you come here like this?" Tauren declared, and then whirled on her guardian and her brother. "Have neither of you a tongue . . . or a spine?" She turned to Holt again. "What do you want with us . . . from us?"

"Only the pleasure of your sweet company," he intoned, with a gallantry that mocked her. His free hand snaked out and caught hers and he kissed it lightly before she could jerk it away.

"The pleasure of . . ." she breathed, unable to believe her ears. He mocked her and flaunted his disrespect for her even now, before her uncle and her brother. Her anger seemed to clear her head of the haze of self-pity that had enfolded her recently, and she knew now why Holt had openly challenged Roger and why he was here.

Stepping a bit closer to him she smiled, knowing that it would lower his guard; then when she was in range, she brought her hand up at arm's length and slapped his bronze-hard cheek with all the force she could muster. "Did you expect your 'prizes' would greet you with open and willing arms? The earl lies barely cold in his grave and you come here to dine! You make me a whore on the lips of the whole shire with your lies and expect me to sit at table with you as if you were an honored guest! Never, Holt Reston . . . I'd sooner roast in hell. Some things are not bought or sold, not even with so dear a fare as blood."

She started for the door, but a hoarse bellow of her name stopped her. She turned with shocked anger to see the duke standing, red-faced, beside his chair, grasping its arm for support. "You will never speak so to a guest in this house again!" he roared. "I and I alone decide who shall dine at my table. Test not my patience further!"

Tauren was appalled, but not to the point of speechlessness. "What will you do to me, Uncle, that has not already been planned?" She stepped back toward the table, her chin high and eyes flashing. "Will you send me to a papist nunnery for the sin of a sharp tongue . . . for telling the truth? Nay, you used that to force me into a marriage with that brute, but it will not work again. You old fool, can you not see what he is doing . . . what he wants? Is it not plain to you by now? Why did you bring us here if only to let us be used and degraded by this rogue?"

"How dare you speak in such a manner!" the duke roared. "Think well before you speak again, for if you do, you will loose every chance you have of making a future. You will obey my wishes in my house or you will taste the consequences." The old man's body trembled from his great effort, but his face was cold, white marble. The silence was near to deafening as Holt and Revan looked on expectantly, seeing Tauren's eyes glittering with determination and finding the same fearsome light in the old man's gaze.

"Then do your worst, Uncle. I'll speak my mind where I please, and if that displeases you, then so be it. I'll not stay in this room a moment longer, not even if I must starve." This time there was naught to stop her as she sailed angrily out, accompanied by Holt's mocking laughter. Revan made to follow her, but the duke's imperious voice succeeded in halting him as it had been unable to his sister.

173

"Nay, boy. You will stay here with me. She has sealed her fate. You will leave her to it." The duke's piercing eyes seemed to draw submission from the boy, and he returned slowly to the table, casting a hostile glance at Holt, who took the chair opposite him.

"What will you do to her?" Revan demanded, his young face a study in misery.

The duke reached a shaking hand to his goblet and drank deeply before turning to the question. "She will remain here in this house. I will not turn her out, but I will not offer her in marriage again. She made the choice. You need not concern yourself about her . . . there are more important things to consider." The topic was closed and Revan fell silent, staring at his plate and swallowing hard. When he looked up again, Holt Reston was watching him intently, a curl of cynical amusement on his handsome mouth.

"Me mam says there's lots worse than not marryin'." Roxie observed sagely as she brushed Tauren's hair the next morning. "Says a man's only good for keepin' warm of a winter and at keepin' scarce the next summer when it's time for the birthin'."

"How do you know about that?" Tauren's face warmed in spite of her. Revan had brought her word of her "punishment" to her chambers late last night.

Roxie shrugged. "I listened . . . like always. But the whole house is talkin' 'bout how ye stood up to the old duke."

Tauren's eyes closed in exasperation. Was this the fate of all ladies of quality, to be plagued by snooping, tart-tongued servants and to have one's innermost thoughts and problems discussed freely by grooms and scullery maids?

"Well, ye'll not be lonesome. . . ." Roxie's eyes twinkled. "Not wi'—"

"Lonesome?" Tauren turned the word over in her mind, not catching the point of Roxie's thinly veiled hint. Yes, that was something yet to be faced. "Nay, I'll not let myself be lonesome. I'll find something to occupy me, something of good to others . . . and there'll be Charlotte Eddys and Revan. . . ."

"Jus' cause a woman ain't married, don't mean she can't have her fun as well as any other."

"Of course— Roxie!" The sense of it finally seeped through to her and she turned an angry scowl on the loyal little servant.

"Well," the girl moaned with a whine, "Master Holt said . . . and ye were out that night. . . ." She swallowed hard and ground to a halt under her mistress' scathing glare, clutching a comb to her ample little bosom.

Roxie believed him! Her own maid . . . and probably the whole household believed she was Reston's leman!

"He lied! The bastard lied through his teeth to goad the earl into a duel and kill him. It had naught to do with me—not a thing, is that clear? I am not now nor have I ever been his or anyone's leman!"

Roxie lowered her eyes from her mistress' burning stare and shifted her feet uncomfortably under her heavy woolen skirt.

"It be no matter to me where ye take yer pleasure, milady." She shrugged and reached for the brush again to continue with her duties.

"I do not take my pleasures anywhere!" Tauren's eyes snapped with frustration at being so dismissed, by her own maid. "Is that clear?" Her frazzled patience was at its end. She paused a moment and then realized dismally that there was nothing she could do or say to turn the tide of speculation Holt Reston had begun with his wretched proclamations.

She sighed disgustedly and turned back to the looking glass on the table before her.

"My Aunt Veldean never married; she's had a good life . . . a useful life. She is something of an herbalist and very knowledgeable of the world. She reads as much as she can, even with her failing eyesight."

"Just like the old duke," Roxie offered, trying to make amends.

"Yes"—Tauren scowled—"except that she used her knowledge to help others instead of hoarding it. The duke has never helped anyone in his entire life, I'd wager. Who knows, perhaps after he's gone. . . ." He could not go soon enough to suit her, she mused vengefully.

What was she thinking? What was happening to her? Wishing for the death of another of God's children without a qualm? She needed a vicar . . . for confession!

"Where is the vicar that serves Lindengreen's chapel?" she demanded abruptly.

"There . . . there ain't one, I don't think." Roxie drew back, puzzled.

"There ought to be"—Tauren drew herself up straighter—"and there will be. There are quite a few things that need doing about here, things a lady could see to. Yes, quite a little number of things. . . ."

*   *   *

"The chapel has not been used for a score of years, my lady," Mrs. Murdock frowned slightly. "Those who attend mass go to St. Edgar's in Keenings."

"A score of years is too long," Tauren declared flatly. "We will open the chapel again and see mass read there regularly. Spiritual nourishment is as important to the future duke as latin or swordplay. Will you send for the nearest rector, or shall I?"

The rector of St. Edgar's arrived late that same afternoon, ushered into the main salon by a dubious Mrs. Murdock. The balding man wore a frayed cassock that Tauren was sure must once have graced a far larger frame. In his thin face burned two brown eyes that flitted about the room and over Tauren too appreciatively. His smile revealed half-empty rows of ill-kept teeth.

". . . so gracious. Yer father was a man of the cloth I was told, a bishop of the church."

Tauren smiled tightly and turned to Mrs. Murdock.

"Vicar Alfred, rector of St. Edgar's," the housekeeper nodded her amusement and withdrew.

"Vicar Alfred, I'm sure you must be busy. It was good of you to come on such short notice."

"Yea . . . busy in this heathen clime. Been a long time since I was called to Lindengreen."

"I wish to reinstitute mass in the chapel here." Tauren plastered a thin smile on her face and put more distance between her and the cleric, noting the telltale reek of rum mingled with sweat.

The little man's eyes glowed. "Too long the chapel has been closed, too long since the word of the church was enforced in this country." He lowered his voice. "No disrespect to His Grace, but there has been no tithe from this house for the parish and, lacking example, none from many other houses in the shire."

"I shall see that remedied." Tauren puzzled over her reaction to this minion of her father's beloved church, then dismissed this question. She would make her own place as the lady of Lindengreen. And this was the first step. "For now, let us go to the chapel and see what will be required. I would see mass returned there before Christ Mass."

Sinking into a chair in the parlor later, Tauren pushed off her slippers, keeping her toes tucked under her hem. She sipped her cup of fragrant tea and closed her eyes. It was exhausting. There was so much to do here. Why hadn't she seen it before? Mrs. Murdock had been somewhat startled by her assumption of authority, but had squared her shoulders and set about showing Tauren the workings of the great household.

Several times Tauren found the housekeeper's curious eyes on her, and she smiled with a bit more confidence than she felt inside. No doubt the duke would receive a full report of her doings. The thought had steeled her resolve further.

In spite of the old man's contempt for her, she could make a good life here. She could be of service to the people and care for Revan's lands while he was away. There were books to read and Revan and Charlotte. . . . She could apply what she had learned of herbal cures and unctuous teas from Aunt Veldean, set them down from memory and learn new ones.

And what of that pale, perfect lass she had promised to become?

"Father, that lass could not bear this shame, nor the solitary future in which I must make my own way. The

178

daughter you had is all you will ever have."

But there were changes in her all the same. At night, after Roxie snuffed the candles and withdrew, glowing, green-brown eyes appeared, mocking and threatening her. Chilled, she trembled beneath the warmth of the down, tortured by the return of startling and fervent sensations. Her lips burned and her loins ached, forcing her to recall her encounters with Holt Reston. The sensations of his lips against hers, of his hard body upon her. Her face flamed in the darkness. She had felt no such confusion, no such shame when Roger touched her . . . only revulsion and disgust. What flaw, what weakness of the soul did she harbor that made her vulnerable to that demon?

She found some comfort in knowing that her reaction was not unique. According to Charlotte, half the women of the shire secretly desired his attentions . . . and a like number had already received them. The swine's attractions were too freely dispensed to warrant coveting for long.

Fourteen

She gave one hard yank, and the heavy, time-corrupted tapestry ripped with a roar and came down atop her, knocking her to the floor amidst a blinding cloud of ancient and venerable dust. A flurry of servants rushed to her aid, peeling back the deteriorated hanging.

"Are you all right, Lady Tauren?" Murdock waved the others back to their work with an authoritative hand and took charge of the lady, brushing the black powdery dust of decay from her kerchiefed head and dark woolen skirt.

Coughing and blinking still, Tauren wiped at her face with the backs of her hands and leaned upon the prim housekeeper as she was led to the lean comfort of a pew in the neglected stone chapel of Lindengreen.

"The thing was rotted," she managed to get out. "This chapel is a disgrace . . . near hopeless."

The housekeeper's face eased. She looked about her at the sturdy stone walls and worn stone floor, and shook her head. "This is part of the original hall. It hasn't been used in many years and was . . . not kept up like the rest of the old buildings.

"I remember the duke's wedding here," Murdock said suddenly, seeming uncharacteristically moved and far away. "'Twas of an evening and the whole chancel was ablaze with beeswax tapers. There was hardly room to even stand for all the folk who crowded in to glimpse the duke and his bride."

She stopped abruptly and shook her head as if to clear it of the vision she had just described.

"There is work to be done." She grabbed up a straw broom and began to sweep the layers of dust and debris from the floor.

The rest of the good daylight was spent removing the accumulated dust and decay of decades of disuse. They scrubbed the flagstone floors with boar's bristle brushes and pumice to take out the moldy blackness, and they carried out baskets of debris, rotting tapestries and straw and the leavings of vermin. The carpenter set about repairing the sturdy oak pews while the smaller, nimbler lads climbed up into the rafters and beams of the high ceiling to wipe down the cobwebs and ferret out the abandoned nests of birds.

The unusual winter red of the evening sky cast a warm aura about the results of their toil, and Tauren smiled in spite of her aching shoulders and back and her cold, throbbing fingers. She started across the side court toward the main wing of the house, with Murdock. The cold air felt good against her flushed face and she was full of the sense of their achievement. It was as if her new life had begun successfully; it augured well.

"Father Alfred was to come for a blessing this eve,

but perhaps he was delayed. We made such progress today, first mass may yet be said this Sabbath."

"'Twill be good to hear the Word read here again," Murdock agreed. "I fear it has been so long, the people will have a time getting used to it again. But they are good in their hearts and willing."

A huge bay stallion, a dark-cloaked rider astride, suddenly pounded into the side court, sending the tired crew of servants scurrying out of the way to avoid the flashing hooves. One glimpse was all Tauren needed to know the rider's identity and the state of his mind. Purposefully, she tossed her head and quickened her step toward the door of the main wing.

But Holt Reston slammed to a halt, blocking her path and pouncing angrily down upon the ground to stand before her, towering black with fury.

Tauren clutched her shawl tighter and dodged to one side, breaking into a run. But he anticipated her move, and his big frame followed her with ludicrous ease.

"No!" she strained against his grip, "have you gone mad?"

Murdock was standing stock-still and the few servants remaining in the yard stared wide-eyed at the spectacle he was making of her.

"Nay," he glowered above her. "I am here to deliver something to you—a message."

"Let me go!" she ordered, twisting her arm and shoulder futilely.

"*Your priest* will not come this eve . . . or indeed, ever again."

She slowed her struggle and stared up into his anger-hardened face.

"He shall ride, or walk, or crawl out of Somerset this

eve, however his wounds hinder him," Holt growled.
"But if sunlight finds him in this shire tomorrow, I'll see
the job done and he'll regret the day his mother
whelped him."

"Wounds!" Tauren gasped, horror creeping through
her. She had seen the overlord's naked wrath before.
"Merciful Father, what have you done to him?"

Holt shoved his hot face down into hers. "I gave him
mercy—thirty lashes. He deserved worse, the sniveling,
filthy hypocrite."

"You whipped a man of God? A priest of the
church?" She could not bring herself to believe that
even Reston would stoop so low.

"A priest—huh," he snorted. "He defiles the very soil
on which he trods. If that be your precious church, let
them all meet such earthly justice—and soon!" He
grabbed her closer to him by the arm he held, and her
free hand came up in a wide arc to narrowly miss its
target, being captured in his much larger one.

"You spoiled, callous little witch," he blazed. "He
said he did it on your order. Did you think to defy me
and control the shire through that wretch's clerical
skirts? I give you fair warning; I run this shire and I'll
not have these people abused by the stupid laws of your
warped, corrupt episcopate!"

"Warped?" She struggled to match his height as she
already did his anger. "You defame the church . . . per-
secute its anointed and ordained. Father Alfred had my
protection! I charged him to see to the church's affairs,
to bring some order back to this godless—"

"Then you must bear the responsibility for his
actions, for his enthusiasm for obedience to canon
law!"

"Gladly!" she spat.

"Then come 'Lady'!" Quick as lightning he hoisted her up and over his shoulder, tossing her unceremoniously across the pommel of his saddle, face-down. "I'll have you see for yourself the consequences you own so gleefully!"

He mounted behind her squirming form and dug his heels into the stallion's sides. The animal burst forward in an explosion of anxious energy and was out of the court and pounding down the lane in seconds.

Tauren flailed and grabbed at the saddle straps to hang on as the hard jolting of the animal's broad withers against her stomach and ribs banged the hot, salty words from her lips. Her rump pointed humiliatingly skyward, right under the bastard's nose. Blood rushed to her head, jumbling her thoughts and perceptions so that she did not feel his iron-thewed arms drag her up over the pommel to nestle her safely across two sinewy thighs.

She had no time to wonder where he took her or what he planned to do. When the great beast slowed his breakneck pace, she did not sense it, and several seconds passed before she realized that her hard support was gone. Strong hands were lifting her down and she felt the blood drain dizzyingly fast from her head as she was set upon her own unsteady feet. There was a pause before a heavy hand on her arm pulled her along, causing her to stumble and barely right herself.

The punishing pounding of the wild ride left her body screaming with angry pain. She could barely breathe because of bruises over her ribs, but she managed a growl of contempt for the great black form that drew her cruelly along in its wake.

They neared a tenant's cottage, with a low thatched roof. A dull glow emanated from the stretched oiled skins over the small widows. Tauren's mind cleared quickly as her breath triggered something in her memory that she could not fit into place. In jumbled ravings she expressed her outraged protests.

They paused as he opened the bare wooden door to the modest dwelling and then pushed her through it forcefully. She staggered into a low room, lit by meager tallow candles and the bright flame of a wood and peat fire in a sooty hearth.

The occupants seemed as surprised to see her as she was them. A middle-aged woman looked up from her seat by a straw pallet near the hearth's warmth and rose jerkily. Three ragged children flurried to their mother's side and she cradled the two smaller ones against her protectively. When Holt ducked through the door behind Tauren, he had to keep his head bent to avoid the low ceiling, and he shoved Tauren further into the room. Seeing him, the woman's distraught face eased and her eyes closed briefly.

"'Tis ye, Master Holt . . . I feared . . ."

A nod of Holt's bent head acknowledged the woman's greeting as he pushed Tauren closer with his hard body.

"See what consequences you own so gladly, lady." He grabbed her arm tightly and dragged her to the pallet where she met the yellowed, pain-dulled eyes of a man with a blood-soaked rag covering one side of his head. Her brow knitted with dread as her gaze flitted uncomprehendingly from Holt to the woman and then to the man on the pallet.

Seeing that she did not yet understand, he reached

down and pulled the rag from the man's head, revealing a gaping bloody wound on the side of his head where once an ear had been. Tauren's stomach surged at the grisly sight and she jerked her face away, only to find it captured by a brawny hand and forced back.

"Look at it," Holt commanded, and with mute horror she obeyed, feeling hot suddenly as the smell of blood and sweat mingled reached her.

"No," she mouthed.

"Your vicar, your precious church did this . . . with your protection. And you gladly own this? His crime was absence from mass last Sabbath. His only cow was calving hard and he spent the time saving what little he had in this world. Now he has paid for that heinous crime with his own flesh! God judge me, I wish I had flayed that miserable bastard of a cleric alive!"

He dropped her arm as if it repulsed him and glowered down at her unrelentingly. Horrorstruck, she turned to the pain-lined face of the woman, but had difficulty seeing what she knew would be hatred for her there. Everything swam and blurred before her eyes as she turned them back on the disfigured countenance beside her, then on the confused faces of the children.

That madman . . . lunatic! A priest of the church—her father's church—rent the flesh of this poor man . . . with *her* protection! The knowledge beat accusingly in her brain . . . *by her word*!

A sob strangling in her throat, she could hardly breathe. Squeezing the liquid from her eyes and onto her burning cheeks, she spun and bolted for the door . . . and none hindered her.

Her aching body and lungs sucked in the cold, dark air wildly as she slowed outside the cottage door.

186

Pausing only a moment with her hands on her thighs, panting, she threw a panicked look over her shoulder toward the open door and then ran for the stallion with all her might.

How she managed to mount the beast she could not later tell, but she was astride him and thudding, careening, down the cart-rutted path—anywhere—but away from here.

The next afternoon it was a grave and sober young gentlewoman who, mounted on a roan gelding, led the stallion and yet another horse on the reverse of that flight. She carried with her several bundles and rode unescorted, her lips a thin, firm line.

"These are herbs to calm the fever and the pain," she told the shocked tenant wife, "and this yellow powder, applied in poultice, should forestall festering of the . . . wound." Seeing the woman's eyes roam to the other cloth-tied bundles, she explained. "You'll need provisions while he mends. I'll see there's more when these are gone." She met the woman's questioning gaze straight on.

"The vicar was wrong, grievously wrong. I beg your forgiveness and would see the matter set to rights." She dropped her head to regain her composure then lifted her chin again. "Send the lad to the great house on the horse I brought if you need me."

Mounting the fine-boned gelding in the yard, she sat a moment, gazing about her, remembering one day they had paused here while riding, she and Revan and Calder. The tenant's oldest boy had picked a sprig of holly from near the cottage and given it to her, smiling

187

shyly under his mother's proud eyes.

Something swelled annoyingly in her chest, making it harder than ever to breathe in the damp chill of late December. How could she have forgotten so quickly? This was the working of the church her father had both loved and hated, sought to right and despaired of saving. It was as most things in this world are, her father had often quoted, neither all bad nor all good. And with hard-won wisdom, she treasured that truth anew in her heart.

Christ Mass came and went, a solemn occasion in spite of Tauren's attempts to bring some life to the cold elegance of the house. Fresh pine greenery was cut and strung into ropes, then draped about the fireplace in the great rooms of the first floor and a yule log was hewn and trimmed for the great fireplace in the main salon. The kitchens and cookhouses prepared sumptuous feasts for the family and servants alike and Tauren saw sacks of provisions readied and delivered to the tenants in the far ranges of the duke's lands; cured meats, flour, dried currants or apples, and a jug of hardened applejack. In spite of Murdock's dubiously lifted brow, she announced that the servants would have the day to themselves for celebration, religious and otherwise.

It was a most somber time for her when Revan stood in the half-filled chapel to read from scripture the story of the Lord's birth. He stopped twice, but valiantly finished the passage before looking at Tauren and reading in her face his own thoughts—how different it had been last Christ Mass.

188

Calder rose from the back of the little congregation of folk and began in wine-warmed voice to sing a Christmas ballad and soon they all joined him. When the first ended another took its place and still another. And the voices and occasional tears did much to salve Tauren's sore heart.

The early year was gray and bleak and far colder than Tauren would have expected in these southern climes. The snow came early, and no travelers that might break the monotony were about seeking hospitality. Aside from Murdock, Revan, and Calder, she saw no one. The duke seldom joined them for supper and for the last fortnight, the galling overlord had ceased to come to Lindengreen.

She set about learning from Murdock the myriad functions of the lady's role in a noblehouse, finding they consumed as much of her time as she would allow. There were always things to be done, even in the coldest of winter; spinning, carding, cheesemaking, weaving, mending.

One early January day, Roxie rushed into the library, hand to her side, nearly breathless.

"You're needed, milady," she puffed. "Important . . ."

Roxie led her to the grand salon where a new fire was laid and candles were lit against the dark winter afternoon.

Holt Reston leaned a shoulder against the mantel, and Calder sat on the edge of the settee with his elegant hat in hand. Murdock clasped her hands before her anxiously.

It was a moment before Tauren realized that the small figure warming before the fire was not Revan.

Holt straightened and wordlessly grasped the fellow's arm, turning him about forcefully. "This fellow demanded to see you," he declared tersely, suspicion bold on his aquiline features.

The slender, bootless young man garbed in coarse woolens, crumpled his knit cap in his hands, one arm still captive in Holt's unrelenting grip. His sober eyes were ringed with a multitude of nameless cares and despite his obvious youth, there was an air of world-weariness about him.

"Walt Sutton?" Tauren stepped forward, then stopped short under Holt's piercing stare.

"Yea, miss—Lady Tauren now, I guess—it's me." Walt stepped forward, glancing anxiously at Holt who released him reluctantly. He relaxed visibly as Holt stepped back.

"What are you doing here? What's happened?" She edged nearer so that he was within reach, but her hands were clasped tightly before her.

"The Scots seized Squire Northings' lands an' turned us all out—housemen, tenants an' all. I come south to Portsmouth. I be headed for the sea, miss."

"Squire Northings?" she repeated as a wave of vivid and awful memories engulfed her with the past.

"Him in prison, now, miss." Walt shook his head and lowered his voice and eyes. "But I was to bring ye word, if I made it this far. Yer aunt, Lady Veldean . . . gone, miss."

Tauren's heart stopped in her chest and her stomach dropped, leaving a huge emptiness in the core of her. She neither moved nor spoke, staring at the wan face of her childhood friend, knowing what it cost him to bring her this news.

She did not see Holt straighten, his face sober, his brow deeply knit. Nor was she aware that Calder had risen from his seat or that Murdock rushed to her side.

"Did ye hear, miss?" Walt repeated. "She's gone . . . died in her sleep, peaceful . . . a month back."

"Yes, Walt." She allowed his voice to penetrate the haze where she was lost and uttered brokenly, "They're all gone now, aren't they . . . all dead."

Tears filled her sky-blue eyes and hung precariously above her lashes. She stiffened, bracing for a lady's duty, and reached out one hand to tenderly touch Walt's pale, concern-lined face.

"It was kind of you to bring me the news." Her chin trembled, and she lifted her head to quell it, succeeding partly. "You must stay with us to allow us to repay your goodness." She turned to Murdock and found the woman's gray eyes awash with unshed sympathy. "You will see to it?"

"Now"—Tauren gathered her skirts slowly—"I must tell Revan." She turned and walked with restrained grief into the great hall.

They followed her out, Murdock leading Walt Sutton away toward the servants' wing and Calder and Holt watching Tauren mount the staircase.

Thinking no one was left to see, Tauren swayed against the banister at the top of the stairs, blinded by a sudden stream of tears and choked by little, shivering sobs. Holt was in motion, but jerked to a halt on the bottom steps. Calder was soon past him and up the broad staircase.

Blindly, Tauren buried her face in the comforting

expanse of the captain's broad chest and allowed him to support her. Above her head Calder sent Holt a grave, uncomfortable look before he led her away.

Holt watched them go, his face a glowering revelation of his thoughts. If he had gone to her, she would probably have shrunk from him or hissed at him. His arms flexed instinctively, feeling heavy and empty.

What did it matter who comforted her? he brooded. But as he took up his cloak and settled it about his stern shoulders, the glistening prisms of her luminous eyes and the sad, whisper-light touch of her fingers on the youth's face returned to him fully. He stiffened and hurried toward the stables, carrying his discontent with him.

Fifteen

"Roxie! Where is that girl?" Tauren muttered, breathing out her exasperation into a little cloud in the cold air of the old hall. She ran her hands up her cold arms and across the raised skin of her chest, regretting her hasty foray into the drafty, unheated part of Lindengreen without a shawl. This wretched January was but half gone and already she was sick of the cold and snow.

"I send her on a simple errand and she disappears for hours!"

Tauren turned the corner of the main hall and paused, putting her hands to her waist and pursing her lips. Where had she seen the marvelous old hand-carved chest?

"In one of these rooms"—she pointed back and forth between two doors—"I told Roxie—" She entered the closest door, finding herself again in the main bedchamber of the old hall. She avoided the great box bed adamantly and scoured the darker recesses of the chamber's sides and corners for signs of the treasure

193

she sought.

Her sky-blue eyes soon lit with satisfaction and she ducked under a sideboard to grasp the handle of a heavily carved teak chest and struggled to pull it out. She would need that footman she had sent with Roxie. . . .

Standing in the midst of the chamber, she waved away a haze of dust motes and found herself frowning and listening, for what she was not sure. A giggle . . . distant, but a female laugh to be sure. She frowned deeper and cocked her head to concentrate. It came again. Roxie.

The sounds grew louder and became all too recognizable as Tauren approached the other chamber, the door of which was left slightly ajar. A male voice uttered something in muffled tones and again Roxie giggled, ending with a moan of delight that brought crimson to Tauren's cheeks. She pushed open the door and stepped determinedly into the chamber, but she was not prepared for what she found.

Roxie lay, bodice open, with skirts raised and knees akimbo on an armless old couch. Atop her lay the eager young footman, nibbling and nuzzling her generous young breasts as she squirmed with delight beneath his bulging livery. Engrossed as they were, neither saw Tauren immediately, and she stared, open-mouthed, unable to speak.

"Roxie!" she finally managed, though her voice cracked strangely. Instantly, the philandering pair were in motion; the footman springing straight up like a tied sapling and Roxie snatching at her garments to cover herself hastily. Tauren's face flamed and Roxie's drained of color as they came eye to eye.

"This is . . . inexcusable," Tauren blurted out, embarrassed by her own lack of words.

"Oh, milady," Roxie's eyes were wide with fear as she hurriedly fastened her bodice together. "We meant no harm, milady . . . honest."

"Be sure, milady . . . we meant no harm," the maid's partner in passion echoed, adjusting his doublet and breeches.

Squaring her shoulders, Tauren turned to him first. "You were sent to move a trunk, not dally with my maid. Your work sits in the chamber across the hall. See to it immediately, or you'll be mucking out the stables from here on." The reedy young swain nearly bowled her over in his haste to be away.

"Roxie"—she turned on a scathing glare on her nubile young maid—"only scullions and strumpets raise their skirts at a footman's wink. You are a lady's maid . . . I demand better of you."

"Oh, yes, milady," Roxie nodded miserably, dropping her head and gripping her apron tightly. "It won't happen again, milady. He teased me and before I knew it, we just . . . I'll see he gets it done proper." She hurried out, and in a moment the sounds of her vented indignation and of the eager swain's complaint wafted back.

Tauren smiled mischievously and began to scan the room for other items that might be of use. She walked about, touching the heavy, faded old furnishings. What was there about this old place that seemed to inspire amorousness?

"What is it about this place that attracts you?"

Holt's voice froze her in her tracks. She found him leaning one broad shoulder against the doorway, watching the slow waltz of her skirts about the room.

She colored becomingly, chagrined by her thoughts. Had they somehow conjured him here? "In the future, please find another passage through to the stables, and spare us your lurking and skulking about."

"This is the quickest way through," he pushed off and sauntered into the chamber, eyeing her appreciatively. "Since I have frequent business with the duke, you'll just have to accommodate me . . . my choice of exits. As you'll come to know, I am adamantly opposed to wastage of any sort." His eyes crinkled at the corners, and his mouth dimpled intriguingly at one end.

Tauren moved anxiously about the room, carefully avoiding proximity to him. The low, silky tone of his voice and the slow bronzing of his eyes as they roamed over her made her jittery inside.

"Which brings me to you." He stopped and crossed his arms, stroking his chin with one lean finger.

"I am absolutely none of your concern," she sailed toward the door, but he grabbed her wrist and held her.

"Everything, everyone in this shire is my concern."

"Let go of me," she balked as he drew her closer, but her smooth slippers and his iron-thewed arms defeated her.

"A woman like you is not meant for wasting away, Tauren." Something in his voice caused her heart to skip, and that frightened her.

"Your lips were made for tasting, your skin was made for touching—your breasts were meant to fill a man's hand."

"Stop it!" she whispered hoarsely. "You're depraved."

"Nay," he held her within arm's reach and took her waist with his other hand. "I only speak the truth. See the way your skin responds when I touch you. You are as hungry for me as I am for you."

Gooseflesh was rising on her chest and shoulder beneath his fingertips. She shivered and shut her eyes tightly against it, feeling herself drawn closer to his dangerous heat. His hand moved up her throat to hold her face gently up to his and he pressed her to him.

Fighting for reason and for her very breath, Tauren opened her eyes only to lose both. His face was dusky, his eyes glowed darkly with the intensity of his desire for her. He lowered his head by tantalizing increments.

"Let me have you, Tauren. Let me love you. . . ." His mouth covered hers slowly tempting, teasing a forbidden impatience from her hiddenmost recesses.

All pride, all indignation, all grievances were flown. There was only the hypnotic feel of his lips on her skin, the hard strength of his body against her, the crispness of his hair curling about her fingers. She pressed closer, mindlessly wanting—needing—the comforts of his body, the comfort of being wanted.

She was weightless, floating in his arms and then coming down slowly, as his body covered her, warming, exciting her. A moan escaped her throat as his hand invaded her low bodice to cup her breast. She nuzzled the smooth base of his throat and sent her other hand up the corded column of his neck into his raven hair. All time, all existence stood still for her, as it had that first time she saw him.

His heavy doublet was cast aside and he peeled her tiered velvet skirt from her gently, never leaving her embrace. Her bodice was opened, baring her satiny skin to his touch even as her face bared the longings of her besieged heart. He traced the curve of her cheek with the tip of his nose and nibbled the angle of her jaw and the oval shell of her ear.

She was unable to speak but her eyes sang for him the harmony of her body and deepest soul, responding to his exquisitely tender caresses. Here there was no history to accuse, no future to defend. Here was only the burning of her flesh where his hands touched it and the hard warmth of his bare chest across her breasts. She clasped him to her, needing his certainty, his strength all about her.

His palm swept her shoulder, her breast, and savored the delectable softness of her hip. "Tauren . . . my beautiful Tauren . . ." he murmured against her chest, not knowing the words found fertile ground in her aching heart.

His face came up to hers, and in the confused wonderment of her pleasure-glazed eyes, he read the time had come and smiled a tenderly knowing smile. In his look she found the same passion and tenderness that had brought her unfailingly this far, and in trust she offered him her lips once more.

Holt held her face between his hands and came to her slowly, drowning the sharpness and stinging she felt in warm, golden waves of pleasure. His movements were careful and restrained, seeking for her that promise of ecstasy that once planted would draw her ever toward its fulfillment. But one word, wrenched from her soul, her longing, exploded his reason and his passion.

"Holt . . ."

His plunging spasms were counterpoint to the pounding of Tauren's blood. A deep, beguiling sense of completion invaded her as he relaxed, surrounding her with his heavy warmth. It seemed a long time before he left her to lie beside her, stroking her face and raining whisper-light kisses over the moist skin of her forehead and temples. He drew her petticoats down over her legs and pulled them protectively between his own. With each hook of her front-fastening bodice he dropped a kiss in the valley between her breasts, until he could no more.

Tauren watched his tender ministries with misting eyes and full, aching chest. She had never guessed such intimacy, such gentleness could exist between a man and a woman . . . between her and this man. Her finger came up to trace the strong plane of his angular cheek and the bold curve of his lower lip. Or perhaps she had known. . . .

Again she felt his firm, gentle mouth on hers and returned his kiss fully, feeling buoyed upward suddenly, as if surfacing from immersion in this marvelous dream.

Holt left her love-reddened lips a moment to raise his head.

"Out," he ordered quietly, returning to her fragrant and responsive mouth.

It was a moment before the sense of what he had said seeped through to her dazzled mind. Only when he repeated it, more emphatically, did she realize what was happening.

"Oh . . . milady!"

Hurried footsteps retreated, punctuated by a muffled giggle.

Tauren's eyes flew wide as she whirled and spiraled upward, then broke through some mystical surface back into suspended reality. She wrenched away from Holt's kiss just in time to see familiar gray skirts disappear through the door.

"Roxie!" she gasped through indrawn breath. Blinking and shaking her head, she was acutely aware of her partner and position. A sickening sense of shame welled up within her. Here she lay, sprawled on that same couch entwined with an infamous lecher . . . her own despoiler!

She pushed savagely against Holt and sat up, dumping him on the floor, surprised. "See what you've done!" She groaned, appalled by the sight of her bare petticoats nestled modestly about her ankles.

"That stupid girl!" Holt muttered raggedly, trying to hold Tauren in place on the couch from his awkward position beside it. "It matters not, Tauren. It changes nothing."

"Precisely," she rasped, taking advantage of his position to twist free and push away long enough to gain her feet. Then she turned on him, backing away as he lurched upright.

"Nothing is changed. You are still the same, arrogant, blackguard that took . . . my virtue and ruined my name. And each time we meet I allow you to add some fresh indignity to your list of wrongs. I must have been mad to let you—" She stopped, bringing the back of her hand to her mouth. Fresh memory spurred her with the sharpness of her own desire for him, and she turned it outward. "I despise you and your constant lust and venery!"

"You wanted me as much as I wanted you. Now you decry my lust because you fear your own. It is a battle you cannot win." His eyes glittered.

"If not, then at least I shall have the satisfaction of knowing you cannot claim victory either," she declared, heedless of the liquid forming in her eyes. "You have what you wanted . . . your famed carnal skills work even on me. But, you'll never crawl beneath my skirts again. Go back to your trollops and your squalid little adulteries; you've finally overreached yourself, bastard."

Flames leaped to his eyes as she delivered that last thrust and she backed to the door and fled.

But Holt stood tautly in the quiet chamber, hearing echoes all about him. Her throaty whimper of surrender as she curled her fingers in his hair and returned his penetrating kisses and the fury of her biting denial grated cruelly along each straining nerve of his rigid body.

"Damn!" he exploded, bringing one powerful fist down hard on a small round table beside him, oveturning it. While he struggled for control, his eyes fell on a swirling heap of velvet near his feet . . . her skirts. He bent to collect the omen, his face and mood as dark as his sober raiment.

Sixteen

Holt paused on a ridge overlooking the river that wound toward the town of Keenings. He had ridden hard for several days, covering the fertile tenant lands that helped to make Somerset a rich duchy. He had been to Portsmouth, the shipbuilding port, for a month and had returned with a compelling need to reassure himself that all was well. He had been eager to see that bustling city and just as eager to escape Somerset and the frame of mind he had found himself in.

He frowned, drawing his heavy woolen cloak tighter around him in the biting wind. His thoughts turned as dark as the sky and ranged as far. With his muscular legs he urged his mount along the ridge and toward a copse of trees that would give him relief from the plaguing wind.

Damn the old man and his precious heir. The whole family was tainted with unholy stubbornness. His warm, hazel-green eyes darkened as he thought of the third member of the family and allowed his mind's eye to trace the gentle curves of her face and voluptuous body. But the skin of his face tightened at the strength of the unwelcome arousal that accompanied those musings.

She deviled him constantly. Never did he close his eyes to sleep that her face, her fire-kissed hair, her sky-filled eyes did not appear to torment him. Again and again he felt her warm lips against his, her firm young body writhing beneath him, and then the heel of her palm smashing into his granite cheek. He ground his teeth in frustration and spurred his startled mount into a gallop that took him headlong into the trees. He could almost hear Calder's laughter ringing in his ears.

When he emerged from the trees on the lea side of the ridge, his ire had cooled and he reined up to a saner pace. From habit, his eyes swept the landscape, catching a lone figure and mount near the frozen millpond above the stone dam. Something about the figure seemed familiar. Holt watched as the fellow dismounted, leaving the horse standing stolidly by as he ventured out upon the ice. The ungainly form balanced precariously with arms outstretched and flailing.

Holt squinted with concentration and felt a prickling of dread as he watched the figure venture farther from the shore. He drew his horse to a halt without knowing why. The fellow slid and spun in a childish way, unaware he was being observed or that he drew ever closer to the dam itself, where, Holt knew from experience, the constant flow of water beneath the surface prevented the ice from thickening. The figure spun once more, and his body registered recognition just as the ice began to give way under the lad's feet.

Holt sat, frozen momentarily by the realization of what was taking place. The heir of Somerset was drowning in the icy water ... the heir ... all that stood between himself and complete possession of the shire, an inheritance.

"Damn the fool!" Holt dug his spurs into the sides of his animal and it sprung violently into action. Whether he cursed the lad or himself he had not time to think. Seconds, that seemed like hours passed before Holt was at the side of the pond and leaping down from his mount, ripping his cloak from his shoulders. Moving in the direction of the frantic and weakening cries, he stepped cautiously upon the ice, unbelting his scabbard as he called to the lad.

"Revan! I'm coming for you. Hang onto the ice as long as you can! Kick your feet! Kick hard and hang on!" Holt kept testing the ice as he inched toward Revan, answering the boy's cries with reassurances that he would soon be safe. When the ice underfoot cracked ominously, Holt knelt and spread himself out upon his belly atop the thinning crust, but he continued to move toward Revan.

"Help me, please ... please. ..." Revan's voice was weaker, his face frightened and blue about the lips. His hands slipped woodenly on the edge of the ice as he tried to hold on with fingers he no longer commanded. Another chunk of the thin ice cracked under his weight and broke off, sending him thrashing under the dark, merciless waters once more.

"Revan!" Holt barked the lad's name, hoarse with tension, "Revan, you've got to hold on! I'm nearly there. ..." He was yelling with all his strength as Revan bobbed once more to the surface, clawing at the edge of the ice frantically. The ice groaned under Holt's weight as he tossed the belt of his scabbard over near Revan's outstretched hand and ordered him to grab it with both hands. It seemed an eternity before the sense of the command seeped through to the frozen youth, and Holt yelled the order again and again, feeling his own panic rising with the boy's unresponsiveeess. Something in Holt experienced a dread, a fear of losing now in this game of life and death, where so often before he had pressed and won.

He held his breath as he watched Revan's frozen fingers reach for the scrap of leather that was his only link with life. "Twist it about your hand!" Holt commanded, watching tensely as the lad obeyed with agonizing slowness.

Then Holt was pulling, and feeling himself slipping toward the lad with nothing to slow his progress. He turned to his side, feeling the ice groan under him, and dug his spurs into the glassy surface, pulling again, straining every sinew of his battle-hardened frame. Revan's stiff, cold body slowly appeared above the edge of the ice, cracking new pieces of the brittle bridge as it came. When Revan was halfway out, Holt paused to change his own position and dug in once more to strain and haul the lad completely out of the murky water. Inching toward the bank of the pond, he pulled Revan's now-unconscious form after him, sitting up only when his feet touched the frozen grasses caught in the ice at the very edge.

Getting to his knees, he dragged Revan to him and pried the belt from his frozen fingers. Holt's heart was pounding in a queer and unnerving way. His mind now raced to determine his next movements as he drew the frozen form against him and half-carried, half-dragged him onto the shore. He wrapped his own cloak about the boy and draped the slender form over the pommel of his saddle until he mounted. Steadying Revan's head against his shoulder and holding him securely with one muscular arm, he spurred his mount, riding hard for the edge of Keenings.

The paneled door shook under Holt's heavy fist and was opened by a surprised little maid who stepped back quickly as he thrust past her into the hall of the modest house. The girl closed the door behind him and blinked, open-mouthed, at the limp form dangling awkwardly over Holt's shoulder.

"Call your mistress," Holt demanded moving down the hall toward a room he knew to be a bedchamber. Ducking to enter the doorway, he saw the girl still standing, staring after him, and bellowed, "Move!" He paused only long enough to see her jolt into action and disappear up the wooden stairs nearby; then he carried his burden into the chamber and deposited it gently on the wide bed.

When Peg Mead appeared in the doorway, Holt was stripping the frozen clothing from Revan's unconscious form. "He's half frozen; we've got to warm him quickly."

"Get wood and build up a fire!" Peg ordered the gawking servants, who scurried to do her bidding. Then she was at Holt's side, pulling the sodden clothing from the stiff, cold body of the lad. Her long red hair fell over her shoulders and absently she tossed it back out of the way, drawing Holt's eye with the movement.

He swept her with a glance, taking in the scanty clothing revealed by her hastily closed wrapper.

"We've come at a bad time, I see," he observed wryly, feeling better, surer by the moment in these familiar surroundings.

"I was . . . resting," Peg retorted. "Who is this frozen stalk of a lad?" She ripped the shirt from Revan's body, feeling the icy flesh of his chest with her slim hand. "He's half dead!"

Holt stripped off Revan's heavy breeches and wrapped the woolen blanket Peg offered about his naked body before answering. "He's the next Duke of Somerset."

The servants had laid a fire in the hearth, and Holt looked about him, his eyes coming to rest on a large sheepskin draped on a chest in the corner. "That skin"—he motioned with his head as he gathered Revan up in his arms and lifted him—"put it in front of the hearth. We'll make him a pallet . . . he's got to be warmed—quickly."

Peg grabbed the skin and spread it in front of the fire as the serving girl flew to rip the blankets from the bed and fold them over the skin.

Holt lowered him onto the hastily prepared bed and knelt beside him to feel his arms and legs. The heat was rising fast as the dry wood caught in the fireplace, but Revan's white limbs were still icy.

Peg knelt beside Holt and touched one icy foot. "He's got to be rubbed. Pansy has a warm enough nature—Pansy!" When the girl appeared, Peg made room for her by Revan's feet and pulled back the blanket. "Rub his feet to get the blood flowing again." As the girl bent to her task earnestly, Peg grinned wickedly at Holt, then at the nubile young girl. "It may be the only time ye'll get to be so personal with a duke."

Pansy paused a moment in her labor, staring wide-eyed at the white-faced lad. "Lor," she murmured, falling to her work with new eagerness.

They rubbed and kneaded Revan's cold, lifeless limbs for what seemed an eternity, sweating with the heat of the blazing fire and their exertions. Peg finally sat back and put one hand to the small of her back, arching it to relieve the strain. "His color's better. I think we can let his lordship rest a bit now."

Holt straightened, running one hand down Revan's arm to assure himself that the blood flowed there again, and running the other through his thick black mane. "He's warming quickly now. Damn fool boy! He could have died out there!"

"The millpond?" Peg asked, laying one hand on Holt's damp sleeve. "That's why you brought him here."

"He would have died on the way to Lindengreen. I knew you'd take him in." His hazel eyes turned on her and she smiled, smoothing back her hair with one hand. Her eyelids lowered, along with her voice.

"I would never refuse you, Holt. You're tired. Come let me get you some brandy and a dry shirt." She was on her feet and pulling him up with her. She laughed throatily at his uncertainty, seeing that his gaze lingered on the sleeping lad. "He needs rest now, you've done all you can. Pansy will see to his lordship, and you can send word to Lindengreen with my man, Frazier." She took his arm and led him from the room, a knowing look on her face.

"Besides, a hero should have a reward."

*   *   *

The sun was well up the next morning when Peg opened her bedchamber door to admit a serving-woman with a tray of tea and scones. She drew her wrapper tight about her and poured a cup of the steaming brew as the stout woman built up the fire in the hearth from the banked embers.

When the servant left, she wandered over to the bed where Holt lay sprawled in raw, magnificent splendor. Her eyes skimmed his powerful chest and arms, black-fringed eyes and weather-bronzed face. Her throat tightened. She should have known it would happen, sometime. They had slept in the same bed, but he had not made love to her nor responded to her sensual invitations. He was distant . . . as if part of him were elsewhere. With the instinct of a woman aware of the ways of men's minds and passions, she knew the cause of this behavior. There was a woman.

Feeling a sudden sense of loss, she replaced the cup on the tray and shed her light garment to climb under the bedcovers. She snuggled over against Holt, pressing her skin against his warm, hard body, and closed her eyes.

Holt opened the door to the room where Revan had passed the night and paused in the doorway. He had not bothered to dress fully, and stood shirtless and barefoot, staring open-mouthed at the sight before him. His initial surprise turned to full, hearty laughter as Pansy, obviously naked, jumped up from the pallet, pulling one of the several blankets with her and wrapping herself in it.

She blushed and stammered, seeing her mistress appear beside Holt. "'E was chillin' in the night an' I jus' thought to keep 'im warm was all."

Revan, now propped up on his elbows, was so chagrined that even the natural red cast of his hair seemed a blush. His eyes were wide and filled with confusion. "Master Reston, I . . ."

Holt's hearty laughter cut short any explanation he might have offered. "And I worried about your health"—Holt chortled—"when it was your morals in the greater danger!" Peg was laughing too and slipped past Holt to collect her overzealous serving girl and usher her from the room.

Holt sobered and went to the fireplace, stirring the banked embers and laying new kindling and logs. From behind him, Revan could see his broad, bronzed shoulders shaking from time to time, betraying his ill-kept mirth.

"She did warm me," Revan declared petulantly.

"I'll wager she did," Holt turned to him, a grin on his rakish face.

"Said her 'mam' taught her it was the best way to stop a chill."

"No doubt." Holt tried to stifle his humor and was only partly successful, his relief at seeing the lad so recovered contributing to his boisterous mood. "How do you feel?" He knelt and tossed back the blanket covering Revan's feet, feeling them warm and seeing them a healthy, fleshy pink.

"Fine, sir . . . ah, hungry," Revan responded, seeming relieved nothing more would be said about the girl.

"Then I'll see you're fed." His big rescuer swung gracefully into action and started for the door before Revan's voice stopped him.

"Master Reston"—he waited for Holt to face him—

210

"you saved my life. Be assured I am grateful. I shan't forget it."

Holt flinched unexpectedly, his face becoming a slate of cold indifference. The whelp learned quickly the barter of the nobility, the brisk, lucrative currency of favor. He bestows it nobly, Holt thought bitterly as he strode out.

They rode side by side back to Lindengreen mostly in silence. Revan was puzzled by this powerful man and his actions, and by the animosity that sometimes surfaced to betray him. He had saved Revan's life, then, when thanked properly, had shown contempt for the effort made. Even now the silence bristled with reined hostility. Why? Why had the overlord bothered to save him?

Only when the walls of Lindengreen were in sight did Holt break the silence.

"I sent word to your tutor and Mrs. Murdock that you were safe and with me. I think the less said on what really happened, the better. I don't think they'll pry."

"And Taurie—Tauren?" Revan asked. "She'll have known I was gone."

Holt merely glanced at him from the corner of his eye.

Something in that look rankled Revan, making him straighten his shoulders and try to seem taller. "I'll see to her," he declared resolutely, instinctively feeling that this was one of those things that were best kept between men. Taurie need never know. In the last day he knew he had aged years. Then he had an "adult" thought.

"I'd like to send Mistress Mead a token of my

appreciation . . . for her hospitality."

Holt nodded, looking straight ahead. Revan smiled, inwardly pleased at his manly insight.

Holt's mouth twitched at the corners.

"And Pansy?" he quipped.

"She only warmed me!" Revan declared hotly, coloring beet-red as he slipped back into the morass of boyhood.

Holt roared.

Seventeen

"I clear forgot the time!" Roxie put one hand on her ample, wool-clad bosom and leaned against the bed-chamber door, breathing hard.

"When don't you?" Tauren retorted.

"Master Holt's come back from Portsmouth and the duke has him to supper tonight. . . . There's a lovely piece of man, the lord."

"He's no lord!" Tauren shot her a stern look of correction, tossing her head to ignore the sudden fluttering of her pulse. "I've lost my appetite. Carry my regrets to the duke and Revan."

Minutes later, Roxie came running back, eyes wide with anticipation as she delivered her message with a breathy bit of triumph. "'E says to come or he'll come after ye."

"The duke?" Tauren was incredulous.

"Nay, Master Holt." The maid leaned heavily against the door behind her.

"The boor." She narrowed her eyes and shook her finger in the maid's face. "Tell them I am taken ill . . . or am in womanly travail. I won't sit at the same table as that lecherous churl."

When Roxie repeated her mistress' exact words before her noble audience, Holt's eyes narrowed and his boots hit the floor with auguring force. "Then the lecherous churl will fetch her himself."

Revan and Roxie had to run along beside him, up the great staircase and along the gallery toward the hall and Tauren's chambers.

"What are you going to do?" Revan demanded, losing some of the effect of his command in the exertion required to stay even with the overlord's long strides.

"I'll not be disobeyed." Holt's eyes glittered strangely in the dim hallway candles.

They stopped at the door to Tauren's apartments and Revan grabbed the dark sleeve of Holt's doublet, his young face colored with exertion and alarm.

"You'll not hurt her!" he demanded.

Holt paused a moment, peering down into the lad's anxious face, and leaned back upon one sinewy leg to clarify his own course. "Not unless she hurts me." Outwardly, his face was like stone and Revan searched it, remembering their recent adventure. Revan let go his sleeve, and Holt pushed back the door left ajar as Roxie had slipped past them.

The little maid squealed with both distress and delight as he stormed into the sitting room. She pressed her rounded form back against the bedchamber door and spread her arms as if to protect it.

"Ye cannot enter, milord, she's . . . she's not dressed!"

Determination lining his finely chiseled features, he

set Roxie aside bodily and proceeded to enter, locking the door behind him and slipping the key into his pocket.

"Out!" Tauren demanded angrily, fighting the weakening of her knees at the sight of him. She stood stock-still in corset and petticoats, furious that he would stoop so low as to carry out his threat.

"I warn you now, I'll brook no more disrespect. You'll dress and come down to dinner now—or I'll dress you myself and carry you down!"

"I should expect such behavior from a baseborn scavenger," she growled and hurled a small vase at him.

He dodged the missile easily, and it crashed ignominiously upon the stone floor behind him. "Yea, being a baseborn scavenger, I have not had the advantages of an elegant upbringing such as yours," he taunted, stalking her and dodging the wooden box she threw at him.

Her back to the window now and no other objects within reach, she swallowed and watched him angle across to her bed, drawing ever closer. He picked up the skirt she would have worn from the bed and held it out to her with one hand. "Will you, or shall I?" His eyes glistened.

Seeing her jutting chin and the clenched, whitened fists at her sides, he started for her, sending her on a desperate flight around the commode table and nearly out of reach. He caught her arm and stopped her with a jerk.

"Don't you dare put your filthy hands on me!" she spat.

"Stand still or I'll turn you over my knee," he growled, dragging her to a chair before the fire and pulling her between his muscular thighs to imprison her. He threw the skirt over her stiff, outraged form and released her arm to pull it down about her shoulders, pinioning her arms to her sides. Her face flamed and her eyes blazed at him.

"You'll pay for this," she vowed tightly.

"The choice is yours, shall I continue?" he smirked maliciously, his hands moving up the heavy velvet of the skirt to the satiny skin of her arms.

Quivering inwardly, she stared straight ahead, finding in his questing touch a compelling motivation for compliance. Her skin was turning to goose flesh under his hands.

"I shall dress myself," she whispered through tightened lips and gritted teeth, anxious to escape his intimate hold. These last weeks had done nothing to bolster her defenses against him; his merest touch still made her want to curl up against his big, hard body.

She was shaking as he released her and she rushed to the other side of the room. Glaring at him, she freed her arms and settled the skirt about her waist.

Holt threw one booted leg over the arm of the stout chair and propped his chin on his fist to watch her every movement. She struggled with the ties at the waist, her shaking fingers fumbling, defying her attempts to retain some dignity. Feeling his presence all about her, his gaze fastened hungrily on her exposed breasts, she walked woodenly to the postered bed and picked up the quilted bodice of her dress, pulling it up, over her arms.

"I'll need Roxie . . . my maid." Seeing his mistrustful look, she darkened. "My laces," she uttered throatily, shamed by the confusing heat his undisguised desire generated in her.

"Come here. I'll be your maid."

She drew breath for a hot retort but stopped as his head tilted and his eyes narrowed in warning. Mentally, she condemned him to every heinous torture she could call to mind but she presented him her rigid back.

He drew a heavy breath she did not see and began to draw the laces with expert hands. She jumped and moved an arm's length away when he stood up. It seemed his hands lingered on her waist longer than necessary, and she jerked skittishly when his fingers brushed her bare skin. Sooner than she expected, he withdrew his hands. She felt a strange drop in her stomach as his touch left her.

She started for the door, but his voice halted her.

"You see, Tauren"—he paused, and she turned reluctantly to look at him—"I get what I want."

"That remains to be seen."

It was a strange procession; Tauren, head high and angry, in Holt's unrelenting grasp, then Revan who was trailed by a wide-eyed Roxie who had listened at the door and heard everything. Holt left her standing unceremoniously by her chair and proceeded down the long table to take his seat beside the duke. Revan moved to assist her but stopped dead under Holt's forbidding glare.

Through supper Holt pointedly ignored her, making her humiliation complete. She must "respect" him— he'd have that by brute force—but he could degrade, even ignore, her at will and she had no recourse.

Twice when she looked up, the duke's eyes were on

her, full of what she fancied must be amusement.

In the nights that followed, there were four at supper. If she were late, Holt sent a polite message of invitation to her chambers, a subtle reminder of her fruitless resistance; one which never failed to raise her embattled pride against him.

The sun of early spring streamed in through the leaded windows of the library, warming Tauren's velvet-clad shoulders. A shadow fell across her page and she shifted in her seat, hoping that such interference did not presage a return of the grinding grayness of the season. But as she returned to her book, she sensed the presence of another in the room and jumped with a start at the deep voice booming near her shoulder and just above her.

"'Behold, you are beautiful, my love; behold, you are beautiful; your eyes are doves. . . .'"

She bounded up, clutching the book to her breasts, eyes flashing. Holt Reston stood like a colossus, fists on hips and jackbooted legs spread solidly. While her face flamed and her lips hardened, he smiled lazily, continuing.

"'The voice of my beloved! Behold he comes. . . . My beloved speaks and says to me: "Arise, my love, my fair one, and come away; for lo, the winter is past, the rain is over and gone. The flowers appear on the earth, the time of singing has come. . . . let me hear your voice, for your voice is sweet and your face is comely."'"

Eyes widening with confusion at his peculiar behavior, she edged toward the door as he spoke. But Holt was quick to read her intention in her eyes, and she found her way blocked by his massive body. Her heart beating a discomforting crescendo, she retreated a few steps from him, back into the strong sunlight that sent fiery streaks along her wrapped and braided tresses.

She made a fetching sight and he crossed his bulging arms over his chest and rested his chin on one finger as he appreciated her openly.

"'Your lips are like a scarlet thread, and your mouth is lovely. Your cheeks are like halves of a pomegranate behind your veil. Your neck is like the tower of David. . . . Your breasts are like two fawns, twins of a gazelle, that feed among the lilies. . . .'"

"Stop it!" she demanded, alarmed by his vulgar and shameless ravings. She started around him for the door.

"'How graceful are your feet in sandals, O queenly maiden! Your rounded thighs are like jewels, the work of a master hand. Your navel is a rounded bowl that never lacks mixed wine. Your belly is a heap of wheat encircled with lilies. . . . How fair and pleasant you are, O loved one, delectable maiden!'"

He had stalked her and now caught her as he finished his soliloquy. He dragged her to him, wriggling with horror in his control. His low rumble of amusement sent scarlet up under her lovely skin and as he continued she brought her hands up to stop her ears.

"No," she panted defiantly, "spare me your lust-spawned ravings in my own house!"

"'I would lead you and bring you into the house of my mother, and into the chamber of her that conceived me. I would give you spiced wine to drink, the juice of my pomegranates. O that his left hand were under my

219

head, and that his right hand embraced me!'" Holt's eyes twinkled with a purposeful light Tauren recognized all too well.

"Let me go," she threatened. "I do not have to suffer your assaults nor listen to your perversions."

"You do not like my poetry?" he looked down into her angry face with mock injury. "I thought you would find it most enjoyable."

"It is . . . revolting!"

"It is scripture," he said evenly, his mouth twitching oddly at the corner.

"You blaspheme!" She was horrorstruck and renewed her struggle in earnest, kicking at his solidly booted leg. "I won't listen to more of your filth!"

"A bishop's daughter and you don't even recognize scripture when you hear it?" His face recoiled in mock horror. "Tsk, tsk, lady. The Songs of Solomon, from our good King James's book."

"Let me go, you jackanape!"

"Or what?" he relaxed visibly, still holding her tightly. "None in this house or in this shire would stand against me . . . or could. They know, as you will come to, that my tax is equitable and my justice sure and fair. I insure the peace such that a mere lass on horseback may roam the countryside unmolested in the dead of night."

Her face flamed at his reference.

"Yes, power you have here, that is clear, but it is extorted power—stolen from those whose right it legally and naturally is!"

Holt's eyes narrowed as he released her. "In that you err, 'lady.' I took power here only after it had been squandered on those unworthy to wield it; I picked it up from the gutters where it had been tossed like so much worldly refuse." His final thrust silenced her with its sharp truth. "Would you rather the noble duke sat judge and bailiff on the lands? I believe you have tasted his justice, his mercy."

Unable to find a quick retort, she whirled and again sought escape. He moved quickly again to block her retreat.

"This is intolerable!"

"Nay, in truth, I am quite tolerable." Holt smirked. "It would come as no surprise to me that you actually like me . . . or perhaps 'like' is not an adequate description. . . ."

"Like?" she squeaked, bringing her arm up quickly to find it seized. His eyes danced angrily, giving her reason to regret her instinctive reaction.

"Twice you have struck me in anger," he growled. "I serve you warning, Tauren, the next time you strike me, I will strike you back. By the time you pick yourself up from the floor, you will have learned a sorely needed lesson in the respect of power." His hand tightened ominously on her arm and he read the shock on her face with short-lived satisfaction. "What more do you expect from a baseborn scavenger?"

He felt her stiffen at his taunt and released her.

"What will it take for you to leave us alone. What do you want of us?" she demanded.

He stood there raking her with his glowing eyes, so big and dark. "I will not bear your open contempt for me. I have not earned it and will not accept it. You will conduct yourself as befits a lady in my presence."

"And what honor, what homage do I owe the man who made me a widow before I was even a wife—a man

221

whose base lies have ruined my name and my future?"

"Lies? I think not. I have stated only the truth where you are concerned, as you well know. As for Sappington, I simply stated my conditions for allowing him to have you. The low-minded fool was gullible enough to believe you had cuckolded him, on the mere words of a man he hated."

"That was your whole purpose, to discredit my brother and me in the eyes of all Somerset. Now you claim my respect, my *gratitude* for defending my honor, when it was you that called it to question! You're mad!"

"On the contrary, I make perfect sense. You would not have liked Sappington's reaction to our regrettably brief loving when you faced him at your bedding . . . and I could not suffer his influence here. I simply eliminated the problem for us both, and at some cost to myself." He rubbed his shoulder, drawing her eyes to it in the process. "I have already paid your blood-price for the pleasure of touching you."

"You," she sputtered, feeling dangerously drawn to his thinking, "you did it to gain Somerset for yourself!"

He glowered, stalking her as she backed away.

"I already have Somerset. I mean to have you as well." His voice had a peculiar, husky quality about it that made her slow and look up into his face. His eyes darkened, but not in anger.

Her lips parted slightly as her breath came quicker. The blue pools of her eyes betrayed her as they came to fasten on his full sensuous mouth. Unbidden, the remembrance of arousing warmth and softness of his lips flooded through her, weakening and confusing her response.

"Then you will have to take me, overlord . . . I'll never come to you willingly."

Dragging her closer to him, he drank in her soft skin, her moist, parted lips, the wisps of coppery hair that curled about her face and throat. Her eyes were now azure, dark and expectant. His head filled with her violetlike fragrance and he pressed her to his chest, one arm capturing her small waist while his head bent slowly toward hers.

His eyes crinkled at the corners and a lazy, half-smile of triumph curled his handsome mouth.

"Never?"

Before she could protest his lips found hers. She lost ground to the volley of trills and ripples that played with excruciating pleasure up and down her limbs and spine. She found it hard to breathe against the warmth and curious hard softness of his lips. His big hand bent to other labor as it flew lightly over her cheek, drawing that something from her which weakened her bones and sent her arms lapping up about his hard back, seeking support and something more.

It was as though one of those shocking, tormentingly sweet night visions that sent whispers of pleasure's promise through her young body visited her waking self. Then unexplainably, his face withdrew, bringing her eyes open wide and causing her to jerk away from him, trembling.

Inwardly aghast at her own behavior, at the degrading tangle he made of her feelings and determination, she managed to clamp an iron hand on her waffling will. Her need to escape was unbearable but her pride would not allow her to run from him again. She resumed her seat, feeling his presence focused on her as she took up her book again.

Moments later, when she raised an inquiring look to him, his angular face was set determinedly against her unwitting challenge. So, she no longer ran from him, he mused. His brow furrowed thoughtfully as he strode from the library.

Tauren's eyes closed, and her head dropped to rest on the side wing of the chair. Why did he disrupt her sense and reason so? She fought when she did not want to fight and she surrendered when she did not want to surrender. Her feelings no longer seemed to be her own, nor was she sure she would want to claim them— where he was concerned.

Eighteen

"Lady Tauren." An insistent hand on her shoulder drew her back from the nether reaches of the mind's world. She started in the gloom of the bedhangings, blinking and squinting toward the meager light of a single candle. Murdock stood by her bed and urged her gently, but firmly, to rouse herself.

"He's taken ill. You must come, there's no telling how much time . . ." Her voice was strangely choked and her words strangled to a halt. While Tauren braced herself with her arms in a sitting posture, Murdock hurried to the bench at the end of the bed to fetch her heavy, fur-lined robe. "Come . . . quickly."

The slippers were cold on Tauren's feet as she shoved her arms into the garment Murdock held for her. She wrapped it about her hastily, her muscles rebelling in the cold as she tried to tie the wrap.

"Ill? Revan is taken ill?" Her blue eyes flew wide with alarm, a searing bolt of understanding paralyzing her.

"Nay," Murdock hastened, seeing her panic, "not the lad, the duke. He's taken ill, likely it's his heart. I've

225

sent Calder for the leech. Hurry, milady." The urgency in her voice and the lateness of the hour caused Tauren to hasten her lagging step behind the housekeeper's retreating form.

They trod the hallway and then the gallery in silence, feeling the threatening damp chill of the great house all about them. When they approached the duke's apartments, Tauren paused at the door, uncertain of what the woman intended her to do.

Murdock's eyes searched her face tensely. "He sent me for you. He would . . . see you." The woman led the way through the sitting room-study and into the sleeping chamber where the duke was propped in the middle of a massive, ornately carved bed. Candles had been lit nearby and a roaring fire dispelled the chill of the room. The duke himself, in shirt and nightcap, almost disappeared into the bedclothes. His ashen cheeks were sunken, and tired lines ringed his closed eyes and slack mouth.

"Your Grace, she is here . . . the Lady Tauren." The answer was so low and muffled that Tauren could not make it out. The age-worn eyes opened slowly, and his lips moved, causing Murdock to motion Tauren closer, into the firelight.

"Your Grace," Tauren stood near the bed a moment as his nut-brown eyes took in her rumpled hair and hastily donned robe. He turned his head to view her tousled tresses and lifted one thin hand to touch them gingerly.

"So like . . . your mother," he murmured only loud enough for her ears and then closed his eyes again.

"Seat yourself, Lady Tauren," Murdock implored. "It is his wish that you sit with him awhile. I'll go rouse the marquess."

As the dark hours stole away toward dawn, Tauren kept her strange vigil at the bedside of the uncle she resented. The grievances she bore against him pressed down upon her, and in those quiet morning hours she learned the meaning of her father's teachings about forgiveness . . . seventy times seven. She wrestled with her feelings and could not deny him his request for her presence.

When the leech arrived, she sought refuge on the window seat some distance from the bed. A shuffle of feet and muffled voices soon burst upon the room, and the door was flung open to admit the officious Baron of Greers, the Bishop of Wellston, and two other men. As she watched their official and proprietary manner, dread sent icy fingers up her spine and her mouth went dry.

"He is resting quietly, gentlemen." Murdock met them before they reached the duke's beside. "My lord, gentlemen, perhaps you could wait in the outer chamber until he awakens."

Quick to seize the advantage, Lord Chester turned to his companions. "Yes, gentlemen, by all means, do go out and have some refreshment after your arduous ride. I shall sit with His Grace and will summon you if he wakens."

Murdock enforced his veiled command and herded them out with her arms spread wide. Lord Chester took the chair Tauren had recently vacated at the bedside. He looked pleased with himself and a bit hungry, like the overeager vulture that his sharp features called to mind.

Tauren watched him undetected, her instinctive

dislike of the man breaking out anew at the assuming way he had barged into her uncle's sickroom and begun ordering others about. How did he know? Why was he here?

The baron's ungraceful jerk when his eyes drifted in her direction pleased her no small amount.

"Lady Tauren!" He bounded on stalky legs over to her place on the window seat and bowed effusively, seizing her reluctant hand. "I did not see you here. Deepest sympathies, my sweet girl." The gray, watery eyes lingered on her unbound hair long enough to make her feel his oppressive longing.

"Your sympathies are extended prematurely, my lord Baron. My uncle is very much alive and may yet recover to outlive us all."

"Nay, I only meant that the pain and sudden onset of this illness . . . it is a hard thing to bear." His staring was blatant, and he made no effort to hide what he was feeling.

"My dear," he squeezed down beside her on the seat and leaned his bulk upon her. "There are realities to be faced. If the duke dies, you must think of your own future. I have never believed the putrid falsehoods of that rogue, Reston. I would be most pleased to make a place for you in my own household." His eyes rested suggestively on the open neck of her robe and she shivered.

"This is my home, my lord. I shall live here."

"Even when your brother is gone?" His arm went about her small waist in a flash, heedless of her attempts to remove it, and his other hand sank into her hair as he tried to turn her face toward his. "My wife is not a well woman . . . she could use some companion-

ship." His gaze smothered her as his lips soon would.
"And so could I—"

Shoving hard against his foppish chest, she barely
escaped his mouth and bounded up, out of reach. She
smiled graciously at the leech and turned a cold glare
and whisper upon the lord.

"I am affronted by your suggestion, my lord. I have
an honorable place here."

"For how long after the duke is gone?" he whispered
loudly. "In my house you will find a generous lord and
a most willing protector. When Reston takes the shire,
you will be in the way."

His fevered words went through her in a blinding
flash of truth. She wheeled and left the room, hearing
them repeated over and over in her mind. "When
Reston takes the shire . . ." What would happen to
Revan . . . to her . . . when the duke no longer protected them from Reston's greed and lust? He had
already claimed the shire for himself in front of her!
What more proof did she need? Revan would be sent
away to Strafford, the calmer portion of her mind
wrestled for control; he would be safe enough and
would have a strong alliance later to help him reenter
the shire and assume control, thank heaven the duke
had seen to that. And what would happen to her?

Tauren was summoned to the duke's bedside that
night and found a motley assemblage in the chamber,
surrounding the great bed where the duke was propped
upright. She avoided Lord Chester's smug look and the
speculative stares of the bishop and the other gentlemen, whom she had learned were lawyers who served

229

the duke. She found Revan and grasped his hand, drawing him along with her toward the old man's side.

Her relief at seeing the duke awake and sitting up was dealt a critical blow as she approached and saw how his pasty flesh sagged upon his bones and his face was sunken, hollow. His eyes burned brightly, with fever or emotion, and his thin hand beckoned them closer until they stood by the great bed. A large, dark shadow stepped from behind the brocade hangings on the other side of the bed. Holt's unusual eyes seemed to glow as he gazed steadily at the pair across from him.

"What is *he* doing here?" Tauren demanded, her face flushing hotly.

"You do not learn quickly, girl," the duke's voice rasped alarmingly. "He is here by my wish and you will keep silence and listen." The old man swallowed with difficulty, revealing the effort the speech cost him.

Tauren knew now, the old man was dying. She clamped her mouth shut and felt her heart hammering uncontrollably in her chest.

"It is meet you hear this, both of you"—the old man addressed Tauren and Revan—"for your futures are decided here. My solicitors, Chester, and the bishop will bear witness to the documents I sign and to the world in the days to come." He paused and breathed hard, one hand going to the rumpled linen of his nightshirt above his chest. The leech brought him a sip of herbed wine but he waved it away.

"With my death, guardianship of Somerset and Lindengreen will pass to Holt Reston. He is now overlord and is named guardian of the Marquess of Wells, my heir, and of my niece. He will act with full authority on their behalf until the day Revan Wincanton comes of age to assume his place. He will carry out my wishes for the boy's future without fail, as stated in these assigns." He gestured to the parchment littering the bed about him. If he said more just then, Tauren would never know; her disbelief deafened her to all but her own voice.

"No!" she wailed. "Don't you see that's what he wants! How long will Revan survive in his charge! You cannot—"

"Silence!" the old man commanded, taxing his already strained body to the limits. "It is my decision! It is done."

"But Your Grace," Lord Chester stepped hastily forward and around the end of the bed, glancing meaningfully at Tauren. "Surely there are more suitable arrangements. I offer my house—"

"Chester, I have suffered fools, but never gladly. My will prevails in this, and if not my wishes, then Reston's strength. Do me the mercy of shutting your mouth in my dying hours," the duke blazed at the imperious lord and the baron stiffened in outrage.

Stepping back, he sought support visually from the bishop and Calder and the lawyers. Finding none, he spun on his heels and quit the room in high dudgeon.

"My lord Bishop,"—Tauren appealed first to the churchman and then to the soldier beside him— "Calder . . . you must speak to him. You cannot let this—" But neither responded to her plea, and with tears welling in her eyes, she lifted her heavy skirts and fled.

Revan cast uncertain looks at the duke and at Holt. He knew both men well enough; there was more here than was yet explained. It seemed final enough—at least none here would dispute it.

"I'll see to my sister, sir, Your Grace." He nodded his deference to both men and withdrew in most adult fashion.

The duke's tired eyes turned on Holt, and he motioned the overlord closer.

"I have not petitioned the king on this matter of the guardianship. My lawyers have drawn the documents; it is signed and sealed and legal enough to infuriate the king. Were it brought before him now, he would retain guardianship himself to have access to Somerset's coffers. I have doubly offended him; first in the choice of an untitled freeman as guardian, and second in not seeking his approval. He may choose to overrule me, but not without recourse to the courts and a lengthy battle. A dead man has lost nothing in being out of favor with his king."

The duke's breath came harder, and his eyes closed briefly to mask the pain that squeezed through his chest and shot down his arms.

"You will know soon enough. I give you your mother's dowry, thirty thousand, sterling." He stared at Holt as if seeing through time and the corporeal world to something, someone beyond. "How much you look like her. It is a knife in my gut even now. If only you had been my bastard instead of . . ." The crusty old aristocrat's eyes grew watery and his head dropped back.

Calder and the bishop advanced upon the bed quickly, then stepped back a pace when the old man's eyes opened again. One thin, veined hand came up to search for Holt's and, finding it, clasped it tightly.

Holt's voice was thick and quiet. "Yea, if only I had been *your* bastard . . . and you my father. . . ."

"I have angered Parliament and now the king," the duke continued in a constricted voice. "I leave Somerset to you after all, but not without perils attached. Now you need defend that which was denied you and given to another. And I give you Tauren Wincanton to do with as you will. I know what lengths you have spent to gain her and it is fitting. You are evenly matched."

His face flushing suddenly, the duke grasped for Holt with his other hand and was comforted by the firm warmth of the overlord's masterful grip.

"Promise me you will carry my wishes out, defend it . . . promise me. . . ."

"I pledge it, before God and this company. Your overlord will defend your heir and guard your holdings . . . all of them." Holt's voice was thickened but audible to all in the hushed room.

"It is good then; all will be well." The desperate edge left the duke's voice, and he sank back limply to the bolsters and closed his eyes. The bishop and the leech rushed to his side as Holt withdrew, and they held a silvered glass to the old man's nose.

"He is gone," the bishop announced in solemn tones.

Holt made his way from the chamber, seeing little until he was atop Atlas and riding hard, shaking the heavy pall of death from his broad shoulders.

Tauren pushed herself up from beside the black-draped bier and stood quickly, trying to sort her tumbling thoughts. The duke had died two nights before and the Bishop of Wellston had led the funeral mass the next day. Lord Chester, under Holt Reston's hostile stare, had departed for Enderfield minutes after the final benediction, and the lawyers were cloistered in the main salon with the new guardian of Somerset for the rest of the day and evening. Now, on the second morning after the duke's death, Tauren and Revan had come to the family mausoleum to pay their respects privately.

Revan touched her arm gently. "Let's go, Taurie. I don't like it here."

Beside her in the crisp air, Revan breathed deeply and scanned the broken sky above them. "The sun will likely come out. Spring is finally coming." Something in his tone drew Tauren's eyes up sharply to his face. He was smiling!

"It'll be all right, Taurie."

"It will never be all right again," she declared tightly, "not as long as we're in *his* power."

"Holt?" Revan seemed surprised. "We could have done worse. He's a fair man and—"

"Fair!" Tauren stopped to face him. What had happened to him under her very nose? Small remembrances flashed before her—long dinners where Revan had talked, listened to, and yes, laughed with Holt Reston.

"You like him!" she charged.

"Well, yes."

"Why?" It was more an expression of horror than a question.

"For the same reasons you do. He's a real man . . . big and powerful and—"

234

"I do?" she squeaked. "I loathe him! He's crude, arrogant . . . licentious, power-mad—"

"You do like him!" Revan stuck his reddening face into hers. "I've seen the way you watch him—and he watches you back!"

"I do not!" she screeched, losing all control.

"You do too! I say you do! I'm the duke now and I say you do!" he stomped.

Horrified by his words and by his sudden acquisition of arrogant lordly prerogative, she glared at him furiously. "You cheeky little brat," she spat. "Go ahead, run after him; lick his manly boots. You'll understand when he does you out of Lindengreen and Somerset and sets himself up as duke!"

When the red haze faded from her eyes she was stamping angrily up the grand staircase of the great hall, head down and muttering. She ran headlong into a housemaid, knocking the little woman down on her seat and sending the garments she was carrying all about them on the stairs.

"Oh, Annie," she sighed, extending her hand to help the woman up.

"Sorry, milady, I tho't ye'd look up in time."

"Let me help you pick them—" Tauren held a rich, brocaded waistcoat in her hand and turned a heavy, questioning look on the uncertain Annie, who retrieved the other garments quickly.

"What's this?" Tauren demanded, holding out the garment and taking in the other clothing the woman bore with a lowering glare.

"We're just . . . cleaning, milady. Master Holt—"

"Reston?" Tauren snapped, and she grasped her skirts and flew up the remaining steps and about the

235

gallery to the duke's apartments.

There were piles of once-crimson, dusty brocades in the study, and in the huge sleeping chamber she found the great bed and windows stripped of their hangings, and house servants busily emptying the wardrobes and chests of the duke's personal clothing and effects.

"What are you doing?" she demanded angrily.

All stopped their work to look at her uncomfortably, shifting their feet or putting down the garments or books they held.

"We was ordered," Ransom spoke up, "to ready the duke's chambers for the new master."

Some of the ire in Tauren's eyes cooled. "The new duke will remain in his own quarters for the present, he has no need of these. The old duke lies barely cold in his grave; this is most unseemly."

"I have need of them." Holt's deep voice rumbled through her. She whirled and there he stood, arms clasped casually across his chest, in bare shirt and breeches. "I would be near my charges." His eyes flickered possessively over her plain black woolen gown, as he recalled the first time he had seen her in it.

"Near your—" She breathed in sharply. "*You*? You intend to occupy the duke's quarters?"

"I am master here. It is best that all understand it from the start. So I shall occupy the master's chambers. They follow my orders that the rooms be freshened and refurbished . . . for me."

"How dare you?" she raged, slamming the heel of her palm into his rock-hard jaw, jarring them both with the impact.

Instantly his fist was back, poised, and in mute horror she recalled his threat to deal with her in like manner. But some unseen force held his brawny fist in place as her face blanched of color and her palm came up to shield her gaping mouth.

What had she done?

She whirled and ran from the room as if the very hounds of hell beset her. All down the gallery and hallway to her rooms, she expected the heavy fall of his boots behind her and felt her heart in her throat.

In her chambers she slammed the doors and locked each in turn, barricading herself against his retribution. "He'll have naught to stop him now." She shuddered. He could beat or deprive—even rape—her with none to stop him. Even her brother was caught in his powerful spell, mesmerized by his presence and power.

But, the uninterrupted silence mocked her and sleep deserted her as the night came and went.

Nineteen

The summons was forthright and to the point.

"Yer presence is commanded in the main salon . . . by the master." Roxie delivered it with an irritating air of triumph. "I'll jus' tidy up yer hair, milady, and add a bit of rice powder, maybe pinch yer cheeks."

"Don't be absurd," Tauren waved the little maid away, summoning every shred of courage she possessed to tread the gallery and staircase toward her fate.

Holt Reston stood, garbed in his regal black, hands clasped behind his back and looking dangerously in control. His raven hair shone with attention and his chin was freshly shaven.

"Go out, Roxie, and close the doors." Roxie bobbed and obeyed, casting a knowing glance at her mistress. Holt approached Tauren slowly and to her dismay, she found herself shrinking backward. He stopped and casually waved her to a chair.

"Be seated," he said coolly. "It is time to discuss your place in this house." He paused and let his eyes tally her assets openly.

Her urge to object was strong, but too well she recalled the murderous look in his eyes only yesterday morning. She seated herself and clasped her hands tightly in her lap, her back poker-straight.

"Every part of the shire must be made to bear a profit in some way, the folk as well. What is your worth, Tauren Wincanton?

"Though sister to a duke, a noblewoman, you are virtually unmarriageable, thus useless for the establishment of alliances. Murdock runs the house and I see to the estates. That leaves only the grand duties of the lady, idleness and entertaining."

Tauren's mouth dropped open unceremoniously at this crass summation of her worth.

"To entertain properly is an expensive proposition"—he cocked his head to one side—"what with clothing, gifts, coaches, wines, and elegant foods and musicians. You could easily become a burden to Lindengreen."

She had to stifle an insanely hysterical desire to laugh. She had worried that he would storm her door to rape her, and here he coldly tallied her up like some bushel of wheat on a clerk's ledger sheet.

The strange look on her face arrested him for a moment, but he dismissed it and resumed his conjectures, pacing now with a touch of a swagger.

"There is more. I have decided to marry and establish a nursery of my own. I have position and wealth enough now. It would prove awkward to bring my new bride here with you about—especially after the boy is gone. You can see that."

"Of course," she choked. "How would it look for you to house your wife and your whore under the same

239

roof?" She swallowed hard as great liquid prisms filled her eyes. "So, you'll separate me from my brother and send me packing, will you? I should expect as much from you!" She rose and was halfway to the door before his hard voice boomed out.

"You have not been dismissed!"

She whirled in disbelief. "I have heard more than enough."

Before she reached the door an iron grip dragged her back to the chair over her outraged protests. He shoved her down onto the seat and trapped her there by standing over her, his face impassive.

"There is another solution."

"You need say no more. Just do what you will and be done with it," she declared mutinously.

"I could marry *you*." He paused, leaning back on one tapering leg to let the impact of his words be felt. "That would insure a place for you and a productive role"—he laughed shortly at his own crude joke—"bearing my children."

He watched her with an intensity that belied the casual way the words tumbled from his lips. "It makes little difference to me where you would go, but go you must if you do not marry me." He saw her struggle to bring forth a hot reply and warned, "I know you think this match absurd and are sorely tempted to refuse and toss it into my face. But think well on it and do not be so rash as to throw away every chance of seeing your dear brother again."

She sat, stunned. He would do it. Revan was all she had left in the world and this—brute—would split them asunder to serve his own passions!

"I am not without recourse," she managed, grasping

wildly for some defense. "If you force me to this I will go to the bishop and seek his protection. I cannot be forced to marry my closest cousin!"

"Cousin?" Holt was genuinely surprised. "You are creative with your parry, I'll give you that. What makes you think we share a sire in common somewhere?"

Tauren straightened and smiled tightly, ready to deliver her final thrust. "You are the duke's bastard, which makes you my first cousin, a degree of relation that prohibits marriage."

"The duke's bastard?" His lip curled lazily upward as his stance eased. He grinned down at her with infuriating insouciance. "Wherever did you get such a notion?"

"It is known . . . and discussed. Mrs. Murdock knows." He accepted her revelation far too calmly to suit her.

"She told you I am the old duke's bastard?"

"She was heard to say as much." Tauren did not like the gleam in his eyes.

"Then you half listened to the gossip, my lady, for I am sure Murdock would not lie about my parentage. Even she does not know who my father was. I am not the duke's bastard, but his wife's. My mother carried me by another when she spoke the vows with the old man. It was a marriage arranged to suit the ambitious young duke, but she had taken another to her— presumably for love." His face lost its amusement. "Had I been the old man's bastard, he would have declared me his heir in spite of my birth."

The shock on her face soon turned to disbelief. "That is a convenient story. Why else would the duke have allowed you free rein in his shire?"

"He allowed me nothing. Everything I have I earned and took. If you would have the whole story, talk to Murdock herself. She was maid to my mother and will verify that what I have said is true."

Her gaze dropped to the floor. Fearing to allow her another argument, he pressed on, shoving aside the oppressive memories that washed over him.

"If you accept, there is another thing you must know. I'll have no reluctant virgin in my bed. I'll not rape my lawful wife nightly. If I marry you, you will come to my bed willingly. I prefer to take my pleasures at home and would chafe mightily at having to keep a mistress when I have already paid for the privilege with a comely, young wife. I can speak with authority that your womanly curves will warm a bed well. . . ."

Awash with angry shame, she fled the room, running straight for the front doors. Holt watched her go, feeling an odd tightness in his throat and shrugging his shoulders to nullify the heavy press of his conscience.

"It is for the best," he declared upon the empty air.

Tauren was barely aware of where she rode, but some contrary instinct led her to the very place where she had first met Holt Reston. There was the tumble-down cottage, the budding, silent trees, the great boulders near the melt-swollen stream. She was irritated, but instead of reining off, she dismounted and climbed up on the same boulder as before.

"He planned it so cleverly . . . like a military campaign. He eliminated Roger and ruined my name, knowing when the duke died and he was in control, he could force me to marry him. As Revan's lawful guardian and brother-in-law, none could question his actions. The marriage will support his claims and power. That's what he truly wants." Her cheeks colored hotly as she recognized the source of a peculiar squeezing in her chest. "He doesn't want a wife . . . nor need one."

But if she fled—escaped—he would have Revan to himself, a gullible boy impressed with his looks and arrogant use of power. And where could she go? She swallowed to relieve the choking in her throat. Lord Chester would likely still take her in . . . as his leman. Charlotte? Could she compromise her friend by asking her protection?

If she married the overlord, she might find ways to temper his dealings with Revan's estates, might intercede, or at least forewarn. Her thoughts flipped and flopped as she tried to reason it out. He had served notice that he would be a demanding husband; she shivered and not from the rising breeze. She closed her eyes against the thoughts of his big hands on her sk— *No!* She was vulnerable to his mesmerizing skills in loving. In his bed, night after night, could she remain true to her purpose . . . to her brother's future?

She jumped up and walked about the remnants of the autumn's leaves on the floor of the meadow. As she rode out of the glade she heard the thudding movement of a horse behind her and whipped her head about. Holt Reston's easily recognized black figure drew closer on the huge bay stallion.

She smiled a bitter smile to keep from crying. He took no chances she might reject his generous "offer."

*   *   *

243

Murdock waited in her sitting room when she returned. The little housekeeper's eyes flitted with concern over her wind-ruffled form and she led Tauren into the bedchamber, pointedly closing the door against Roxie's prying ears.

"I was Lady Anne's maid," she began.

"You really don't have to do this," Tauren interrupted her.

Murdock frowned and her face became wistful. "Holt said you wouldn't marry him because you think he's your cousin. But that isn't true. He is not the old duke's bastard. He was Lady Anne's son, by a man she never would name." Seeing Tauren's disbelief, she grabbed her hands and pulled her down upon the padded bench at the foot of the bed. "It's all right, you'll be able to marry him."

Tears long held in check sprang to Tauren's eyes. Murdock thought she wanted to marry Reston; that was why she had come to make this explanation. Murdock put her arms about Tauren and held her comfortingly, offering her own handkerchief.

"I was a young girl, just come to service as lady's maid for the new duchess. She arrived late for the wedding and I saw her only briefly before I had to prepare her for her bedding. When I was dismissed, I had a bad feeling about it. She was distraught and weeping, more than I expected. She told him that night; she carried another man's child."

Murdock's eyes were far away and her words were soft with memory. "The duke had fallen in love with her and made a deal with her father, without her knowledge. He had such plans, built much of this house for her. When he learned, he was murderous with rage and packed her off to the seashore to have the child in secret. He said he'd not claim her bastard as his heir, insisted they have another child . . . his child. I went with her, stayed with her for her time.

"When the baby was born, the duke came and sent it off, up country to live with a squire's family. But the Duchess Anne, she never really recovered from the babe. She died a few weeks later. The duke went wild with grief . . . raving mad. Holed up in his rooms for days at a time, seeing nobody." Murdock shook free of those awesome memories and proceeded.

Into Tauren's waiting gaze, she poured her own love and pain. "Holt was here in the summers, with us. Later he went abroad . . . fought in their wars as a paid soldier. Then, almost five years ago, he came back. He used his sword here too. But the duke deserved the ringing he got."

She patted Tauren's hand and smiled reassuringly. "He's not your cousin, lass. Marry him."

In the great hall, after supper that evening, Holt dismissed Revan to his rooms and confronted her.

"Join me in the salon."

Feeling her heart drumming steadily against the wall of her chest, she nodded, avoiding his gaze, and walked silently into the elegant main salon. The rustle of her silk underskirts was loud in the room and the dull wheeze of the draft on the embers in the hearth kept an expectant tempo.

Holt poured himself a brandy from the decanter on the ornate sideboard, but hesitated and left it to come and stand near her. Her hands fidgeted with the lace at her cuffs and she stared at the ancient portrait above the massive marble mantelpiece.

Holt cleared his throat a bit. "You talked with Murdock?"

"Yes."

He drew a long breath. He had not exactly expected her to be pleased. "Tauren, I would have your answer now."

Something in the way he said her name or in the odd tenor of his voice caused her to look at him. His great, green-brown eyes glowed as they met her own. For a time they searched each other, and she felt as if he examined her every secret thought, every private feeling. The experience sent an all-too-explainable shiver up her spine, but she would not let it best her.

"Yes." She tore herself away from the raw intimacy of his probing eyes and put a safe distance between them, missing his reaction altogether. She paused at the door and looked back at him, so dark and compelling. There was no assumption in his handsome face, no taunt, no leering. His usually hard-set mouth seemed softer. She turned away to seek the peace of her rooms.

Holt stood a moment, watching the sway of her hips as she disappeared, a silly grin of delight spread over his face. He'd forced her to it, but she'd get over that when he showed her the full delights of a marriage bed. He retrieved his brandy and closed his eyes a moment, savoring her as well as the burning amber fluid. Her sky-blue eyes, the creamy skin of her breasts, the pouting curve of her lips—they would be his by week's end. He downed the brandy as if to extinguish the fire in his loins and poured another quickly.

The next morning, Roxie stumbled and banged her way across a trunk, two chairs, and a table that were meant to blockade Tauren's bedchamber door. The racket roused Tauren from the middle of a rumpled bed, and in a flash she was on her feet, clinging to the bedhanging for support.

"It's . . . you," Tauren breathed relief.

"And who else would ye be expectin'?" Roxie looked askance at the ineffectual barricade, drawing her own unerring conclusions. She drew a regal glare for her unuttered barb and set about laying a fire.

"If ye fear for yer safety, of a sudden, perhaps we'd best call Master Holt back from town to stay 'til the weddin'."

"Town?" Tauren stopped with her robe half on. "He's gone to town?"

Roxie sat back on her heels as the wood splinters caught and shrugged. "Mrs. Murdock said so this morn when she told us about the weddin'. Says he'll stay at Keenings till the vows are said proper." Her face was exaggerated innocence.

"How . . . civil of him," Tauren bit out, "to consider my good name, too little and too late."

"I think it's right gentlemanly of him." Roxie lifted her chin resolutely.

"Precisely what he wants you to think, and everyone else on the staff as well." Tauren read in Roxie's stubborn jaw the success of that tactic. "But I don't care if the whole house thinks him a bloody prince!"

"I don't think he much cares what *we* think," Roxie observed tartly. "He'll not be beddin' the lot of us in six day's time."

"Out!" Tauren's face flamed. *"Out!"*

All stood as she entered the chapel of Lindengreen on the arm of her younger brother. Her costly gown of heavy ivory satin lay in a heap on the floor of her bedchamber. At the last moment, after Charlotte Eddys had left, her gaze had fallen on the scandalous French Puritan dress in the wardrobe and she had shed the gold-embroidered gown in a vengeful whimsy.

The shimmering ivory satin of the wide collar threw flattering lights into her long chestnut hair, a tamed fall of fiery softness. The glistening black brocade clung tightly to her small waist and spread with tantalizing meagerness up over her creamy breasts, shielding little from the crowd's lurid curiosity. Every element of the gown was Puritan, and yet none of it was.

Holt's expression was dark as he scrutinized her gown, his eyes resting hotly on her liberally exposed skin. He took her from Revan's arm and wrapped her slender hand in his large warm one. Despite her resolve, she trembled.

The uncanny match of their garments and the near physical perfection of the pair caused a murmur through the crowd. The overlord had found his true match, it would later be said.

The vows were short and most solemn. A heavy golden ring set with rubies was slipped on her finger and in a breath she was turned to face Holt. He seized her shoulders tightly but then kissed her on the forehead before claiming her trembling lips gently.

A shout went up from the back of the chapel where Calder's cavaliers were crowded in a sea of scarlet, and Tauren found herself swept away and into Charlotte Eddy's crushing hug, then kissed lustily by Lord Cedric and Calder and bussed excitedly by Revan before being returned to Holt. Her new master swept her up and cradled her against his chest, striding through the noisy press of the crowd of servants and tenants toward the main hall and the waiting feasts.

The afternoon wore on, the food seemingly endless and the toasts growing noisy and more ribald. The great hall was filled with makeshift planking tables that continued into the dining hall itself. Soldiers, tenants, and servants alike reveled in this privileged glimpse of noble life, being guests at their lord's wedding feast. The noise grew to drown out the reedy music of the lute and pipes, and occasionally good humor soured under the wine's influence and an argument or fight broke out. Calder's lieutenants quickly restored order in every case and the festivities went on.

Charlotte posted herself beside Tauren at the long table in the dining hall that had been reserved for the bridal party and patted the bride's hand reassuringly. "Have some more wine, dear"—Charlotte poured from the silver carafe at her fingertips—"you look as if you've just been pinched."

Tauren turned a surprised look to her friend and found an understanding glint in the older woman's eyes. "Oh, Charlotte," she whispered, the chaos of her inner state distilled in the tightly uttered words.

A sympathetic, then mischievous grin played at Charlotte's mouth. "After all, this is only the wedding feast; the real fun starts tonight." She giggled wickedly, drawing Holt's attention to them, and he pulled Tauren's nearest hand through his arm, bringing her snugly against him.

Tauren managed a sickly smile at the gesture and felt his ribs vibrate against her as he laughed.

"Come, Tauren, don't be such a prude," Charlotte chided. "He'll be here any moment now."

"We could bolt the door," Tauren muttered grimly, her mouth drawn into a thin line, as she plopped onto the bench at the foot of the great ducal bed.

Charlotte sighed her exasperation and, pouring a goblet of rich amber wine from the tray Roxie had brought, shoved it toward her. "I can understand nerves, dear . . . a little crying, a little maidenly reluctance, but it's bound to happen to a girl sooner or later—and better sooner with Holt Reston to manage it. You'll get little sympathy from me on that account. Half the maids of Somerset, and as many dames, would gladly scratch your pretty blue eyes out to have your place in that bed tonight." Her lively eyes narrowed with determination. "Drink it," she ordered, tilting the cup with one finger toward Tauren's lips and applying pressure to see it downed.

"Help me get her out of this gown and brush out her hair," Charlotte ordered Roxie, who sprang to life from her seat on the bed with annoying enthusiasm. They peeled the shocking, black brocade from her stiff limbs, and Roxie carried it reverently to the tall, ornate wardrobe.

"And build up the fire as you warm the bed," Charlotte ordered. "It wouldn't do for her to have chills in her marriage bed." She fingered the heavy gold bed drapes appreciatively and ran a hand up the sleek, polished bedpost. She gawked about the great bed-chamber unabashedly. "Ye gods! This place is as big as a banquet hall!"

"With me the main course," Tauren responded tartly.

"Well, well . . . there is a spark of life in there yet!" Charlotte poked her good-naturedly with one finger. "Now, off with this." She reached for the bottom of Tauren's only remaining garment, her chemise.

"No! I'll . . . leave it on," Tauren declared adamantly.

Charlotte hissed her disgust and seized a brush for the bride's hair.

Just then Holt burst through the door and slammed it shut on the few tipsy comrades who still had legs enough to escort him to his marriage bed. They banged ineffectually on the door, calling the advice of drunken sages and fading away quickly when no response was raised.

Tauren stood near the fire in her thin chemise, flame-burnished hair unbound and flowing all about her and eyes wide like purloined pools of summer sky. Holt stood, looking at her, drinking in every detail of her ripe form silhouetted alluringly against her loose garment by the firelight from behind.

Charlotte smiled contentedly as she followed his eyes to the enchanting effect of Tauren's position before the

251

hearth. "They won't be needing you, Roxie girl." She marshaled the little maid from the room brusquely and turned to Holt's wine-warmed grin.

"I hope you haven't left Cedric drunk under a table somewhere. I've better use for him this night." With a spirited laugh and a coy wink at Holt she waltzed out.

Twenty

Tauren watched her husband bolt the chamber door and walk purposefully toward the hearth . . . and her. She bit her lower lip from within to quell her fright and breathed again only as he extended his hands to the warmth of the fire.

"You've a head start on me, wife." He nodded to her scant dress and Tauren's cheeks flamed. He set about unbuttoning and removing his sleek velvet doublet and his elegantly embroidered shirt to expose an awesome chest and shoulders to Tauren's shamed curiosity. She watched as he poured water into the basin and began to wash but the heat that crept into her face was too humiliating. She must not let him see her blush, nor cringe from him.

But as his great boots hit the floor one by one, she felt her heart thudding anxiously and her mouth became dry as thistledown. He approached and she turned quickly to the fire, making a show of warming her bare feet and calves.

"There were few noble guests at your wedding," Holt

remarked, testing these new waters of his marriage. "On such short notice—"

"A week is not much time. Those who mattered were here."

Holt braced himself to try again. She'd declared her resistance to the marriage in the choice of her wedding gown. But he would see she proved reasonable in this marriage business, remember his conditions and honor them.

"You are a beautiful woman, Tauren. You made a fetching bride. It pleased me that you chose your wedding clothes with me so clearly in mind."

Her little gasp and flashing eyes produced a deep rumble of laughter in him. She jerked her head about. Any normal, upstanding man would have been mortified by her behavior. But then, her deeper recesses taunted, Holt Reston was no ordinary man.

Holt plopped down on the heavily carved chaise, swinging one leg casually over the end and leaning back on one elbow to study her. His eye wandered up her trim and shapely calves and, with their aid, remembered the richly rounded taper of her thighs and hips. He felt a stirring within him and stood abruptly, noting with some satisfaction that her eyes sometimes lighted shyly on his half-bare, stocking-clad body.

He approached her slowly and sat down in the chair beside her, within arm's reach. He tilted back his head, his index finger tracing the bold curve of his lower lip and drawing her eyes to that subtle invitation.

"I have been of the opinion that noblewomen are a spoiled and lazy lot—of little practical worth, even for pleasure. They make demands constantly, both of goods and attention." Seeing the firming of her jaw, he continued, "But I have not yet decided about you. I have selected a wedding gift for you, one that you alone might enjoy."

She frowned her mistrust, forcing herself to stay in place and yet bracing for what must be his physical assault. She knew where he was leading; she was not the naïve little virgin he had once dazzled and despoiled.

He smiled lazily, showing in one cheek that dimpled slash that had proved her undoing before and revealing white, even teeth behind his full lips.

"Your brother, Revan . . ."

She startled, suddenly all enormous blue eyes and proud, pouting lips as she turned to him.

". . . he will not go to foster. He will stay here at Lindengreen with us." Any guilt he felt at putting it to her thus was soon bludgeoned and bowed beneath his pleasure at the hope that filled her face . . . and the anticipation of knowing her delights fully at last.

"How? Why? The duke was so determined. Are you sure?" A cloud of painful doubt drew her lovely features into a wistful frown he longed to kiss away.

"I have decided. He will stay." Holt rose and stepped near, towering over her, his eyes drawn to the sweet curve of her cheek and the ripe roundness of her partly revealed breast. "There is much for him to learn here and there is too much unrest in London to risk him in observance of a rite of noble antiquity. Does it please you, this gift of mine?"

Her eyes came up to his, filled with liquid that hung precariously in them, and they stabbed him sharply, unexpectedly. Her next words made a sweet carving of his carnal scheming.

"Nothing could please me more." She responded with total honesty and in that vulnerable moment she threw down every gate and door that guarded her tenderest feelings.

Staggering slightly with the heady victory of his game, Holt put one hand out to touch her face, tracing her lips and chin, letting it fall upon the silken skin of her chest. She stood perfectly still before him, barely breathing.

With his other hand he traced her shoulder and arm to capture her slender hand and press it gently to his bare chest.

"My wife," he murmured softly, not realizing that he had spoken his thoughts aloud, "I would make this perfect for you."

Her eyes flitted wonderingly over his muscular, bronzed shoulders as her hand, held against his chest, longed to. She pulled his hand on the back of hers to her lips and touched it. All other thought vanished as he put his arms about her gently and drew her to him, holding her in the comforting hard strength of his big body.

He carried her to the great bed and set her down beside it, slipping the thin straps of her French chemise down over her shoulders and watching with fascination as the fabric slipped past her taut, darkened nipples and fell, unhindered, to the floor. Instinctively, her arms came up across her full, satiny breasts but he caught her hand and raised it to his lips. His face was darker now, his eyes glowing hungrily in a way that both frightened and excited her.

Feeling her shyness, he stayed the urge to feast with his eyes and sent his hands instead to savor her bounty, slowly tracing the blades of her shoulders, her spine and the erotic roundness of her buttocks.

He watched the nuances of her kaleidoscoping feelings in her eyes, and in the parting of her lips, in the tilting of her head. Then he lowered her to the soft cradle of the waiting bed and sank into the down beside her, feeling the coolness of her soft skin all along his lean heat.

Before he drew the cover up he swept her entire length with one hot, sensuous look, stopping her breath with the raw desire in his face. His hand found hers and placed it upon his chest, near his shoulder, guiding her toward her own exploration.

"You are more beautiful than I dreamed, my wife." He kissed her shoulder then her lips lightly.

His hand stroked the elegant curve of her waist and came up to cup one rose-peaked breast. He felt her draw breath sharply, but her hand on his chest began to move shyly and he wondered at his own restraint—and the sweet pain its exercise with her gave him.

Her slender arms came up to cradle his head and draw it to her waiting lips. She returned his kiss deeply, running the tip of her tongue experimentally around the corners of his lips and tasting the wine-warmed sweetness of his kiss. Exploring his mouth with hers, she felt that curious, drawing sensation in her loins. His lips pulled away from her, and she made a small noise of distress, such that they returned to reassure her for a lingering moment before proceeding down the slim column of her neck toward the twin prizes that had often deviled his peace at night.

He nuzzled and kissed her breasts, lavishing attentive devotion on each, and she began to move under his masterful touch. Her body seemed on fire, each part crying out for his touch, his exquisite attentions, wanting, needing more. . . .

Strange, she thought hazily, to be so full of pleasure as to feel like bursting and yet be drawn higher, on to fuller, greater feeling—more intense, clearer. He moved his hard, muscular weight above her slowly, parting her thighs with his knees and seeing her eyes fly wide as he spread himself atop her and between them. His hardened staff lay against her, and for a long moment he did not move but stroked her gloriously tangled hair and kissed her face and throat lightly.

His lips found hers and with their lush response he entered her quickly, stopping her sharp moan with his loving kiss and ceasing to move further until he could measure her response. When her eyes opened again, they were misted and for a moment, he stroked her face with his bristling chin to bring her back to him.

In her loins was a deep, warm fullness that invaded her, the rest of her, with its wonder. She ran her hands down the heavy muscles of his back to his firm buttocks and caressed them hesitantly. Taking her lead, he began to move within her slowly, feeling her body accept and welcome him. His fingers stroked her body in luscious lazy circles, making her wriggle as his nails crossed sensitive spots on her sides. Then her legs wound up about him as she reveled fully in this shattering new pleasure.

"Holt," she breathed his name, and it drove him faster until the tightness and the sweetness were all he could bear and he burst inside her with the racking spasms that she seemed to feel even as she witnessed them.

He collapsed atop her, bearing part of his weight to one side, and she looked with awe on the glistening bronzed face of her husband. His heavy black lashes were closed and she reached one finger up to cautiously touch those lips that had given her such pleasure. At her touch his green-brown orbs flickered open, their dusky glow mirroring her own satisfaction with the moment.

After a while he withdrew and pulled her against him, cradling her head on his shoulder and feeling expansive, soaring.

"It was," she murmured sleepily in response to his quizzical gaze, "perfect."

The rumble from deep in his throat let her know he agreed and was pleased. "Then we'll do it again sometime." He grinned lazily from beneath heavy-lidded eyes.

Again, she thought sleepily, satisfaction glowing through her very skin. Other nights like this . . . every night . . . imagine . . . again. Then she was asleep in her husband's embrace.

Again . . . She wandered back through the haze to the present world, her bed . . . her newfound self. Her heavy eyes refused to open, and one by one her other senses clamored for and captured her full attention. The delicious feel of the soft muslin sheets against her startlingly bare flesh, so different from the cling of her heavy nightdress. Her lips felt exceptionally sensitive as her tongue flicked out to moisten them, and at their corners they tasted slightly of salt. A sweet musky odor filled her head—a compelling remnant of the night's heated passion and of the one who had evoked it.

She smiled and shifted slightly, lying curled on her side, afraid of dispelling this new and intensely pleasurable awakening. "Again" . . . She moved her lips silently to repeat its magic . . . there would be "agains." A shifting near her on the bed brought a long, sinewy thigh up along her buttocks and behind her thighs, and a heavy arm dropped across her side.

She jolted rudely awake at the strange heat of Holt's chest and belly pressed against her from behind. He cradled her in his body as if seeking to touch every inch of his skin against hers. But from the slow, even rhythm of his breath against her hair and the steady drumming of the pulse in the arm he'd placed about her, she knew he slept and was grateful for it.

She wanted time to think about what had happened between them and about this marvelous— Marvelous? Her heart leaped, beating faster, as her mind swept coolly backward past the heated events of her bedding to recall the events of the several days before.

In an instant the skin of her whole body colored hotly with the realization of where she was and what had happened to her. She longed to jump away from the dark, possessive form that entrapped her so completely. Laboriously, she inched away from him, peeling her damp, reluctant skin from his by agonizing increments. Slowly she extricated the thick locks of her hip-length hair that had become his casual cushion, and she breathed a silent prayer of gratitude for what she was sure was the heaviness of wine-sleep.

Creeping gingerly to the edge of the bed, she shivered as the damp morning chill penetrated her stiff body. She hurried to a wardrobe and opened it slowly lest a creaking hinge give her away. Her first thought was to cover her nakedness. She hissed with silent ire at the stark blackness that greeted her . . . his clothing.

His garments . . . his house . . . his shire . . . *his* wards . . . and now *his wife!* He marked everything with the seal of his possession, brought all under his hand by the raw and naked exercise of power. And last night, she burned to admit it, she had succumbed to the bold extension of his power into the realm of the flesh itself.

How willingly she had served his pleasure . . . and how strange that now in the coolness of dawn she could remember none of the gratitude, the startling feeling of physical awakening that had pushed her blindly into his waiting embrace. But now she was truly herself, married or not; and she would fulfill her vow to see to Revan's welfare.

She pulled on a heavy, beaver-lined robe from her closet and walked to the washstand, feeling the stickiness of her spilling onto her thighs and hearing the loud complaints of the muscles of her abdomen and legs. It all served to remind her of his effective use of her body's stubbornly wanton impulses. She seized a soft cloth to scrub her skin relentlessly, squeezing her eyes shut against the memory of his hands caressing the same soft places.

A soft rapping against the door sent her flying to unbolt it before the sound carried to Reston's sleeping ears. Roxie's nose peeked in first; then she waddled in heavily, balancing a large copper kettle of hot water in one hand and a tray of tea and crusty, hot scones in the other. Puzzled by the finger Tauren put to her lips, she gawked past her mistress toward the great bed.

Tauren scowled and took the tray from her. "My clothes," she whispered angrily.

"That will be all, Roxie," the voice boomed from behind Tauren, and the little maid blushed and stared eagerly at the revealed form of her master, propped on one arm in the midst of the rumpled bedclothes. Her speculative gaze returned to Tauren's disheveled hair and gaping robe. She rolled her eyes impudently and, with a flick of her skirts, exited.

Holt stacked the bolsters behind him, leaning back luxuriantly and stretching his full length. The muscles of his arms and chest flexed visibly through his smooth, tight skin. He called her to him as she opened her closet again.

"Come here, wife, I want to touch you and see you in the sunlight."

Her mouth dropped open at his raw command and she turned to him, clutching a petticoat to her bosom.

"Husband, we have guests and the sun is well up. I must dress and see to them."

The finality of her rejection as she returned to her dressing stung him, and knitting his brows, he felt the languorous satisfaction of the night vanish like some sweet mystical vapor. "Come to me." His voice carried steel beneath its huskiness.

She met his hardening gaze with a determination of her own, but she was unwilling to test her rein in so close a quarter. She complied but at a maddeningly slow pace.

He beckoned her to his side. "Closer, wife." His voice had a velvety tone now that Tauren was surprised to recognize. He wanted her again, to lie with her.

Her eyes flitted about, carefully avoiding the great

bronzed body so disturbingly displayed, and she halted at the edge of the bed.

So she avoided looking at his body, would play the reluctant wife now that she knew how the game was fully played. One of his brows flicked up at the recognition. His big hands reached for her as she came within range, and her late resistance was easily overcome as he pulled her effortlessly up and onto his sheet-covered lap.

Quick hands slipped beneath the heavy robe to caress her silky hip and back as he pressed her bared breasts against the lightly furred bronze of his chest.

"*No*!" she pushed ineffectually against him as his mouth came down on hers. This time her resistance survived long enough to forestall her succumbing to his tantalizing ministrations.

In a single, clever maneuver her bottom hit the down mattress beside him and his legs came from beneath to cover hers while his torso pressed her bare breasts down into the tousled bedclothes. His weight atop her drove breath from her momentarily and desperately she breathed him into her with his penetrating kiss.

She jerked her face away and his lips, undaunted, nibbled the fragrant column of her neck as she pressed ineffectually against him from below. She watched his face darken and the light of passion begin to burn in his eyes as they struggled in silence, neither willing to surrender.

She began to wriggle beneath him, rolling to one side, attempting to unbalance him and escape. But he carried too much weight, and he laughed at her method, knowing she did not realize the erotic impact of her wriggling bottom.

"Very nice, wife," he whispered lustily near her ear, giving her to know that he interpreted her movements as enthusiasm. "The duke was wrong . . . you learn quickly."

"You insuf—" But he stopped her words with his mouth and set one large hand at her breast, touching, teasing her dusky nipple. She felt the tingling from her breasts down into her very womanhood. It startled her, stopping her futile wrestling and making her concentrate all her efforts on stillness—and on those incredible caressings that caused her body to sing for him.

"Tauren," he whispered huskily, "let me love you, let me pleasure you and discover the delights of your beautiful body. Let me have you. . . ."

His mouth followed his hand and she felt the gentle tugging and the delicious flicking of her nipple in her loins, making her woman's hollow ache for filling.

With a will beyond any she thought herself capable of, she remained still beneath him. Through her red haze shot streaks of silver as his ripe, hot staff penetrated her moist, eager flesh. She shuddered beneath him, an unuttered sob in her throat.

He murmured her name over and over as he moved inside her. His hoarse whisperings and tender, agonized endearments washed over her like warm, fragrant oil while those powerful thrusting spasms surged deep inside her. His eyes closed and his lean muscles jerked awesomely, as though some part of his life itself was wrenched from him.

Tauren lay beneath her husband, quivering and relieved it was done. It was small consolation that she had managed little outward response for inwardly she had been writhing under his expert touch. She felt him withdraw and squeezed her eyes shut tightly, feeling them burn with gathering tears. *No*, she ordered herself sternly, he must not see how he had shaken her just now!

But Holt Reston lay beside his tantalizing young bride, matching her confusion with his own at what was happening inside him. His body was drained of its charge, its fire, in the explosion of his passion for her. But part of him was left unsatisfied, still hungry, wanting. In the light of the sun his eyes feasted with awe on the sweetly exposed body of his wife. Her full, rose-tipped breasts fascinated him, as did the sinuous curve of her tiny waist and full hip, the taper of her calf to her slender ankle.

She was his by force, her accusation was plain; and he had won. He would have his pleasures however she resisted. The grim set of his jaw muted subtly into resolve. This temper and determination of hers were but extensions of her passionate nature. . . . Yet, after the promising start of last night, she had cooled considerably and his sharp sigh of irritation surprised even him.

It would come in time, her willingness, he vowed sternly. He would see her eager—willing—to share his bed.

Twenty-One

The bride and groom descended the great stairs together, Tauren's hand captive in Holt's. Her dressing had taken far longer than usual, with Holt scrutinizing every part of the process. Her hands trembled uncontrollably under his glowing eyes . . . and Roxie nearly had to be dismissed, she gaped and giggled so. But the results were gratifying; the deep emerald of her velvet gown made her creamy skin seem translucent and gave her luminous eyes an enchanting sea-green cast. Her hair was bound up in heavy braids that were rings of burnished copper at the sides of her head, after the fashion of married noblewomen. Holt's uncon- cealed appreciation perversely both irritated and pleased her, and she found crimson flushing her skin betrayingly.

Holt held her close to him as he greeted his men who lingered at the makeshift tables in the great hall. Something inside his chest swelled as he savored each ordinary little movement of her hand or tilt of her head, and for the hundredth time that morning he felt a rush of heat rampaging through him. He was unable to take his eyes or hands from her and for some reason it didn't bother him. He had never had a woman of his own before . . . only and always his. . . . When he thought of the night ahead he grinned broadly with anticipation.

All evidence of the night's revelry had been swept away from the dining hall by Murdock's efficient minions and the fragrance of warming foods greeted the overlord and his lady as they entered.

"You look terrible!" Holt clapped Calder's back and gleaned a jaundiced look in response. ". . . And you, not much better, young lord."

Revan's mottled face jerked up from its cradle on his arms atop the table, his blearing eyes bearing testimony to his first unabashed indulgence in strong spirit the night before. Some of Calder's men had taken him under their wing to teach him the manly sport of drinking. Now he paid the manly price for his evening of fallow sport.

Tauren smiled tightly, accepting Calder's unsteady bow with a gracious nod, and she shot a spitefully cheery look at her younger brother. Seeing him in such distress was the bright spot in her day thus far, the little sod. He had become annoyingly "noble" and excruciatingly patronizing during his week of dukedom. When informed of her upcoming marriage to their overlord and guardian, he had judiciously pronouced it "an excellent solution to the problem of what to do with you."

Holt seated her first, at his right, and then smiled his annoyingly knowing smile at her. "I'll not ride out today, nor for a while yet. The old law said a man

267

should not work nor war for the entire year after he was married, that he might see his wife well contented."

Irritated by his scriptural jibe, she retorted venomously. "Do not neglect your 'work' on my account, husband. I shall not take offense if you have frequent need to be away."

"Ah," Holt stilled her moving hand with his as she reached for her pewter mug of steaming tea. "I do not intend leaving you lonely, wife. I take my husbandly duties seriously, as you will discover." He lowered his voice for her ears alone. "I expect the same from my comely, young wife. Such were my conditions."

They stared at one another, each assessing the determination in the other's face. When he released her hand, she reached for a warm oat cake and spread jam on it, trembling visibly. His eyes were full upon her, and she tried to appear unconcerned, knowing that her rich emerald velvet and their audience offered paltry protection against his searching, caressing gaze.

But his quiet reminder gave her cause to think, and she stole a look at him with new eyes. He wanted her and had her, but for some reason it seemed to matter to him that she come willingly to his bed. Her uncooperative manner this morning displeased him, she was sure of it, despite his formidable countenance and impenetrable self-assurance. She straightened in her chair with a greater measure of confidence. She would think on it, this new bit of information.

"One doesn't have to ask how you two fare this morning! Ye gods! It's written all over them," Charlotte crooned annoyingly as she dragged the suffering Cedric into the dining hall and seated herself beside Tauren. Her smug, insinuating little smile

268

grated on Tauren and worse, sent telltale heat into her cheeks. By the time they quit the dining hall not a person present, including the pallorous bishop, had failed to raise her wrath with a remark and scrutiny.

She tried to go about her normal routine, consulting with Murdock on supper and matters of household order, visiting the dairy and weaving room; yet she found herself shadowed incessantly by the familiar dark figure of her husband. He was everywhere; beside, behind, leading or trailing her. His hand was at her waist, his arm steadying her step across a puddle, his heavy boots clearing a path for her through a flock of ducks near the mill.

Let him follow, she fumed silently, let him see how worthless, how unproductive a "lady" can be. But it was with genuine pleasure that she received the smiles and greetings of her people and answered their shyly offered best wishes, for it was evidence of the affection they held for her. At such times, she refused to look at Holt, knowing that he watched her with that possessive pride.

The sun was quite strong in the noon sky when Tauren returned to the house to spend time with their guests. She paused in the side yard to inspect a newly spaded plot of ground between the pavingstones of the court and the wall. Holt was beside her instantly.

"What's this?" He gestured toward the dark, upturned soil.

"I've ordered it tilled for a new planting." She met his gaze and under his strikingly forest-flecked eyes, felt her stomach fall toward her weakening knees. This was the very thing she had so assiduously avoided all morning.

"I've married a goose girl, a dairymaid, a clerk, a weaver, and now . . . a farmer," he quipped. "Which did I have in my bed last night? I would have that wench back."

She sighed sharply, her patience in tatters from the strain of the morning. "'Tis for medicinal herbs and seasonings. I have learned some of the herbalist's art from my Aunt Veldean. I would use it to benefit the people of Lindengreen."

One of his brows shot up as he rocked back on one leg and swept her with an insulting thorough look. "An alchemist as well . . . Wife, I find more to you with each passing moment. Knowing the passion and tenderness you bear for me, should I look to my food and drink with caution in the future?"

"Oh-h-h." She ground her teeth in frustration. "Why don't you leave me alone? Go! Ride out. Go back to spending your days oppressing the people and your nights in dissolution and debauchery. I care not as long as you are away from me!"

"My nights in debauchery?" He snorted a laugh, his eyes twinkling. "Woman, even an overlord is not always fortunate enough to find a good 'debauch' about come nightfall. Why do you think I married you?"

Tauren gasped slightly, her eyes blazing with the true state of her feelings. He was laughing at her!

"You married me to legitimize your hold on my brother and the shire," she lashed out. "I see you for what you are . . . a pretentious, power-hungry rogue, so used to having your own way you cannot abide the thought of anything withheld from you. You married me so that none disputed your power here—and to punish my audacity in rejecting you. And how long will my brother survive under your careful tutelage? How long will it be before he meets with some tragic mishap or contracts some strange, wasting illness?" She was shouting at him and his face sharpened and lost all hint of amusement.

"Had you thought, wife, that it might depend on you? On how faithfully and sweetly you ply the role of the eager, cosseting mate?" A muscle in his firmly clenched jaw jumped, betraying his anger with her. How he wanted to grab her and shake some sense into that maddening little head of hers!

Tauren looked as though she had been doused with a pail of icy water but he pressed on rashly. "Who knows but that I might content myself with being simply the power behind the title . . . if I found other compensation."

Each word drilled its way into her inner being. She realized now that her deepest fear was that she would be right in her suspicions. And he had confirmed it with his biting sarcasm, his iracund arrogance.

The shock on her face stopped him and he scowled fiercely, in deepening anger toward himself as much as toward her. He had just given her the very reasoning and evidence that could be wielded effectively against him when he sought her willingness in their marriage bed.

She whirled, and her angry gait became a full run as she fled his growing rage and sought refuge in the great house. He watched her go, skirts billowing to reveal her trim ankles, and her hips swaying. His inflated temper was effectively punctured by a sharp pang of wanting. He stood with feet solidly planted and hands on hips, his body as adamant as his thoughts, and together they combined in overpowering force against her. She'd fight him, there was no preventing it now. But if there was anything his warring days had taught him, it was that every opponent has a weakness—and he knew exactly where to find hers . . . both of them.

Night came all too quickly and Tauren's dread grew as they and their guests quit the dining hall to take their ease in the salon. Calder had joined them, no longer walking as if his head might roll from his shoulders. When Charlotte picked up a cittern and began to strum the strings and sing, Calder surprised them all by joining her and Lord Cedric in a lusty ballad.

The contrast between the singers was overwhelming but their voices blended miraculously and drew a smile of delight from the bride of yesterday. Holt watched her as they began a second song, and he noted that her blue eyes took on a sparkle and her chin lowered. His breath caught at the sight of her womanly softening, and he glanced enviously at the trio on which her delighted eyes lingered. He felt a quickening in his loins and relaxed his tensed shoulders and arms, remembering that she was his now—his to enjoy, to pleasure.

Holt applauded loudly when the ballad ended and was on his feet in one energetic bound, bidding their guests good night and drawing a humiliated Tauren with him out the door and toward the stairs.

"What are you doing?" she demanded, jerking him to a halt along the gallery. "Whatever will they think?"

He waggled his brows wickedly. "They'll think they've attended a wedding yesterday and that the groom is hot to enjoy his new bride's obvious delights."

"You're disgusting," she managed to say sourly.

He pulled her along the hallway toward the ducal apartments. "You didn't find me disgusting last night, nor this morning." He pushed her through the door to the study. "Nor, I'll wager, will you tonight."

He turned from locking the door to see a tight expression about her mouth and a glint in her eye, which disappeared so quickly he wondered if he had imagined it.

"Roxie—" she began, eyeing the lock.

"Won't be needed," he finished for her. Taking her hand, he drew her into the bedchamber where a huge, beaten-copper tub sat before a well-made fire. She looked at him questioningly and he replied, "I thought you might enjoy a soothing bath before . . ."

She stiffened visibly and he laughed.

"I bathe frequently as, I have learned, do you. So I had your maid prepare us one. She's a most willing girl, that little Roxie of yours . . . a most desirable trait in a woman."

Her suspicions must have shown on her face for he chuckled and pushed her toward the tub. "You first, wife." Instantly, his dexterous fingers were at her lacings and she jerked away from him.

"I don't want to bathe just now."

"Good," he leered openly, pulling her to him and nuzzling her neck. "There'll be more time for—"

"I'll bathe," she declared hurriedly and pushed away from his light hold. Her face flamed at his low rumble of amusement. He toyed with her, the masterful bastard . . . flaunted his power over her at every turn, before every eye.

Her garments were laid carefully across a chair and in her batiste shift she stepped into the hot tub and sank slowly into the water. Holt's eyes narrowed as he watched her simple defiance from a chair near the fire.

She scrubbed her skin slowly with the richly scented rose soap and rinsed it thoroughly, delaying her exit from the vessel as long as possible. When at last she rose from the concealing water she knew her error instantly. Her gauze-thin shift clung to her like a second skin, revealing every curve and hollow of her ripe young body more alluringly than nudity itself.

Aghast, she covered her breasts ineffectually with her arms and stepped from the tub. But her linen toweling was not on the chair by her clothing where she had left it. She looked about in confusion, to find the cloth stretched neatly across Holt's knees.

"My towel," she complained, stepping toward him but stopping at the blend of arousal and amusement in his hazel-green eyes. His lips curled upward on one end and he rose.

Pressing her shivering breasts closer against her with her arms, she backed away and stopped when he stopped, maintaining the distance between them.

"A charming display, wife." His eyes mocked her. "You do know how to hold a man's attention." He handed her the linen and watched attentively as she wrapped it about her chilling flesh.

Holt turned and in what seemed seconds divested himself of doublet, boots, breeches, and hose to step into the tub fully bare. Feeling Tauren's surreptitious gaze upon him from where she huddled near the fire to dry, he stretched luxuriantly before sinking into the water. The slight jerk of her head brought a wicked laugh from him.

Through his short bath, Holt's eyes never left her, and when he finished drying, he strode directly to the great bed and sat down. "Come to bed, wife. We can share our warmth here."

She turned her damp back to the fire and faced him. "I must dry my chemise first," she stated flatly.

"Dry? It would not need drying if you had not chosen to bathe with it on," he declared testily.

"Most gentlewomen bathe so," she tilted her chin and eyes away from his disturbing nudity.

His feet hit the floor and she froze, knowing he was about to force his will on her again. She shrank from his hands but they easily grabbed the toweling from her and tossed it aside.

"Gentlewoman or no, you'll bathe and sleep to suit your husband." His big hands locked into the top of her fragile garment and with a sickening rip, tore the front of it from her.

"*No!*" she bolted away as he tossed the ruined piece from his hand and reached for another, catching her by the arm instead. In seconds she was divested of the remaining shreds of the garment and he held her against his lean hardness.

"'The wife hath not power of her own body, but the husband.' Do you not agree St. Paul was a wise man to order it so?"

"St. Paul!" she gasped her disbelief even as she struggled.

"From the good James Authorized Version . . . the writings to the Corinthians . . . You do not know it?" Seeing her speechless with impotent rage, he continued adamantly, "In my bed you will sleep without

275

cumbersome clothing, for you have nothing on your comely frame to give affront to the Lord or your husband. We have both seen you at your barest."

"You viperous heretic!" she shrieked, pounding his chest with constricted movements. "You blasphemous—" But he picked her up with ludicrous ease and deposited her quickly on the great bed with a plop, falling beside her and holding her there with his leg across hers and his hands restraining her flailing arms.

"I hate you!" she shouted. But he stopped the stream of words with his mouth on hers and pressed his hardening manhood against her wriggling hip from the side. Instantly she was still and he murmured into her ear, "'. . . And likewise also the husband hath not power of his own body, but the wife.'"

Her struggles ceased so abruptly that a knowing smile came to his full lips and was soon drowned in the fragrant warmth of her mouth. He stroked and touched and teased her sinuous curves, feeling the tiny quivers of excitement he sent through her in her skin and fluttering pulse. His mouth and hands caressed her body lovingly, devotedly, missing no part of her enchanting womanliness. At last he sought relief within her unresisting warmth, barely feeling the belated press of her arms about him.

His head cleared quickly as he eased his weight from her and displeasure quickly replaced the languorous release he had grasped so fleetingly with her. Her face was turned from him, her hair still bound in its heavy braided coif, and she lay as he had used her, legs parted slightly, limp upon the soft bed linen.

Anger replaced his disappointment in full as he

recognized her game and his bare feet hit the floor hard as he rose to dress.

An hour had passed and the single candle at the bedside was guttering when Holt returned to his rest. Tauren had taken her hair down herself and brushed it carefully before climbing back into the great bed and falling quickly asleep with the down coverlet tucked securely under her chin. As Holt slipped beneath the covers, his searching hand encountered satiny, bare flesh and he smiled wryly. Why did it seem for each step forward he made two back?

The Bishop of Wells and Cedric and Charlotte Eddys departed the following morning, and all were pleasantly surprised by their hostess' sweet humor at their leaving. Tauren personally oversaw the packing of hampers of good wine, tasty cold meats, and sweet pastries to send along with them. Then she kissed Charlotte and hugged Cedric warmly. She accepted the bishop's awkward bow amicably and then joined her husband and brother on the steps of the main entry to see the carriages off. Smiling fondly, she waved enthusiastically, accepting Holt's arm about her waist without demur.

As the coaches quit the gates, she let out a contented-sounding breath and turned on her heel to make her way to the duke's library, leaving Holt and Revan to exchange wary looks.

"Join your tutor for the morning's lessons, Revan,"

277

Holt ordered, then followed his bride inside.

Tauren had selected a large leather and brass-bound book from among the shelves and was seated at the reading table, turning the ornately illuminated pages gently when Holt appeared.

"What are you about, wife?" he demanded, watching the sweet curve of her cheek and the maddening hollow at the base of her throat as her face came up with a cool, little smile.

"I would remedy my ignorance of the scriptures, *husband*." Her emphasis on the last word mirrored his taunting use of her new title and belied the pleasant expression she affected. "I am well educated in many areas and would not bring the harsh judgment you extend to gentlewomen in general upon myself. I wonder, *husband*, how came you to be so learned in them?"

Holt approached her cautiously, unsure of her motives and uneasy with her calm, saccharine manner. "My tutor was enamored of the language of the Authorized Version and instructed me in it tirelessly. He was a learned Catholic monk, defrocked and in name converted."

"Well"—she turned her eyes to the page before her and spoke her taunting approbation casually—"what better source of sound morals and theology than a hypocritical, defrocked papist."

She heard the pounding, hollow ring of his jackboots on the polished marble floor as he strode out. The bow of her lips curved upward.

Twenty-Two

After supper, that same evening, Holt surprised Tauren by requiring Revan to read for them in the salon. The young duke was vexed at having to provide the evening's entertainment and halted and stumbled in his reading, hoping that his inadequate performance would bring swift dismissal. But the reverse proved true, and Holt kicked back his chair to prop his spurless boot up on a low table nearby, settling in for a stay.

Revan regarded his move sourly and read only a few more lines before slamming the book of history shut and rising.

"Why did you stop?" Holt demanded calmly, tilting his head slightly to view the lad.

"I'm tired of it . . . it bores me," Revan informed him with an affected sniff.

"I found the subject worthwhile, but the presentation lacking. I think you need more practice—read on." Holt's voice was calm but carried a clear command.

"Then read for yourself." Revan thrust the book

toward Holt and seeing the overlord made no move to accept it, tossed it casually onto the small table by Holt's feet, starting for the door, chin in air.

Tauren watched, fascinated, gazing from her brother to his guardian. This was something new, this test of wills, and for the life of her she could not say whom she wished to see win.

"Your Grace!" Holt bellowed, setting the window-panes arattle and bringing a startled Revan about in his tracks. Holt lowered his feet slowly, deliberately, and leaned forward in his seat as if coiling for action. "You have not been given leave. You are required to read further until your tongue no longer stumbles doltishly over the passage."

"*Required* to read?" Revan echoed, assuming that lordly air so recently copied from the imperious Baron of Greers. "I do not wish to continue. I shall not. I am the duke."

Holt rose slowly, appraising the novice nobleman narrowly from beneath a lowered brow. His voice dropped an octave, laying open its raw rasping core.

"It is time, my vain young lord that you were tutored in the first lesson which every true nobleman must master—the substance of power. Only when your power is established and recognized will your wishes matter in the least."

Committed on his hasty course, Revan's eyes hinted at his uncertainty as they met Holt's hard unflinching, stare briefly.

"You daren't hurt me, sir . . . I have my men. . . ."

Holt smiled coldly. "*Your* men? Who hired Calder and hand-picked his cavaliers, Duke? Under whose command have they ridden against outlaw bands, sharing hard ground for bed in cold and damp and tossing strong ale and willing wenches in good times? What obedience do they owe you, Duke? What loyalty have you earned?"

Revan's face was candescent in the hot silence as he sought reply. "What can you do to me if I refuse?" He found his last leg of defense rang hollow even in his own ears.

Holt's muscles had slowly tensed and he seemed in his heavy black garments to grow subtly before Revan's eyes, looming large and powerful. His eyes glowed like molten copper, such that Tauren's breath stopped in her throat. The tension crackled on the air of the room as the overlord smiled with cold determination.

Some almost imperceptible shift of body signaled the lad's surrender, and Holt commanded with less virulence in his voice, "Read now, and show your best endeavor."

Holt returned to his seat with deliberateness and again propped his feet upon the table. Revan paused, not wanting to surrender so completely. Holt watched his defiant slowness but said nothing and eventually Revan picked up the book and glanced at Tauren's pale face before turning to his place and reading again of Alexander the Great.

When the flawless performance was ended and he closed the book, he looked at Holt, who nodded approval, before he again placed it on the table.

"Think, young lord, on what I have said this night and take note of what I did. Here lies true power, the might to win by force, without the necessity to use it. Alexander, of whom you just read, took whole cities without a drop of blood shed or a weapon raised. You may go to your rooms now, Revan, for we ride out early tomorrow."

Relief at this calm dismissal blatant in his face, Revan took his sister's hand with as much dignity as he could muster and then to Tauren's complete surprise, he nodded gravely toward Holt before departing.

Holt sat for a while studying the floor before him over his templed fingers. Tauren glanced at him covertly while she continued her stitching. Something in his pensive mood tugged oddly at her stomach, and she mused on the overlord's way of dealing with the naïvete and insolence of a youth thrust into a privileged role in so green a year.

"Let's to bed, wife." He rose at long last and cocked one brow inquisitively as she put down her needlework immediately and made her way to their shared apartments. He shrugged and, after dousing the candles with wetted fingers, followed her, a satisfied grin stealing over his roguish face.

In their bed, Tauren fought valiantly to contain her rebellious desire for him, but as his expert kisses drifted lower on the cool satin of her skin, she shuddered and began to move beneath him. His deep, leisurely kisses pulled something from her farthest recesses and left her limbs aching with a delicious madness. When he arched and plunged above and in her, her arms clasped him tightly, recklessly, only to withdraw as if scorched the moment his passion was spent.

Holt turned away from her tempting, womanly profile onto his side. In the quiet darkness he found his own unique torture in feeling so deprived, so hungry, even after having his fill of the very thing he had bargained for, coveted, demanded. The time would come, he vowed grimly, when she would come . . . she would come.

Beside him, Tauren's mind was in similar turmoil, torn between her body's vibrant and haunting responses and her pride and mistrust of her husband. She sighed silently and chewed the corner of her lip, remembering his stunningly effective demonstration of dominion over her brother earlier. She knew well that another would not have taken such pains to use the confrontation for teaching an important lesson. She smiled wanly at the lesson she had learned as well. In her he had met his power's limit. He had her to serve his pleasure—but she was not his. His kind of power did not extend into the heart itself.

The next morning and each morning of the week that followed, Holt left their bed early and roused Revan to accompany him as he rode out to see to the business of the shire. They returned late each night and after the second evening of delaying supper until it was nearly charred, Tauren retired early to her rooms leaving the servants to see to their comforts.

When Holt crawled between the sheets late and his hands came roaming over her body, her anger did little to bolster her indifference toward him. She felt his fingers stroking the curve of her waist and gritted her teeth; he kissed the bends of her arms and legs and she made whitened fists of helplessness. When he returned to her mouth she pushed her arms wide and grasped handfuls of the linen sheets and feather ticking to keep from embracing, from exploring his tantalizing body.

When he reached his shattering, convulsive conclusion, her eyes filled with tears of frustration that she would not allow him to see.

By week's end, the duration of his nightly attentions had dwindled noticeably, in direct proportion to the increase of his irritability and the shortening of his patience with seemingly everyone. Roxie's wry observations and precious snippets of gossip affirmed her hope that he was just as miserable in this sham of a marriage as she was.

May saw an end to the gray dampness of the season of preparation and a resurgence of travelers along the roads. Murdock, skirts billowing and her starched day cap bouncing airily, hurried to the side court to find Tauren. She directed the planting of the precious day's garner of herbs and woodland unguents.

"Milady," Murdock panted, "there are travelers come—a young lord and some men. They've asked for the young duke."

"I will come." Tauren wiped her gloves hurriedly on the cloth that aproned her soft woolen gown. "Who are they? Where are they from?" Her heart began a drumming of excitement.

"Young Brighton and three others . . . I know not their names." A slight frown creased the housekeeper's brow. "We should send for Master Holt." It was a statement and something of a question all at once.

"Yes." Tauren sent a hand up to smooth her hair as she turned to the staunch Murdock. "Send Ransom for him . . . if he's told *you* where he was bound." She strode inside leaving Murdock frowning concern after her.

"Gentlemen," she addressed the small delegation in the main salon. She had paused only long enough to check her appearance in the looking glass and to shed the calf-skin gardening gloves and apron before sweeping into the room. To a man they rose and greeted her with wonderment as she announced herself as sister to the duke. Her pale blue woolen gown followed closely the lines of her firm young body, dipping low at the neckline to reveal the pearl-like skin of her chest and breasts, belling at the sleeves that were embellished with stiff lace and velvet cording.

"You have come to see the young duke? He is out with . . . his guardian, riding. I have sent for them; I am sure they would not want to miss your visit." One by one the young men introduced themselves, taking her proffered hand gently: David Barrent of Brighton, Thomas Didwell, Houghton Kidry, and Maxwell Payden of Essex.

The young nobles were dressed in traveling clothes of costly tailoring; soft leather jerkins over richly colored woolen doublets, snowy linen collars edged in fine, muted laces, and dashing knee-high jackboots fitted with elegant silver spurs.

"Where are you bound, gentlemen?"

"We . . . um . . . are traveling to Portsmouth but thought to make the acquaintance of His Grace the highlight of our journey." Maxwell Payden answered for them smoothly, his eyes alight with admiration.

Tauren noted how deftly he had evaded her inquiry.

"Then by all means, gentlemen, your journey has not been for naught. And you must taste Lindengreen's hospitality this night in the bargain. Provender your mounts in our stables and dine and take rest this night with us."

"Your beauty is equaled by your generosity, Lady Tauren." Young Brighton nodded flamboyantly. "That makes us fortunate men indeed; being beneficiaries of both."

"You can repay the kindness, sirs"—she waved them to seats as she seated herself—"with information. . . ." Seeing Brighton glance meaningfully at Essex, she continued. "I mean to know all I can of London—the fashions, the pastimes, the society—will you prove worthy sources? We are so far from it here. . . ."

"But of course!" they chorused.

Holt entered the salon with a heavy stride to find his uncooperative bride awash in a sea of openly enamored young bloods, and the sight rocked him back on his own spurred heels momentarily. He paused inside the archway and set fists to his waist, a frown brewing on his sharply chiseled features.

"Gentlemen." His voice boomed to capture their attention as the purposeful hard clack of his bootheels had not. Their heads snapped up from gallant attendance upon the mistress of Lindengreen, and Tauren's face colored suddenly like the blush of ripe peaches as she halted in midsentence.

Houghton Kidry jumped up quickly and ap-

286

proached him. "Master Reston, good to see you, sir."
He bowed slightly, drawing the others into the
greeting. Tauren looked at Holt with surprise; these
noblemen of court knew him, greeted him with respect.

"I see you have been properly welcomed to Lindengreen already," Holt nodded to their silver cups and his
gaze turned on Tauren.

"Most delightfully," Barrent agreed, grinning.
"Lady Tauren has enchanted us completely and
extends to us the night's hospitality at Lindengreen."

"Such generosity." Payden nodded with exaggeration.

"Nay, such beauty and grace—" Thomas Didwell
began.

"Then my *wife* has welcomed you fully," Holt
declared pointedly, "and there is little I may add except
my company."

"Wife?" Barrent expressed their collective surprise,
and Holt noted with grim satisfaction a subtle, but
general distancing occurring between the young bloods
and Tauren.

"The vows are over a fortnight old, gentlemen.
They were read just after the old duke died."

"Felicitations, then." Payden beamed the good
humor of the graceful loser. His hand went to his chest
to assuage some phantom pain. "Ever my lot . . . to be
too late to capture the prize." He lifted Tauren's hand
to his lips. "Reston, that explains why you've shown
little of yourself in London lately, you sly fellow. If I
had this beauty to wife, I'd not set foot outside my door
either. Would that our intelligence of you were as
thorough as yours is of us."

Intelligence? Tauren looked at Holt. She recalled Charlotte's comment about his influence reaching beyond Somerset. He had sources in London . . . friends?

"Surely our local affairs would be of small concern outside Somerset," Tauren demurred. "I believe you are given to flattery, my lord, and no doubt quite successful at it." She turned a dazzling smile on Payden who had remained boldly seated by her. His tongue tripped and stammered over some courtly inanity as he took refuge in his cup under Holt's hardening stare.

Tauren's new womanly sense flawlessly intuited the reason for Holt's dark mood and she found it a deliciously promising revenge for her humiliation of recent days. She rose gracefully, drawing those seated up with her.

"Holt"—her use of his given name caused him to look at her strangely—"I would see to supper. Perhaps our guests would enjoy a tour of the hall and grounds." She was at his side, her slender hand touching his dark sleeve with a casual intimacy that drew the eyes of the room. "I shall send Revan to you, then I must dress more suitably for the evening."

Unnerved by her changed mood, Holt watched her glide away from him and turned to the noble delegation with squared shoulders and a formal smile. What were *they* doing here?

Tauren dressed in her golden velvet and green brocade for the evening's sumptuous dinner, and thoroughly enjoyed the ill-concealed admiration she

288

inspired in their noble guests. They were at pains to compliment her appearance, the food, the elegant dining hall; and each bit of praise seemed to abrade some hidden nerve in Holt's usually unshakable presence. He brooded over his plate, scarcely tasting the delicious duckling and lamb, his hands toying first with his linen, then his knife, then his goblet.

Holt commented only when spoken to and then rather coolly. Each smile Tauren aimed at one of the young blades seemed to mock him, piercing pride's stout armor in places he had not considered vulnerable. Even knowing she laughed more gaily and her eyes sparkled brighter when he turned his stern gaze upon her, he could not stop the tightness of frustration in his stomach and the feeling of lead in his limbs and on his tongue.

She never lowered her eyes flirtatiously toward him or smiled so intriguingly at him. She never laughed— that lilting, musical sound—in his presence, nor paid him charming compliments. Her chin was always hard set against him, her frame unyielding and stiff or limp and unresponsive, her words curt or bitter. She bestowed the sweetness, the magic of her enchanting being on these total strangers while to her husband she gave nothing—only relinquished what he took. Nor would she accept anything from him; her disapproving looks and impenetrable hauteur soured even heartfelt compliments on his tongue. Seeing this previously unrevealed side of her, he felt all the more deprived and resentful, angry with her selfish pride that denied him that ill-defined something which was the first thing in many years he was unable to obtain by the exercise of his raw power or persuasiveness.

In the salon later their visitors spoke of the state of the government quite openly and Tauren was surprised to learn how far the conflict between King Charles and Parliament had progressed.

"His support dwindles with each passing week. With Laud gone—"

"Gone?" Tauren spoke up from where she quietly engaged Revan in a half-hearted chess match. "Archbishop Laud is gone?"

"In prison, my lady, for these last several months. Likely his head is forfeit. Had you not heard?" The lanky, aristocratic Barrent turned a quizzical frown upon Holt.

"News travels slowly to this part of the country," Holt stated flatly, causing Tauren to turn to him with a troubled expression.

"But you have had word, Reston. That you have sources in London is well known," Payden of Essex charged amiably.

"Charles has troubles enough to keep him busy," Houghton Kidry sniffed a scented handkerchief with a satisfied expression. "Now that Strafford is dead and half his ministers flown, the privy council is a shambles."

"Strafford!" Tauren choked out before she could check her reaction. "Dead? How can that be? He is the king's first minister! When? How?" She seemed so deeply shocked, paling, that stout Didwell rushed to take her hand while Kidry continued.

"Strafford was beheaded a fortnight ago—or more. His trial for treason was a bitter, divisive one. He was most eloquent in his own defense and turned many undecided hearts in his and the king's favor. Fully half of London thronged about to see him done and most of them cheered. I was there myself. I can't say I agree with it all, but he was a damn—"

"The glibness of his tongue cannot belie the callous politics he enforced!" Barrent interjected. "He backed the repeal of tenants' rights, the fencing of the commons—condemning to starvation the peasant classes—the rape of Ireland—"

"I think we have had enough of dire politics for my lady's sake," Didwell interrupted, gazing moonily at Tauren's paling face.

"By all means," Payden observed with authority, "a pleasanter topic is needed . . . to be sure."

What more was said, Tauren could not be sure later, for she found her eyes drawn to Holt's lean, finely chiseled profile. Strafford had been sentenced for treason . . . beheaded . . . Revan's foster father— almost. If Holt had sent him . . . A fortnight? Holt knew! With his spies in London he knew Strafford was beheaded and his well-timed "gift" was a total sham! Strafford was gone, the duke was dead, the king was occupied with the state of the government; here was Holt's chance to have the shire and the title, with naught to stop him!

She rose shakily and called Revan to retire, her eyes flashing at Holt as she took her leave. The masterful bastard! How she loathed him!

Holt watched her go, wondering at her confusing

switch of moods through the evening. He dismissed the bright gleam in her eyes as she bid them good night and turned his mind to the urgent matters at hand.

Barrent rose to refill his cup and glanced meaningfully at Payden before summarizing their commonly held opinion. "Your bride is a rare beauty, Reston, witty and charming. Marrying her was a stroke of genius. The lad seems quite bright and not unhappy in your charge. You seem to have arranged things quite nicely here."

Holt eyed him coolly and said nothing, prompting Payden to take it up.

"Charles was insulted by the old man's 'novel' guardianship arrangements. It has been the talk of the salons of London since. Most think he would not hesitate to move against you openly, except for Parliament's broad opposition and the fear of further confrontation. That you have . . . friends in Parliament is known."

Stout Thomas Didwell sat forward, watching Holt expectantly. "It is clear you are in charge here, Reston; Somersetshire is yours. The time for straddling the damnable fence is long past. We are here to urge you to declare yourself an ally of a free Parliament."

There it was, said and in the open. Holt toyed nonchalantly with the stark white linen of his cuff as he framed a reply.

"The old duke has given me a charge—" Holt began.

"Damn the old man! He's dead!" Barrent burst out. "It's no secret you want a title, Reston. Here's your chance for it. When the fighting is done, there'll be a new order and plenty of reward for those who helped

292

bring it about."

"Fighting?" Holt turned to Payden with an uplifted brow.

"We have evidence that the king tallies his stores and arms and may quit the city soon. Further antagonism can only lead to armed conflict. We will be prepared for it when it comes. And you must determine where you will side, Reston. A freeman like yourself stands to gain more with us than with the arrogant Royalist cause and a king who may move against you at any moment." Payden smiled—a cold, brittle expression—as he drove what he knew would be his winning point home.

"And if I were to agree to help you, put Somerset's resources at the call of the Parliamentary party, you would not interfere were I to declare myself duke?" Holt's face was flawlessly dispassionate.

"We could arrange a resolution in the Commons supporting you . . . perhaps discover a witness or documents. . . ."

Holt's face reddened slightly but his features retained their deceptive calm. "And the boy?"

"He is in your care," Barrent insinuated. "Once the fighting has begun there will be many martyrs for the cause of rights. Then who might say you nay if you assumed the title fully?"

Holt rose solemnly, pulling his doublet straighter and straining for control. "Gentlemen"—he engaged each pair of eyes, one by one, with his burning forest gaze—"your intelligence of me is indeed inferior to mine of you. Were I such a man as you think me to be, you would sully your cause by asking me to join you. Or perhaps you would but welcome me into your cutthroat band."

His voice rose to drown their indignant clamor. "You prattle about the honor of the nation being in the will of its people and claim your cause to be the just voice of that agency. Yet here you run like jackals in a pack, sniffing out a juicy morsel to feed your own ambitions. You have just advocated openly the betrayal of an oath of fealty and the convenient death of my young ward—the brother of my wife." His fists clenched at his sides as his face became dark granite.

"What you have heard of me, no doubt, is true. I get what I want. I make no secret of it. But neither is it a secret that I never prosper at another's expense. When I take control as I have here, I see to the welfare of others in the bargain. I do not see your strain of ambition as more noble than that of current authority . . . nor in basis more just."

"Parliament is the voice of—" Payden began.

"Then where are the land reforms and easing of the burden of tax? Where is the relief from the hideous oppression of speech and religion? Nay there is none pending and none will be produced. Your mob is driven wild by a taste of blood and now will stop at nothing to gain and enforce its own power while the rest of the country rots."

"Don't be a fool, Reston," Barrent growled and was on his feet in an instant, barely restrained by Payden. "You sit here snug in your little southern nest, but not for long. The conflict will reach even here; then God help you, for you'll see no mercy nor aid from us if you reject us now."

"Come ahead, lord," Holt spat, his eyes flashing with warning fires. "I care for my own and have nothing to fear from the likes of you."

Didwell and Kidry approached Holt with hands outstretched in supplication. "See here, Reston, you have us wrong. We do not advocate—"

"Save your breath. I have heard all I care to hear. You may abide in this house for the night but will leave tomorrow at first light. Be out of Somerset by nightfall. My men will see you to your rooms."

Holt strode out and angrily waved the order to the waiting Ransom and two dozing cavaliers. His boots pounded fiercely against the hard marble of the grand staircase and he found himself turning about the gallery toward Revan's quarters. He went quickly inside and lit a candle, standing at the lad's bedside a long moment.

He felt an odd catch in his throat as he watched the calm, untroubled breathing of the boy's deep sleep. Each feature of the young duke's face recalled a similar curve or hollow of his wife's. Moments later he left and, encountering Ransom returning from posting a pre-arranged watch on the guests' chamber doors, ordered him to spend the night in the boy's rooms. He was to come immediately if aught seemed amiss. The boyishly fair young man nodded, puzzled, but obeyed.

In the duke's study, Holt poured a brandy and downed it quickly, savoring the fiery sweetness and casting a troubled glance toward his bedchamber door. He doused all but one candle and sat in the darkness, stewing on the confrontation and wondering at the anger it produced in him. He frowned deeply. It was not like him to let his anger rise so blatantly, or to condemn so righteously the ambitions of other men. He was often—and rightly—labeled an ambitious man himself. Few men of true personal worth could be found without a streak of it in them. No . . . It was this matter of Tauren and Revan. He had summed it up better than he had intended. He would allow nothing to harm what was his . . . his wife, his young ward.

His eye wandered to the bedchamber door. From beneath it came a low beam of light. It shot through him and he sat bolt upright, a grin stealing across his face. Tauren had kept the candles lit, and waited up for him!

"You did not tarry with your friends over spirits?" Tauren stood before the fire in a light wrapper, brushing her long chestnut hair as she turned to him. The bright look on his face stopped her for a moment, but she shook free of the feeling and placed her brush on the dressing table. "I would have expected such. What better occasion to celebrate your nearly completed mastery of Lindengreen than with your traitorous friends?"

"I choose my friends more carefully than that," he stated flatly. "And I far prefer the unique delights of your own delectable person to their worthless prattle."

"Is it so worthless when they bring you such valuable news as that of Strafford's death? Or could it be your spies had already informed you of it? Perhaps a fortnight ago . . . just in time for you to present a 'gift' to your gullible young bride?"

His eyes narrowed as he pondered the challenge in her questions and the reason for her ire. He put his fists to his waist in a display of unaffected determination.

"A man cannot be condemned for wanting to please

and cosset his nervous bride."

"Please!" she spat contemptuously. "Your own pleasure was what you sought, lying and deceiving—"

"It was no lie!" Holt barked. "I decided, as was my right, to keep the boy here."

"After you were sure Strafford was dead!"

"Nay! He was only taken to trial and we awaited the outcome. The old duke knew the outlook was dire and in the assigns of his will left it to me to decide whether to seek another foster or to keep the lad here. I thought it would please you to know he would not be sent away."

"You played me false that night to secure my . . . cooperation, and Lord knows how many other times yet to be discovered!"

"Lady, your cooperation is not so cheaply bought as I well know! You let me taste your pleasures fully that first time because you wanted me as I wanted you." His hot eyes seemed to scorch her skin through her clothing, making her feel naked.

"You are so accustomed to it, now you deceive even yourself!" she declared hotly.

"Your complaints could well be pressed in full against yourself. You parade your precious honor about like a banner when in truth you do not honor your word or your lowly vows. I warned you I'd have no icy virgin in my bed and you agreed to that bargain in accepting me. You pretend you sacrifice your body on honor's altar to protect your dear brother"—he blazed, his words of white hot anger, meant to scald her stubborn pride—"when in truth you married me because you like the way I can make you feel!"

"No!" she shouted, her eyes wide with her fear that

297

he spoke the truth.

"I would have that honorable willingness you promised me, wife!" he growled, starting for her as she backed away, clutching her wrapper together.

"Very well!" she stopped unexpectedly, bringing Holt up short with the unexpected change. "I'll come to your bed without being dragged, but my willingness is of my heart and that is mine alone to give. You cannot *take* that overlord!" She pulled the tie of her wrapper and jerked it from her shoulders to toss it from her angrily. She stood, bare-limbed, in a clinging, light chemise, her fiery hair flowing long about her in sable waves. Her eyes flashed as she grasped the low neck of her meager garment in her hands.

"Shall I, overlord, or do you wish the pleasure?" she taunted with a smile of malice. Seeing a dark frown creeping over his angular face, she pulled savagely and the chemise was ripped asunder, revealing her ripely curved body in full. With angry movements she pushed the useless straps from her arms and stood, shoulders high, before him in all her taunting nakedness.

His face showed surprise and bewilderment at her startling behavior, and he stood motionless, looking at her tempting nudity and glowering.

Her arms came up to reach out toward him even as her eyes blazed, daring him to come. "Take me, *husband*," she gritted out from between her teeth, "it is your right."

Instantly his face was dull red with rage. He took a step forward, then stopped. His arms twitched convulsively and his fists clenched impotently at his sides. A muscle in his firm-set jaw was jumping furiously.

He wheeled, slamming open the door with such force

298

that the wall trembled as he stomped out of the great ducal chambers.

She had *won*! And for no creditable reason, Tauren began to laugh and to sob simultaneously, racked with a cacophony of feelings that screamed for expression. She flung herself down on the great bed, more miserable with each falling tear.

Twenty-Three

Holt did not return that night and the next morning early, Tauren learned that their noble guests had departed at dawn and her husband had escorted them partway to Portsmouth.

"When will he return?" she questioned Murdock as she tried to hide her surprise and annoyance.

"He did not say." The keen, gray eyes observed her disguised irritation, and the housekeeper put a reassuring hand on Tauren's arm. "I am sure it won't be long; he took only Calder and two of his men. He frequently travels to Portsmouth to trade and buy . . . of late even more so." She looked as though she might say more, but stopped.

"Well"—Tauren's cheeks reddened—"if he has not the courtesy to inform me of his comings and goings, I need not worry that his comfort is met. I have other concerns." And she was off in a flurry to see to the cabinetmaker's ailing wife.

*　　　*　　　*

But late that same evening as they dined alone in the hall, her responses to Revan's queries were not so adamant.

"I'm sure he would have taken me with him. When did he decide to go to Portsmouth? He promised to take me someday. . . ."

"No doubt it was late when he decided and he left at dawn. You have your lessons and—"

"But he promised me another lesson with the sword today."

"Sword? He's been teaching you the sword? When did this start?" she demanded irritably.

"Last week. I've had two lessons already. He says I'll be good at it."

"He said nothing to me," she remonstrated, "nor did you. You're too young for that sort of training."

"No wonder he left!" Revan threw down his napkin and rose defiantly. "You argued with him again didn't you? You never smile, never sing, hardly talk anymore. You're always angry about something, especially when he's around. And the only time you talk to me is to order me about like some baby!"

Before she could recover her voice he was quitting the door and she sat a long while looking after him, stung by the truth of his assessment. She seldom talked to him, never laughed—hardly smiled. A quick and nasty vision of herself as a wasting, dour old prune blossomed before her and she fled the hall into the sweet heaviness of the spring evening.

In her solitary bed that night she reached one slim hand beneath the coverlet to touch the pillow where

Holt usually slept; then she drew back sharply with annoyance that melted into confusion. Holt was right . . . she wanted him, almost more than anything else. In his arms, feeling his lips on her face, bearing his hard, driving weight on her body, she thought of nothing but him and could not keep her arms from clasping him to her in the final throes of his passion. It took every shred of her will to carry off the deception. . . .

Carry it off? She flushed in the darkness; he was right again, for the only one deceived was herself. Trying to hide her feelings—her passion—from him, she only succeeded in denying herself. And the whole household suffered from the strain it caused her.

How could she care so about a power-hungry rogue who had stolen her virtue, openly declared his claims to her brother's inheritance, forced her into marriage, and even deceived her at her bedding?

Perhaps he was right, she was totally without real pride or honor, for she longed to give herself to him fully—to please him. She wanted to watch him, learn about him. His rakish smile turned her stomach over to pour heat into her loins and the stride of his muscular legs drew her eyes like a moth to the flame. He could be so breathtakingly gentle . . . and so ruthlessly controlling. Oh, why could her father have not married her off, dowerless, to some nice, dull farmer's son? Then at least she would not have to spar her way through every meal or wage battle nightly in her very bed.

She sniffed and realized that her face was wet; the tears were falling in profusion again. Revan was right, she was turning into a shrew, a sour and miserable thing to be around. The constant tension of their nightly war permeated the days as well and took its toll.

"If only I could trust you, Holt Reston . . ." She reached out to grab his pillow and hug it against her as she turned on her side. It smelled faintly of his musky, masculine scent, and she stroked her damp cheek against the soft linen, sighing tiredly. "If only . . ."

Holt strode the dark street more from memory than by sight, his hard jackboots announcing his presence recklessly as his thoughts were concentrated elsewhere. The shadows along Portsmouth's shabby waterfront concourse flitted and deepened in ominous conspiracy, but Holt took little notice.

Suddenly, a human shape loomed up in his path. Holt's stride slowed and his mind rushed back from the day's business. A small man dressed in coarse sea clothes, stood square in his path. The fellow seemed to weave and hailed Holt as "mate."

As he passed the drunkard, he heard a rustling and scraping behind him. He whirled, sending one hand instinctively for his short blade. A stout club swung upward, catching his head a glancing blow, and he dodged a dark blur, dazed. Suddenly there were fists and clubs coming from all directions, and his lean, iron-thewed arms shot out in self-defense, slashing and connecting savagely, twisting and distorting flesh.

In the fuller light of the middle of the path, Holt could see the thugs outlined as they came at him, swearing and grunting advice and encouragement to each other. He could not tell how many there were; they thudded and rolled and seemed to pop up again to charge anew. Then two came at once, one taking the brunt of Holt's fist and the other smashing his face with the massive knuckles of a hamlike fist. Another blow to his jaw, then his eye, and another fist from somewhere rammed into his gut, doubling him over.

Confusion broke out among his attackers, and Holt heard violent cursing and wild scuffling. "Sons of perdition . . . spawn of hell, I'll send ye to yer evil master this very night!" Then something in Holt's head exploded and a blinding flash of light preceded blackness.

He did not hear the scrambling retreat of the remaining pack of thugs nor feel the tugging and jostling that raised him, like a giant sack of barley, atop burly shoulders.

The sour, musty smell woke him first, that, and the pain in his eye, the ache in his jaw and gut. His one good eye came open quickly into the dim light of a single candle. He searched the corners of the low ceiling of the dingy room and started up from his bed of soured straw.

"Nay, lad." A deep voice enforced by strong arms forbade him to rise. "Ye've had a bad knock on the head. Best ye not get up as yet."

His eyes still blurred, Holt looked up into a fleshy, red face, pierced by two dark eyes that glowed strangely. His tongue filled his mouth as he attempted to speak, and he produced only a dry, croaking sound. Instantly a cup of cool ale was put to his lips and he drank gratefully with the man's assistance.

"Where am I?" Holt managed.

"Safe enough," came the response. "Though I come too late to save yer purse. Ye took down one and I took down another."

"How many were there?" Holt raised one battered hand to test the damage about his stubbornly shut, swollen eye and cut lip.

"Five, I saw."

"Seemed a dozen." Holt grimaced with the pain in his stomach and head.

The man laughed roundly and Holt looked at him through his narrowed good eye. His rescuer's face bore broad, clean features, and beneath his blocklike shoulders rested a broad girth covered in worn and dusty black broadcloth that stretched down to the man's skirt. Holt's face jerked up quickly with its question.

"Who . . . are you? You helped me?"

"Yea, it was me that set that wretched dross to flight. Me and this . . ." His brawny hand patted the ornate bronze handle of a long sword slung about his ample middle.

"What are you?" Holt frowned in confusion.

"I was—am—a priest of the true church . . . the Anglican Church."

"A sword-wielding vicar?" Holt snorted his disbelief.

"Yea, it is true." The portly man defended himself sternly. "In these perilous parishes, a vicar must first survive in order to serve. And often the Lord's justice and protection must be lent a more temporal arm."

"A vicar with a sword . . . it takes getting used to." Holt's frown brought a grimace of pain as if to censure his incredulity. "You must own some skill, routing four thugs."

305

"Right enough. I am handy with a weapon, and my bishop declares I wield the scriptures in the same fashion. It does not make me popular with him, nor with fat, wealthy parishoners. Haldan is an old viking name and I fear I inherited a regrettable dose of my forebearers' love of battle."

Holt grinned crookedly and tried to sit up.

"Nay." The vicar's stout arm pushed him back down. "Ye're not ready yet."

"I'll be right enough again as soon as I down enough wine to ease this pounding in my head," Holt declared. "Then I must send word to my men—" This time when he struggled up, nothing hindered him and he felt a hefty arm about his waist as he made to stand from the low pole-and-rope bed.

"You did not ask my name," Holt leaned on his rescuer.

"Ye be a child of the Almighty, sorely beset. Ye need be no more," came the terse reply.

Holt laughed gruffly. "You are a true priest after all."

The vicar stared up at him warily then, his broad face split in a contagious grin. "Right below is a tavern that serves unwatered wine. Likely we can find some generous body to ferry a message for ye." He steadied Holt as he tried a wobbly step.

"I have . . . no coin. My purse . . ." Holt ran one hand up and through his disheveled raven locks.

A loud, rumbling guffaw came from his broad support. "My credit here is the innkeeper's tithe; ye'll not go thirsty."

"Master Holt's come!" Roxie ran into the ducal

306

bedchamber, out of breath and cheeks flushed rosy with her haste. "He's callin' for ye, milady . . . in the great hall."

Tauren put down her brush and slipped her wrapper about her. "At this hour?" She glanced at the tall window near the great bed, where the earliest morning light streamed in through the beveled, leaded panes. "Are they just come? They must have ridden all night. Is something amiss?"

"I don't think they rode all night"—Roxie followed her mistress quickly through the portal and along the hall—"not by the smell of 'em."

Roxie's last remark drifted short of Tauren's hearing as she rushed along the gallery, her heart drumming steadily faster. As she started down the grand stairs her eyes widened at the sight of three sprawled figures near the entry doors below. Nearing them, she slowed her steps and stopped dead, several paces away.

Holt stepped away from the frame of the huge front doors and swept his plumed hat downward in a wide, unsteady arc. Calder parodied his movement, weakly, from his seat on the nearby marble bench, failing to rise and quickly propping his head on his fist again.

"My love," Holt began, swaying slightly and tucking his thumbs into his belt to steady himself. "I haf . . . brought you a gift . . . one only you could ap-appreci-ate."

"What's happened to you, Holt? Are you all right?" The sight of his much-abused face sent a wave of anxiety through her, and she had to force herself not to run to him. She stopped as the sight of his bloodshot eyes and the overpowering reek of rum assailed her in the same instant. She recoiled, drawing a hot breath.

"You're . . . you're sotted!"

"Nay . . ." Holt stepped a wobbling bit closer. "We've but tos-ssed a few. I bring you a vicar to replace the one you los-st. A fine man . . . a defender of the faith . . . a true s-soldier of the cros-s-s." His brows lifted and a lopsided grin appeared as he congratulated himself, with rum's sophistry, on his elegant turn of phrase and wished Haldan were conscious to hear himself described thus. His hand swept toward the black-clad form propped against the end of the marble bench Calder occupied. Booted legs were outstretched before the cassocked figure and a fleshy chin rested stolidly on the man's broad chest.

"A vicar?" Tauren felt a double heat warming her veins. Here, she taunted herself snidely, was the irresistible tempter of her body's perversely sensual responses. Then she looked askance at the silent, disreputable form draped across the floor and turned on Holt with a fury.

"You *lout*! How—" She stopped, choked completely by her rage. It was a long moment before she would trust herself to move, her urge to violence was so overwhelming. "After four days' absence, off without a word, you return, hail fellow, well met, with a drunkard who lies senseless on the floor, claiming my welcome and bearing that as a *gift*!" Her voice rose shrilly at the end when she flung an accusing finger at the cleric.

Holt's grin wilted a bit but was still present as he gazed raptly at his beautiful young wife. Her hair flowed past her waist in sinuous waves, her blue eyes flashed becomingly . . . that was all he could take in.

Seeing her words made no dent in his drunken sense,

308

she whirled away to find a raft of whispering servants and a pale-faced Murdock behind her.

"*You* take care of him . . . him and his playmates!" she charged angrily, then stomped up the stairs to her chambers.

Later, Murdock threw open the heavy brocades at the windows of the master bedchamber to admit the strong sun of late afternoon. She turned to the bed, with narrowed eyes, and pulled back the heavy green velvet bedhangings to direct the bright, intruding rays upon a sprawled, sleeping form.

"Up, Holt!" she barked. "Up and wash now and make yourself presentable before supper." When the figure sprawled on the bed failed to respond, her brow furrowed dangerously and she put both hands on his shoulders and shook him soundly. "Up! I say, and wash! I've brought you a tub."

Holt jolted up shakily, disoriented at first and nearly blinded by the light. Shielding his eyes with one arm and blinking, he muttered thickly, "What is it, Murdock?"

"Time for you to be up and about, Master." The little woman put a telling sneer on the last word. Seeing his hand at his grizzled head, she smiled saccharinely and shoved a vile-smelling tankard under his nose. "Down it," she commanded, "before it downs you. It'll clear your head."

"Ye gods!" he pulled his nose away and shoved it from him, feeling his stomach roll. Insistently, Murdock pushed it back.

"Drink!"

His reddened eyes peered mistrustfully at the stern housekeeper from darkened sockets, the one nearly swollen shut, all purple and ghastly green. His two days' beard and still swollen lip made him look every bit as bad as he felt. Seeing him hesitate, she pushed the tankard closer still and leaned toward him to lend force to her command. He held his breath and downed the concoction, gasping for breath as the last of it cleared his throat, searing a path downward to his stomach.

Smiling beatifically upon his instantaneous writhing, Murdock intoned, "Lady Tauren showed us some marvelous bitter herbs for just such cures. You'll feel better after you've got the poisons out of your system."

Holt raced for the chamberpot stowed beneath the bedskirt, and purged his stomach while the housekeeper stood watching with jaundiced eye.

"Serves you right, Holt. A pure disgrace, you are. Look at you!" One thin hand swept the length of him contemptuously as he sprawled, half-sitting, beside the bed on the floor, clothing mud-stained and disarrayed.

Holt's face was pure agony as he bleared up at her. "Spare me your sermon, Murdock. I could be dying. She may have poisoned me and your lecture will be for naught."

"I've always borne pride in you, Holt Reston, like you were my own in some ways. Now I shudder to think I was a party in the making of this. . . ." Again her hand waved its contempt.

His head was clearing remarkably fast and he sent one hand to his now quiet stomach to press and test it cautiously. What was Murdock prattling on about? It wasn't like her to carp.

"Had us all worried sick . . . especially her ladyship."

"Ladyship?" Holt grunted as he made to rise, waving away Murdock's tardy assistance. "She's a plain madam now, she'll have to be content with that."

"She'll always be Lady Tauren here, Holt Reston. Shameful how you ran off without a word to the girl . . . her sick with worry."

Holt had made his way to the washstand and splashed his face with water, but it was the housekeeper's words and not the water that smacked him awake. From behind a towel he mumbled something unintelligible, then peeked his good eye over the cloth at her.

"*She* was worried?"

"Not that she had reason to be, what with thugs nearly making her a widow before she's a bride a month. And what with you out carousing and drunken for days. And not a civil greeting for your wife upon your return—looking like a half-carved leg of mutton. Nay, she had little enough cause to wring her hands over you, but—" She stopped suddenly her lips drawn tight against saying more and went for the kettle warming at the hearth and poured the hot water into the large copper tub.

Holt watched her, frowning, as he began to strip off his dirty doublet and begrimed shirt. Tauren now claimed the staunch housekeeper's loyalty, to be sure. He didn't like her accusatory tone or the guilty way he was beginning to feel.

"Make yourself presentable," Murdock commanded, crossing her arms over her chest. "That 'vicar' of yours was up an hour ago. I've laid the law to him— no bath, no supper. It appears he'd rather starve. But I won't have him thinking he can abuse milady's hospitality just because her husband has no consideration for her tender feelings." She sailed toward the door, permitting herself a smug, little expression of satisfaction when her back was to him.

Holt stood, watching her go, feeling his irritation rise. His indignation was supplanted by another, more interesting thought. Tauren had missed him . . . well, worried about him. He slipped into the steaming tub and sighed with relief at the welcome warmth. A warped, crooked grin reappeared. That was something to think on.

Tauren absented herself from the main house most of the day, putting as much distance between herself and that madman of a husband as she could. It was with lagging, scuffling steps she made her way inside as the sun was setting past the great old oaks in the side yard. Her head throbbed and her back ached, her limbs were pinging from the day's stresses. The worst was yet to come, she knew, for she still must deal with her profligate mate and that sotted miscreant he had fetched home with him.

Relief filled her as she discovered their bedchamber empty, but while she dressed her ire was fanned anew by remembrance of the morning's unpleasant scene.

"'E was sore set upon by thugs, a pack of them." Roxie had volunteered the gossip begun by Calder's recounting of the tale to Murdock. "The priest, Vicar Haldan, happened by and saved 'is skin. His face ain't as bad as it looks . . . and that's a mercy. 'Tis only sin itself would mar so handsome a face."

Tauren had drawn a long breath and silenced Roxie with a warning glare. She was tired of the lout's praises being sung by every servant, stableboy and servingmaid.

Now every eye fixed upon her as she entered the warm candlelight of the dining hall. The dusky rose of her gown threw crimson lights across her half-bound hair, and her warm blue eyes were luminous with the light of many candles. Revan, Holt, and the hard-drinking vicar were gathered before the fireplace, all three freshly scrubbed and clothed. She avoided staring at Holt, denying the urge to search his face and make sure he was all right. He was dressed immaculately in his customary black, and in spite of his grotesque eye and damaged lip he was awesomely masculine.

She would have been pleased to know how Holt's eyes ached with sudden longing for the soft beauty of her and how his head spiraled unexpectedly.

"My wife, Tauren," he announced her to the vicar as he pressed a warm kiss upon her hand. "This is the Vicar Gateson Haldan, Vicar Haldan as he prefers."

"You are welcome at my brother's table, sir," Tauren said coolly, as determined not to show her contempt for him as she was that he would not be staying at Lindengreen.

"How beautiful and gracious you are, my lady." The stout, dark-clad man dipped his head respectfully. "Master Holt is indeed blessed beyond most men in his marriage."

Tauren smiled reservedly, appraising the vicar openly and in telling silence.

"The vicar can sure enough hold his liquor," Revan blurted out, drawing her shocked stare. "He slept a few hours and then was up and about in fine fettle." Holt was chewing the unscathed part of his lip, and the vicar had the grace to redden.

"How fortunate for him," Tauren mused from between terse lips. She sent a narrow look at her brother that deterred him little.

"I showed him the chapel and he thinks it's fine, don't you Haldan?"

"Indeed, a pleasant and agreeable place for worship of the Almighty . . ." The rotund rescuer, usually voluble, slowed to a stammer under Tauren's skeptical gaze.

"He knows Latin and Greek and French and Italian and lots of other languages and things . . . history, too!" Revan sought to defend the companionable cleric.

"How commendable." She turned and found Holt striding beside her, holding his arm under hers in escort. He held her chair properly before seating himself at the head of the table. The vicar was given the chair beside Revan and across from her. The empty plate beside her caused her to puzzle a moment.

"Calder won't join us this eve; he's off his feed. I've given him over into Murdock's loving care. He'll be better by morning . . . or dead." She looked at him as the others laughed and he caught her gaze warmly.

Fully ten different emotions flickered across her features in that brief exchange, and she lowered her eyes to her goblet in confusion. The swollen eye and cut lip on his usually clean, angular face jolted her as Roxie's words rushed back. She felt her stomach lurch downward, and she was nearly sick at the thought of what might have happened to him. How could he be so careless with his safety? He was a man with responsibilities now, with duties, and a wife. She scowled darkly,

314

concentrating on the blessing, which Haldan delivered with a simple grace that nettled her further.

"I hope you fare better than our past vicar," she observed tartly as they were served.

"And what became of 'im?" Vicar Haldan stuffed a boiled potato into his mouth and tore a hunk from the fragrant loaf of dark bread Revan offered him.

"My husband had him whipped and banished," she retorted with taunting lightness. She cut off a piece of roast hen with her knife and enjoyed his reaction.

Haldan's head snapped up to search first Holt and then her as he swallowed his food hard. "What was his offense?"

"My husband did not care for his brand of orthodoxy."

Holt watched her keenly, knowing her displeasure was aimed at him. "I am overlord here"—his strong voice sallied forth—"and I will allow no cropping of ears in this shire, nor any time spent in stocks unless sentenced by civil magistrate."

The intensity of the reverend's face eased and he shrugged his broad shoulders, returning to his now-heaping plate. "The powers of church and state are best kept separate, to my mind. A pity my superiors do not favor my views; I'd be well set now in a rich parish with a fat wife and a dozen children."

Holt smiled broadly as the vicar passed the first of Tauren's tests and noted his wife's brief scowl of disappointment. He drew from his cup as he studied her.

"My wife has a keen interest in the spiritual affairs of the Lindengreen and the shire. You see, her father was a bishop of the church. He served the North Country—

Northumbria, I believe." Tauren registered mild surprise as she looked at her husband.

"Northumbria?" Haldan turned to Tauren as he swallowed a tasty morsel of lamb and quaffed it with wine. "Where, my lady? Who was your father?"

"He was Bishop of Greaves, Edward Wincanton. He died last September." For some reason as she said it, a huge lump rose in her throat and threatened her composure completely.

"Edward Wincanton, true?" the stout cleric echoed with surprise. "Tall, lean man with a red cast to his hair and burning gray eyes that could light damp kindling?"

"That's him," Revan answered, his face alight. "Did you know of him?"

"Yea, he was my bishop in my first vicarage in training and petitioned to have me assigned there. But it was not to be. . . ." The cleric's eyes wandered off as if seeing some memory live again.

"Now, there was a man," Haldan pronounced, nodding affirmation, "and a true priest of the Almighty if ever there was one."

Tauren sat, stunned. Either the man was a colossal liar or an outrageous saint.

Vicar Haldan put down his knife almost reluctantly and wiped his greasy fingers on the linen. "You two be Edward Wincanton's children," he pointed to Tauren and Revan with a light of recognition in his eyes. "It's a true honor to serve ye." The broad face was genuine and so full of respect that Tauren felt a sharp pang of unwelcome guilt.

"No boughten office, your father's. He earned it well and bore it with more grace and dignity than any of the rest, even after they sentenced him to that godforsaken—" Seeing the strange look on Tauren's face he paused.

"When I was at the vicarage, we had a cursed and stubborn old farmer who had not set foot inside the church for twenty years. He always had some excuse and the rector was at wit's end with 'im. His wife was a devout woman and brought the young ones for instruction. 'Twas time for confirmin' the eldest but he refused to come, sayin' he 'ad a cow stuck up to her belly."

Holt glanced at Tauren and found her mesmerized by the vicar's tale, her eyes rimmed with beautiful liquid crystal. He had not thought of her as having a father, as being someone's little girl. It unnerved him to see her now as the loving, grieving daughter of a good man.

"Well, the bishop had come for the blessin' and he went personally to fetch the old rouser. Me and half the kirk trailed behind. Right into the muck he went, robes an' all. The old coot just stared whilst the bishop pulled that bawlin' creature out single-handed. Then he said, 'I suppose she'll be needin' milkin' as well.' Milked her, he did, then dragged the old backslider by the ear all the two miles to the church. That ornery old rouser didn't miss another mass for the two years I served."

All were silent as the vicar shook his head fondly. "He knew to be a priest a man must both command and serve."

"He caught hell's fire from Aunt Veldean when he came home, his best robes caked with dried mud," Tauren spoke softly. "I remember it, the man with the cow. I was but a little girl. . . ."

Something in Holt's chest tightened at the sweet pain

of memory in her face, the tears in her eyes of sky blue. Just then he wanted to gather her up in his arms, to comfort her, and he ground his teeth in frustration for he knew she would not allow it.

In the vicar's warm eyes and generous features, she saw compassion and it was all she could do to keep from bursting into tears. She wrestled inwardly with her emotions for a moment before she could speak.

"I hope your room is comfortable, Vicar Haldan."

Twenty-Four

The fireplace in the salon was cold for the first time that spring as Holt sat alone in the meager candlelight, having sent Revan and Haldan on to rest some time before. He dreaded mounting the stairs to his bed to discover what awaited him. And then there was this uneasy feeling he had about himself and the way he had reacted to Tauren at supper. This was not simply desire for a beautiful woman, nor male pride of possession, nor the challenge of conquest. It had somehow become far more complicated than that. Just how complicated he was in no mood to ponder. Murdock's words returned to him; Tauren had worried about him. Perhaps she was coming around. . . .

When the heavy door to the bedchamber swung open, Tauren bolted upright in the chair she occupied by the dark, silent hearth. Her sleep-heavy eyes echoed the soft blue of her light wrapper and her cheeks seemed dream-blushed.

Holt smiled to himself at the sight and strode briskly into the room. "I see you have waited up," he stated

319

calmly. "Did you want something, wife?" He proceeded to peel his rich black velvet doublet from his broad shoulders and to unbutton his shirt.

She tore her eyes away, irritated with herself for watching raptly. "Nay," she declared hastily, busying herself with her sewing basket. What she had to say would anger him, she was sure. The lusty curl of his lips let her know his expectations.

When he had stripped and washed, he carried the candelabrum to the nightstand by the great bed and climbed between the cool sheets. "Come to bed, Tauren." His voice was low and silky.

She removed her wrapper and laid it neatly aside, approaching the bed dressed in a heavy nightdress. His eyes roamed her and lit with ire at this evidence of her continued resistance to him.

"We have fought this battle, wife. Get that thing off!" He pointed to the offending garment.

"No!" she answered, her face hot with the explanation to come. "I am . . . it is . . . my time." Her pride faltered at this humiliating exposure of her body's very intimate functions and she lowered her eyes, vowing to bear his wrath with some dignity. "I could go to my own bed for the time. . . ."

"*This* is your bed," he declared loudly and was out of bed and around the end to her before she could retreat. He scooped her up against his hard, naked chest and plopped her on the bed gently. Angrily, he tucked her feet under the coverlet and pulled it up about her chin, then doused the candles and crawled in beside her, lying on his back with his arms crossed beneath his head.

Angry confusion filled him. Why had he not

recognized that this must inevitably occur? As intimately as he knew women, it seemed there were some things he had not yet experienced. It struck him that despite his varied experience, he was as much a novice at this "marriage" business as she.

A muffled sniff from beside him brought back in a rush some of his old boyish lore about women's special pain. And again he felt some of that boyish awe of women's secrets.

"Are you . . . does it . . . hurt?"

"No." Her voice was tiny with the small lie. Tears clogged her throat, and she made whitened fists of her hands. Why did she have to hurt and cry, now of all times?

In the dim moonilght he searched her motionless form, but her face was turned from him. He tossed back the covers and felt her recoil as he reached for her.

"No!" she gasped in a strangled voice. "You cannot—"

He dragged her to the middle of the bed and turned her resisting form over onto her stomach, pressing her buttocks down firmly with his hands as she tried to roll away.

"I'm no beast!" he growled defensively. "I'll not hurt you."

Her strained, tensed flesh was evidence of her disbelief as he sat up beside her and began to gently knead the muscles of her back and shoulders with his strong hands. He remembered well the soothing power of such treatment on battle-weary limbs.

Tauren could scarcely believe her own senses as his caressing hands made butter of her tensed and aching muscles. She had not expected such understanding, such . . . tenderness, from him, with no hope of his own carnal reward. Her thoughts convicted her, and she stifled a sob in the pillow.

He felt her sudden tension and the small jerk of her head, and rested one hand on the small of her back. "Did I hurt you?" he whispered anxiously.

She raised and shook her head, thankful for the thick fall of hair that hid her tear-swollen face. Reassured, he proceeded to her thighs and calves and stroked and pressed and massaged until the aching melted away. A blessed numbness enveloped her well-tended limbs as he proceeded to her arms and slender hands. Soon she surrendered her whole body to it and, lastly, her jumbled thoughts themselves.

From the shallow evenness of her breathing, Holt knew she slept and smiled tightly to himself. It was a solemn, thoughtful overlord of Somerset that gently cradled his sleeping wife's body with his own. She made him feel, think about things he hadn't considered in years. In this marriage, he had learned, very little was in his control.

In the cool stillness of the early dawn, Tauren lay watching Holt's sleeping face, so near her own she could feel his breath moving her hair. Secretively, she touched her fingertips to her lips then applied them to the battered green-purple ring about his left eye. He did not stir and his breathing was slow and deep. Then with her fingers she bestowed another kiss-by-proxy upon his wounded lip. Feeling oddly content with these unacknowledged mercies, she drifted back to sleep.

*　　*　　*

Spring settled fully on the land, her warmth drawing forth a verdant response. The cool green of new leaves gave way to the lush emerald of maturity and in the grasses, snowy starflowers and violets appeared. Lindengreen buzzed with the work of beginnings, planting and lambing. But there was also the ending work, the shearing and winter cleaning of stables and outbuildings.

Tenants came to Lindengreen from all over the duke's lands to get seed for their new crops, using the occasion as a time for visiting and breaking a keg of the lord's ale and for hearing the news of the shire. The harvests had been good last season and the rents reasonable. Some had grumbled when the overlord taxed them extra grain to fill a common storehouse for the next year's seed. But now they saw the wisdom, for their contributions had been carefully tallied and tended in Lindengreen's ample granaries to prevent the mold and rot that often plagued the storage of seed.

As Holt walked among the tenants that came to Lindengreen, he kept Revan by his side and listened intently to the freely expressed opinions and complaints of the people. He often stopped to inquire about the condition of a farmer's land, a herd of sheep or cattle, or a new addition to a family. He commented to his young ward on the merits of a method of farming, the nature of a rivalry that flared, or an anecdote involving a particular family. Revan attended it all with an unusually sober mein and a genuine interest.

Some of the tenants brought gifts to their overlord, carvings, weavings, or tools made during the long wait of winter. Others petitioned for the felling of certain trees in the duke's forest to provide lumber for the building of homes, the making of tools or furnishings.

Holt saw that each request received due consideration and all came away knowing their overlord had done what was best and right.

Adding color to this hectic scene was Vicar Haldan, who came daily from the rectory in Keenings and threw himself vigorously into the task of acquainting himself with the stream of parishioners and their various religious needs. Since the ignominious departure of the Vicar Alfred, which he had heard retold a dozen times, a dozen different ways, there had been no one to bless the graves, baptize the babies, distribute the sacraments, or marry the feverish young couples. It was pointed out that Vicar Alfred had seen little of his flock before his banishment and it was clear most people felt that an agreeable situation.

But this stout, broad-faced man seemed to them to have possibilities, what with his hearty laugh, his substantial clap on the back, and his twinkling brown eyes. He made it his business to see that every sack of seed grain that left the granary yard was duly blessed. And better yet, he promised a marrying soon at a nearby squire's farm to allow the anxiously awaited start of several new unions and to letigimize a few already begun. It would be a huge, libatious celebration, a fact not lost on the gusty cleric.

Among the last wagons to arrive for seed were two from the Earl of Rentings' household. Seeing the wisdom of Holt's scheme, Lord Cedric had voluntarily provided a portion from his tenants' grain to insure proper storage and good seed in the spring.

Behind the wizened little man who drove the first wagon, rode a smartly dressed older woman holding a young child on her lap. When the wagon stopped in front of the granary, the old man helped the child and the woman down first, then sought out the overlord to complete his business.

"Old Clayton Healey," Holt greeted him by name, surprising the man.

"Yea, lord. Come to get the earl's seed." He wiped one weathered hand on his rough cambric shirt before taking the one Holt extended to him.

"And who's this you've brought with you?"

"That be little Eden Eddys, Lady Eden . . . and her nurse, Mistress Culwain." Old Clayton leaned close and lowered his voice as the two approached them. "I hadta bring 'em. Little missy wanted a ride and tossed a fit. She's spoilt a bit, them always doin' for her." The old man lumbered off to see the steward.

"Mistress Culwain," Holt swept a hand down before him, and Revan stood quite erect and nodded as the solemn woman bobbed before him.

"Your Grace, Master Reston."

Suddenly the white-haired moppet tore free of the nurse's restraining hand and headed straight for Revan, grabbing him about the leg in an unbreakable embrace.

"What!' the young duke exclaimed, looking desperately from Holt to the stoic Mistress Culwain and back. "What's she doing?" he demanded, unused to children and half afraid of being bitten.

"Ah, Your Grace, she's taken a liking to ye. She wants you to pick her up . . . hold her, like her brothers do."

Revan looked stricken at first and Holt laughed, bending down to peel the child's arms from Revan's leg and lift the angry, rebelling form up into the young duke's stiff, uncertaim arms. Immediately the child

325

quieted and stared unsteadily into his face as if expecting something.

"What do I do?" Revan jerked his chin back cautiously.

"Talk to her, Your Grace, she likes that." The nurse folded her hands proudly and beamed at her feisty little charge.

Revan then asked the perennial adult-to-child question. "How old are you?"

"Two!" came the enthusiastic response, with two chubby fingers held up in evidence. Grinning with delight, she threw her arms around Revan's neck and shoved her face into his.

"Her eyes," Revan said suddenly, still wary of her quick movements, "what's wrong with them?"

"Wrong?" Holt frowned concern.

"They're orange in the center, like a ring and blue in the rest. Are they all right?" He stared into the huge, lash-rimmed orbs framed in a cloud of white, silken hair.

"That's just their color, Your Grace. Nobody can figure how they came to be such . . . so different."

"It's like the sun at dawn in the middle of her eyes." Revan grinned in bemusement. "She's kinda cute," he declared aloud, and immediately the flaxen-haired pixie pressed a wet resounding kiss on his cheek.

"He-ey!" Revan drew back as if poisoned, unaware his voice had just cracked.

"You've a touch with the ladies, Your Grace," the nurse chortled. "She don't take up with just anyone."

"Take her!" Revan croaked in a strange voice, all high and low, trying to pry her chubby arms from his neck while he balanced her on one arm.

Holt laughed roundly at Revan's red, mortified face and nodded to Mistress Culwain to take the child. "Try the kitchens," he offered over the cherub's wail, pointing the way. "A jam tart and she'll forget all about her new love, here." He watched the nurse's futile attempts to console the child, who hung over the woman's shoulder, flailing and stretching her arms to Revan until they were out of sight. Then the overlord turned to the young duke, who faced him with alarm.

"What's happening to me? Can a baby give you something . . . make you sick?" Revan gripped his throat, forgetting all about his embarrassment.

Holt frowned thoughtfully and shook his head with the realization of what had transpired. "Nay, you're in no danger. Now, if she were fifteen, you'd have cause to worry." He laughed at the stricken look he received. "Nothing's wrong with your voice." He sobered and put one hand on the lad's shoulder. "But it's time we talked about that . . . and a few other things."

Tauren had watched Revan and Holt with the child, as she had other incidents, from the upper window of the women's house where candlemaking was in progress. She ignored the chatter and clamor about her as she watched Holt lay a hand on her brother's shoulder and lead him away. In the last week she had seen that happen several times, and a fullness that was almost painful rose in her chest. Revan needed a man's guidance, a man's strength, a man's wisdom to serve as template for his own developing character and spirit. It seemed now by bold design, Holt Reston commanded that role in his life, whether for good or for ill. Tauren found a fervent prayer escaping her lips that Holt's influence would be for the good—for both their sakes.

327

She had watched the comings and goings about Lindengreen with curiosity and some amusement as she went about her familiar spring routine. There was much to be done: waxing and polishing both furnishings and floors, airing bedding, plucking geese for new tickings, lowering and cleaning the sooty chandeliers, gathering bloodroot and gentian violet for dyes, gathering mosses and wild onions, calendula and teaberry. . . . In the women's house there was the washing and carding of the wool for spinning. The outside servants consulted her on the planting of the kitchen gardens and she oversaw the general pruning and cleaning of the grounds.

She often wandered toward the graneries, the smithy, or the carpenter's shop. But even as she sought a glimpse of Holt, she reminded herself it was to keep her vow of watchfulness on his care of Revan. That did not explain the fluttery feeling in her stomach or the weakness in her limbs as he laughed or listened intently to their visitors, or displayed a rippling back as he lent a hand with loading sacks of grain or helping to pull a broken wheel from a cart for repair.

Certainly no lord would put his hand to such tasks, but would feel demeaned by even the suggestion of such labor. Holt Reston seemed to enjoy it. And none could call the looks of admiration the overlord received from his people, or the soft, fluttering glances of the women present demeaning. Holt retained his dignity, his presence, no matter what the occupation of his hands . . . even, she groaned to admit it, quite sotted.

Worse yet, something between them had changed this last week, something Tauren refused to ponder, while feeling its comfort, its familiarity. Each night he

328

had delayed his own retiring until he saw Roxie exit their chamber. Then in the darkness he would slip in beside her and kiss her lightly, his hand caressing her shoulders experimentally before encountering her nightdress and turning away onto his side. She was aware that he lay awake for long periods and knew that each passing day brought them closer to renewed confrontation.

Several large barrels, trunks, and crates cluttered the great hall as Tauren entered late that afternoon. Holt's determined words to Murdock and Calder ceased abruptly upon her entry but remained in effect to redden the usually calm housekeeper's face and turn Calder's normally jovial visage to stone. Both looked at her oddly before returning their eyes to his warning glare.

"You do understand me?" Holt lifted one arched brow as he examined each of them.

"Yea," and "Yes, Holt" came their tardy responses, and still they hesitated.

"And is there more you wish to say?" he challenged them.

"Nay, no more." Murdock shot a disapproving look at him before departing for the upper chambers of the old hall. Calder simply settled the elegant crimson hat with its jaunty white plume upon his head and strode heavily through the front portal.

"What's happened?" Tauren frowned her concern at the crates and barrels and then at Holt, whose pensive gaze seemed to touch her intimately from several yards away.

"Nothing to concern you," Holt declared off-handedly. "Some things no longer used and in need of proper disposal." He swept the lot before him perfunctorily with one hand.

"But what—"

"Come walk with me awhile," Holt interrupted, seizing her arm and drawing her outside with him.

Frowning and looking doubtfully back over her shoulder at the baggage, she replied, "I really should go to see about the kitchen gardens. . . ."

"These are busy times," Holt mused, stopping to look down into her sweet frown, "and perhaps dangerous ones. You may as well know now, the king is angered at your uncle's will." He waited for the impact of his words to register on her face before continuing. "He would like the rich prize of Somerset to bolster his sagging treasury and your brother to support his precarious position. I would have you know, I will not let him take the boy. I will do everything in my power to prevent it."

Doubt of his motives showed in the furrowing of her brow. "The king may send for him? But surely the king would see no harm to a loyal—"

"Strafford was most loyal of all and the king sacrificed him to the Parliamentary mob. Once in London the boy would be little more than a prisoner of his own title and wealth, kept apart and watched closely by the king's lackeys while Somerset was slowly bled."

Her eyes were undecided as they searched the depths of his angular face. He took her hand and drew her along toward a stone bench beneath a sprawling oak. Her thoughts were disconnected, and her heart skipped and fluttered annoyingly. He sat beside her, holding her hand in his much larger one.

She stared at the yellow ruffle that rimmed the overskirt of her dusky gold muslin dress. The rustle of leaves, the chirping of sparrows, the smells of the damp earth and new grasses; all seemed magnified to her. With him so near, her senses came alive. Tiny shivers darted through her and she struggled unsuccessfully to recall what objection she had been about to voice before he touched her.

He cleared his throat quietly, small evidence that what he would say made him uneasy.

"I know you do not trust me, Tauren." He lifted her chin on one finger so that her eyes met his. "You have taken pains to tell me so. But I would do nothing to bring harm to you or to Revan. I am sworn to you in vows and to the boy by oath of honor." His voice dropped and softened. "There are times when one dream must be abandoned to seize another fate has brought within grasp." His free hand came up slowly to touch her cheek gently and trace its curve downward to her throat.

She was mesmerized by the touch and immobilized by the fear and hope that struggled within her. His eyes glowed suddenly with his desire for her, and she closed her own in distress. Lightly he pressed his lips against hers.

When he withdrew, her eyes flew open and fastened on his full, curving mouth that had the power to drive her beyond all limits. A second wave of heat poured through her, totally unlike the first.

"Time will prove you, Holt Reston, one way or another." She jumped up shakily and made her way to the graveled path to the great hall.

Holt sat a moment longer, pondering the encounter as he had the week that preceded it. Perhaps tonight he would know.

But that night his hopes fell short of accomplishment again. He waited in the study for Roxie to leave, but Tauren was already abed. When he joined her there and his hand went searching, he encountered that wretched nightdress that told him he must bide awhile longer.

Disappointment brought to his mind the suspicion that she was purposefully prolonging this miserable abstinence. But to confront her on so delicate an issue might be to undo any progress he had made with her in these last days. If she spent more time with him, saw him in other circumstances, other surroundings. He reached out and drew her to him, resting her head against his shoulder and curling about her, spoon fashion. If she were still awake, she made no effort to move away and in this small intimacy both found rest.

Twenty-Five

The low stone wall of the paddock both enclosed the small tenant pasture and served as Tauren's perch for watching the well-tended birth in progress. In the unusual strength of the morning sun, Holt had removed his doublet and shirt, and knelt in the muck of the paddock by a young heifer in the throes of a difficult calving. The young tenant farmer knelt beside him, frowning and Revan, having removed his own doublet, knelt by the poor beast's head.

"It's that bull what's done it," the ruddy-faced farmer complained gruffly before catching himself and tossing a sheepish nod to Tauren nearby. "Sorry, milady, no offense." To Holt he turned a bit and lowered his voice. "'E sires 'em too big for the cows. She'll need a rope, I reckon. Brought one just if we might need it." He retrieved the coil from a worn leather pouch.

"Is this your first from the new . . . animal?" Holt caught himself in time as he took one end of the rope from the man's hand and watched as the farmer tied the other end to the protruding forelegs of the yet unborn calf.

"Aye, me first. And likely me last if Hessiah here dies birthin' it." The man squatted by the beast, looking askance at Tauren's elegant dark riding skirt and jacket; then he turned his back and lowered his voice again. "Ain't right, her ladyship bein' here. It's no sight for—"

"Her ladyship has seen as much before." Holt overrode his concern with an amused glance at Tauren who was rearranging herself gently on her hard seat. The pronouncement settled the matter, but the man shrugged and wagged his head in disapproval as he strained at the rope. Holt flashed a disarming smile at Tauren before lending his back to the effort as well.

Tauren watched it all, bemused. She could not fathom what she was doing here, witnessing Holt and her brother groveling about in the muck of a cow pasture. Just before sunrise that very morning, Holt had awakened her with a smart whack to her lightly clad rear and had ordered her from the bed and into her riding clothes. When she had protested, he had genially reminded her of her vow to "obey," and had snatched up his doublet, belt, and blade as he'd sauntered out.

He seemed far too pleased with himself later when she appeared in the morning room, garbed for an outing in her best dark blue, velvet riding skirt and fitted jacket. He gave Calder cryptic orders about some supplies to be delivered somewhere and dragged her to her waiting mount before she could taste a morsel of the generous feed that lay ashambles on the buffet.

She balked when he made to seat her on the mare, demanding to know where they were going, and received a typically obscure quip about her learning what real debauchery was about.

So, he was tutoring her on the work of an overlord, was he? She shooed a fly from her face with one hand. And just what did he think he'd prove by that? Furthermore, why did he bother? He had her in his power . . . mostly.

But the day wore on and two more tenants received their duke and their overlord before midday. Unfailingly, they were polite, but Tauren perceived a distance they maintained with her that did not mark their interactions with Holt and Revan. At the third farm, Tauren grew tired of the talk of shearing and small legal matters, and drifted toward the small stone huts where the tenant's wife and his mother grappled with their own duties.

Holt found her there later, holding a cuddly, begrimed toddler on her lap while the mistress of the cottage sat beside her plying a churn briskly.

"What a domestic sight you are, wife."

"You might try a weak willow-bark tea for when the teething fever comes on him," she concluded, ignoring Holt. "But add a drop or two of honey, it's bitter." Handing the child back to its mother, Tauren bade the woman a warm good-bye and received a tired smile in return.

She stalked past Holt to where the horses stood tethered and waited while he caught up with her.

"Is it your intention to starve me on this epic jaunt of yours?" she asked, masking her discomfort with a sardonic tone.

Holt stood beside her, gazing down on her upturned nose and pouting lips. He grinned and put one hand to his lean belly as his gaze roamed her. "Nay, I'll not starve you, wife . . . I enjoy your well-nourished curves too well." He lifted her up into her saddle and reluctantly pulled the soft velvet of her skirt down over her shapely calf. Suddenly his head was pounding, and his reddening face betrayed his instinctively lusty reaction.

"I feel hunger's pangs too, wife." He lay one hand on hers where they gripped the reins, and his look stopped her breath momentarily. Not a single tart remark or sharp rebuff could she raise against such honesty. For a minute, they searched one another's eyes, and when Revan came jogging up, he released her and mounted.

"It's a fine day for business," he declared, "and I think I know where tasty fare is to be had."

Calder met them at an old mill site by the stream that meandered through Lindengreen proper. Amidst the downcast and overturned stones that once served the estate, they feasted from a hamper of delicious cold foods from Lindengreen's kitchens.

Tauren plopped down on the grassy slope beside the basket and scrutinized Calder's retinue. Four of his men rode with him while another drove a cart that was covered by heavy canvas. "Calder, what have you in the cart that merits so august a guard?"

"Provisions, milady." The genial captain seemed to color.

When no further explanation was forthcoming, she shrugged away her annoyance and stuffed another bite of the cold beef pie into her mouth.

Holt sat near her while they ate and watched her every movement, as if proving his earlier remark. Even as he ate, she could see the hungry gleam that lingered in his eyes, meant for her alone. His double-edged remarks set Calder and Revan laughing, at her expense, but oddly, she found herself laughing too and swatted him good-naturedly. Her eyes sparkled brighter each time they fell on Holt's manly frame, sprawled casually within reach.

Calder withdrew abruptly, insisting Revan accompany him to see a part of the old mill and learn a bit of local history. When Revan balked, Calder tossed a discreet, meaning-filled frown toward the couple, and the young lord bounded up enthusiastically.

When they were alone, Tauren plucked some grass and began to plait it while she let the easy silence between them prepare the way for her question.

"Why did you bring me here?" She shaded her eyes against the midday sun with her hand and watched his face.

He took a deep breath and sat up, seizing a twig and snapping it into ever smaller pieces as he sorted and narrowed his thoughts.

"I thought it would be good for us to be together somewhere besides Lindengreen. There it is too easy for you to think of me as a power-mad tyrant. And I have work to do here, in the shire. I care about these farmers and their crops and their beasts."

He reached out to stroke one of her hands lightly. "If there is nothing else between us, I would have you know—believe—you can trust me."

She met his eyes fully and felt them pulling at her, turning her inside out. For a long moment they sat, so engrossed that Calder had to clear his throat twice to gain their attention.

"I'll be leaving now." The captain donned his elegant, cuffed gloves and smiled cryptically. "I'll see

337

you on the morrow at the squire's, for the marryin'."

Holt nodded and rose as Tauren made to pick up the cloth and pack the remains of their meal in the basket. She watched him stroll slowly with Calder toward the already mounted cavaliers, and she turned his words over in her mind. Trust. It was what she needed most. But what she wanted most set her hands trembling as she watched the strong easy movement of his muscular legs.

The village of Berensa was little more than a huddle of small, whitewashed dwellings roofed with tired thatch and separated by low stone walls and meager wooden sheds. They stopped to rest and water their horses at the local well. Holt asked a wizened old woman who came to draw water about the smith, who for reasons of ill health had shut down his forge and with it the main source of income for the burg. Nearly every family's survival depended on the forge in some way: wagonmaking, supplying the forge, or feeding and lodging those who came to do business there.

Holt took Tauren by the hand and pulled her along as he paid a call on the ailing smith. They found him on his bed, weak, but well tended by his youngest daughter, a sweet doe-eyed girl of about sixteen. In the end, Holt promised the old man a well-trained apprentice to reopen the forge, ignoring Tauren's quizzical looks. The gratitude in the old widower's eyes was almost painful to behold, and his brown-eyed daughter grabbed Tauren's hands and kissed them with joy and thanks.

When they were a safe distance from the cottage,

Tauren stopped in her tracks and waited for Holt to face her.

"Where will you get a trained apprentice smith?" she demanded irritably.

"Why, Lindengreen." He puzzled over her irritation. "Daniel Fahlen is quite capable and has no family I know of. He'll do well here."

"But what of our smith? He's old—"

"But is strong as an ox and has plenty of time to finish training the two younger lads." He started to turn away, but seeing her scowl, turned back.

"How do you know he'll want to come? Maybe he won't like it here!" She was exasperated with his cool answers and the smug handsomeness that made her lose control.

"Did you see the smith's little daughter? He'll like it here." This time he strode away and Tauren traipsed after him angrily, seeing the full scope of his plan.

"How do you know she's not spoken for already? Maybe she loves someone else!"

Holt stopped and breathed out heavily, making his sufferance plain. "If you knew this village, you'd know, there are no families with sons of suitable age. With the forge down there's little possibility she'll make a match outside the burg. At sixteen, why do you think she's still at home?"

It all fit, Tauren realized furiously, every single piece! "Another bit of the world laid to rights by the mighty overlord of Somerset," she bit out caustically. Was this how he planned her future?

"Don't you ever get tired of arranging other peoples' lives? What makes you think you can do it so much better than they can?"

Holt's face tightened. He was trying to show his best self, to rein his temper, but was losing to that something in her that defied his neatly logical grasp on his world. She was the one thing in his life he could not control, and increasingly, the only thing that mattered to him. This ridiculous sojourn was proof enough of that.

"I do it because I do it better!" he yelled, propping his fists on his hips and sticking his square chin out adamantly. "Most people don't really know what they want or what they need, and they're ignorant of the possibilities all around them. I simply save them the time and effort they're too ignorant—or indolent—to put forth. In short, I do it well because I do it well!"

"That's why you killed my betrothed and forced me to marry you! Because it was what I needed and wanted, but I was too stupid to know it!" She was nearing fever pitch and Holt's stubborn honesty had dispensed with verbal combat in one last revealing blast.

"No! With you it was different!" he bellowed. "It was a matter of time, as much as anything. It was obvious Sappington was repulsive to you and the wedding was set too soon."

"Repul—"

"Afterward"—he shouted down her protest—"you had no inclination to let me woo you and court you properly and I couldn't wait around forever for you to fall in love with me. When the duke gave you to me, I decided to see the vows read first and let the rest come later. I wasn't about to lose you!"

"Well, this time you were wrong, overlord," she spat out. "I didn't want you!"

"But you do now, that's all that matters."

She should have shouted her denial at his hard, retreating back but for some reason she stopped, floundering in angry confusion and unsure where to proceed next.

They were mounted and riding toward another farm before she ventured to look at him. His mood was as dark as the color of his garments, his face seemed carved from dusky granite. Knowing herself the cause of his distemper, she felt no triumph at all.

Why did it infuriate her that he was always so cursedly right . . . about everything? The arrogant rakehell! Disposing of her as though she were a dumb beast—chattel—then expecting her to fall gratefully into his bed at the first opportunity! Did he think she had no pride at all? The thought pinched her sharply. Pride. Of all the deadly sins, she had been taught, pride was the most insidious, the most corrupting . . . and the most eagerly defended. Now she experienced the truth of the good bishop's teaching all too vividly, in herself.

What honor was there in this ongoing battle that neither won and both despised? How would it hurt Revan if she overcame her pride to find some joy, some peace in her marriage . . . in her days and nights with her husband?

It all came back to the same point, a wearisome and disturbing circle. If she let down her guard, gave in to her feelings and began to trust him, would he betray them if a more promising opportunity presented itself? His arrogance was astounding, no matter how uncannily the circumstances seemed to bear out his judgments. Could she trust her husband with their

341

future . . . with her heart?

That evening they stopped at the house of a prosperous tenant who delighted in sharing the fare of his table with them and offered his own down-soft bed for the night. To Tauren's aching horror, Holt refused, accepting only a few blankets with the announcement that they preferred to try the hay loft in the new barn. Tauren was bone-weary and past argument as he helped her up the short ladder to their rustic bed. She spread one heavy blanket on the hay and collapsed atop it, caring little for the humbleness of her surroundings. She breathed deeply of the pleasant, clean smells of new lumber and sweet hay and was instantly asleep.

Holt smiled at her relaxed form and slipped down beside her, spreading another blanket above them and molding himself protectively about her. Revan had found a soft place nearby and rustled about until finally comfortable. When all was quiet, Holt nuzzled the nape of Tauren's neck and realized she slept. A wry smile admitted his defeat—for the night.

Holt shouldered his way through the press of onlookers and assumed the magistrate's seat, his customary black seeming more somber and settling a grave, important air about his raven hair and intense forest-hazel eyes. Once each fortnight he served as magistrate in the four major villages of the shire, today in Cornis.

Tauren sat beside Revan and Calder at the back of

the taproom where court was held and watched his entry with a strange twinge of pride in his powerful bearing and striking figure. She was disposed to judge his justice harshly, but as the day wore on, she found nothing to fault and much to ponder, if not admire.

The court witnessed a stream of small complaints and petty offenses, each of which was treated with the same even-handed consideration. Holt's standards of justice were simple and his punishments likewise; each member of the village or farm must both conform and contribute. Therefore, drunkards were barred from alehouses and made to work, vandals became indentured to their victims, poachers and animal abusers were themselves whipped, and slanderers and other cheats stood in the stocks.

At midday, a paunchy, officious young squire dragged a rebellious tenant before Holt, demanding his imprisonment for the debt of rents not yet paid. Holt heard both sides and his tone was even as he pronounced his decision.

"You, sir,"—he addressed the squire—"are apparently correct, the rents are in arrears. To you goes the judgment—though not as much as you desire and more than you deserve." He looked pointedly at the smooth, fleshy hands of the faddishly dressed young owner and smiled contemptuously. "Seeing it was your land that failed this farmer's seed, you too must bear some of the loss. You will return his seed to him immediately so that he may plant anew. And you, farmer"—he shifted his burning gaze from the blustering squire to the slack-jawed tenant—"you spent precious little time plowing and planting for it cannot be done from the taproom of an alehouse. Your family is hungry and your squire is angered. To send you to debtor's prison would assure you better treatment than you have afforded them. You will work hard this season under the squire's watchful eye and will pay double rents for this new crop. Then you will work the winter in the squire's barns to provide for your family."

Next he sentenced a poacher to prison for a second offense and, after calling witnesses to testify to the destitution of the man's family, arranged that the wife and two children be brought to Lindengreen to work for their keep until the man was released.

Tauren watched, spellbound, as Holt sat, judging and arranging the lives of these people as though he were born to the role. Some of his judgments were harsh for the offender, but mercy always tempered his dealings with the families and victims of the miscreants. She watched the clean, angular features of his face, the moods and emotions that this stream of humanity produced in him working like a subtle sculptor upon them. Occasionally, he glanced toward her while deliberating, and always he looked thoughtful, not self-assured, nor concerned, only thoughtful. Tauren's heart never failed to tumble into her stomach.

It was a long and tiring day and in the afternoon when the hearings were done, Holt ordered the taproom reopened and the tavernkeeper provided them with a tasty meal of cold meat pie, tangy cheese, and fresh bread topped with pale, creamy butter. When Holt ordered their horses brought around, Tauren felt like moaning, "not again!" Her whole body ached at the thought of climbing aboard that beast.

Some audible evidence of her thoughts must have escaped her for Holt took her hand and squeezed it, an understanding look on his square, handsome features. "It's only a short ride to Squire Dennison's. Haldan is no doubt there already, preparing for the festivities."

"Festivities?"

"The marryin'. Don't tell me you've forgot!" He waggled his brow in mock horror.

"All right," she murmured. "I won't tell you." He chuckled and pulled her against his side with one arm in a half-embrace. Hearing his irresistible good humor, she couldn't stop herself from smiling, or from enjoying the feel of his hard, muscular arm about her. When he put her on her horse, her ladylike expression of gratitude became instead a cozy smile that lingered on her lips for at least a furlong.

Twenty-Six

The small, cobblestoned court of the squire's comfortable, half-timbered house hummed with activity as Holt's bay stallion threaded its way forward through the mob of people, carts, and animals. Near the door of the main house, Holt helped Tauren dismount and watched raptly as she brushed her skirts and straightened her fitted dark blue jacket about her waist. The heavy oak door of the house swung open with a bang and a pleasant, graying man of middling years emerged, his arm outstretched in welcome.

"Master Holt, you honor us at last." The squire beamed his delight, clasping Holt's arm and shaking it vigorously. "Double the honor at such a festive occasion! And this must be Lady Tauren . . . and welcome to Your Grace." He bowed smartly before a rumpled, but still noble Revan. His deep voice and lively brown eyes exuded a contagious good humor. Tauren liked him immediately.

A thin, smartly dressed woman came from the house

behind their host, greeting Holt stiffly and Tauren not at all.

"Mistress Claire," Holt responded formally. "May I present my wife, Tauren Reston . . . and of course, you have met the young duke."

The narrow eyes flitted coldly over Tauren's finely tailored blue riding skirt and lace-trimmed jacket, and she nodded slightly before turning to Revan. "Welcome again, Your Grace." Her smile was forced, its unpleasantness accented by her pinched features and small chin.

The dame's tacit disapproval slapped Tauren with unexpected virulence. She glanced at Holt from the corner of her eye, wondering what could have made her this enemy without her even knowing it.

The squire took her hand as if in apology and hurried her toward the house. "I've given orders to prepare our own rooms for you and Master Holt—"

"*Our* rooms?" The mistress of the manor whirled on him and halted him in his tracks. He turned to face his choleric wife with a meaningful look of warning. "I knew you would want Master Holt and his lady to have our finest, wife. Is that not so?"

The woman's face tightened, and her arms crossed and tucked tightly about her waist. The silent wait for her response belied her control.

"Yes, of course . . . the best. And where will His Grace sleep? And us, of course?" This thinly disguised challenge to her husband's generous impulse was clearly understood by all. She would not honor Holt and Tauren by abandoning her own comfortable quarters to them easily.

"We have a slew of rooms, wife. I leave the selection to you." The squire quickly ushered Tauren and Holt inside.

The good Vicar Haldan drew himself up straight and smoothed the split collar of his office that lapped over the neck of his black cassock. With august bearing he called for the nine pairs to come and stand before him in the lowering evening light of the courtyard. He personally positioned them, two by two, in a semicircle around him to better view them as he spoke the words of union. Then he began in somber and sonorous tones.

It was a motley group of varying ages, mostly poor tenants dressed in rough woolens and scrubbed cleaner than was their custom. One young woman was seven months gone with child, and another held a small bundle in her arms, rocking it gently to preserve the hushed silence that had fallen upon the participants and those who watched. No lofty cathedral could have inspired more reverence than the commanding devotion of the good vicar.

From her nearby seat at a makeshift planking table, Tauren listened to Haldan's clear, resonant voice and the weighty words of the honored prayerbook. She had heard them read over herself barely a month before, but had not truly listened. She listened now.

"Holy," "honorable," "obey," "comfort," "love" . . . It was what she had promised Holt before God himself. Her throat tightened and her eyes stung. Their marriage was a mockery—a lie to the world and before the Almighty. Her hands were tightly balled into fists in her lap, and her back was rigid as she sat on the rough bench. She wanted to be anywhere in the world besides here, suffering this excruciating reminder of all she was not and had not.

Something brushed her skirt at the side, and she turned to find Holt squeezing down onto the bench beside her. She jerked her head quickly back to the rites being performed, not wanting him to see the telltale moisture in her eyes. For a long, breathless time she waited, focused entirely on the absorbing press of his lean body along her right shoulder and side. It sent a shocking course of warmth through her, causing her to shiver with surprise. Her heart picked up its pace, and her face flushed annoyingly with the strength of her attraction to him. Something in his hypnotizing self-assurance, his mastery of every situation, the raw physical power of his unusual eyes, the easy grace of his magnificent body brushed aside her burdened reflections.

He claimed her hand with his and drew it over onto his hard-muscled thigh, placing it palm down and covering it gently with his own. For some inexplicable reason she left it there, even when he loosened his grip and began to stroke its softness reassuringly. It was a small, quiet intimacy, one a true husband and wife might share. Her body sprang to a life of its own, humming with this awakening. It was all she could do to sit still. She stole a look at Holt and found him staring down at her, an exceptional softness in his forest-flecked eyes.

This time she did not turn away, but allowed him to touch her fully, intimately with his gaze. And when his

349

eyes flickered briefly toward the good vicar and returned to her, she felt the eloquence of the gesture all through her and affirmed it with a new warmth in her face. It was as though Vicar Haldan read those words for them too; they shared the same thoughts, the same wonderment.

How much time passed before the reverie broke around them, neither could say. It was Tauren who tore herself away and plunged back into the present, blushing prettily and looking around at the crush of instant merriment that assaulted them. Holt still clasped her hand tightly beneath the table and she smiled at the knowledge.

Her forced interest in the commencement of the music, the congratulations, and the tapping of a monstrous keg of ale was rudely arrested when she spied Mistress Claire across the table and several seats away. The lean, uneven features of the woman's pinched face were sharp with an open malice which took Tauren's breath momentarily. She stood up, bringing Holt up quickly with her since he would not relinquish her hand.

"We should greet these newly wedded couples," she said quickly, desperate to find a reason to escape the woman's unmerited wrath.

Holt's sinewy arm helped her across the bench, and with a murmur of approval, he pulled her hand through the crook of his arm and led her into the noisy throng of celebrants. She was introduced over and over to a sea of bright and joyful faces, slowly comprehending that Holt seemed to know every one of them by name and residence. They greeted her warmly and offered heartfelt congratulations to the overlord on his marriage as well.

Squire Dennison's ample voice rang out above the burgeoning celebration, to call them to a toast—the first of many to be offered—to the king's health. Next he toasted the newlyweds' happiness, the young duke's prosperity, and the overlord's bride. And on it went until a short, stocky fellow with the neck of a bull and a shock of wheat stubble for hair, jumped up on a bench to lift his mug to the overlord of Somerset who, he announced, had provided this generous wedding feast himself!

Tauren stared at Holt with surprise and he grinned sheepishly.

"It doesn't do to run out of ale or wine in the middle of a good debauch, nor to drink copiously on an empty belly."

Tauren looked hard at him, but a betraying laugh escaped her and she pushed him away good-naturedly. "You!" she complained, recalling the cart of provisions that had several of Calder's cavaliers as escort. "You might have told me when I asked what was in the cart."

"You would only have accused me of stealing your brother blind." Holt eyed her warily.

She gasped indignantly. "I . . ." She blinked and looked perplexed. "I . . . probably would have." She laughed at her confession. It felt so good to laugh . . . with him.

Holt stared at her, oblivious to the press of people about them, treasuring the warm, velvety feel of her laughter against his pride-chaffed heart. Her slender hand was on his full, dark sleeve, resting—perhaps,

351

testing—and he covered it with his own.

Later, the reedy, thumping strains of a country tune wafted toward them as they finished their plates of lamb pie, sliced ham, tangy cheese, and dark, nut-rich pudding. Tauren had downed half a flacon of ale which, with the rich food, conspired to make her feel oddly content, sleepy.

Holt leaned toward her and murmured, "The night is young, but if you would seek our bed . . ."

Instantly, she was wide awake, straightening her drooping shoulders and forcing her eyes open. "Nay," she answered nervously. "I enjoy a wedding dance." The torches, lit and bracketed on posts about the courtyard, bathed Holt's handsome face in bronze, and she had to stay her hand from seeking it. She turned to the dancers whirling and stomping nearby.

"Then, dance with me, wife."

Later Tauren sank gratefully beside Revan on a bench set beside the brick wall that enclosed part of the front court. She pushed back a wisp of her usually tidy hair and loosened the top few buttons of her jacket, wondering idly what she must look like after two days without so much as a brush, sleeping in barns and enduring sun and wind. She smiled contentedly. Whatever the state of her dishevelment, it did not seem to deter her husband.

Revan was pulled to his feet by two giggling young girls and was shamed by their teasing into enduring the dancing. While she was pleasantly engaged in watching the amusing spectacle of *His Grace* trying to tame his gangling frame in imitation of the other dancers, someone claimed the seat her brother had vacated.

Tauren found Mistress Claire examining her with icy eyes and a frosty smile on her thin lips.

Tauren acknowledge her presence with a controlled nod and turned her gaze back to the dancers that swept by her. What had she done to draw this woman's blatant censure upon herself?

"'Tis the curse of the low classes"—Mistress Claire's hand indicated the pregnant bride who sat sprawled on a nearby bench fanning herself—"rutting and breeding without honorable vows." Drawing Tauren's wary eye, she smiled maliciously. "But then you would already know about that . . . your background being what it is."

It was a crude slap, and the woman gloried visibly in the duplicity of her phrasing. But at least now Tauren knew the reason for the woman's hostility toward her. Mistress Claire had heard and believed gossip about her previous relationship with the overlord. Tauren stood abruptly, squaring her shoulders proudly.

"Yea, my father was a bishop of the church, and he often lamented the weakness of morality. But he detested even more those hypocrites who presume to piously judge others while their own hearts are filled with hatred and pride. He advocated Christian charity in dealing with all men."

Mistress Claire was on her feet. "Charity indeed! And is it your Christian charity that enables you to ignore the overlord's crime, the murder of the good Earl of Sappington? And that while Roger sought to defend your . . . honor?" She spat the last word as if it befouled her mouth.

"It was well witnessed, a fair and proper duel,"

Tauren's face burned and her voice rose as she struggled valiantly to control her careening anger.

"You defend him, then . . . your husband? You prefer the bastard to a true nobleman of honorable and ancient family?"

"Honorable?" Tauren nearly choked with rage. "I do not presume to judge any man's motives, but I assure you, we will differ on that which we name 'honor'! A man cannot help how he is born, but can learn to bear himself with dignity and courage. And he can deal with others honorably as Holt Reston has dealt with my brother and with me!"

"You made the worst of the bargain, lady. Blood will tell in the end. You'll rue the day you bedded the common bastard to cuckold my cousin!"

Cousin! So that was it!

"How dare you!" Tauren raged, incensed and seeing only red before her eyes. Instantly, her hand went back in a wide arc and just as quickly was caught firmly by some unseen force. She stumbled back and found herself clasped tightly about the waist and being hoisted up. She knew instinctively it was Holt's iron-thewed arm that held her securely above the ground so that her toes barely dragged it despite her struggles. He carried her quickly away from the fracas and toward the limit of the circle of torchlight.

The music wheezed and swayed on, but several of the dancers and some seated at the tables had stopped stock-still, staring at the confrontation of the squire's haughty wife and the tempestuous lady of the shire. Across the widening distance, Tauren saw the furious, scarlet-faced squire dragging his snapping, snarling

354

wife into the manor house, and it gave her grim pleasure to witness this scene. Only then did she notice the faces that followed her own departure, the bewilderment and lurid interest her outburst evoked.

"Let me down!"

Holt laughed and put her on her feet only when they reached the shelter of a massive oak tree, where he turned her about to face him, searching her face in the bright moonlight.

"I'll thank you not to interfere."

Holt laughed broadly, putting his hands to his waist and bringing her thoughts to an embarrassing halt. "Sweet, you can't go about bashing other women in the face, no matter how richly they deserve it. Real ladies are well above such things."

"Don't you laugh at me, Holt Reston!" Tauren realized furiously that he must have observed the revealing exchange. "She insulted my honor, my marriage vows, and my husband! Do you expect me to stand there and suffer that viperous old crone in holy silence?" His refusal to see the seriousness of the incident flamed her anger.

"I won't be ridiculed and defamed to my face by that vicious, ferret-faced— I'd sooner be impaled! And you . . . She called you a bastard and a murderer!" She poked his hard chest forcibly with one outraged finger.

"So have you, my love . . . in most ungracious and unrelenting terms." Holt's eyes danced with amusement in the intimate light.

She snapped her chin back abruptly, struck dumb by this potent reminder. She *had* accused him of being both—and worse! Now she defended him and her

355

forced marriage like a she-lion defends her cubs! What was happening to her?

"Still," Holt drawled and eyed her speculatively, "it's heartwarming to know you're so willing to defend me, despite my decadence and debauchery. Or better yet . . . that you're changing your opinion of me."

"Don't be absurd." Tauren reeled from the accuracy of his assessment. It was true. His unsubtle and well-charted campaign to win her trust—or at least her cooperation—had proved a resounding success. And something in her was perversely pleased by that patiently pursued triumph.

"Are you?" He moved forward stealthily.

"Am I what?" she demanded irritably, finding her gaze transfixed on the knowing curve of his full lips.

"Warming to me?" he murmured, quite near and filling her senses.

"I . . . don't know," was the best resistance she could muster when her knees were turning to water and her stomach was aching hungrily.

He engulfed her, crowding out her indigation and surrounding her with his all-encompassing presence. He touched her face gently with the back of his knuckles.

"I think you are." He bent slowly toward her, holding her heart-shaped face and pressing her lips with his.

Her limp arms gradually came to life as he folded her close against him and they circled his waist eagerly. Her embrace caused him to straighten and he drew her lips along with his, pulling her up onto her toes.

On the lids of her closed eyes, Tauren saw bright and

dazzling lights; the hot, molten reds and flame-seared golds of ransomed passion. They burst like colored chinese rockets, sending a shower of burning sparks through her entire body. His strangely hard and soft lips tugged at something in her chest as they poured over hers, imploring, then demanding a pliant response.

The warm buzzing of the night air about them found resonance in Tauren's blood, and her hungry young body molded itself against Holt's tempered and potent maleness. He was raw power, ruthless potential, now focused on the giving and sharing of pleasure with her.

Holt's head was pounding and soaring in dizzy spirals as his hands caressed her back and the tantalizing curve of her small waist. Her sweet, cloverlike scent filled his head. The ripe softness of her breasts burned into his chest where they pressed against him, and his hands searched lower for the maddening roundness of her hips and buttocks.

He shifted his kisses downward, nuzzling open the unbuttoned top of her jacket to claim the warm fragrant flesh of her throat. His mouth burned a trail along her skin and when it could go no farther, his hand worked the hindering silver buttons that winked invitingly in the moonlight. He captured her breast in his lean, supple hand and teased it until Tauren was limp against him and gasping. His tongue followed his hand, pushing aside the thin gauze chemise and tantalizing the dark, erect nipple that was linked inexplicably with her woman's hollow.

When his hot kisses continued down, across the light barrier of her garment, she felt the erotic chill of the night air on her damp nipple and the excruciating tightness of Holt's arms about her waist and hips. It was a moment before she comprehended that he held her off the ground completely, his bulging, corded muscles crushing her to him and his muscular thighs flexed and braced to support them both.

"Holt," her husky call brought his face up to hers and she took its raging heat between the slim coolness of her hands. His eyes were glazed and heavy with desire for her and Tauren responded with a passionate look that snatched his hard-won breath.

"Put me down," she ordered gently.

With a sanity that Holt himself disbelieved, he complied, holding her gently against him, knitting up his tattered control.

"Let's go back," he rasped with all the smoky, dark persuasion of the conspiring night. His lips were against her hair and through her open jacket she could feel the jumping of the muscles of his arms. The sheerest margin of will maintained his control.

Tauren pushed him back a bit, her head throbbing as she nervously fumbled with the buttons of her bodice, still encircled by his magnificent arms.

"Where can we go . . . to . . . sleep?" her thoughts were clearing and she recalled the reason she had been dragged from the celebration.

"To our rooms, love," Holt murmured, wondering if she would find in these awkward logistics a new reason to deny him.

"I'll not sleep in that cloying old harridan's bed!" her eyes flashed with remembrance.

"No doubt you won't," Holt observed dryly, finding

the perfect goad. "Knowing that, Mistress Claire would be incensed—probably consider it defiled—and never sleep there again." His knowing look conveyed the teasing challenge.

"On the other hand," Tauren took up his line wryly, "the squire would be embarrassed if we spurned his fine, soft bed for the cold comfort of a crowded, drafty loft. He's a good man. . . . We daren't abuse his hospitality." She waltzed away from him, finishing the last buttons of her jacket, and swept him a thoroughly desirous look before swaying back toward the flourishing celebration . . . and the squire's big, inviting bed.

Holt rested one spurred jackboot on the bench by Revan, laughing with Calder and the young duke as Tauren entered the manor house ahead of him.

"I never thought to see the day she'd defend the likes of ye, Holt Reston. Seems right pleased to be married to yer bastard hide." Calder shook his head with exaggerated wonderment, grinning. "And the old dame— Lord! I've waited years to see her made speechless!"

"Taurie's a sight when she's got her temper up," Revan observed sagely, burying his nose in a mug of ale.

"And when she doesn't," Holt agreed wryly, glancing toward the door of the manor house where Tauren had disappeared.

Calder caught his eye with a knowing, almost envious, tilt of brow, and Holt found his own face reddened by the captain's clear access to his thoughts.

He straightened and took the mug of ale from Revan's surprised grasp.

"Enough of that for you, Duke. Calder, see this young man gets a night's uninterrupted rest—and soon." Revan's belated protest fell unheeded on the cobblestoned paving at Holt's back, mixed with Calder's stoic laughter.

Twenty-Seven

Inside the squire's big, paneled bedchamber, Tauren's fingers fluttered nervously about the heavy braids of her hair. A little maid hurried about, turning back the soft linens of the draped poster bed and setting out clean toweling and fresh water in the pitcher of the washstand. Tauren did not see the girl leave nor did she hear the door as Holt opened it.

Holt found her seated before Mistress Claire's mirror, bodice unbuttoned, her hair a rippling and waving mass of soft tangles. He watched her tame the wanton mass as he removed his jacket and poured water to wash. He felt every stroke of her brush as a touch of her hand down across his loins. Finishing hastily, he took the comfortable chair near the cold hearth to watch her.

The time for decision was past. Tonight Tauren would give her husband that which he had learned was hers alone to give—herself. She looked at him and found him staring at her, a strange softness on his sharp, aristocratic features.

She slipped the jacket from her shoulders and soon undid the ties of her skirt and single linen petticoat. She turned to Holt in her thin, knee-length chemise, hair rippling in burnished sable waves across her shoulders and swinging about her. Her hands trembled.

Holt sat, index fingers posed against thoughtfully pursed lips, studying his beautiful wife. She knelt before him and surprised him by tugging off his massive boots, leaning them carefully against the cool stone of the dark hearth. Her determination to trust him, to play the willing wife, was written calmly in the firmness of her jaw, and a sudden painful squeezing grabbed Holt's chest. Reaching for her hands, he drew her up on her knees before him. Her sable-rimmed eyes were the color of robins' eggs as she knelt intimately between his legs; they darkened to azure.

Tauren saw the frown that flitted across his brow and paused, wondering, until it passed. She could not have known the irony that produced it; the heady wine of victory which, when fully drunk, led only to greater thirst. She was his now; in moments he would claim the smoldering prize of her full passion. But now he felt a more relentless and terrifying hunger that would not be sated even by the feast that would soon be before him.

He shoved these disturbing thoughts aside and drew her lightly clad form up onto his lap. She laid her head against his shoulder and sent one hand to explore his aquiline nose and the granite plane of his cheek, stopping to press a fingertip against that place where, infrequently, a dimple appeared that ruined her resolve. She leaned up to kiss the spot as she had often longed to do and found her move produced an embarrassing tenderness between them, more intimate than anything that had gone before. It was the first kiss she had ever given him of her own will.

He was up and striding quickly for the bed with her in his arms. He placed her in the middle of the bolsters and stripped off his remaining clothing. Sinking down beside her, he kissed her deeply and felt the warm delicious dartings of her tongue in response. One of his hands traced her curves through the light garment, fluttering down across her flat stomach and raking across the inner curve of her thighs. A tremor surged through her and her pliant hands began a long-sought exploration of his hard, fascinating body, discovering the sweet spots on his back and sides that made him writhe eloquently when she raked her nails across them.

Holt showered light kisses on her cheeks and nose and chin, flowing on to the hollow of her throat where he nuzzled and tasted the faint saltiness of her cool satin.

Even with her eyes closed she could see his dark head; his hard, arrogantly sensual features; and the shining, raven blackness of his shoulder-length hair as he teased and nibbled her tingling nipple. His hand captured her other breast, kneading and caressing it expertly . . . lovingly.

He tugged impatiently at the bodice of her chemise and she pushed him back abruptly, smiling coyly as she grasped the hem of her garment and drew it quickly over her head. It floated to the floor somewhere, and she braced herself, her hands on her knees, as she shook her chestnut hair about her.

"If I'd let you do it, I'd have had naught to wear tomorrow." She laughed huskily. Her eyes caressed his lean belly and well-muscled chest unashamedly, and her hands soon followed, wandering up to encircle his neck as her lips came to his and her silky legs slid down his length. His laughter died, a mere gasp in his throat.

He let her stroke his chest, his hip, his thigh experimentally, surprising himself again with his restraint, marveling at the pleasure she gave him freely.

They lay facing one another and Holt reached down to draw her leg up about his hip. He felt her startle as his hand cupped and stroked her buttocks. His lean fingers stirred her woman's body like some primitive unction meant to salve his inflamed passions. She lost track of thought, even breath, as he drew her deeper into the plummeting vortex of sensual pleasure. She felt his hardness, his strength all about her and she clasped him to her with complete abandonment, pressing against him in a sweet agony of arousal.

Suddenly she was on her back, his hard thrusting weight above and between her damp thighs. She pressed her quivering breasts upward against his chest as she urged him inside her. He devoured her skin, her lips, then her breasts in a frenzy of desire, pushed to the edge of oblivion by her throaty moans and murmurs.

Her cool hand on him, jolted him back from the precipice, and he drew back, still joined to her, to look at his Tauren. Her dark-fringed eyes were closed and her passion-bruised lips were parted by short, quick breaths. She arched exquisitely with each deep, sure thrust.

He saw no more. All his reason exploded in a blinding crimson flood of feeling and response. She grasped him to her tightly, hoarsely uttering his name over and over, meeting each surge with an eager motion of her own. He carried her deeper, faster, no longer separate from her, unable to distinguish boundaries between her body and his own.

The burning, unbearable fullness of her loins suffused her entire body, robbing her of breath and blinding her with sharp flashes of silver in passion's pervasive crimson. The blaze exploded from her loins, searing up through her to send burning cinders against her skin from within. She was drowning, suffocating, clasping Holt's plunging form to her savagely, feeling through this maelstrom his simultaneous eruptions in her very veins.

They hung together on the edge of existence, souls torn from flesh and fused inseparably in the white heat of passion's forge. When they returned to the corporeal, it was as two keen edges of some rare, marvelous blade—separate, yet only together were they fully one.

Some time later, Tauren spiraled back to reality as Holt lay beside her, drawing her against him. Contentment flowed from her every pore and she nestled cozily within his familiar, hard frame. Her hand searched above her head to trace the lightly bristled outline of his jaw. He caught one finger playfully between his teeth and ran his tongue over its soft tip. Tauren tilted her head back and found his eyes glowing golden upon her. She smiled contentedly and stroked the crisp hair of his chest with her cheek.

"I thought for a while I might be dying," she murmured softly.

His amusement reverberated in her ear, and she

looked at him with puzzlement. He tucked her head back against his chest and stroked her face reassuringly. "Such pleasure never killed anyone."

"If it had"—she threaded one silky arm about his waist and hugged him briefly—"I wouldn't have minded." Again she felt his amusement as it found resonance in her body.

So that was it, she mused sleepily . . . his "special power" with women. Roxie seemed to know about it, the way she flirted and ogled him openly. And Charlotte too. Charlotte had openly praised his prowess. . . . Suddenly she was not sleepy at all.

"Do . . . your others . . . feel this pleasure?" she blurted out, feeling her face redden at the naïvete and jealousy her query betrayed.

Holt tilted her chin and shifted his position to better view her. He knew what she was asking and it sobered him. His lips brushed her forehead.

"There are no others now, nor will there be," he declared softly. "Pleasure such as we have made for each other is rare, Tauren."

"But . . . after so many others . . ."

"Tauren." He stopped her with a warm, searching kiss. "I have never felt such pleasure with a woman before. You are very precious to me, wife." His hazel-green eyes reached inside her, caressing, convincing her of his truth.

Whatever reply was half-framed in her mind, it was obliterated by his earnest assault on her heart. She curled her fingers about his damp, raven hair and pulled his mouth down to hers, possessing it boldly.

The exhaustion of the long day and the celebration

finally overtook them, entwined about each other, and they slept until the earliest morning beams found their windows.

Tauren's waking was slow and warm, nestled as she was against Holt's side. She forced her heavy lids open and turned to look at Holt, finding his profile silhouetted by the waxing light of the dawn. A smile born of contentment was on her lips, and it soon took on a knowing curl. She was abed with her husband . . . with Holt. And yet she was still very much herself after the night's wild loving, even after the shattering discovery of her own woman's pleasure.

She flushed bodily at the recall of it, feeling the tactile memory spreading through her loins and under her skin. Her lightly bruised lips and rosy nipples tingled and her fingertips and palms itched with eagerness. Shocked by her wanton responsiveness to the strong memory, she sat up quickly, only to find herself stopped short. Part of her heavy fall of hair was tucked securely under Holt's relaxed shoulder. She chewed the corner of her tender lip in concentration on the hopeless task of freeing it.

She did not notice his hand moving up behind her stealthily, just out of sight, nor the widening crescents of his eyes.

"Oh-h-h!" she squealed as Holt's arm snaked out and clamped about her bare waist. In an instant she was on her back with Holt's dark, perfect face above her, his body covering hers.

"Holt!" She meant to sound exasperated, but it came

out too husky, too earthy, to be a true reproach.

"I like the way you say my name." He grinned wickedly, then imitated her passion-hoarse whisper from the night before. "Holt . . . you work a certain magic with it. I've never particularly cared for my given name, but when you say it like that I'd not be called anything else in the whole world."

Tauren flushed deeply, seeing his hazel-green eyes roving over her bare shoulders to fasten on her taut nipples.

"You . . . surprised me. I thought you were asleep." She could hardly bear it when he talked of her and him . . . of them being together, loving. It made her ache all through.

"I have further surprises in store for you, my little wife." He winked at her and his smile curled insinuatingly as one hand slid down her bare side. Her blush and sputter of embarrassment brought a rumble to his chest, and he shifted higher and to one side, propping himself up on one elbow to watch her. He dropped light kisses on her forehead, eyelids, and the tip of her nose before claiming her mouth sweetly.

"You're what must be called a 'blushing bride,' love. An enchanting term . . . I never fully appreciated it before now." She turned her head slightly away and Holt guessed rightly the source of her chagrin. "Tauren, there's no harm in a man's honesty with his wife, even in matters of the bed. I expect—nay—demand the same of you."

Her face came quickly back to his and he kissed her pert nose and fully curved lips to staunch her protest.

"I pleased you last night, did I not?" He trapped her gaze with his, and beneath his hard, warm weight, she had no recourse but to answer.

"Yes." She became scarlet.

"And you, enchantress, drove me to the ends of sanity—beyond mere pleasure. I knew all along how it could be between us. This"—he ran one big, sinewy hand down her bare side and felt the trill of her response—"is what men and women were made for—each other. The two become one flesh . . ."

She parted her lips to speak but lost the will in her confusion and wonderment at her acceptance of what he espoused. His kiss probed the inner depths of her response without the need for words.

"Wife—" He drew back, his eyes changed and glowing darkly.

"Tauren," she corrected him, sending one hand to trace the well-defined outline of his lower lip. "I am Tauren and you are Holt." The tip of her tongue peeked out to trace her own lip even as her fingertips followed his. "I am your wife and you are my husband." Her voice was low and full of promise as she declared and affirmed their changed relationship.

"I've asked no more of you, Tauren, but to be my true wife." His face sobered momentarily. "I would replace the past with sweeter memories . . . for us both."

His earnestness, his entreaty filled her chest and threatened to pool in her eyes. A moment passed and then she nodded wordlessly, her eyes admitting that she wanted nothing more in the whole world.

His face relaxed, and Tauren realized that in the pause tension had collected there. He really wanted this marriage, wanted her. She was stunned by the knowledge and in equal measure by her joy in it.

"My beautiful wife, my Tauren," he stroked her, making a thorough, loving inspection of her face with his lips and gentle hand. "I can hardly look at you without my blood stirring. Whatever wrongs you think I may have done you, I have been punished twice over with the agony of wanting you."

Suddenly light and almost floating, Tauren clasped his heated face between her hands and stared up at him with seductive smoke in her gaze.

"You were a beast . . . it served you right," she murmured, her mouth curving into an inviting bow. "But justice must be tempered with mercy."

She pulled his head down sharply and possessed his lips, holding nothing back as she blistered his mouth and body wherever he pressed against her. They rolled and pressed and kissed, exploring, joining, yielding to the hunger in each other as they came together with the hot brilliance of colliding stars.

There was no reining Holt's long-checked passion, nor curbing Tauren's long-denied response. They arched and coupled in nature's most sublime and primitive rhythm. All time and existence—the very cosmos itself—hung suspended about them before they plunged into the violent waves of searing heat and blinding, pulsing light.

Later, Tauren turned drowsily to Holt and ran her fingers through his raven's-wing hair as he slept. This coolness, this peace, she thought, was worth everything else. It had taken so long, on so perilous a path, but now it was theirs . . . always.

*　　　*　　　*

Summer settled unusually dry upon the lands of Somersetshire. Lands often too damp for planting were seeded and the meager rainful kept them well nourished. The unseasonably early cessation of frost had resulted in an abundance of apples, plums, and pears in the orchards, and a profusion of walnuts, hazelnuts, blueberries, and raspberries. Lindengreen's modest vineyard promised a full, sweet crop for the making of wine, and the kitchen gardens flourished under Tauren's watchful care.

The harmony of the season was echoed in the blossoming relationship of the overlord of the shire and his lady. Many pairs of eyes witnessed Holt's eagerness to be near Tauren, to lend a hand or a strong arm as she went about her numerous duties. More than once, he saddled horses and escorted her to a tenant's sickbed to administer her herbal cures. They smiled and laughed openly, and teased in the way of courting lovers, touching hands and stealing sweet kisses, mindless of the inquisitive and sometimes envious looks they drew from soldier and servant alike.

Tauren seemed to glow every time his unusual, forest-filled eyes fell upon her; it was a change so dramatic and genuine that all witnessing it wagged their heads at her demure smiles and charming manner with her husband. All too well the staff and guard recalled the violent sparks of their clashes, the lady's openly displayed contempt and the overlord's arrogant determination. But there was no denying the change in them, nor the positive effect it had on everyone they touched.

Roxie was quick to display her wholehearted

approval on the change in her lady's attitude and comportment. "I was beginnin' to fear ye'd never learn what a man is for," she declared saucily one morning as she worked her mundane miracle with Tauren's locks. "Master Holt's such a lovely piece of manhood it brought tears to me eyes to see him goin' to waste so."

"Roxie, you surprise me," Tauren countered, not affronted. "I never dreamt you had so thrifty a nature. Perhaps I should watch more closely to see just where you apply yourself to such frugality."

For once, Roxie reddened and clamped her mouth tightly shut. The response was so uncharacteristic that Tauren laughed and made a mental note to be more observant in the future.

Calder occasionally laughed and chided Holt about his monkish habits of early-to-bed-and-early-to-rise and his sparing indulgence in spirits or games or company of an evening. Holt smiled with decidedly unmonkish satisfaction and quipped that the captain should consider the compensations of taking such vows himself—if he could find a woman dim-sighted and simple enough.

Revan's rapidly maturing eyes searched with new-found eagerness for the opportunity to turn the happy situation to some benefit for himself. In such a blissful atmosphere he might ease the one real discomfort left in his easy, privileged life. When he approached Tauren on the subject of his tutor, he was considerably put out to have her defer thought on the matter until Holt could consider it as well. He took it up after supper one night.

"Master Wickestrom's health is poor and Calder

already instructs me in riding and archery; you teach me the sword." Revan had worked out a plan and now, with Holt's thoughtful nod of encouragement, he launched forth upon it.

"Why not allow the good master to retire to his books . . . give him a modest pension," he added with a judicious flash of inspiration.

"Then how would you continue your studies? Training on a field is no substitute for a sound knowledge of law, history, and letters in the world of courts and powers." Holt glanced at Tauren and found her particularly engrossed in needlework of some kind.

"I'd thought of that," Revan countered solemnly. "Vicar Haldan is most accomplished in history, philosophy, and languages . . . even geography. I could study on my own—and he could examine me."

Holt was silent a long time and Revan hastened to add weight to his argument.

"I know the vicar is busy, but surely he could spare us a day each week to hear me and assign my studies. We get on well . . . I'm sure he wouldn't mind."

One day of the week? Holt smiled, knowing now the aim of the young duke's maneuvering. "A fine proposal," he declared, slapping his palms down hard on the arms of his chair. "Well thought out and succinctly expressed."

Holt caught Tauren's gaze as she lifted a puzzled brow. The glint in his eye both piqued her curiosity and reassured her that he had more in store for the innovative young lord.

"What do you think, Tauren?" Holt drew Revan's

uncertain regard to his sister's calm, beatific countenance.

"I?" Tauren's astonishment was a bit too wide-eyed. "I have full confidence in your judgment, Holt. Do as you see best. You are his guardian."

It was Holt's turn for bemusement as he watched her return casually to her stitching. She had sweetly thrown the decision at his feet, and he turned to find Revan rocking up onto his toes, satisfaction oozing from him.

"Then, we'll have Haldan moved in by week's end . . . and you may begin lessons even earlier." Holt rose and smiled judiciously at the lad.

"Moved?" Revan puzzled. "Start earlier?"

"Excellent idea, Duke. But if one day a week is helpful, think of five or six. We can get another vicar to help with the parish duties and Haldan can serve Lindengreen's chapel and your tutorage exclusively."

The full picture was dawning in his mind and Revan didn't like the looks of it. "But, I only meant to—"

"No expense is to be spared for your education, Duke, and no effort unmade."

"But"—Revan was grasping for objections—"Taurie might not like having *him* living here."

They both turned and Tauren lifted a sweet smile to their inquiring looks. "I admit I had reservations about the vicar in the beginning, considering our unfortunate introduction." She cast an eloquently reproachful glance toward Holt. "But he has proven himself a devout, if unconventional, man of God. He works hard and is pleasant of countenance and conversation."

Revan's face fell as the hoped-for dissension failed

374

to materialize.

"It's settled then," Holt declared genially, clapping the red-faced Revan on the shoulder. "We'll ride to Keenings tomorrow morning to fetch Haldan and I'll arrange a pension for old Wickestrom." Holt paused, watching Revan struggle manfully with his disappointment. "I'm glad to see you show such interest in your preparation, Duke. Learning to shoulder such responsibility willingly is a hallmark of maturing."

Revan mumbled something approximating gratitude and withdrew to his chambers, scuffling his bootheels despondently on the way.

"Well done," Tauren was chewing her lips to still her mirth and finally gave way to a low musical laugh. "If Haldan applies his usual brute enthusiasm to Revan's education, Revan will soon rue the day he advocated sacking old Wickestrom."

"Um-m-m-m," Holt agreed, resuming his seat and watching her speculatively. "You played the reasonable, deferring wife quite well."

"You musn't let my performance mislead you," she warned with a twinkle.

"Nay, I have run afoul of your well-disguised shoals too often for that." He grinned, stroking his chin with one knuckle and roaming her with his eyes. He was remembering the previous night's romp with a demanding vixen in his bed. Her darkening, lowering eyes betrayed her recall of the same.

"I thought it best you handle Revan, man to man. He is of an age now, and certainly of a size, which makes that desirable, and his gambits are increasingly clever. Dealing with him, I think we'd best present a united front."

Holt was on his feet.

"Do you think we'll make an effective alliance?" she murmured as he took her in his arms and bent his dark head to nibble her neck.

"Um-m-m," he growled agreement from against her throat, ". . . formidable."

Twenty-Eight

"Ouch!" Holt cast a leery eye at Tauren and shoved his injured finger into his mouth. "Are you sure those things are so important to our health and well-being as to hazard my blood in obtaining them?" He inspected his pricked digit and pouted.

"Rose hips are very important, Holt. They're wonderful cures for a host of common winter complaints"—Tauren pocketed her small knife in her apron and went to inspect his damaged hand—"ague, croup, pleurisy . . ." It was as she expected, a scratch or two and a prick here and there. "Poor dear, you're much abused by this arduous duty." She chewed the inner corner of her lip and eyed him appreciatively. Then she kissed his reddened fingertips in leisurely fashion, allowing her tongue to wander over each one. She looked up at him through her dark, feathery lashes and tilted her chin down. "Perhaps I've worked you too hard."

"That you have, heartless hoyden." Holt's muscular arms enclosed her in a flash, his lean hands playing up and down her back as her face turned up to his. "I demand compensation." His lips covered hers hungrily and she rocked up on her toes to meet him.

The afternoon sun was strong for early autumn, and on the air were the sweet smells of drying grasses and of the summer's last roses fading nearby in their thorny bower. A light breeze ruffled Tauren's loosely bound hair and tugged at her soft woolen skirts, but she was aware of little besides Holt—the comforting hardness of him about her. It was always like this for her. His touch seemed capable of ridding her of all other thought, and sensation. He filled her arms, her head, her heart, whenever he pulled her to him and began that mesmerizing prelude to loving.

"I think"—she struggled to speak against his mouth—"we have enough . . . rose hips for today." Every word seemed a sacrifice to sanity.

"Um-m-m, perhaps you have—but I never get enough." His hands slid lower to her well-curved bottom, and he caressed it expertly, even through her skirt and petticoats.

"Not enough . . ." she murmured and abandoned herself to his kiss, his overpowering sensuality. In a fleeting return to reason, Holt grabbed the blanket from the hamper that had carried the food for their outing and drew her to the privacy of a thick copse of trees near the secluded glen. Tauren sank to her knees on the leaf-cushioned blanket and drew him down with her.

Holt entwined about her, reveling in the softness and coolness of her skin, the crisp resistance of her corset, and the yielding, rose-tipped mounds above it. His bare chest covered her breasts, and he felt her wriggle maddeningly against him. She returned his kisses eagerly, pulling that peculiar, chest-crushing wanting from his once impenetrable recesses.

Holt caressed and excited every part of her, finding her scant clothing more an enticement than a barrier to his attentions. She encouraged him, sending her hands along his sides and over his muscular back.

It was enchantment: the sun-dappled warmth; the early autumn smells of dark earth and forest bed; the tall, graceful canopy of trees sheltering them. When Holt came to her, completed her, Tauren cried out, lost utterly in the powerful grip of her feelings. He moved gently at first, then, as she matched his eagerness, he rolled to his side and onto his back, carrying her with him, until she rode astride him, still joined to him.

Instinct overcame her surprise and she seemed to know what he wanted. She moved above him, lost in the bold, uncharted realms of pleasure where he led her. Experimentally, she sat upright and produced in Holt a shattering explosion of passion that spiraled her upward in its wake until she, too, seemed to burst the bonds of human form. She extended, expanding as pure light, beyond mortal substance and infinitely one with the elements of being.

Holt held her close to him, feeling the wetness of her face against his shoulder and the shivering little sobs she tried in vain to quell. He was at a loss to explain her tears, knowing she found the same joyful release he had reached in their loving. But this time, there was no chest-wrenching pain, no bewilderment, only a small, painfully sweet ache near his heart as he drew her still closer. He smiled wistfully. It was almost gone, that anger, that hunger, that wretched agonizing need. It was Tauren who produced it in him, and now it was his lovely, infuriating Tauren who supplied the remedy. How had he? . . .

. . . gotten so mixed up inside? She sighed, stopping the trail of one salty tear with a quick dart of her tongue. It all seemed so simple now, loving him as she did—*loving*! She started so that Holt tilted her tear-streaked face up to his. Yes . . . She was instantly lost in the warm, verdant forest of his eyes. They were soft, giving, perhaps even a bit . . . loving. She loved him! The idea settled in with astonishing speed, and once expressed, it seemed so completely entrenched that she wondered how long she had been concealing it from herself.

Watching the play of his own passions, his own overwhelming emotions in her eyes, he smiled sympathetically.

She sighed. It was as if he read her heart each time he turned those extraordinary eyes upon her. No doubt he already knew just how she felt about him and waited smugly for her to discover the truth of it. He was always so right, always so perfectly in command . . .

. . . never predictable, always clever, ever desirable. . . . Whenever he began to feel sure of her in his grasp, some new aspect of her asserted itself to elude him. But this, he had this much of her . . . and perhaps a bit more. . . .

"Had I guessed the potential in such outings, you'd have had a constant companion." Holt broke the long, productive silence.

"Had you assisted me so ably on other outings, our herbal stores would be nil." She found herself blushing for no reason she could name.

"I'm glad you find my 'assistance' pleasing. You were not always so complimentary," he teased.

Tauren turned onto her back, still snuggled close to his chest. "Strange how things work out," she mused. "A year ago we met in a glen not far from here, on an afternoon much like today."

"From that day I've been a marked man"—Holt groaned, touching his lip—"bitten, then gone mad with some delicious, exotic fever that recurs whenever I see you, touch you, or even think about you."

"You function marvelously for a man afflicted with such delirium."

Holt's face brightened. "You think so, eh?"

"Um-m-m." She copied his customary affirmation and kissed him soundly. "Marvelously." He hugged her so tightly, grinning broadly, that she could barely breathe but had no desire to protest.

"I wish we didn't have to go back." Some time later she stared up at the boughs high above them and at the patterns their graceful wind-dance made on the sapphire of the sky beyond. His only response was rubbing his cheek against her hair near her temple. She turned her head on his arm to look at him, needing to search out and deepen this incomprehensible something between them.

"Sometimes there, at Lindengreen, I look at you and you're a stranger to me. I cannot fathom your moods or motives. Here it seems so different—you seem different."

He shifted slightly, searching her. "Here there are no decisions to be made, no mischievous young lords, no

Parliament, no greedy squires, no boundary disputes . . . only warm sun, soft grass and a delicious young wife to share them with." The sharp lineaments of his face seemed softer and the lines of strain she never recognized until now had eased to erase several years from his handsome countenance, both delighting and disturbing Tauren.

This was new, this awareness of her overlord-husband. She had never imagined him as anything but controlled, powerful, compelling. With a flash of insight, she knew that such control had a cost for him as well. Men like Holt, and her father, disliked their world's assumptions, givens, and limitations; and they set about reshaping it, each in his own way. And each willingly paid a price for the control they seized.

"Tell me about you—when you were a boy . . . where you lived, who raised you . . . where you've been." She ran her hand down his braced arm to draw his hand to her lips and kissed its slightly salty palm. She sat up as he rolled to his back, tucking his hands behind his head.

"It's not a particularly edifying tale," he declared flatly.

"Nevertheless . . ." Tauren pulled her knees up to her chest and rested her chin on the little valley her petticoat made between them. She watched him expectantly and he looked at her thoughtfully, making his decision.

"Nevertheless." He surrendered and received a warm smile for his tractability. "I was sent to a small manor on the northeast coast to be raised by the good squire Jennings Ryton. They had two sons and three daughters before I came and they gave me their family name, although I later learned that the duke prevented them from adopting me fully." He paused and shifted his gaze upward through the boughs above, as if seeing through the past to that time and place. He spoke slowly as the images appeared before his mind's eye.

"They were good people—I grew up thinking I was their son. I had a plump, motherly nurse, a raft of playmates, and my own pony to ride. When I was seven years old, the duke sent for me during the summer, and I had a hard time understanding it, them making me go. But he insisted and slowly I began to realize there was a tie between the old man and me. I spent those long summers here at Lindengreen—in the kitchens, the barns, the stables and mill.

"By the time I was twelve, I had heard enough servants' gossip to guess the old man was my true father. It explained the way he watched me and quizzed me and seemed to evaluate me constantly. I suppose I was proud, thinking I was the duke's son.

"He sent us fine tutors and books; he set a generous income that meant a comfortable life for the squire's children as well as for me. We all had education and introduction befitting nobility."

Tauren found herself frowning with bemusement . . . the old duke had behaved more generously than she would have expected. . . .

"When I was seventeen"—Holt's voice lowered— "the squire died and it was then I learned the truth; I was not the duke's bastard, but his unlucky wife's. I discovered, too, it was no tender motive that commanded my yearly sojourn in Somerset, but the old man's gnawing, perverse desire to see my mother's face incarnate in me and perhaps by some physical

383

similarity to divine my dishonorable paternity." He stopped and swallowed the bitterness that rose inside him afresh with the remembrance. His hand came up to bridge his nose and press away a phantom pain at the corners of his eyes.

Tauren reached for his other hand and squeezed it tightly, as if to apologize for insisting on his painful revelation. It jolted him and he stared at her, his eyes filled with uncertainty. A small, tight smile under warm, sympathetic eyes stopped him for a moment, and then he too smiled, a wan expression unusual on the overlord of Somerset.

Tauren could see the young lad he had been, not long past Revan's age, still in Holt's face and in his seldom-revealed heart. She longed to gather him up in her arms and love him fiercely until all the hurts of his past melted away.

"That year, I left the squire's house and changed my name from Ryton to Reston. There was little honorable to do but go to sea or soldier. I chose the latter. My size and training at arms insured I did that well from the start. I crossed the channel to find employment in the wars of France and in the Baltic." He spoke slowly, seeming very remote. "A man far removed from the true source of his hatred makes a horribly efficient soldier.

"It is the smells of battle that seem to stay with me—fresh blood, the acrid burning of the timber skeletons of dying villages, the stench of the unburied. . . . I killed that old man a hundred times over, in battle. When I thought my anger spent, I came back to Somerset five years ago.

"The shire was a sty of corruption and abuse—both

of power and of people. So I took it from the old reprobate. I felt he owed me something. I still believe that, only . . . now the debt is mostly paid." He stopped suddenly to look at her, slightly embarrassed by his own loquaciousness, his unusually free revelations.

"Paid?" Tauren shrugged.

"He gave me my mother's dowry upon his death . . . a considerable sum. And that is my mother's ring you wear." His voice softened a bit.

Tauren stared down at the heavy gold and ruby ring she had received at their vows, the ring she had considered the degrading symbol of his ownership of her. She had difficulty seeing it just now.

"And of course . . . he gave me you."

Holt sat up and drew her into his arms, his brow furrowed with some unshared concern as he struggled for words.

"Tauren, I am not an easy man, I know. I have many responsibilities I cannot share with any other. But, I do what I know to be right, even when it is unpleasant to me personally."

She pushed away long enough to nod. He wanted her, and it seemed he needed her as well. There was no other he could trust and confide in, no other with whom he could share his private self. She could be that for him—woman to his man—the compliment and completion for him that he might be for her. Here, in his arms she felt love, given freely, now returning fourfold.

Their ride back to Lindengreen went all too swiftly. They chatted about small things and laughed together, their minds and hearts delightfully truant from the press of duty. But as they crested the rise nearest the sprawling great hall of the estate, a scarlet-clad figure on horseback kicked into action and made for them at breakneck speed. Tauren looked at Holt and saw once again the erect shoulders and firm, faintly disdainful expression of the overlord of Somerset. How easily the mantle of duty slipped back upon his broad shoulders. She felt a sharp stab of regret.

"King's men!" the cavalier declared as he reined up before them. "The captain set watches out to warn ye." The pleasant-faced young soldier nodded to Tauren respectfully and cast a sidelong glance at her while he lowered his voice. "We knew not where to find ye, sir."

"How many?" Holt demanded, urging his mount forward at a walk, forcing the soldier to fall in beside them.

"A full score, Master Holt. Escort to a court's officer . . . a lord . . . somebody."

"When did they come?" Holt's expression was firm and calculating. "Did they present credentials?"

"Something, sir. Mistress Murdock sent for Calder over an hour back. He set men about, conspicuous, and sent us out."

"Holt!" Tauren turned to him in alarm. "What do they want?" His stony silence gave her the very answer she feared. The king had finally made his move on the young duke and the shire. "What can we do?"

"You"—Holt turned to her forcefully—"will go straight to our chambers and stay there, whatever befalls." He turned to the soldier as they entered the side court. "Where is the duke?"

"I cannot say, sir."

"Then find Murdock and see the boy joins his sister in my chambers . . . *go!*" The young cavalier wheeled and dashed for the rear of the great hall.

Tauren started to protest her orders, but Holt's horse was already halfway to the main doors. Her eyes narrowed. She'd not be relegated to cowering in her chambers, even if it were for her own protection. He must expect some violence!

Dear God! He would not let them take Revan . . . he'd fight first; he'd declared it! She drew up quickly by the side court entrance and slid from her saddle.

She ran a hand over her untidy hair and rumpled skirt, thinking quickly. She was in no condition to confront an emissary of the king. She would go to her chambers . . . but not to hide!

The front court was ringed with a handful of men in plain scarlet, tensely juxtaposed against an equal number in the distinctive black and red uniforms of the king's personal guard. Both sides waited anxiously for a sign from the great house before them. The swift arrival of the big man dressed in somber Puritan garb arrested the invaders' attention and several fingered sword hilts nervously, looking to their sergeant, who also seemed uncertain.

Holt bounded from his mount at the marble steps and stood atop them surveying these potential adversaries with a serene, commanding manner. When his piercing eyes fell on the sergeant they persuaded the seasoned soldier against any restraining action. After all, the sergeant reasoned conveniently, the Puritan was but one man. What harm could he do? And there were these others to watch. . . .

Tall, slender Ransom opened the massive door and to Holt's terse inquiry responded, "In the salon, with the captain . . . and them."

When Holt gained the door to the great room, he found Revan seated in the middle of the room, looking strangely small and drab in his plain woolens. A stout, florid-faced man in extravagantly multicolored clothing hovered menacingly above him. Spotting Holt, Revan stood up abruptly, banging against the colorful lord in his haste to be away.

"Here is my guardian now . . . Master Reston." Revan escaped the man's range to stand near Holt, shifting his feet awkwardly. "This is Lord Auden, Earl of Claxton."

"Sir." The overdressed nobleman eyed Holt's dark, meaning-filled raiment and raised one brow loftily. "Then it is to you that these are addressed." He recovered two rolled and sealed documents from the nearby table and presented them matter-of-factly to Holt at full arm's distance.

Holt made no move to accept them, placing his still-gloved fists on his hips instead. "The royal seal . . ." he mused openly. "The king sends a better class of messengers these days. Things must be dire indeed."

Lord Auden stiffened as if slapped and his face reddened. "The royal prerogative may not be ignored."

Holt paused as he took stock of the young lieutenant who stood near the front-most window. "You can tell me the contents; there is no need to waste time." He crossed to the sideboard and placed his hat there, removing his dark gloves with deliberate slowness. "What would the king have of us? You do know your

388

mission, do you not?" Holt's eyes were flinty as he turned again to face the portly lord.

Auden drew up to his full height and tapped the rolled parchments against his open palm angrily. "I remind you, Reston, that I am an agent of His Majesty"—by Holt's continued display of indifference, he was goaded into revealing—"sent to bring the young duke back to court."

"Ah-h-h"—Holt smiled humorlessly—"that." He propped one shoulder against the great arching doorway, reading Calder's cautionary frown. "My Lord Auden, what is there in London, at court, that is counted so irresistible that grown men prance and posture to receive that coveted bid?"

"His Majesty wishes to become acquainted with His Grace the Duke of Somerset." Auden's voice dropped and his irritation rose in direct proportion to Holt's disdain.

"A friendly little invitation, issued at the point of a score of blades," Holt jibed.

Auden followed Holt's gaze to the young officer. "They ride as escort—protection for the young duke and myself on the way. We are to depart as soon as possible. Charles is most anxious. . . ."

"To inspect the boy firsthand?" Holt finished disagreeably. "When will he be permitted to return?"

"I . . . am instructed only to fetch the boy. You will make him ready at once."

"Him alone?" Haldan filled the portal behind them with his ample, cassocked frame, his incongruous blade hanging at his side. "Nay, it cannot be. No nobleman appears at court without his retinue, his company. And for a proper court invitation, a stay of at least three

389

months is required. Is he invited to the palace, or must he provide the expense of his lodgings as well?"

"Who are you?" Auden demanded imperiously.

"Vicar Haldan, counselor and tutor to His Grace. The lad has never been to court, indeed is new to the ways of nobility."

"All the more reason for him to be at court, finding his proper place."

"Surely the king has more pressing business. . . ." Holt interrupted, drawing the lord's ire back to himself.

"The king would know who his supporters are."

"The duke is loyal to King Charles. Indeed, the old duke was most generous with his sovereigns. The young duke is prepared to show his loyalty in similar largess." Holt smiled coldly.

"Coin is not my concern," Auden declared irritably, noting the slow drawing together of the priest, the soldier, and the guardian about the lad. "We will take the boy with us to the palace."

"The duke stays here in the safety of his home." Holt's right hand went to the hilt of his blade and at that signal, Haldan and Calder copied him.

Auden glanced hurriedly at the young lieutenant and back at the threesome angrily. He would not see his mission come to failure. Charles had entrusted to him the securing of the boy, and thus Somerset's coffers.

"You, Reston"—Auden forced an easing in his own stance and noted uncomfortably that it produced no corresponding relaxation in the overlord and his men—"you are a powerful man here, I am told; there is power to be had in London also. The king has no commanders well versed in warring; there has been peace in England for more than seventy years. You could be near your charge and yet make your own place at court."

"You offer me a commission in a nonexistent army?" Holt snorted his contempt. "My concern is the duke's welfare. His place, and therefore mine, is here in Somerset. The lad was to foster with Strafford . . . and the king tutored us well on the fate of those he offers his confidence and protection. Half the ministers are fled; there are riots and civil disorder everywhere in London and war hangs imminent in the air. Into this the king commands a young boy to see to his courtly education? I think not. Tell me, my good lord, if the lad were to die in one of these unfortunate upheavals, to whom would the estates fall? Would they not be crown property by nightfall?"

"How dare you intimate—"

"I dare because I am an audacious bastard who will not deal in lies!" Holt snarled, his dark face a dusky red.

"Then we must take the boy," Auden threatened, casting a look at the officer that started him for the window and for his blade.

"Gentlemen!" Tauren's richly feminine voice and instantaneous presence between them threw both sides into confusion.

"Holt, dearest." She flew to him and under his furious glare, she put her hands on his and forced his partly drawn sword back into its sheath as she talked. "Something is amiss? There is bad news from London?"

Holt watched the careful expressions she made for him alone change from astonishment to determination and back again. "Lord Auden has come to escort your brother back to London—to court." He wrestled with the urge to grab her and shake her. This was his arena . . . and his duty. Before he could act, she was out of reach and facing the stout nobleman.

"Lord Auden?" She felt the man's hostile glare pressing on her, examining her; but she did not shrink from it. She would endure anything that might forestall the bloodshed that would bring the king's wrath crashing down upon them.

"An escort for the duke to court?" she echoed, a bit too blankly to the ears of those who knew her well. "How gracious of His Majesty. But of course he cannot go." She whirled on Holt. "Holt, you cannot let them take him!"

In the silence that seethed and crackled about them, Holt ground his teeth in frustration. The stubborn little fool! If only he had grabbed her when he had the chance.

"Tauren—" Holt growled, starting for her.

"Well, just look at him!" Tauren avoided his grasp smoothly as she grabbed a reluctant Revan and dragged him between the antagonists with her. "He has not a thing to wear," she declared, drawing several pairs of incredulous eyes to her slender hand as it swept the lad in demonstration.

Revan glared stonily at her, failing to comprehend her ploy. "Tauren you meddle in things which—"

"—are rightfully my concern, your education and presentation at court." She turned sleekly to a slightly unnerved Lord Auden. "Forgive us, but there have been so many changes in so short a span. We have concerned ourselves with my brother's education and training, never dreaming a summons to court would come so quickly."

"Tauren—" Holt was beside her, taking her arm tightly in warning but she ignored him except to pat his constricting grip in what appeared an indulgent, wifely gesture.

"Let me see," she brought her fingertips together against her thumb as if mentally reckoning an important sum. "The tailor in Keenings is adequate, though unimaginative . . . fittings"—she nodded against that mental tally—"and of course, I must have new gowns. I could never be seen in these old things." Her disdainful expression and disparaging hand indicated her violet velvet and brocade, cut in the latest fashion and worn over the indispensable farthingale. No one could have mistaken the gown for an "old thing" and Holt's shoulders eased of their own accord, seeing her game played so effectively against the ostentatiously attired lord. She had intuited his vanity, and with feminine charm had exploited it unabashedly.

"Of course, there will be servants—and likely a house to procure, unless we're all invited to the palace. Ransom, Roxie, Mrs. Murdock"—she enumerated them on her fingers, acutely aware of every disbelieving eye turned upon her—"Richard, the young duke's valet, and Vicar Haldan, so as not to interrupt his lessons. I doubt we've even proper trunks!"

She stopped abruptly, pressing her fingertips to one temple and closing her eyes against the awesome task of preparation she detailed so dramatically.

"And of course, the duke will have to make his sovereign a gift—that will take some thought." She snapped back to the present. "If you are to accompany

393

us, my Lord Auden, you will have a long wait—two months at least. You're most welcome to stay with us. . . ."

"That is quite impossible, my lady. I must return to London within the week . . . and with His Grace."

Tauren shot him a dazzling smile, perfectly calibrated to warm his chilled resolve. "Sir, my father and my husband have positively convinced me that *nothing* is impossible." She smiled with an engaging hint of mischief. "We shall see."

She left Holt's side to extend her hand to the king's messenger, and he took it with a wary look at Holt's granite-hard countenance.

"I fear we've forgotten our manners, my lord. You and your men must be famished. . . ."

And she led the lord past the bemused assembly and into the great hall where Murdock had nervously awaited the outcome of the lady's gamble and now hurried to do her part.

Late that night, after Holt had bolted the door of their chambers, he tucked his arms across his broad chest and turned a solemn stare upon Tauren as she lithely tread about their room in her wonted rhythm of evening.

"I could have strangled you this afternoon," he scowled, "interfering . . . you might have been caught between blades or taken hostage."

"But I was not." Tauren stopped folding a towel and laid it on the washstand. "Nor could I have slunk to my chambers and cowered under my bed while the blood of my husband and brother stained the floors of

Lindengreen. I would and will interfere again to prevent such folly." Her jaw was firm and her eyes flashed her determination, even as she held her breath. She had dared much with him and was not assured of his forgiveness.

"It would not have been our blood—"

"Nay." She set her hands to her waist, her face reddening. "Likely it would have been the king's man, a member of the ton and a peer of the realm who lay dying in a sea of gore in our salon. Then with you and your men declared outlaws and murderers, what would happen to us, Holt . . . to Revan and me?"

Holt was silent a long time as he searched her eyes, his thoughts as clouded as his face. She had interfered with his duty . . . and worse. He had dropped his guard in the warmth of an afternoon's tryst and she had used it against him. A sharp stab in his chest tripped his breath. It was something he would not forget.

"You've saddled us with him for at least a week. What makes you think you've won aught but a few days. Auden may yet fight for the boy. He is not as soft as he appears."

"The count is plump and highly placed." Tauren explained her reasoning for the course on which she had launched them. "I think we may gamble that his desire to prolong his comfortable and privileged life exceeds his zeal to accomplish Charles's errand. In this week, he will see us begin to make plans to come to London . . . probably after Christ Mass. He will take that and a fat purse back to the king and will explain most nobly."

"Um-m-m," Holt pondered her reasoning and reluctantly affirmed her statement. "Charles does not truly want the boy, he wants Somerset. He wants financing and support . . . and one day soon, he will want men at arms." He stopped abruptly, his expression unreadable, and began to unbuckle his sword and prepare for bed.

"We will send Charles a fat purse indeed and some trinkets as tribute. It will pacify him for a while." He sat down heavily in the chair near the fire, resting his elbows on his knees and gazing at the flickering halo of destruction about the logs.

Tauren rested one shoulder and her head against the massive mahogany post of the bed, and watched him. She had never seen him so pensive, so . . . troubled. Instinctively, she knew the weight he bore; he held all their futures in his hands. And she recalled her own insights of the afternoon . . . which now seemed strangely distant in time.

As he pulled off his boots, she went to help and then sank to her knees and sat by his feet, leaning her head against his thigh.

"I'd hate to see Lindengreen and the shire stripped of its riches," Holt mused, "but it may come to that."

Tauren looked up at him with all the warmth of their afternoon in her face. "Holt, the land will always be here. The other—the gold and silver—what is that compared to having Revan safe with us . . . being together?"

His smile was tight and brief. "I do not trust Auden."

"Then watch him," she adjured.

"I sent Ransom to sleep in Revan's chambers as a precaution. I think it best he be under escort until Auden is well away."

Tauren's eyes widened slowly, and her smile became

a giggle that grew to hearty, musical laughter while Holt's frown deepened.

"You sent Ransom . . . I sent Roxie!" She gasped, adding an insinuating wiggle of her brow.

"Um-m-m." Holt nodded, breaking into a wry grin as he made sense of her statement. "Then perhaps I should send someone to guard Ransom."

Tauren was in his arms, showering his chest with kisses that dropped mischievously down across his ribs. He caught her up against him and ringed her neck with nibbles, laughing at her shivering squeals. And for a brief time the doubts and tensions of the evening melted away before the warmth of their loving.

Twenty-Nine

The next day, Lord Auden toured Lindengreen, escorted by Holt, Revan, and Tauren. His lieutenant was never far behind, but the outward tensions were greatly diminished. He was impressed with the granaries and stables, and rose to near eloquence in praise of Lindengreen's fine kitchens. But the old duke's library was of particular interest to him, and he returned there repeatedly in the evenings, always escorted by Holt.

During one of Auden's inquiring strolls, he came across the upper doors leading to the old hall of Lindengreen. They were chained heavily and padlocked, bearing dusty evidence of their disuse. That afternoon, Auden confronted Holt in the great hall to inquire about it.

Holt was quick to reply. "I've had it locked until repairs are made—plaster falling, beams and braces weakened. I'd not endanger His Grace, nor even the servants, in that wing. We'll see it repaired during the winter when there is little to do outside."

"Of course," Tauren murmured, hiding her surprise. "I thought . . . but we certainly would not endanger Lord Auden. Well, do you drink tea, my lord? It is becoming our custom to have it every afternoon about now."

As they wound their way into the main salon, Tauren wondered at Holt's statement. She had never witnessed falling plaster nor unsound beams or stone in the old hall. She did not even know it had been locked. Well, she told herself, perhaps it was a ploy to hide some of Lindengreen's treasures from the lord's appraising eye.

As Tauren had predicted, Auden departed a week later bearing generous gifts and the young duke's pledge of loyalty along with his own thorough intelligence of the shire. With his departure, the great house resumed its routine of preparation for the coming winter months . . . and now prepared for the journey as well.

The Earl of Claxton took his time along the way back to London, feeling unwelcome ambivalence about the course he had been persuaded upon. He stopped that night at his favorite inn, only to find his customary accommodations occupied by . . .

"'t other gentleman." The innkeeper blinked balefully. "I didna know ye were coming and I let 'im 'ave it." The little man cringed from the portly earl and the thought of his imperious wrath.

"Then give him your second best . . . move him out!" Auden demanded.

"Move out whom . . . and by whose authority?" came a thin, nasal baritone from behind him.

Auden turned to encounter a tall, lanky man of fastidious dress and a hauteur that fully matched his own. Auden's bushy brow shot up with irritation. "It seems this lout has let my usual rooms to someone else by mistake. I am on a mission for the king and cannot be hindered and delayed by such bungling. Who are you, sir?" A man of some substance, he thought privately, tempering his tongue and manner.

"Glenford Chester, Baron of Greers," Lord Chester intoned importantly, appraising this potential adversary with like frankness. He was not in a mood for generosity just now, his pride having been dealt a crushing blow by Charles's refusal to hear his protest of the young Duke of Somerset's guardianship. He had not even been granted audience, only informed that the king would not discuss the matter with him and dismissed.

A mission for the king, eh? Chester mused. A careful bit of politicking might turn this irksome clash of rank to some advantage. His instant change of heart was manifest on his long face.

"This churl failed to inform me the rooms were promised to another." Chester tossed a sneer at the innkeeper. "Whom do I have the honor of addressing?"

"Auden, Earl of Claxton, emissary from His Majesty, King Charles."

"Sir, I am delighted to make your acquaintance." Chester's hand went to his chest and he dipped his head slightly. "As a loyal subject of our gracious king, I insist you take the rooms and I wish you godspeed for your mission." He barked at the anxious innkeeper, "See to it, man!"; then turned to Auden with a fresh expression of elegantly casual interest.

"Allow me to offer the best wine this humble establishment may offer." Chester postured carefully, sniffing his lace handkerchief and fluffing his ruffled lace cuffs. He gestured to a modest wooden table near the fire of the inn's taproom and followed the stocky earl there.

As the tavern maid poured thick, red wine into the pewter wine cups, Auden removed his butter-soft riding gloves and shrewdly appraised the gentleman before him, wondering what the man sought to gain from him. When Auden responded to the baron's inquiry regarding the location of his mission, he noted the lanky lord's eyes lit.

"You saw the young duke, then?" Chester intoned. "A sad lot, his . . . captive in his own house . . . his sister forced to marry that base-born usurper. I have just been to London to petition the king on his behalf . . . and it seems my efforts were unnecessary. The munificent Charles had already taken the situation in hand. No doubt you will report it all to him soon. . . ."

Auden was too skillful to answer directly. "The boy is young, his loyalties are not yet fully formed. Charles will see to them well."

"I fear for him under Reston's hand. The bastard is no friend of the crown. He has openly entertained Parliamentary rabble at Lindengreen . . . and no doubt secretly aids them. He tricked the old man on his deathbed into giving him control, then forced the

401

duke's sister to—"

"Lady Tauren?"

"Yes"—Chester softened affectedly at the mention of her name like some smitten swain—"the lovely, sweet, gullible Lady Tauren . . . forced to marry him; for what else could it have been?"

Auden studied the man before him as he tested Chester's revelations against his own keen observations. Lady Tauren was far from gullible and the attraction she covertly displayed for her striking husband was unmistakable. The lad seemed well treated, certainly no prisoner, and was given a thorough education. Reston himself, despite his cursed Puritan garb, was a strong, shrewd, enigma of a man who wielded power well and who was loyal . . . at least with his gold.

But these were perilous times. Despite the generous gifts Auden carried, the king might be angered by the delay in the boy's appearance at court. It would be wise to present him with an alternative; a foil for future use—a malcontented lord willing to testify to the sordid state of affairs in Somerset. He would present both sides to the king, his mission a complete success, financially and politically.

Lord Auden smiled with judiciously measured approval at this unexpected boon. "Indeed," he answered at length, "you must tell me more. The king must have all the information I may glean for him."

"He hoards you like some craven old miser," Charlotte Eddys declared. "I'd boil in envy if it weren't so obnoxiously sweet. The way you look at each other—"

"Charlotte, you embarrass me," Tauren chided, her face coloring becomingly under the older woman's inspection.

"It's true. You're positively lost to all other mortals when around each other." She ran a smoothing hand over her dark, elegant coif and arranged herself on a pillow-strewn window seat in the upper solar of Lindengreen. "To think I actually worried about you. But we went so long without word . . . and with things as uncertain as they are, we wondered if . . . That's what prompted this visit. I hope you don't mind."

"Charlotte," Tauren stopped her with an upraised hand of approbation. "We're glad to have you here. And you must tell me all you can about London and court. You have been introduced at court?"

"Of course, but that was long ago. Things change so."

"We had a visitor a fortnight past . . . the Earl of Claxton. He came from the king to fetch Revan back to Charles's court. We persuaded him to return laden with gifts instead, but had to promise we would appear at court after Christ Mass. It seems we shall pass the winter in attendance on our sovereign's whims."

Charlotte's frown had grown deeper with each new revelation and she smoothed the heavy wine brocade of her ribbon-pierced overskirt as though studying it for a reply. "Will Holt really let him go?"

"We shall have to, the king commands it."

"I cannot imagine Holt being constrained to a mere king's will." Charlotte laughed nervously.

"He is difficult; I won't deny it. He almost drew his blade on the earl; I had to put myself between them." Tauren felt her friend's uneasiness creeping into her own stomach. "I finally promised to have Revan in London. . . ." Her voice trailed off as her thoughts traced new, unwelcome paths to disturbing conclusions. Holt had never actually consented to take Revan to London; neither had he protested her assurances to Lord Auden. She knew his thoughts on Charles's motives and knew Holt well enough to be aware that his audacious self-assurance often made his opinions immutable.

"I shan't pry." Charlotte caught her hands and her gaze, bringing her back to the present. "But in this matter, I think you'd best let Holt decide the course. No." She silenced Tauren's protest. "I know he's headstrong and difficult to persuade, but politics is his sphere. And he has friends in high places. Tauren . . . things in London are very bad. Food shortages, intrigues, arrests on every hand. Charles may have to quit the city soon. He's sent Queen Henrietta across the channel, ostensibly for a visit. Cedric says it is but a matter of weeks until some fool in Parliament is killed and that motley rabble of an army moves against the king's men."

Tauren's face was pale and her heart dropped to her stomach. "Army . . . what army?"

Charlotte gazed at her intently, puzzled. "Surely you have heard. Essex, Cromwell . . . that lot. They're organizing volunteer brigades, arming themselves openly. Charles is powerless to stop it. They withhold tax from him to prevent his raising his own forces, so he depends on those loyal to the Royalist cause to pay for his small guard. 'Tis a pathetic state . . . family against family, brother against brother." Her face tightened and she shook her head gravely.

"Our eldest, Frederick, is sixteen and he itches to try his blade in the king's service. Cedric won't allow it, of course; he's far too young. But where's the end of it in sight? I have four sons, Tauren—four heartaches to be suffered as they face manhood and duty." There were tears choking her voice and she pressed the heels of her palms to her eyes.

"Oh, Charlotte." Tauren groped through her shock for words of comfort to her friend. "I had no idea the situation was so dire. 'Twould be civil war. Holt knows this and he keeps it from me?"

"No doubt he spares you the worry. There will be time enough for that later." Charlotte paused, seeking composure. "I must tell you . . . in a month, the children and I sail for Italy. I have a cousin in Florence we shall visit while we look for suitable living quarters." She paused and looked earnestly into Tauren's disbelieving face.

"We won't return until the government is settled. The Almighty alone knows when that will be."

"You're fleeing?" Tauren said weakly, unable to give credence to her own ears. Auden's sparse tidbits from London often included the departure of some noble family for an extended time on the continent . . . was this what he meant?

"I hate it, but it is true." Charlotte's eyes dropped to where her hands wrung a lacy handkerchief. "I'll not stay and watch my family—my sons—made pawns and

405

destroyed in some mad contest for power. Cedric will stay awhile longer, then will join us when he's made suitable arrangements here."

"But, Charlotte, this is your home."

"Yes, it is my home"—her eyes flashed angrily—"but not one of those petty tyrants on either side has seen fit to consider that . . . to allow that some loyal subjects might desire only to mind their lands and bring up their young ones in peace." She jumped up and paced the room to employ her agitated limbs.

"They hurl us all into the jaws of destruction, in the name of some high-sounding principle. Tauren"—she stopped and grabbed Tauren's hands in hers—"you must come with us . . . you and Holt and His Grace. Call it a voyage for His Grace's health!"

"Charlotte!" Tauren pulled her hands back and stood before her distraught friend. Her heart hammered wildly in her chest with the fear that Charlotte spoke the truth and counseled her wisely. It was Tauren's turn to pace and rub her hands together, her fingertips lingering over the heavy golden band on her left hand.

"Revan is due at court soon . . . we cannot just ignore the royal command. Even in his tender years Revan feels his obligations, and Holt seems to know the politics. We could not leave England. Holt is the only protection Somerset has now . . . nay." She swallowed hard and blinked back the tears. "We can only wish you godspeed and a swift return to us."

Charlotte's revelations had cast a pall over Tauren's

delight in the Eddys' unannounced visit to Linden-green. Each conversation, each simple act of hospitality shouted to Tauren that it might be her last with her dearest friends.

Over and over she pondered Charlotte's conclusions and found herself watching Holt for signs of some unexpressed concern or strain. But in everything he was the genial host, the commanding overlord, the attentive husband; and it caused her a moment's shame to realize that her old suspiciousness was not yet fully laid to rest. She had given Holt her trust when she had surrendered her willingness—and her heart. She could not recall it now. But her innermost self scoffed at her delusion of control in the matter of her feelings for Holt. It was impossible to love cautiously, to free passion and rein emotion as though they were separate entities.

At night she lay by Holt, feeling in the iron-thewed arm that encircled her, all the security and strength she needed. When she was tempted to speak to him of Charlotte's worries, she would recall the sober strength of his gaze upon Revan or the open warmth with which he faced her in their chambers, and held her tongue. She would trust him, her husband. It was what she wanted and what she owed this maddeningly absorbing man.

On the day of the Eddys' departure, Tauren and Charlotte lingered in the morning room over cups of cinnamon-spiced chocolate and the Lady of Rentings watched her friend with discernment. She placed her cup on the china plate before her and smoothed the snowy table linen with her long, tapered hand.

"He doesn't know, does he?" Then she answered herself. "No, of course not! He'd be carrying you about on a pillow if he knew."

"What are you babbling on about?" Tauren protested, a guilty stain on her cheeks.

"You're with child, of course," Charlotte charged, smiling broadly. "I must be nearing my dotage not to have seen it before now." She waggled a finger scoldingly. "But you're a clever one. . . ."

Tauren could not meet her eyes and clasped her arms across her still narrow waist as if to hide it from Charlotte's amiable prying.

Clapping and chortling with mischievous glee, Charlotte dragged her chair closer to Tauren's. "How many months gone?"

"Months?"

"How long before the babe comes?"

"I . . . I don't know, quite a few I guess. I've gone three months now."

Quick arithmetic on Charlotte's fingers produced the answer. "June then, or late May. Oh, how I wish I could be here for your lying in."

"How . . . did you know?"

"My dear, you were positively ill at the sight of the sausages and your cheeks are a lovely moist pink. And naturally, seeing how things are between you and Holt, I supposed . . ."

Tauren managed a tentative smile. "I wanted to be sure. And there's so much to do, I didn't want it to complicate things."

"Complicate!" Charlotte laughed heartily. "Dear, sweet Tauren, things will never be simple again. You're to be a mother; that's quite as complicated as things may ever get! You'll do well to get used to that at the start. Besides"—she lowered her voice conspiratorially —"I think the overlord is quite man enough to handle this burden his much-relished pleasures have brought down upon him. There's no better time than the present to begin training the great and mighty ruler of men in the proper cosseting of his breeding wife. Make sure he pampers and fusses over you . . . taking care of you will give him something to make him feel important and a part of it all. It's just another step in bringing along one of the great hunter-warriors toward usefulness about the hearth."

Tauren was first amused by Charlotte's smooth condescension toward the lords and masters of the earth, but a conspiring glint was forming in her own eye. Then she laughed too as she realized that Charlotte's wise counsel was just that which sustained and bound together women of all ages and times. Men might rule the world, but there was another power, unique and God-given, that rested securely in the hands of women. The hunter-warrior—the overlord— needed a compliment, a mate, a comfort, a counterpart . . . sometimes even a spur. From that moment on, the cosmos assumed a slightly different order of rotation.

"I have not told Holt lest he seize it as a pretext for making me stay here while Revan goes to court. I do not trust the combination of his prejudices and his temper to keep them out of trouble, nor to endear a young duke to his suspicious sovereign."

"You are too wise to inhabit so youthful and so lovely a frame." Charlotte laughed. "I can see you have this campaign well planned. You needn't fear I'll give you away, though I confess the temptation will be monstrous."

"That's not all. I've ordered new clothing for Holt in beautiful browns and sedate, sendal greens. I only hope he won't be so angry he refuses to wear them. I fear his 'Puritan' garb will go against us at court, given the avowed disloyalty of so many of them."

"Then I'll light candles for your success, for you will need more than mere mortal assistance in these next months." Instantly Charlotte's bright smile faded. "I shall worry for you. I can hardly abide the thought of not seeing you again . . . of leaving my home. . . ."

She stopped, making a little choking sound, and Tauren flew to put her arms about her friend's shoulders. They sat together in the poignant silence for some time.

"Not a word!" Holt commanded, his eyes burning with hazel fire. "So it was begun and so it shall stay, until I am ready to reveal it to her."

"She has a right to know." Calder bristled defiantly. "It's her future . . . and the duke's."

"She'll do as she must . . . and in time she'll see it is best. Until then, let her go on with her preparations; they serve us well, do they not? By the time she learns her true destination it will be too late for any of her clever maneuverings or headstrong defiance. Have you forgotten Auden's visit?"

"Ye owe it to the lass, man; she's yer wife! Explain it to her . . . reason with her."

Holt's face was as brown as his thoughts, and in the uncomfortable silence he considered the situation again for the hundredth time.

"She'd accuse and rail . . . or try some stupid—"

"The Almighty knows why, but she's daft about ye, man. She'll listen. And when she hears what's happening in London, she'll agree to it. Ye should never have held it from her this long."

None but Calder could dare such an open challenge to his judgment. And none but Calder would confront him with his own worst fears spoken right aloud.

"And if she doesn't?" Holt rubbed his thigh briskly, as if massaging an aggravating old wound. He did not like the uncertainty he felt, a nagging sense of betrayal of his recent intimacy with Tauren. "She seems contented enough, but she does not yet trust me fully. . . ."

"Or is it ye don't trust the lass?" Calder's heavy brows knitted, and his mouth tightened against a stream of unweighed words.

Holt's boots hit the library floor hard as he rose angrily and jerked away to recover his self-control. "That's naught of your concern. Keep your meddlesome thoughts to yourself."

"Jesus, man, will ye never listen to reason? Must ye always battle yer way through things by yerself?" He paused and studied Holt's unyielding back.

"Well, I've done with ye." Calder rose and grabbed his distinctively plumed hat from the littered writing table, jamming it down on his head with uncharacteristic roughness. "Ye'll go on yer own stubborn, pigheaded way in spite of us all. Ye needn't worry I'll betray yer bastard hide. But it'd be a mercy if someone did." As his hand touched the latch he was stopped by a rumble from deep in Holt's throat.

"You'll see the documents and the crates safe into Cedric's hands?"

"Yea," Calder gritted out, "I'll see to it." And he was gone.

Thirty

"It's magnificent!" Tauren ran her hands over the shining bands of beaten brass binding a large oak chest that sat in the midst of the great hall. "Surely there could be none finer in London itself!" Her total admiration and engaging smile brought a gruff stain to the cheeks of the rough-clad old man who stood nearby, crumpling his weathered woolen hat in his gnarled hands.

"Thank ye, milady," Old Jerome Corbin, the carpenter, bobbed his torso stiffly. "I'll have t'others ready directly. A day—no more."

Tauren slid her hands over the oil and beeswax finish, tracing the elaborate, bold grain of the aged wood. "Ah, Jerome, I wish I had a whole stand of oak trees for you. . . ."

"And what would the old coot do with 'em?" Calder strode into the hall from the salon, pulling on his immaculate black gloves, his broad-brimmed hat set at a cocky angle. He laughed away Tauren's gathering frown. "He'd kill himself just cuttin' them down, and we'd be stuck with a pile of useless, rottin' lumber."

"I be plenty sound of wind an' limb, yet, Captain." The aging carpenter shoved a grizzled chin out in defiance. "I live a healthy, God-fearin' life—not carousin' nor drunken—keepin' to me own wife and mindin' me own business. I'll be goin' long after me betters is molderin' in the shades."

Calder laughed heartily at the steely glint in the old craftsman's eye. This was not the first such exchange between them.

"Here, old man"—the barrel-chested captain tossed his cloak on the nearby marble bench and pushed back his dapper cuffs—"I'll help ye take it up the stairs." He made a show of reaching for one of the handles and the hoary craftsman pushed him away.

"'Tis me made her and 'tis me will set her in milady's chambers. Take note, ye high livin' scoundrel, what an honest man can do!"

Calder stepped back a pace and before the incredulous eyes of the lady, the captain, Murdock, and several house servants, the cabinetmaker tugged on the ropes that bound the great trunk and stood it on end. Through clever working of the ropes and experienced leverage, the massive chest was pulled up and onto the wiry old fellow's back and balanced there while he started, bent double, for the stairs.

Tauren gasped and urged Calder forward by his sleeve. "Help him!"

"Doesn't appear he needs assistance just now." Calder rocked back on his polished bootheels and grinned broadly.

"But he'll hurt—"

"Nay, milady," Calder stopped her and lowered his

voice. "'Twould hurt far more to take away his fun."

"Yea, old man," Calder bellowed out after the retreating chest and bearer, "ye have the back and the constitution of a mule. I concede ye this one. But I'll have me own way yet with a Corbin, I'm determined."

A short, labored laugh wafted from the top of the stairs and Tauren shook her head, smiling her amusement and relief. "Who'd have thought it?"

"He's a tough one, him." Calder retrieved his cloak and settled it about his shoulders. "His granddaughter is the same . . . only more comely. I've yet to win one with her either."

"Granddaughter?" Tauren puzzled for a moment.

"Cassie Whitelaw, cook's widowed sister-in-law. Old Jerome's her grandsire. . . ." Calder reddened uncharacteristically and stopped short. "Good day, Lady Tauren."

He was out the door before Tauren made all the proper mental connections and so he escaped her sympathetic laughter. So Calder was a smitten man . . . and brown-eyed Cassie was responsible for the hours the captain whiled away in the kitchens of Lindengreen. Tauren smiled, recalling Holt's recent advice to Calder. Again the overlord had been right.

When the servants left and Murdock returned to her duties, Tauren continued on her way to the library. Christ Mass was over a fortnight past; already they would arrive in London weeks later than they had agreed. What a time she had had in getting Holt to send word to the palace of their delay. He seemed especially difficult these last two weeks . . . or perhaps it was within herself the difficulty lay. Her hand went to her blossoming waistline and she sighed wistfully.

She paused in the doorway of the library where Holt and Calder had spent much time of late, pouring over charts and documents . . . discussing something. Whenever she entered their business was curtailed, and Holt wryly poked fun at her curiosity, dazzling her with his smile and showing his incessantly amorous admiration for her in his eyes.

The room had a faintly musky, masculine smell that pressed her physically with the recall of frequent encounters with her husband: in the salon, the granaries . . . their bedchamber. She saw him everywhere she went and always a giddy lightness rose within her, giving her to wonder if it were the babe or if the mere sight of him could send her waffly head into dizzy spirals and shorten her breath.

Holt. She stood in the midst of the bright room seeing nothing about her. Of late he was so thoughtful, so . . . tender with her. She wanted to tell him what she felt, or as much as she could decipher of her baffling and sometimes contrary impulses. But there was some last bit of her yet unable to surrender that last bit of power to him.

She sat down at Holt's writing desk, brought from his modest house in Keenings to spare his knees the banging they took from the one that formerly stood there. Old Jerome Corbin had made this one for his overlord in appreciation of . . . something neither he nor Holt would talk about. Her abject fondness for her remarkable husband showed in her face again and she gingerly stroked the polished, dark wood before her with her fingertips. There was no life he left untouched.

And again her hand sought the waist of her gown.

Enough of these doting musings! She opened the one free drawer of the writing desk, searching for some vellum on which to begin an inventory of the things they would take to London. She sifted through a stack of uninteresting-looking papers, blotched scraps, and crumpled quills lying amongst blotters and overturned sand. She gave up quickly. Her shoulders slumped with disappointment, and idly she tried one of the three locked drawers. It slid open, surprising her. She stared a moment, thinking it strange; Holt always kept these drawers locked.

There was no vellum in the first drawer, only a stack of sealed documents, half-folded maps and ledger sheets. . . . She picked them up to look beneath and dimpled one corner of her mouth in disgust, closing the drawer and trying another on the off chance it might too be open. It was.

Some letters, a deed—duly sealed and witnessed— and a bill of sale . . . Something written on the document of sale snared her interest, and she pulled it back out a moment to study it, frowning with the pang of guilt she felt for such prying.

"Sixty fertile acres of prime river-bottom land . . . adjacent the stream known as 'Potter's' and marked due west by a stone fence along the boundary of Burrow's land. . . ." Holt was purchasing more land?

Then her eyes fell to the bottom of the document where the ducal seal and Holt's signature, as legal guardian of the duke, were affixed. Seller? Holt was selling part of the old duke's—Revan's—lands? She scowled and worked harder at deciphering the legal phraseology, hardly able to fathom why Holt would

417

take it upon himself to sell part of Revan's lands without consulting her . . . and Revan, of course. Revan would have told her if he had known, wouldn't he? Perplexed fully, she picked up another document to peruse, seeking some further explanation.

She found a second bill of sale prepared much like the first, only for "the meadow and tenant habitation, twenty acres in all, located in the glen known as Craven's Bend and stretching from . . ." Another sale. Holt's signature and the ducal seal were prominently displayed. Craven's Bend? It was a part of the duke's lands bordering the estate of Lindengreen itself—the place where she and Holt had first met.

She took another parchment from the stack and found it to be the legal deed to yet another, larger parcel of land at Lindengreen's edge. And under that was another. This one she recognized as a part of the estate proper, though some distance from the main house.

Her eyes widened as she tried to drink it in. Holt was selling ducal lands, pieces of Lindengreen itself? She looked quickly at the names and titles of the buyers . . . "honorable" somebody's she didn't know. For some reason her mouth was dry, and she felt an oppressive cloud stealing over her faculties, preventing her from comprehending what she held in her hands.

Her muscles slowly contracted all over her body, as if bracing for a shock; and her heart began an agonizing crescendo against her tightly laced bodice. As the thought formed, she tried futilely to evade it, then to suppress it.

No. It could not be. Holt was slowly, secretly selling off Revan's inheritance! No!

She dug frantically into the drawer and brought up three more deeds and bills of sale, each larger than the last and each closer to the heart of Lindengreen itself. And there was more. An inventory of items: paintings identified as ancestral portraits in enough detail so that she recognized some of them as being from the old wing, tapestries by date and description, plate silver, candlesticks and lamps, chests containing the armor and battle gear of Wincanton forebears . . . By each listing was a note in Holt's distinctive, blocky hand detailing the value and a set of initials, no doubt the buyer!

A wave of dark nausea slammed through Tauren and she stifled it with one hand to her mouth as she leaned her head back against the chair. She closed her eyes and shook her head to rid herself of this wicked delusion. She would not believe it . . . could not. Surely there was an explanation. Read, search out more, her cooler, logical self commanded; and she collected her scattered wits enough to rush to the door and close it, sending the bolt home.

Holt! Bound for Keenings, then Barensa to see about the young smith. Haldan rode with him. No one else would disturb her here.

She rushed back to the unholy find, feeling her heart banging in her chest, seeking escape from the revelations yet to come. In the third drawer she found a leather-bound packet containing letters from bankers in London, Amsterdam, Geneva, and Paris, addressing Holt and acknowledging receipt of large sums of gold and silver . . . and an astonishing assortment of jewels. These were the proceeds from his surreptitious sale of Revan's inheritance, there could be no doubt. And jewels—she staggered into the chair—she was so new to the nobility, she had not even wondered about the family jewels, of which there must be many with so rich an estate. She looked at the costly band of rubies and gold on her hand. Did she, even now, wear the spoils of Lindengreen?

More papers surfaced, receipts for payment rendered, a letter or two from a Lord Calvert and a handbill advertising investment in the American colonial ventures.

She dropped them to the desk as though they scorched her hand and jerked back in the big chair to stare in mute horror at this trove of deceit she had unwittingly uncovered. Taken together, there was but one explanation for these documents. For the past several months, her husband had been methodically selling off her brother's inheritance and secreting large sums of gold and silver—even the family jewels—out of the country.

The man who had so earnestly pleaded for and finally commanded her trust was bleeding the shire of its wealth while claiming to protect the young duke from the greedy manipulations of their rightly sovereign. Was this why he was so anxious to keep Revan from London . . . and access to the king? One horrifying conclusion lead inevitably to another.

Once Revan was in London, the king might question the powerful commoner's stewardship of the estate and demand an accounting, perhaps might assume the guardianship himself. Chances of the detection of Holt's scheme would be dangerously increased with each day they passed at court.

Why else would he have stalled and delayed their

journey? Tauren's fingers were bloodless as she gripped the arms of the chair. He didn't want Revan at court at all; he'd said it openly. How far would his widely vaunted ambitions for the title of Somerset push him?

She swallowed hard, trying to dislodge whatever it was that threatened to choke her. How far would Holt Reston go to have that which he deemed his by right?

He had killed the Earl of Sappington to eliminate the man's influence in the shire! But he could not kill the king . . . so why not merely eliminate one vulnerable, impressionable boy?

No! She jumped up and stood repeating it over and over to herself. No . . . no . . . not Holt! Not Revan!

The battle raged viciously within her as a collage of her times with Holt engulfed her. For every tender moment, there seemed a damning counterpart. For every kindness she recalled a display of arrogance, for every enforcement of justice there seemed a claim of special privilege.

Hot liquid seared its way down her cheeks and she crumpled into a heap on the overlord's chair. Sobs racked her entire body, snatching her breath so that she heaved and gasped like a devastated child.

"Why couldn't I see?" she wailed. "I was supposed to protect Revan. I've only led him into betrayal. If only . . . I hadn't . . . begun to love . . ."

It was some time before Tauren could collect herself enough to consider her future course. She replaced the documents carefully, exactly as she had found them. At the back of one drawer, her fingers touched something cold, metallic. She brought up a solid iron key. The key to the old hall . . . the part Holt had sealed away even before Auden's visit! She had been so preoccupied, she had not even remembered it until now. The relics and artifacts—they had been plundered from the old hall itself. He had stolen them from beneath their very noses and showed his contempt by forbidding them to venture into part of their own home. And they, like dumb sheep, had obeyed.

Her mind flew now. Where could she go to seek help and protection for Revan and her? The only rightful choice was the king himself . . . he already expected Revan at court. Lord Auden's insinuations had made her believe it would take little to persuade Charles to act swiftly to restore the pilfered lands and wealth. She must get Revan to court, immediately!

Tauren slipped from the library up the stairs and into her chambers, carefully avoiding contact with servants who were about. She bolted the door to the bed-chamber against Roxie's untimely entry and splashed her face with cold water from the basin. Pacing the polished floors frantically, she felt time slipping through her fingers. Holt would return and she must be prepared. He must not know she suspected him of anything.

But how could she get Revan to London? There would be the court to negotiate, a request for a private audience. . . . She hadn't the faintest idea where the palace lay, much less the protocol for the granting of an audience. But they were not ordinary petitioners. Revan was commanded to court. Surely their appearance would be welcomed.

The journey . . . They would need guidance, perhaps protection. Would Holt hunt them down when he found them gone?

She shook her head. Cedric? In Portsmouth or in London . . . They could not wait for his return. She rubbed her hands together distractedly. Surely there was someone. Of the other nobility hereabouts they only knew Lord Chester. . . .

Tauren shuddered, remembering his grasping nature and his lechery at the old duke's deathbed. What price would he extract for aiding them? Whatever, he could not be sure of recompense until Revan was safely in London. That would be their assurance against his duplicity. And her motherhood should forestall—

Motherhood! The thought felled her where she stood and she sank to her knees. "Dearest Heaven, help me," she anguished. She carried within her a new being, part her and part Holt. How could this be happening? "How could he make love to me, look at me with such tenderness, all while he was plotting Revan's ruin? What future will this babe have, conceived by such monstrous deception? His father outlawed by his mother's word . . . Nay! Not my doing, but his own.

Her heart seemed to be crushed within her, unable to withstand the onslaught of such bitterness and of the hopeless tenacity of her love for Holt. It was a love based on falsehoods, but undeniably there. The hurt was killing.

"You're back late," Murdock greeted Holt in the great hall well past nightfall. She took his cloak and cast a disapproving eye on his mud-caked boots as she spoke. "A body would think ye had more important things to do than gad about the countryside in

423

questionable company." She shot a challenging look at Vicar Haldan, who scraped his boots against a rough-woven straw mat near the door.

"Haldan"—Holt's eyes glinted as he stared into Murdock's china-gray gaze—"methinks you've a fence or two to mend hereabouts. I'm not sure you've ever overcome that unfortunate introduction to Murdock, here."

"Aye." The girthy cleric stuck his thumbs in his belt and set his jaw determinedly as he returned the housekeeper's close scrutiny tit for tat. "I been thinkin' on that. 'Tis time she learned to appreciate me better side, for lately I've come to favor hers quite a lot."

Murdock reddened and sputtered uncharacteristically as she snatched the vicar's outstretched cloak. "I . . . never . . . well . . . there's a cold supper on the buffet in the dining hall. My lady and His Grace dined earlier and my lady retired straight away. She wasn't feeling well."

"Not well? . . ." Holt asked her fast-retreating back. But she was set on her course and did not respond. He shrugged, frowning, and vowed to make this meal a quick one.

In the darkness Holt crawled between the cold sheets and shivered, sending an arm over to clasp his sleeping wife to him. He encountered a heavy linen nightdress instead of the satiny skin he had grown accustomed to finding. It puzzled him and then one brow shot up with rueful understanding, and he pulled her stiff form against him. He nuzzled her fragrant hair away from

424

her neck.

"Are you all right?" he murmured, kissing her ear and feeling more than seeing her wakefulness.

"Y-yes." The wavering answer was long in coming.

"Shall I knead your shoulders and back?" he persisted.

"N-nay." She shivered in his warming grasp. "I only need . . . rest."

He frowned as he felt her pull away and released her to her own side of their great bed. Whatever the state of their relations, it had been a long while since she had refused to share warmth with him. It must be the whims of the female condition . . . it had been awhile and he had nearly forgotten. . . . A thought jolted through his entire body. Awhile . . . it had been *months* since that wretched garment had intervened in their bed. Months! He was sure of it. Even with his admittedly incomplete understanding of women's things, he understood the ramifications of that! His jaw dropped with astonishment.

Tauren . . . with child? He'd been so preoccupied with his plans and preparations that he'd failed to notice what had transpired beneath his very nose—in his very bed.

Fatherhood! The prospect rattled him, as did Tauren's unexpected rejection of him tonight. Could it be she did not relish bearing his babe? The thought pierced him briefly, but his customary self-assurance quickly rooted it out. Nay, she was but tired and quirksome.

He tucked his arms behind his head and smiled shakily. Tomorrow, when she was rested, he would

425

press her for his answer.

The great chamber was warmer than usual when Tauren awoke that next morning. Her face felt tight and swollen as she shifted in the cool, gray light to peer at the fireplace. A cheery, warming blaze crackled a greeting, and in the same instant she spied her husband, fully dressed, sitting in one of the big chairs near its warmth. He seemed to be watching her. Instantly her mouth was as dry as thistledown, and she clenched her hands into white fists beneath the covers to steady herself.

"You are in chambers late this morn," she observed steadily.

"Aye." Holt templed his fingers and pressed them against his lips in thought. "There's no hurry to be out in this chilling, uncertain weather. Are you feeling better?"

"Yes." She pulled the heavy, down comforter up with her as she rose to a sitting position. "It must be forbidding weather indeed to keep you warming your knees by the hearth."

He smiled rather cryptically and stood, taking her heaviest, fur-lined robe from the nearby chaise and holding it up before the heat emanating from the fireplace. After a silent moment, he folded it together and brought it to her bedside, opening it in invitation to her.

"What's this?" Tauren stared uncertainly at the garment.

"To warm you. Hurry, before it cools."

Fearful of betraying herself in a show of obstinance,

she slipped from the bed and donned the well-warmed robe. This was new, this cosseting manner. Clever of him to play the role so faithfully—down to the very last.

But his arms closed about her from behind, and his big hands slid inquiringly over the soft velvet of the robe. She stood motionless, holding her breath and wondering at his strange behavior. When his questing touch reached her waist and the rounding mound of her belly, it stopped inquiringly and his deep voice reverberated in her ears.

"Have you some news for me, Tauren?"

Her eyes widened as she realized what was happening; he suspected she carried his child.

"News?" she managed, though the word sounded suspiciously strangled.

"I think you know what I mean."

She abruptly pushed away from him, unable to bear the sheer torture of his arms about her another second. "You imagine things. I never realized the cold could effect a man's logical humors so." She hurried to her wardrobe and pulled open the door to begin dressing. Where was Roxie?

A heavy fist on the chamber door just then transformed Holt's frown of bemusement into a scowl of displeasure, and he whirled away. "Enter!" He was confused and irritated by Tauren's odd, aloof manner and by her off-hand rebuff of so vital an inquiry.

Calder opened the door and swept the room with a wary gaze, smiling apologetically at Tauren before turning to Holt.

"A messenger, Holt—with important tidings. Ye must come."

Holt read in Calder's face the validation of the captain's concern and set his own jaw sternly, assuming his mantle of authority.

He murmured something to Tauren and was gone. She stood, stunned and aching, grasping the heavy, carved door of the wardrobe for support. Likely it would be the last time she would see her husband.

Thirty-One

The horses' hooves thudded on the cold-hardened ground. It was the only sound in the gray cold that had chilled both body and conversation. Revan rode beside her roan mare on a dappled gelding, wearing a beaver-lined cloak, a studied concern on his face. He stole looks at her from time to time as his puzzlement mounted.

They paused at a faded signpost at a fork in the road. She scanned the lettering then indicated the road to the right and kicked her horse forward.

"Where is this tenant in need of such special care?" Revan turned sideways in his saddle and pushed himself up to survey the countryside. "We've left Lindengreen's lands an hour ago," he mused testily in that deepening voice that still unnerved Tauren whenever he spoke unexpectedly.

"It shouldn't be long," Tauren assured him quite determinedly and fell silent again. It had been no small feat to drag Revan with her this morning, ostensibly to visit a seriously ailing tenant. She dared not tell him their true destination, knowing how besotted he was with Holt's power-driven character. Likely he would not have believed her, and there was no time for convincing him. Their departure had come just after Holt and Calder rode hurriedly out of Lindengreen. Roxie had made suspicious remarks about the heft and girth of her herbal pouch and about Tauren's insistence upon carrying it herself.

But they were well away now and even in this miserable cold and dampness that seeped through her clothes, she felt a sense of relief. She was doing right.

"Where are we?" Revan demanded angrily, feeling Tauren's adult condescension all through him as they rested on a rise overlooking the baron's hall.

"Enderfield." She started for the gates, feeling her heart thudding anxiously. When she realized she was alone, she stopped and called back over her shoulder. "We need call on the baron about some matters. Come, Revan." She ordered her horse forward again, gambling that he would follow and sighing with relief as she heard the thudding of his mount catching hers.

"What business have we here, Tauren?" he demanded in a voice so like Holt's that Tauren jerked her head about to stare at him briefly. Her heart quivered strangely in her chest.

"I don't know what you're planning, but you can count me out. The man's a viper. He'd sell his own mother for a few farthings—probably has." Again Holt's phrases, but this time she would not look.

The court of the large, stone manor house was littered and ill kept, and the stone wall that enclosed it lay in disarray, its mortar crumbled and unrepaired. Tauren could see the roof was in sore need of repair, and here and there the broken glass of once-elegant windows was stuffed with rags against the winter elements. This deteriorating house was a far cry from what she would have expected of the fastidiously fashionable Baron of Greers. She shuddered unexpectedly, but refused to allow herself misgivings now.

Inside the weathered and unpainted front doors of Enderfield, they were greeted stiffly by a frail prune of a manservant who took their cloaks and led them to a poorly warmed parlor filled with faded and well-worn furnishings. The windows were small and stingy with the lowering daylight, and as yet the tapers had not been lit. The room had an air of decay about it that only served to send Tauren's spirits lower.

"I'm warning you, Tauren, whatever you're up to, I'll have no part of it—or of him. I'm riding back to Lindengreen with or without you." He pushed past her and she caught his sleeve tightly, straining to hold him as she stared up into his tight, angry face.

"Revan, you must hear me out."

"Your Grace! Lady Tauren!" The penetrating, nasal voice arrested their conflict. "I could scarcely believe my ears when told you awaited. You honor my home greatly by your presence. My wife is away until tomorrow; she will be devastated to have missed you! Pray, be seated. . . . I shall have the fire built up." He rubbed his clammy hands down over his napless velvet breeches and self-consciously adjusted his worn and wine-stained doublet as he reached for a brass bell on the sideboard and gave it a vicious shake.

"Thank you, my lord Baron," she slipped her arm

through Revan's and discreetly dragged him to the threadbare sofa near the meager fire. She sat down wearily and settled the bulging pouch beside her feet on the faded rug.

"More wood for the fire!" the lord ordered the ancient manservant. "And my best sherry to warm my guests." Chester ran a hasty hand back over his untidy hair, then joined them on the sofa.

Tauren had to clamp a hand on Revan's arm to prevent him from rising.

"Now then, sweet lady, Your Grace . . . how may I be of service to you?" The lord's long, sallow face seemed cold but for the lights that flickered at the backs of his eyes.

"We've come to enlist your aid, Baron, in a cause it gives me great pain to relate." She felt Revan's arm grow still under her grip, and she glanced at his guarded face before continuing. "We are at this moment bound for London . . . and an audience with King Charles, to lay our case before him. There are some, at least one, who would prevent our arrival. . . ." Her voice cracked ignominiously, threatening her composure completely. She could not look at Revan but felt his hot accusing look upon her, and she swallowed hard.

"Dear Lady Tauren"—Lord Chester restrained his glee manfully and reached over to pat her hand consolingly—"you must unburden yourself and make my arm your strength."

"Revan"—she turned to her brother and took his hands as she spoke, leaving the baron her back—"you will find this difficult, but surely no more than I. Yesterday when I was in the library I came across

432

documents that show, beyond any doubt, that . . . the overlord . . . has parceled and sold large parts of the ducal lands, including a significant part of Lindengreen itself." His scowl caused her to hurry on. "He has stolen and sold many of the family's priceless heirlooms, emptied the old hall of its relics and treasures. *No!*" She shook her head violently at his angry disbelief. "You must listen to me, Revan. I saw—read—them with my own eyes. I can show you some of them I've brought as evidence. He's sold half your inheritance and secreted the gold and silver outside England."

"I never dreamed you hated him so," Revan declared angrily and shook free of her, attempting to rise.

"I don't—didn't—hate him, Revan." She pulled at his hands. "Hear me out!"

"Nay! I won't listen to you plot against him! I don't know what you saw, but there's a reason for it . . . an explanation. Holt can explain and I shall see he has the chance!" He twisted in her grasp and Lord Chester was on his feet and about the sofa, blocking Revan's way, even as he gained his freedom. He turned from the shabby baron to his sister, face flaming.

"From the start you resented him, resented the time I spent with him. I know he forced you to marry him, but I thought you'd made, peace with that . . . these past months."

"Revan!" Tauren was on the brink of hysteria, her face wild and frightened. Tears poured down her cheeks, arresting him. "You accuse me of hatred, jealousy, spite . . . but the deception was his, the betrayal, his! He played his game with my heart until I came to care for him—and ceased to question his management of your affairs. You think I lightly charge the father of my unborn child with thievery and treason?" Her hand grasped her waist as the tears dropped slowly from her chin to her chest.

"I cannot choose between my brother and my husband, but I can protect you from his demented schemes and see what is rightfully yours restored to you."

The long, shocked silence lengthened unbearably as Revan wrestled visibly with his maturing view of his sister and her marriage. And a child . . . Taurie would never lie to him about such a thing. But Holt, who had saved his very life, would never steal from him; he was sure of it. What had really happened?

"Tell me what you saw . . . show me," he commanded in deep, solemn tones.

Tauren felt her knees buckle and she collapsed with bitter relief on the sofa. From beneath her closed eyes squeezed large, golden drops; and she clutched Revan tightly as he sank stiffly beside her. Her world was shattering and she was too numbed to avoid these jagged, merciless shards of the future that might have been.

The coach that took them to London was little more than a wooden box set on an unsprung wagon, and it jostled them about mercilessly on the rutted road. Revan sat beside Tauren, holding her cold hand in silence. Across from them, riding backward, the lanky Lord Chester was once more resplendent in his peacock finery, trying to maintain a mein of solicitous concern as the hard wooden seats rattled his very bones.

Tauren roused slightly from time to time, only to reflect how like that first journey this one was, she and Revan being propelled along a rutted and uncertain path toward an unknown future—accompanied by that same disagreeable agent. Only now, there were three of them, and instead of comforting Revan, he held her head against his broadening shoulder. How cruelly the past seemed to haunt the future.

The coach slowed unexpectedly and Lord Chester bolted upright, peering out the wavery glass window, then craning his neck outside the door.

"Greetings, friend!" he shouted a bit too loudly. A male voice outside the coach spoke, but the sound was muffled. Tauren and Revan exchanged worried glances.

"We are bound there ourselves! I insist you join us! Tie your horse and ride inside where it is warmer." The baron turned to them with reddened face and eyes gleaming strangely. "I hope you don't mind—a business associate of mine."

"Shouldn't we—" Tauren began to object.

"He is most discreet, I assure you. Our mission is not compromised at all . . . in fact, it may be enhanced by his presence."

A pair of muffled voices outside caused Tauren to glance anxiously at Revan; then she forced her grip on his arm to ease. Likely the man spoke to the driver.

The wooden door swung open and the man climbed in, removing his hat to enter. Tauren gasped involuntarily, causing the man to level a cold, hard gaze at her from above his false, silver nose. Immediately she averted her eyes from the unfortunate man, but not before noting that over his head he wore a tight-fitting

435

cowl. Her hand was instantly captured by the baron as he introduced them.

"Lady Tauren . . . and Your Grace, may I present to you Esmond Meeks, an associate of mine, a man of noble birth and bearing."

"Delighted to meet you at last, Your Grace. And to think I sit in coach with the lovely Madam Reston. My joy is complete."

Tauren noted with a shiver that there was little joy in his disfigured face, and she doubted whether there had ever been. His metal nose gleamed dully in the dim light of the coach windows and she shivered anew, hoping her revulsion would go unnoticed.

"We are pleased to make your acquaintance, sir," Revan responded for them both, noting that Lord Chester looked a bit too pleased with something. Instantly he mistrusted this stranger and wondered at the coincidence that set him in their path at so precarious a time.

In the awkward silence that befell them, Revan reviewed it all for the hundredth time in his mind. The bills of sale and the deeds, the listing of heirlooms that Tauren had secretly removed from Lindengreen and had produced from her herbal pouch—all bore Holt's hand and signature; there was no mistaking it. Taurie was with child, that was certainly true. Alone together in their shared rooms last night at Enderfield, Revan had seen the depth of her despair. However they ranted, fumed, and clashed, Taurie had really cared for Holt, that much was clear to him now. This man-and-woman business was far more complex than he'd realized. His adamant, boyish perceptions were slipping from beneath his feet, and he scrambled to retain some balance in his whirling, maturing world.

They traveled through midday, sharing the scant nourishment provided by the baron's kitchens and little else. Esmond Meeks's strange visage unnerved Tauren and increased her irritation with the pompous Chester to the level of wrath. Why did he insist on inflicting this macabre companion upon them all the way to London?

Sunlight surged into the coach in a welcome flood late in the day as the clouds parted for the first time in a fortnight. The sudden bright rays beamed through the uncovered windows and caught Tauren and Revan unawares, full in the face, and both raised their hands to shield their eyes.

"Would you have me trade seats with you, Lady Tauren?" Chester was poised on the edge of his seat like a raptor about to strike.

"Nay." Tauren tried to affect a genial expression. "It is a small price to pay for such a swift conveyance north to London."

North. Revan froze as the sun's filtered rays beat full upon his face, his recent lessons with Haldan ringing in his ears. He had been made to recite it over and over. . . . *The sun's lowest zenith occurs at Christ Mass. The winter sun, when seen, stays in southern skies.* He held his breath and waited to test his growing fear. The sun still glared into his face however they pitched or turned. They traveled *south*, not north to London as Chester said!

"Where are you taking us?" Revan demanded, his youthful face sharpening with indignation. Tauren

437

jerked her drooping head up from his shoulder and stared, slack-jawed, at her brother.

"Revan—" she began.

"By the sun, we set a southerly course, sir. You cannot deny the clear evidence of my own two eyes. You do not take us to London. Where do you take us?"

Tauren was suddenly awake, staring first at Revan, then at Chester and the setting sun. Heaven help them, he was right! They were not traveling toward London at all.

Chester glanced knowingly at the shadowed aspect of his associate, then he turned an ugly smirk upon them. "How clever you are, young Duke. We are so near our destination, you would have learned soon, anyway. For your own protection, we've arranged a suitable safe haven while this ugly business of the guardianship is settled."

Tauren gripped Revan's arm, hearing him, but disbelieving her own ears. They were betrayed by Chester!

"You will be the guests of the Earl of Sappington for a while," Chester crowed.

"Sapping—" Tauren's words were strangled. "He's dead!"

"On the contrary," the menacing Esmond Meeks sat forward into the brighter light, his yellow-ringed eyes gleaming malignant wrath. "I am very much alive. I suppose in a way I have you to thank for my succession to the title, and when the time is right, you'll feel my gratitude fully, Madam Reston." His pock-marked face was distorted as he raked her ominously with his burning feral eyes.

"How dare—"

Chester laughed mirthlessly at her impotent rage; then a gloating sneer settled on his face, his relish in their plight further revealed by his next words.

"Esmond was cousin to your dearly departed betrothed, and since there was no other family, Esmond inherited all from poor Roger. You might think him eager to thank your husband for the deed that made him an earl, but that, I fear, is not the case. There is yet another score that Esmond has to settle with the overlord, one that eclipses his gratitude for that fortuitous duel."

"Your husband, Madam, decreed this my punishment." Esmond ripped off the silver cast to reveal a grisly, gaping hole in the midst of his face where his nose should have been, and in a moment the cowl joined it on the floor of the coach. The side of his head was a hideous mass of flesh scarred from searings where an ear had been.

"Agghh—*No*!" Tauren jerked away and covered her face with her hands to blot out the sight. Revan grabbed her protectively while struggling not to avert his own shrinking gaze.

"Each day of my life since, I've vowed to have revenge on the almighty bastard of Somerset . . . and you have brought the means within my grasp. I could not have planned it better."

"Better than you know," Chester interjected fervidly. "She bears the bastard's brat."

The laughter must have roiled forth from the bowels of hell itself to send Tauren's flesh crawling.

"You won't!" Tauren raised her horror-filled face

from Revan's shoulder and launched herself across the coach at Chester's surprised face, nails bared. She dug furrows down his pasty cheeks before he could react and shove her back against the other seat. Revan scuffled with the hideous Meeks, and the last thing Tauren saw was Chester's contorted face and his fist slamming toward her head.

Thirty-Two

"Where is she?" Holt demanded, his face darkening dangerously beneath his broad-brimmed black hat.

Murdock's distraught shake of head was the only response, and he stared at the young houseman, Ransom, then at the servants assembled in the great hall. None would—could—meet his eye.

His heavy black cloak swirled closely about his lean body as he stormed up the stairs and about the gallery to the ducal chambers. Roxie sat in a miserable huddle before the fire of the bedchamber, her face red and swollen.

"Where did she go?" Holt grabbed the girl by the arm and glowered into her retreating face.

"She didn't say, Master Holt—honest. Only took her pouch of herbs, filled heavy."

"Was she angry, upset?"

"Yea, she . . . snapped at me and argued with His Grace."

"Anything you know," Holt commanded. "Think, girl."

He eased his tight hold on Roxie's arm and clamped a tighter rein on his anger.

"I don't know . . . but night before last she asked the way to Lord Chester's house, said it weren't for no reason . . . she only wondered. Then they were gone for a ride to see to an ailin' farmer, she said . . . her and His Grace."

But Holt was at the door and through it.

The great house was hushed, expectant, when Holt and Calder had returned from their grueling ride to be met by Murdock and Haldan with the news that Tauren and Revan had ridden out yesterday morning and had not returned. Now Murdock's only other information was that Tauren had spent some time in the library and seemed out of sorts, distracted, when she sent for Revan and ordered horses made ready.

A suspicion and a quick look at the broken locks of his desk drawers confirmed his fear. He had forgotten to lock the desk a few days ago and now he knew Tauren had found that which he held secret for so long. And she had fled, taking Revan with her, the little fool!

He joined Calder and a tight-lipped Haldan in the great hall, avoiding Calder's righteously accusing stare.

"Roxie says she asked the way to Enderfield . . . it's all we have. Calder I must put the plan into action now. You'll stay here and—"

"The hell, I will!" Calder bellowed. "I'll not be stuck off here like— Let the vicar here handle yer clerk work. I go with ye! Ye might need a blade at yer back!"

"Clerk!" Haldan growled, reaching for the hilt of his

442

ever-present blade. "Not while there be a chance for a bit of swordplay. Let me lady here do whatever it is ye yammer on about. I be ridin' with ye."

Holt closed his eyes briefly as he assembled his fatigued wit. "I'll need three of your men," he directed Calder. "Set the rest at Murdock's call for handling the wagons and carts. Murdock, we'll need three days' provisions and oats for the horses." She nodded tightly as he turned a grave face to her.

"I know you have not approved of this and now I must ask you to—"

Her upraised hand stopped him and her gray eyes were filled with caring born of their long history. "It will be done as you've said. Rest your mind on that. Go with God, Holt. . . . Find the duke and your wife."

Tauren awakened shaking with cold, and the unremitting blackness all about her made her doubt her senses. She lay on coarse ticking, straw-filled from the musty smell of it. She ventured a trembling hand out beside her until she found the edge of her support. She ran her fingers along it . . . a rope and post bed. And over her, a coarse woolen blanket that did little to relieve the cold.

She sat up slowly, testing the blackness above her with a waving arm until she was sure no barrier existed immediately above her. She pulled the blanket tight about her and curled her quaking legs up under her. Her hands went to her abdomen and she felt the little mound with pure relief.

She had only to blink in the blackness to recall how

443

she came to be here and to experience the full terror of her predicament.

"Revan?" she called out hopefully, but was answered with uninterrupted silence after the last fluttery echo of her own voice died away. They had been separated. She bit her lip to keep from crying out.

The metallic scrape of a key in a lock froze her. A dusky slice of light appeared around a doorway not ten feet from her. Light from several candles nearly blinded her, and she threw up one arm to shield her eyes.

"So, you are awake at last." It was the voice of Chester, and Tauren was aware of a certain relief that it was not the hideous Meeks that came to . . .

"I've brought you a tray." He admitted a hunched and ragged old man who deposited a tray of food on the stone floor and then shuffled out, closing the heavy door that was the only break in the solid stone walls of the chamber. She glanced warily about her, at her prison, while keeping a sullen eye on the traitorous baron. He sat down on a low, three-legged stool.

"Your disposition has improved somewhat." He sent one hand to his red-streaked face and his mouth tightened. "I am here to announce your fate."

"Where are we?" she uttered hoarsely, wetting her dry lips and realizing her need for the liquid in the pitcher on the tray.

"The Earl of Sappington's estate. A safe haven until I am made your brother's guardian and have married his widowed sister." He waited a moment for the words to register on her face. "No doubt your husband will come for you and the boy; we have planned a misfortune for him . . . a fatal encounter. We have already dispatched to London the evidence of his crimes you so providentially provided. When he dies it shall be as an outlaw—and one who has barbarically murdered the Lady Glynis of Greers, my wife. After a decent interval, the poor victims will marry and console one another." He rose and grabbed her up from the cot.

"You will consent to marry me, or your dear brother shall die . . . and before your eyes."

She managed to spit into his florid face, and he pushed her away violently.

"You stupid slut!"

"Did you forget that I carry his child?" she snapped.

Chester wiped the spittle from his scarlet-scarred cheek, and his frame trembled with unvented rage. "I trust, by then Esmond will have relieved you of that odious burden." He stomped out, slamming and locking the massive door behind him.

Tauren's cramping legs gave way and she crumpled into a heap on the cot.

Holt and Haldan covered the distance to Enderfield in one-third the time it had taken Tauren and Revan. Fearing they might have already fled, Holt had sent Calder and three of his men off on the London road from Lindengreen with instructions to stop all travelers for news of them. The overlord and the vicar now slowed their horses to a fast walk as they approached the gates of Enderfield.

Suddenly, there was a thundering of hooves and a cacophony of shouts about them as a dozen riders

445

appeared from nowhere, blades drawn. In only a moment, Holt recognized the threat for the ambush it was and shouted to Haldan who was already drawing his formidable weapon.

When the first riders reached them, they were met with blue-honed steel and experience, and two attackers dangled uselessly from their mounts before the others could press in. The clang of steel, the snorting and rearing of horses, the muscle-wrenching swings and jarring blows—it was battle again. Holt fought to his right, his horse jammed against Haldan's sturdy mount, and Haldan brandished his blade in his left hand as effectively as most men could with their right.

Four attackers had been dispatched when one dismounted and darted in to slash the rear legs of Holt's mount, sending it screaming and thrashing to the ground. Holt quickly regained his footing, and in moments, Haldan was at his back, praying loudly and slashing savagely in the fray.

They were pressed on all sides by the hireling cutthroats whose bladework was no match for Holt or Haldan taken singly, or even in twos. But, as a force, they would wear down two lone men, however skilled. Holt took a sword tip along his cheek, and the pain spurred him on, teeth gritted, to slice into the mercenary responsible.

"Riders!" one ambusher yelled to the others, and the furious pace of the attack eased as each of the paid assassins weighed the value of his own life against the few farthings they were being paid. The two still mounted kicked their horses into a gallop and were soon beyond reach, riding north. The others, six in all, fought on even when Calder and his men rushed headlong to attack their rear from horseback.

For a few moments the little valley rang with steel, and the screams of horses frightened by the smell of blood. When it was over, Holt stood for some time, unable to clear his ringing ears of the sounds or his mind of the gore of battle.

Calder lay a firm hand on his shoulder and dragged him away. Holt looked at his friend, and between them was the silent acknowledgment of all that men can be to each other as they lay down their lives for one another in battle.

The captain reached inside his spattered doublet and pulled out a packet of documents. "He was sendin' them to London—we found the courier first. They blame ye for the death of Lady Glynis, Chester's wife. No doubt it was their next job." His head indicated the inert forms of the thugs. "And they charge ye with theft of a treasonous nature—the young duke's estate."

"Where are they?" Holt's eyes lit anew with angry fires. He had much to settle with his wife and with the opportunistic baron.

"Chester took them to . . . Sappington's estate."

"Sappington's?" Holt scowled his disbelief. "Whatever for? He's—"

"Esmond is back . . . made the new earl."

Holt blanched, and his stomach turned over at the thought of Tauren and Revan in that madman's house. The degenerate had sworn revenge on the overlord; and now he had the cruelest possible means to extract his vengeance. Whatever Holt's anger at his wife and her distrust of him, his concern for her safety and for their child would override it.

"We have no time to lose."

Tauren prayed earnestly, not knowing what to pray for . . . except deliverance. She had doused all but one candle in the battered candelabra to save them for the interminable darkness ahead. And in that gentle golden flame she searched for hope.

There was no one to rescue them, save the king, and from Chester's letters he would think them cosseted and well cared for. Holt— She winced and bit her lip trying in vain to shove aside the memories of him—of them together. Heaven help her, she could not stop hoping he escaped the country before Chester's treachery caught him. He was no murderer. . . .

Guiltily she recalled her vivid imaginings of Holt's plans, perhaps even a convenient death. . . . They seemed pathetic now. Fleeing him, she had experienced true evil, real greed and debasement. She knew that by comparison, Holt's raw exercise of power and high-handed dealings were almost saintly. Perhaps if she had told him about the babe . . . No. That would not have changed what he had done, his betrayal of the trust, the love she had given him.

Likely Holt would think them cozy beneath the king's standard and seize the chance to flee the country . . . to enjoy his looted treasure. There was naught to hold him once he returned and realized he'd been discovered. Again, she could not bring herself to think of him captured and executed . . . on her distorted word.

Her tears had been shed already, but she sat for a long while in the midst of her poor bed cradling her abdomen in her arms, bereft of all feeling.

The key sounded in the lock, and Tauren jerked around to stare into the dreadful countenance of Esmond Meeks.

Thirty-Three

The fine drizzle falling about the neglected hall of Sappington's estate wet the faces of those who hid nearby in a dark grove of bare trees. Holt pulled his cloak up tighter about his throat and wiped his dripping chin with one rough movement. He glanced at the men who also awaited the signal from the silent manor house.

Haldan and Calder scouted the hall while Holt waited in the miserable cold rain and his innards roiled at the thought of what might even now be taking place in that cursed den. The limp, brutalized forms of two young girls rose before his mind's eye to torment him afresh. His wife, his child . . .

"There 'tis," came a relieved voice from his right and instantly he was in motion. His men followed on unspurred boots; to wagon, to barrels, to stone fence. One by one they slipped into an open door at the rear of the house, where moments before the signal had appeared. Haldan pulled them into what appeared to be a servants' pantry, empty of all but stale air

450

and litter.

"We haven't found them yet, likely they're well hid. Calder is searching upstairs," the vicar announced hastily.

"How many?" Holt peeled the sodden cloak from his shoulders.

"Six—and Chester. Square enough odds. The way they loll in the kitchens they don't expect trouble."

Holt's eyes burned amidst dark, sleepless rings, and he ran one bronzed hand back over his damp hair.

"You take the ones in the kitchens," he ordered Haldan and the cavaliers. "Then find me when you're through. I'll be wherever Chester and Meeks are."

Revan turned his raw wrists beneath the stiff, new ropes that bound him to a rough-hewn chair in the empty hall of Sappington's house. The bonds grew tighter with each struggle. He breathed out heavily, his young face a study in defiance.

"You need not suffer this indignity, Your Grace," Chester taunted. "If you would come to your senses, agree to abide peaceably under my terms, you could be free of those crude restraints."

"Strut while you can, Chester." Revan leveled an intensely hostile glare at the lord, catching the baron off balance for an instant.

The boy has grown much in the last year, Chester mused; he is no longer the malleable young whelp I escorted south to Somerset . . . Reston's influence, no doubt.

"Be reasonable." Chester approached him slowly, his bootheels clacking ominously on the bare stones of the floor of the empty hall. "There is more than your own comfort to consider. . . ."

"If that monster harms Tauren in any way, I'll see you both dead, I swear it!" Revan's gray eyes seemed paler, icy, and his low voice sent vibrations of warning through the treacherous nobleman.

"Your cooperation could procure her safety. I have no desire to see your lovely sister harmed."

"That is well." A deep voice echoed about the hollow chamber, sending the baron's flesh crawling. "Your very life depends upon her safety."

The baron whirled and reached for the blade he had carelessly tossed on the planking table nearby. The action produced a macabre, magnified laugh that Revan recognized and welcomed, though it made the hair on the back of his neck rise.

Holt swung down from the railing of the old musicians' gallery above them to stand squarely between Chester and Revan, a dark specter of retribution.

"Holt!" Revan called out his relief.

"Meeks! Cartiers! Jenkins!" Chester shouted, backing away as he handled his steel uneasily. Too well he knew the ramifications of Holt's startling appearance. His plans were discovered. . . .

"Meeks may come—and let him—but I will finish what was started years ago. Your hirelings are even now in contest for their own skins; they'll give you no heed. You have only yourself to count on."

"You're an outlaw, Reston—a thief and a murderer. Killing you will only add spice to my acquisition of Lindengreen."

"Murderer?" Holt laughed steadily and without mirth. "Nay, Lady Glynis is quite alive and soon to become your widow instead of your victim." Seeing Chester's eyes widen, Holt pressed on. "We found your messenger." He made visible the packet of rolled documents tucked inside his doublet and brandished his blade in lazy, menacing circles.

Chester swallowed hard, his sallow face draining of its meager color as he searched the doorways for aid. None was forthcoming and he began to stalk the exit.

"I hoped you'd come," Revan pronounced in a choked voice. "Esmond Meeks has Tauren somewhere. . . ."

Holt's face hardened into dusky granite, and with a careful slice of his blade on each rope, Revan's arms were free. Chester saw his chance and darted toward the arched doorway behind him.

"Nay," Holt snarled and lunged forward viciously, halting Chester's retreat. "You've come to a reckoning, coward."

The cornered baron brought his face and his blade up together, jolting into action and whipping at Holt while his skin flushed to match the crimson streaks down his face.

Revan was standing now, rubbing his cold limbs as he watched the struggle anxiously.

"Find Tauren!" Holt ordered over his shoulder. Revan bolted toward a small arched door tucked away near the corner of the hall, and Holt marked it mentally.

The baron's flaccid face and mincing manner belied the force and stamina of his lanky frame. Holt drew on

453

every shred of skill and experience he possessed, knowing what danger lay in underestimating an opponent.

They thrust and slashed, parried, and dodged. There was nothing in the barnlike hall to put between them, and they came at each other full out, each man keenly aware of what was at stake. Both pulled on their reserves, and there was no time for draining talk.

Suddenly Holt lunged, missing Chester's chest by a hair's breadth and slamming into his blade. Their weapons were hilt to hilt, and their faces were very close. Whatever Chester saw in the overlord's strange eyes, it unnerved him for an instant and as they shoved apart, the ambitious baron felt a cold draft of air flooding up and about him. Sweat beaded on his forehead as he recognized the chilling swirl of death about him.

Holt read the lord's face with seasoned judgment and in a feinting move to the right, drew Chester's lame parry as he reversed direction to sink his blade deep into the baron's chest.

Holt was panting, the red that obscured his vision lifting. His jaw set grimly as he darted for the doorway where Revan had disappeared minutes before. The passage was narrow and ill lit, but he moved along it swiftly, guided by his hands and by the echo of his own footfalls.

A sudden downward slope took him by surprise, but he maintained his footing and continued to feel his way along. His heart pounded in his head, and his mouth was dry with the dread of what might await him.

A golden shaft of light split the gloom, and he hurried toward an open doorway, slowing to approach cautiously.

"There you are, bastard!" came an ugly, rasping voice as Holt flattened himself against the wall by the open portal. "Do come in. I've awaited this meeting for a long time."

Holt whirled into the doorway, braced for attack, sword moving eagerly. Revan lay sprawled on the floor, senseless, and Meeks stood in the center of the stone-lined chamber, holding Tauren with her back against him, a knife blade pressed to her throat. Bile rose in Holt's throat at the ravaged, mute plea of his wife's face. She had a bruise on her chin and another beginning on her jaw; her eyes seemed glazed with terror or pain. Her gown was ripped from one shoulder to her waist, baring one shivering breast.

"Whoreson!" Holt exploded. "You'll die this time! Chester has already tasted my retribution!"

"*No*!" Meeks warned, pressing the blade tighter against Tauren's pale flesh. "Press me and she'll bleed slowly!"

Holt's growl of rage reverberated about the chamber, and a slight trickle of crimson showed down the column of her throat.

"I warned you, Reston," Meeks exulted in this perverse, long-savored vengeance. "For each step you make I'll open your little whore's throat wider!"

"Murdering slime! I should have killed you then . . . but I'll see the job done now."

"*Holt*!" Tauren's agonized face stopped him, wrenching his stomach sharply. "Take Revan . . . and go. . . . Please!"

Holt stood, feeling some of the rage draining from him, and again allowed his reason to dictate his course. Tauren's blue eyes were glazing gray, and Holt's arms twitched for action. He lowered his blade and rolled

Revan over, noting a small lump had appeared on his left temple. Holt raised Revan up and onto his broad shoulder, and paused in the doorway.

"I'll be wherever you are," he warned the one and promised the other. "Watch for me."

Tauren nearly screamed as his large form disappeared into the darkness beyond the threshold. As Holt's footfalls receded into terrifying silence, Meeks listened too; then from the befouled depths of his soul came an eerie laugh as he loosened his grip on her benumbed arms.

"Now, slut, *move*! I would finish it here, but you will buy me safe passage awhile longer. *Move*!" He shoved her forward again, still holding one arm and resting a dagger's point at the side of her throat.

The next moments in the darkened passage, feeling death's breath upon her shoulders, Tauren suffered the torments of hell itself. Meeks forced her along before him, alternately shoving and dragging her, banging her against the cold stone walls as they groped along.

Revan is safe, she repeated over and over in her mind so that it became a chant. Holt will not harm him. . . . But now she would pay for his freedom with her own life . . . and that of her unborn babe—Holt's child. She choked back a sob and Meeks laughed at this sign of distress as he pushed her onward.

The dim night seemed like midday as they emerged from the black tunnel into the quagmire of the unpaved rear yard. Meeks cursed savagely as she stumbled before him. Her shoes were sucked so deep into the mud that she lost one. He pushed her onward, jerking her by the arm to change course until they neared an outbuilding.

Meeks shoved Tauren into the little-used stable and called out to someone. He waited testily for the response and when no sound broke the expectant silence, he cursed again.

"Here, bitch." He shoved her against a post and tied her hands with a ragged rope he found hanging nearby, securing her to the post by the free end. Hurriedly, he saddled a horse, watching over his shoulder as he worked. Tauren's heart stopped. If he meant to keep her alive for long, he would take two horses.

An odd jumble of desperately final thoughts bombarded her, and in their chaos she found a curious calm settling over her. She did not resist further when he undid her tether and pushed her toward the beast. She was numb, a spectator.

A howl of rage like an ancient battle cry rattled the timbers of the decrepit stable. Without looking Tauren knew its source. Holt materialized from the blackness of the doorway, a fearsome spectator bent on vengeance.

"Meeks!" he thundered and his scarlet-stained steel hissed eagerly in the air between them.

A rushing explosion of fury knocked Tauren back and she staggered, her bound hands unable to balance her. She fell against something strangely hard and soft, something that engulfed her in its blackness.

Her scream clotted in her throat as she struggled against the force that half-lifted, half-dragged her away from the sound of scuffling, the clanging, and the guttural sounds of blade battle.

"Merciful Heaven!" came a muffled, but recognizable exclamation, and Tauren tussled to right herself on her feet, shoving against her odd support to stare up into Haldan's red, fleshy face. For a moment the pandemonium about them bombarded her senses and rendered her incapable of response. The sturdy cleric clasped her to him and worked at the ropes at her wrists. She buried her face in his chest, and he dragged her along with him, away from the fighting.

When she tried to halt him to look back, he turned her about sharply and pulled her onward. "Nay, lass, ye do not want to see it. Be ye all right?" He stroked her wet, disheveled hair.

She tried to nod but could scarcely move in the vicar's tight hold. All she could think was that she was safe in arms like her father's, smelling the musk of wet clerical wool that had always meant security to her. She clung tightly to him, and he pulled his cloak over her quaking shoulders.

"By the saints, woman, ye had us worried out of our wits!" Haldan uttered, a strange tightness in his voice.

"Revan?" she managed.

"Safe enough, I trow. Holt's taking care of Meeks proper." For a moment both listened to the strangely singular sound of rain dripping into puddles by the open door. There was nothing else to be heard. "'Tis finished then."

Tauren pushed violently away from the surprised Haldan and was out into the mired yard, running toward the house. Revan! She must get to Revan. . . .

Holt caught her halfway across the field of mud and jerked her about to face him. In the dim light he could make out little of her state, but she shrank from him and twisted in his grasp as he tried to draw her to him.

"Let me go!" She sprang to life and grappled earnestly for her freedom.

"Tauren!" he warned and shook her. But he ceased abruptly and stooped to jerk her off her feet, lifting her up into his arms to cradle her against him. Wary of her anger, he caught her one free arm and pinned it to her side with one hand as he strode for the house.

Just inside the doorway near the servants' pantry Holt set Tauren on her feet, ignoring her struggles to make a thorough inspection of her in the dim light. He touched the small bruises on her chin and jaw, and glowered as she pulled back furiously. He could not have known the pain his gentle fingers inflicted was felt most deeply in her heart.

"Why did you bother, overlord?" she lashed out. "We were little enough threat to you. You were free of us. Chester and Meeks would have saved you the trouble—"

"Tauren . . ." Holt warned, his eyes glittering angrily. His grip on her shoulders tightened.

"What have you done with Revan?" she demanded.

"The boy is well enough," Holt bit out. "Fortunately, your friends were not as thorough as I am."

"Then you've come to finish the job yourself!" Tauren slipped beyond all reason, finally conquered by the pain and terror of her ordeal.

"Stop it!" he commanded, giving her a shake and scarcely keeping his frayed temper in bounds. He turned her abruptly and dragged her by one arm along the hall to shove her into a small room and close the door behind them. He fumbled for a candle and set flint to steel to light it, holding it up to view her.

"You?" he demanded. "You've not been harmed?" His eyes were dark as they fell across her half-bare breast to her waist.

Tauren lifted her chin defiantly and clasped her arms across her shoulders to shield herself from his appraising stare. When he drew the candle back, she was jolted by the lines of fatigue in his face and the deep, bruised circles about his eyes. His raven hair was wet and rumpled and his chin bore several days' beard.

"What will you do with us now?" Tauren grimaced with self-loathing at her impulsive concern for him. Why was she unable to despise him wholly after all he had done to them?

"You'll know when the time is right. You're in no fit state to reason with, and I'm in no state to attempt it."

"Thanks to you." Tauren's blue eyes filled with sparks.

"Nay, I'll not take credit for what you brought on yourself, running straight into that degenerate's arms."

"I sought Chester's help to petition the king . . . to see the lands and treasures you stole from Revan restored to him."

"To be restored, they must first be lost. His inheritance is—has always been—secure," Holt contended.

"In your pocket!' she charged anew. "You said it over and over; the shire is yours. You boasted you always get what you want . . . why didn't I listen!" She steadied herself against the bare, dusty shelves of the abandoned storeroom. "You were stealing Revan blind all the while you were mewling about and cajoling me into trusting you. I let my feelings for you lure me into your snare. I trusted you, and you took everything we had . . . now perhaps our very lives!"

Holt's fists clenched at his sides, and that same angry muscle in his jaw jumped furiously. His voice was low and threatening. "I have stolen nothing. You did not come to ask me to explain the documents you pilfered . . . you tried me and your precious wounded pride condemned me. Contrary to your fevered little mind, not only Wincantons can have a noble motive."

"You lie." Tauren gritted her teeth. "The facts speak plainly for themselves. You sold off parts of Lindengreen and stripped the old hall. Small wonder we never saw any of the family jewels."

"There is an explanation, one I would have given freely if you had trusted me enough to ask."

Tauren's laugh was thin and bitter, evidence of her tautly stretched endurance. "What do you plan for us now, overlord? Exile? Imprisonment?"

"Good God, Tauren, you go too far!" He pounded one fist against the beam supporting the shelves and set it to rattling. "What have I done to make you hate me so?" His voice was hard now but had lost some of its anger, and his eyes seemed to dull.

"I did not tell you of my plans because after Auden's visit I was not yet convinced I had your trust. In that I see I was right. Do you believe me so depraved as to destroy my wife and unborn child for a few gold farthings?" He paused and his eyes seemed to penetrate her cold shell to reach the heat of her anger beneath. His shoulders seemed to slope a bit more and his jaw set grimly. "If you loathe and mistrust me so; then it is indeed a bitter thing I have done to us all." A dark swirl of his cloak moved the air about her as he left, and she heard the key click in the lock.

Tauren stood looking after him, aching, as if some vital part of her was ripped away. She knew with certainty the source of that poignant pain which began

461

the instant he touched her. How could she still love a man who misused her to gain power over her lonely, vulnerable brother and his wealth? He had not denied it—could not—and pretended her ignorance of it was due to a flaw in her!

Her legs gave way and she gripped the shelves beside her as she slid down to the floor.

Thirty-Four

An hour later two young cavaliers appeared at the door of her temporary prison. They lifted her gently and wrapped her in her own warm cloak, meeting her half-coherent queries with embarrassed silence. The stout young sergeant lifted her into his arms and carried her from the house to Chester's waiting coach. Carefully he settled her silent form among the furs and lap robes, asking after her comfort before he closed the door. There had been no sign of Revan nor Haldan, nor the overlord.

Men's muffled voices and the snort and movement of horses meant her escort had mounted. The coach lurched forward, and Tauren found her eyes dry and burning with unshed tears. A brazier of hot coals sat near her feet, dispelling some of the chill and dampness. As she warmed, her tensed, aching muscles relaxed and she fell into an exhausted state of unconsciousness that approximated sleep.

*   *   *

Tauren roused when strong arms lifted her from her hard pallet and bore her out into daylight and salty air. A confusion of light and sounds assaulted her and she squinted and shielded her eyes with one arm. The same young sergeant now carried her along a stone street that was steps away from a wharf. She was lost momentarily, confused by the bustle in the street, and she stared wonderingly at the great, silent hulks of ships berthed all about the harbor.

Alarm filled her. "I can walk sir, unless you fear I'll try an escape."

The sergeant stopped at once and set her on her feet. "Sure you can walk, milady?" His expression was solicitous and apologetic at the same time.

"Yea," she answered tersely, her mouth unbearably dry. She winced as one stocking-clad foot hit the cold pavingstone of the street. She looked up and scanned the wharf where they stood.

"Where are we? Where are you taking me?"

"Here, milady." Her escort took her arm and gently urged her forward to the plank gangway of a large ship which throbbed with activity. "'Tis Portsmouth, ma'am. You'll be safe enough here."

"Safe?" Tauren turned a cold eye upon the sergeant who again took her elbow to usher her along. She noted for the first time that three more of Calder's men encircled them at a distance as they walked and each man grasped his sword hilt in readiness.

"Is he so unsure of himself that he sends a regiment to guard a mere woman?" She stopped halfway up the gangway and faced her guard. "I'll not go a step farther until I know where I'm being sent. What hellhole has he planned to hide me in? Where has he taken the duke?"

"I cannot say, milady. If you will not go, I shall have to carry you."

The sergeant's face was heavy with determination and not a little regret. Tauren's fatigue and consuming thirst and hunger conspired to dissuade her from a fiery response. She turned and mounted the gangway.

She was shown to a comfortable cabin where a cheery fire burned in a small iron stove. The quarters were paneled with mahogany and furnished with a heavy, eye-pleasing table, spindle-back chairs, and a mahogany and marble washstand. The deck was highly polished, and near the wide, built-in bed it was covered with a thick woolen rug containing all of nature's own pallet of color. Two generous, beveled and leaded portholes looked out over the harbor and admitted plentiful light. Another time, she might have been delighted with such comfortable accommodations; now she could only stare disbelievingly at them. She turned to her escort, but he was gone and the lock clicked softly behind him.

Tauren kicked off her remaining slipper and threw it violently against the stoic door. Taking a deep breath, she collected herself and removed her cloak. Before the stove, she warmed her hands and stared down at her ripped and mud-spattered gown. Any activity would work a charm against the tears that threatened to flow again, so she set about warming water and soon washed the dried blood from her throat and continued on to her feet and stockings.

Possibilities paraded through her thoughts relentlessly. Always, Holt's impenetrable face appeared to awaken that unbearable ache in her chest . . . and so she forced her thoughts away from him, exploring the

465

shelves and furnishings of the cabin instead.

Soon the door opened to admit a bent little man in rough sea garb. He carried a tray of plenteous, good food and warmed wine. After he was gone Tauren attacked the sumptuous fare voraciously, groaning with relief and pleasure. At least she would not be starved.

Having satisfied her thirst and hunger, she crawled up into the midst of the wide bunk and pulled a heavy down comforter up over her. Instantly she was asleep.

How long she slept, she could not know, but it was dark when she was roused by thumping and banging in the companionway outside her door. She fumbled to light an oil lamp and watched with amazement as two of old Jerome's beautiful chests were carried in by her escorts. When the doorlatch clicked behind them, Tauren rushed to kneel before one and turned the key in its lock.

It was filled with her clothing, carefully tended and neatly organized. She felt a warm flood of relief to have some of her things about her. She stroked the heavy velvet of her fur-lined dressing gown. Now she could rid herself of this cursed rag that bore so many hateful memories.

Her joy was short-lived, however. The second trunk bore a somber cargo of black woolens that sent her back on her heels in angry confusion. What were *his* things doing here . . . brought to her?

Furiously, she pulled the Puritan doublets and breeches from the chest and stood, searching the cabin for some means of destruction. Failing to locate a sharp knife or a pair of shears, she turned to the stove and her hand was on the iron handle before she paused to think. There would be much smoke. She turned to the portholes and opened one to stare down at the night-blackened water lapping below. Out they went, the whole armload and she flew to the chest for the rest, disposing of them in like manner.

The black in the trunk soon gave way to lush sendal greens, rich amber, and soft sable browns that stopped Tauren's destructive binge. These were the clothes she had covertly ordered made for Holt. They seemed the embodiment of all she had hoped for, of all that had proven false. She slammed the lid of the trunk down to blot out the sight. Her throat tightened and she fled to the comfort of the wide bed.

The next day passed with excruciating slowness in Tauren's shipboard prison. She was well fed and given the unbelievable luxury of a full tub of hot water for bathing and washing her hair. She slept long and soundly, the rest renewing her strength though not her temper.

The morning of the second day she stood by the square-paned porthole, staring out into the moving harbor. It took her a long moment to realize that the unsteadiness of the floor beneath her feet and the changing relative positions of the ships berthed nearby signaled that they were underway. She steadied herself by the porthole, feeling despair flood through her. In her anger with Holt, wielding her sharp tongue, she had failed to learn where he was keeping Revan and what his plans for them were. The ship might even now be putting distance between them. . . .

Revan had needed—trusted her, and she had failed

him. She had wanted them both—Holt and Revan. Holt's open assault on her heart was masterfully executed, though one-tenth the effort would have sufficed. He had claimed her well before she had surrendered to him, but she had no right to love him, then or now.

Her hand went to the budding roundness of her belly. At least he knew of the babe's existence. Perhaps his dealings with her would be tempered by some consideration for what he knew to be his child. As she turned back to the wooden chair by the little square stove, she felt a curious, fluttery affirmation in her womb. Her eyes misted, and she wrapped her arms across her belly to cradle and comfort them both.

The key clicked dully in the lock later that same morning. Tauren turned, expecting the cabin boy who usually brought her meals, water, and fuel for the stove. She drew her emerald, fur-lined dressing gown closer about her and rose, her word of greeting dying on her lips.

"Revan!"

They were in each other's arms, Tauren feeling as though a great weight had been lifted from her heart. She was soaring with relief.

"Let me look at you." She pushed him back, running her fingers through his tousled hair with thorough joy.

"I'm fine, Tauren, truly . . . I am." Revan squirmed under her authoritative attentions and strove to maintain his manly demeanor. "You're looking fit. Do you feel well? I mean, with your . . . condition?"

Tauren radiated pleasure. "I feel fine now that I know you're here and safe. *He* let you come? He does not keep you locked away?" She was suddenly very puzzled.

"Nay, I have the run of the ship." Revan pulled her to a chair near the stove and gently pushed her into it. His young face was serious and his voice deepened impressively. "I have much to tell you . . . some of it you will not like. But hold your judgment until you've heard me out."

Tauren watched him with new uneasiness. "Where have you been these last two days? What's happened to you?"

"I've been with Haldan, Calder, and . . . Holt. Holt explained a lot of this to me, Taurie. It's a bit complicated, and I'm not sure you'll like it. But you'll have to agree it was the best thing to do."

Tauren's blue eyes steeled and her lips became a thin, hard line. "He's sold your lands, Revan."

"But not all of them. All of the original Lindengreen is intact, still mine. He only sold off parts Duke Geoffrey acquired. All were sold with the provision of repurchase or reversion to Lindengreen when the present owner dies."

Tauren's scowl deepened. It was little comfort that she was not the only one beguiled by Holt's manly persuasiveness. "He secreted the funds out of England—with bankers in Amsterdam, Geneva, and Paris. He's pocketed the proceeds, Revan!"

"The accounts were drawn in my name," he responded defensively. "I've seen the documents . . . they're in my cabin, in my possession. It's held in trust for me."

"I cannot believe my ears!" Her face was scarlet as

she grabbed his hands tightly. "Revan, he's sold your lands and disposed of the family heirlooms and jewels."

"He didn't really sell them. Many of them are in the hold of this ship. I saw them. Most of the others are in Lord Cedric's care. I saw the letter Lord Cedric wrote agreeing to safe-keep them."

"Letters may be forged," she charged. How could he be so besotted with the man as to swallow such obvious concoctions? Guilt washed over her anew. She had encouraged Revan by her own ignominious example.

Revan was on his feet and towering above her. "I don't know why you're so set against him, but you're wrong about what he did and why he did it."

"Then where are we going . . . and what assurance do you have that we'll ever reach our destination? What makes you think he's not waiting for the chance to finish—"

"He'd never do anything like that! Holt's a good, honorable man! He saved my life."

"He only wanted to be sure Chester had no chance to accuse him before the king; that's the only reason he 'rescued' us."

"Not then." Revan spread his gangling arms wide with exasperation and paced away and back.

"A year ago, last winter . . . long before the duke died . . . I sneaked out to ride by myself and I fell through the ice on the mill pond near Keenings. Holt was nearby and heard me and pulled me out. He took me to a woman's house in Keenings where they warmed me—saved my life. He bade me tell no one, and I wouldn't tell you now except you're so pigheaded about him. You're his wife, Tauren"—he sounded oddly adult and paternal—"you're supposed to honor and help him."

Tauren stammered and fell silent as her mind whirred and careened. He saved Revan's life! Her hands were white knots on her lap.

"Old Duke Geoffrey and Holt made plans a long time ago. If the king tried to assume guardianship as a royal prerogative, then Holt was to seek aid from his friends in Parliament. But in the end it was a choice between the wolf and the jackal. Even Holt is not strong enough to fight both Charles and a hostile Parliament. The only recourse was to leave England until the quarrel is settled and I can return to claim and wield the power that rightfully belongs to the Duke of Somerset."

Revan stopped and shoved his hands into his pockets for lack of anything better to do with them. His voice was low and uneven. "We're bound for America."

"America!" Tauren's mouth gaped. "Dearest God! It's a wretched, heathen place! Half the colonists die of plague or pestilence . . . the others slowly starve. He's taking us to our death!"

"Tauren!" Revan grabbed her shoulders and shook her. "Listen to me! Holt has bought tracts of land there for me and for himself in a colony chartered to Lord Calvert. It's a going settlement already, and the soil and climate are good. It's his chance to make his own place, to make a home for you and the babe. Don't be so pigheaded, Tauren! He's done it for you!"

When he finished Tauren was stiff, reeling. She stared at him with new and disbelieving eyes. When had he become so adamant and self-possessed? When had he begun to dictate to *her*?

His failure to convince her was reflected in his

flushed face and troubled eyes. "If it will help, I'll bring the documents and maps and deeds. . . ."

She turned her head away and he stopped, unable to fathom why she took this so hard when it was his inheritance at stake. She acted as if she were the one injured. If he could accept it, believe Holt and go on, why couldn't she?

"I don't understand, Taurie—he's your husband."

"Exactly!" She turned on him, eyes flashing anew. "But I'm not the one who forgot it."

Revan frowned and searched for a rebuttal in the scuffed toes of his jackboots. He found nothing to add weight to his argument, and under her piercing gaze, he backed to the door and was gone.

Thirty-Five

Holt opened the unlocked door to Tauren's cabin and bent his head through the doorway, filling the chamber as he straightened. He kicked the paneled door closed behind him, producing a key and blatantly turning the lock. Tauren watched him settle a bottle of wine on the table, noting irritably that his appearance had vastly improved since their last meeting. He wore only a white shirt, open at the neck, his plain black woolen breeches, and his ever-present boots. His face was freshly shaven, and his black hair gleamed with attention. When he faced her, his eyes were bright, no longer ringed from sleeplessness. She felt her stomach drop at the sight of him.

"More light," Holt commanded to no one in particular. When he had set a splint to the dimly glowing brass lantern and transferred the flame to another lamp, he held it up a moment to look at her before hanging it on a notched peg above. He crossed his arms over his chest deliberately, seeming cool and foreign to her.

Tauren stood by the stove in her warmest robe, framed in a chestnut fall of hair. Her blue eyes were tinged with the green of her robe and the brown of her thoughts, making them seem even larger and darker against her creamy skin. Holt's mouth went dry as he stared at her.

"You saw Revan," he both stated and inquired.

"He was here. His performance was admirable. Perhaps he even believes your convenient stories. You will not find me as gullible."

"Nay, I would never use that word to describe you," Holt's forest-dark eyes glittered. "Stubborn, foolish, prideful, ridiculous—those would do well enough."

"Ridiculous, am I? Did you come to insult and degrade me further, overlord? I would have thought you above such mean sport . . . or perhaps not."

"Nay." His face darkened. "I came to talk and just perhaps to reason with you. Charles quits London for Newmarket, where he rallies his forces. The Round-heads of Parliament are gathering a small force nearby; we received word this morning before we sailed. England will soon be at civil war."

"So you say now. And if it is true, why have we not heard of it before this? If your motives were so honorable, why did you conceal all this from us?" Her tone was acid.

Holt leaned toward her, setting his hands to his hips, his face tight with self-control. "We have fought this battle before, Tauren. I will not answer a spurious charge. The old man and I planned for this possibility a full year ago. I had Phineas Pitt himself design and build this ship to stand at our disposal. I worked out a plan to divest the estate of minor holdings and portable wealth to see the young duke would have resources for the future. We planned for the safekeeping of the family heirlooms. I arranged it all to appear as sold so that any seizure of Revan's property in his absence would exclude it."

It all fit, Tauren ground her teeth; it was perfectly in keeping with Holt's self-appointed dominion over the lives of all those he encountered! Her knees weakened suddenly, and she felt she was being swallowed up, surrendering. She countered with the instantaneous rise of both her pride and temper.

"You send us to the *colonies*," she spat, noting with satisfaction that his scowl returned with an added element of puzzlement. "You pack us off into hardship and disease. I am not totally ignorant of the world, overlord! I have heard of these 'death Colonies.'"

"I do not *send* you wife, I *take* you there myself!" Holt exploded. "I will make a new home for us on the land I purchased with my own coin. It is our possession and someday it will be our fortune!"

"*Home!*" she sputtered. "How dare you pretend you did this for my sake—for the sake of building some glorious future! You planned and carried it out without a word of explanation or counsel to your wife . . . you didn't honor or trust me enough to tell me the government was coming down about our very heads! Am I some drooling idiot that you hold me in such contempt? You treat me as you would not the lowliest drudge on Lindengreen."

"Trust you!" The idea struck him like the back of a hand. Trust her . . . Calder had accused him of not trusting her. The sting of truth caused him to redden. "Don't bait me, Tauren."

"And what will you do to me, overlord, that you have not already done?" she choked out, and her face went scarlet. Instinctively she copied his stance, her fists set to her waist. "You called me rightly, overlord. I am the fool. I ceased watching your care of the estates and watched only you. I put my trust in you from the first night I came willingly to you. I was even simple enough to think you might need a wife to share your burdens as well as your bed. But you've never needed anyone . . . and you never will!"

She advanced toward him as hot, angry tears spilled down her flaming face. "You don't want a wife—that's clear. And I won't be your plodding broodmare."

Holt's head swam with startling insight as she advanced on him. That's what this was about? She did not refute his plans, but was angry because he had not trusted her . . . treated her as a true wife. The irony of it hit him, and he grinned—a crooked, bemused expression that he regretted instantly. "Tauren—"

"Get out!" she growled, flinging one hand angrily at the door while she hurried to the great trunk that held his clothing. She surprised him by jerking it open and pulling garments from it to throw at him.

"Take your chattel with you! Find some trull to mend your shirts and warm your bed . . . you'll never share mine again!"

"Tauren," he uttered a low warning, as he caught the clothes she hurled at him and tossed them away. "You're behaving daft, woman. . . . Let me explain."

"*Out!*" she screamed, now beyond pride and reason. "Get out and leave me be!"

Holt turned slightly as if to leave, only the crinkling of his eyes hinting at something else. Then he leaped

476

forward, surprising her and grabbing her to him.

In one whirling, dark instant she was crushed against his unyielding body, her arms trapped uselessly between them. She twisted futilely in his relentless grip, feeling the floor receding from beneath her feet as he lifted her against him.

"Let me go, overlord," she spat. "You'll rue the day you do me violence, I swear it!"

"What will you do to me, wife? Have my heart for dinner? Appeal to your lordly brother? Nay"—he struggled with her over toward the wide bunk—"this will be far simpler. I should have done it sooner."

She tried to kick him but found her heel banged painfully against the wooden edge of the bunk, and then she was falling backward, toppled, followed by Holt's hard body.

A guttural cry escaped her as she wrenched her hands free when Holt caught his own weight to keep from crushing her. Her nails were dangerously close to his face when he recovered enough to catch her wrists and pin them above her shoulders on each side. She struggled on the rumpled blankets, sinking into deeper restriction with each movement. She gritted her teeth and fought for her breath under his massive frame as she panted her threats.

"Liar, cheat . . . you wretched, scheming son of perdition—"

He grunted what passed for a laugh and covered her insults with his mouth. When she tossed her head frantically to break the contact, he followed her movements with uncanny precision until her head was still. His kiss deepened as she quieted and her relaxing limbs elicited a corresponding easing of his rigid body.

Just as he thought she returned his ardor, she brought her teeth together hard on his lower lip, sending him up above her, yelping in pain.

"Dammit!"

"If you take me, overlord, it will be by force." Her eyes glistened with this small triumph.

"You dictate terms to me?" he snapped. "This time you have no place to run. You are my lawful wife and you bear my child. You'll stay here with me as long as it takes. . . ." The purposeful, hard weight of his body and the harder light in his eyes made her know the futility of her continued physical resistance.

"As long as it takes for what?" she jeered.

"Till you believe me and admit your love for me." His face was fierce with determination.

"Love?" she sucked in her breath, fighting the pressure of him even to speak. "You're mad as well as degraded."

"Aye, that's true or I'd have done away with you long before now, wife." There was a sudden twinkle of amusement in his tone, and Tauren slammed her eyes shut against the bold assurance of his perfect, angular face.

She still saw him in her mind's eye, and a shaft of pain went through her as she tried to maintain her shamed anger. The masterful bastard . . . how he enjoyed tormenting her!

"Tauren." He called her name and she felt the unexpected warmth of his voice along every nerve and sinew of her body.

"It's true I had to see Revan away from England, but I chose this new colony of Calvert's because of you." Feeling, rather than seeing her attention to his words, he chose these next ones carefully. "You often accused me of coveting Revan's lands and title. It was true, at first, before I knew you. But from that first day, I wanted you and I knew in time you'd want me. To have you, I had to forfeit Somerset. So I looked about for lands I could make my own, a place where I could build something for myself—and for you."

She opened her eyes and turned her head as far away as possible. She lay motionless beneath him, her aching heart absorbing every word. It would hurt too much to have him again and, knowing what he was capable of, never be able to trust him.

She swallowed back the tears that collected in her throat. How could she still love a man who—

"Tauren." Holt's voice was little more than a rumble that reverberated through them both. He released one of her wrists, and with his work-toughened fingers wiped back a tangled lock of her hair from her face, lingering over its silkiness. Her distant eyes glistened at the corners, and the angry stain of her cheeks subsided into a blush of moist warmth.

The slim column of her neck and throat lay bare to his gaze beneath the strain-parted velvet robe. He let his hand trace its smoothness, pausing over the small greening stain on her left jaw and the small red line on her throat. She did not see him wince at the hurt that had caused it. The perfect symmetry of her profile was at once familiar and yet unnerving to him.

Then for a startling instant he glimpsed and felt fully the frustration of exclusion that seemed to cause her such pain. This excruciatingly intense oneness of feeling astonished him . . . as did his awareness of it. Holt's deepest instincts surfaced, and he sought to close the gulf between them before this tide of feeling was gone.

"Tauren." He repeated her name again, only now with all the wealth of feeling she stirred in him. The strange fullness of his voice lodged in her heart and turned her to him with doubt and determination in her face.

"If I had known how much you love me," he stated solemnly, "I would have done things differently."

It took a full minute for her to respond. "Love you? You callous, arrogant—"

"Deny you love me," he challenged, but this time with a cockeyed grin that creased one hard cheek with that dimpled groove.

"Swindler . . . freebooter . . . fraud—"

"Deny it!" he taunted handsomely.

"How could I love a man who would betray his own family to fatten his filthy purse?"

"You couldn't . . . and you don't. You love me, and I am none of that, as you well know."

Tauren opened her mouth for a hot rebuttal, but the turmoil of her heart and the deep, forest depths of Holt's matchless eyes quelled it before it was even formed. Heaven help her, she could not deny it . . . not with him so tormentingly close and so exquisitely persistent.

Holt bent his dark head to claim her parted lips, and in the soft-hard warmth of that kiss a special sense of oneness that had once begun between them was completed.

"Say it."

"I . . . love you, Holt."

His face nearly split with unabashed delight that

480

contained a measure of triumph. But his kiss was one of pure joy.

Accusations, betrayal, power lust fled like misbegotten minions of estrangement before the greater unity of love's power.

Deeper and deeper into love's bottomless chasm Tauren felt herself falling, unable to check her descent. Holt's big, warm hands on her face and shoulders wove his spell of caring about her so that the falling became like floating and the last traces of anxiousness were drawn from her lovely brow.

Her arms came up hesitantly about him, testing the promise of this accord. Once again the smooth, hard strength of his back comforted her questing hands; once again his heavy, powerful body seemed her gentle protection. She returned his penetrating kisses measure for measure, lost forever to that perverse, prideful maiden that had vexed her for the weakness of loving.

Reluctantly, Holt pulled away from her to move over and beside her. He dropped light kisses on her forehead, temples, and ears as he ran one hand gingerly across her slightly rounded stomach.

"You might have told me, Tauren . . . about the babe. You must have known how I wanted that."

"I was afraid you'd forbid me to go to London at first. Then after . . . I was in no mood to see you add my child to the booty you had already claimed from us."

"*Our* child." Holt's eyes were luminous, dark windows on his soul as he touched her cheek and met her heart in her gaze. "It is hard for me to trust another—any other. I was wrong . . . not in the ends I sought, but in the means."

"I cannot be your wife, Holt, unless you will let me be a part of you as you have become a part of me."

As his answer covered her lips tenderly, she hugged him to her joyously. Her heart swelled to near bursting and she wanted to laugh, sing, cry—all at once.

She grabbed his heated face between her cool hands and pushed him back. He blinked uncertainly at her quick change of state.

"Say it!" she commanded.

"S-say . . . what?" he uttered hoarsely.

"Say *you* love *me!*" An impish glint in her eye brought forth an uncharacteristic redness in his face.

Well, he had demanded such of her and she had given it. He loved her more than life itself . . . what could be changed by admitting it to her?

"I . . . love you, Tauren."

She sat up completely, pushing him up before her. "Say it again!" she commanded, her chest rising and falling quickly as the light in her sky-blue eyes became a familiar wayward gleam.

"I do love you, wife . . . more than anything in my life."

"Then show me." She grabbed the front of his sober linen shirt and pulled it open, sending white, bone buttons flying. Holt gaped in astonishment as she wreaked similar havoc with the frogs of her elegant robe and shrugged it from her shoulders. Clad only in a thin chemise, she tucked her feet under her and shook her tousled mass of hair about her. He could not move.

"Have you forgotten how?" She grabbed the collar of his shirt and pushed it back and down over his shoulders, binding his muscular arms at his sides. Her fingers left the fabric to trace a tantalizing path about his arms and across his bare ribs. Her palms drew lazy, inviting circles up from his lean stomach and across the furry hardness of his chest.

The shirt was hopeless by the time it hit the floor, followed quickly by heavy boots and somber black breeches.

Tauren opened her arms to her husband and laughed exultantly as he filled them. He lowered her to the bed once more, his hands eager upon her.

Heedless of the damp chill invading the secure cabin, they arched and pressed together, legs intertwined and arms embracing; their only heat born of loving. Their curves and contours, flesh on bare flesh, molded in candescent synchrony.

Holt left her fragrant mouth to spend small kisses on every inch of her face and throat. Then Tauren nuzzled the base of his throat, kissed his ear and the square of his jaw. When he tenderly caressed each breast she wrapped her fingers through his thick hair and brought his kisses lower, moaning sharply when he captured the rose-tipped treasures she offered him.

She wriggled exotically under his touch and giggled wantonly at the effects of her movements on him. They came together joyfully, as if discovering—reveling—in each other for the first time. They stroked, tickled, and laughed, celebrating the revelation of their love.

Intimate play soon gave way to more serious endeavor as their kisses grew longer and sweeter. Holt's hands grew hot upon her thighs and curving waist. She guided him above her eagerly and her rounded hips surged upward to meet his.

Their eyes met and in all their loving never parted, each feeling this subtle and splendid communion more intimate than the sensual feasting of their bodies. There was no reserve in either of them, only the desire to join, to love uncautiously. Their primal rhythm exploded into searing heat and dazzling light, obscuring all but the image of each beloved's face.

Tauren curled against Holt, listening to the slowing rhythms of his body as they echoed her own. A small shiver raised her flesh, and Holt quickly pulled a heavy comforter over them, garnering a murmur of thanks and a small hug. Never had she felt such contentment.

"Say it again," she asked sleepily.

Holt smiled and pulled her into his arms, resting his chin on the top of her head. "I love you, Tauren. You are precious to me above all else." His brow ceased. "I died a thousand times over, imagining you tortured or abused."

She stopped his words with her hand. "It is over. We have a new life before us. Let's not look back." Her faced turned up to him, and she drew back a bit, resting her head on his arm. Her eyes crinkled suspiciously. "I demand an accounting, Holt Reston. I want to know everything you know about this wilderness you've decreed my home!"

He tucked her head back under his chin. "It will be wonderful."

"Um-m-m," she murmured, "no doubt. Tell me."

"Um-m-m," Holt teased, "tomorrow." His lips found hers again.

The cabin was fully lit by the bright sun streaming in

the portholes when Tauren woke the next morning. The hissing sound from the stove and the soft pad of bare feet on the polished boards told her Holt was up and about. She opened her eyes to witness Holt, fully bare, upended in his huge sea chest. She clapped her hand over her mouth but some sound must have escaped. He was up and about in a flash, his hands full of rumpled velvets and woolens and dangling linen.

She sat up, greeting him with a warm, sleepy smile. "Good morning, husband. Are you not just a bit cold?" She blinked innocently and was rewarded by a dusky flush on Holt's bronze face.

"Where are my clothes?" His exasperation was clear. "And what is all this?" He held up the garments spilling over his hands.

She sat up on her knees and pulled the comforter up about her. "If you mean those miserable black shrouds you wore, they're most likely at the bottom of Portsmouth Harbor. Those 'things'," she pointed to the garments he held, "are your new clothes."

"Portsmouth Harbor!"

"I threw them out." She held her ground, just managing a small, neat expression of contrition. "You will recall, I was quite angry. You're fortunate the new things I had made for you didn't join them." She folded her hands in her lap expectantly, feeling this a test of their new closeness and hoping—believing—they could endure it.

"You tossed my clothes into the water?" he echoed incredulously.

"I thought of burning or shredding them, but giving them a heave seemed quicker." A nervous little smile played on her ripe, dream-blushed lips as she rose from

485

the bunk and reached to the floor for her robe. Aware of his eyes on her body, she took her time with the garment.

"Burning them?" he repeated angrily.

"It was a futile, childish thing to do, I admit—but I had no access to your throat at the time." She paused, feeling his anger was on short rein, and thought it best to apologize. "I'm sorry, Holt."

She stood before him, her large sky-blue eyes entreating him from beneath a canopy of soft, dark lashes, and the luminous softness of her bare skin beckoning from her conveniently parted robe. She pulled a shirt of fine linen from the mass in his hand and held it up for his inspection.

"They're tailored just as you like them . . . only I've added a ruffle or two." She dropped it on the side of the trunk and wrenched free a heavy, quilted doublet of rich brown velvet that was embroidered with flaxen silk. Holding it up to his shoulders, she tilted her head to eye him admiringly.

"These are perfect for you, Holt . . . you'll be so dashing in them." She pressed against his lean body and released the garment so that it was trapped between them. A small, knowing smile curved her lips upward as his whole body tightened with response to her blatant maneuver. "Of course, you're a fine figure of a man just as you are."

"I see why some men take to beating their wives." Holt's voice was frayed and betrayingly husky.

The tension was broken. Tauren laughed and wrapped her arms about his bare waist. He dropped the garments in his hands to follow her lead. His mouth descended on hers voraciously as he clasped her to him.

486

It was a long, productive union, and when it ended, Tauren was certain no clash over mere property, however large or small, would ever part them again.

"You'll get cold," she ran a suggestive hand down over his flanks. "Either dress in your new clothes . . . or . . ."

They laughed together as he made his choice clear and scooped her up into his arms, making straight for their bed.

Thirty-Six

The sapphire sky was dappled with thin, white clouds; and the cold, crisp air was dizzying as Tauren made her way on deck later that morning. She had dressed in a warm, practical woolen dress and had gathered her beaver-lined cloak about her. The cold brought a blush to her cheeks and her eyes sparkled like the unveiled jewels of the sky.

She shielded her eyes from the brightness and surveyed the deck of the long ship from her spot near the hatchway. There were seamen about, seeing to the water barrels, mending sail, and climbing up into the rigging. Above, the great sails of Phineas Pitt's marvelous ship flapped in chorus with the rhythmic beat of the waves against the hull.

An arm slipped about her from behind, and she turned about to find herself secure in Holt's brown-clad embrace. "You've decided to join us at last." He smiled. Tauren felt as though the sun itself was contained in that smile.

"To join *you*," she threaded her arms about his waist and found herself staring up into the unabashedly tender gaze of her enigmatic husband.

"Are ye not just the tiniest bit curious about who ye'll be sharin' this new home with?" came a familiar voice from behind Holt's square shoulder. The tip of a saucy, white plume preceded the scarlet doublet into view.

"Calder! You've come too!" Tauren was out of Holt's arms and into the stout captain's before another word could be uttered. She gave him a resounding hug, then, sensing his courtly discomfort, released him and clasped her hands before her tightly to contain her joy.

"Here, now. Ye'll be making this strappin' great husband of yours jealous. I'd not want to be testin' his generosity with ye too far. 'Tis not conducive to long life." The deep resonant tones and dancing eyes were filled with humor.

"Um-hum," came a féminine voice from behind him.

Calder jumped and put his arm about a dark, petite woman Tauren recognized immediately. "And I'm not a free young buck meself anymore."

"You and Cassie? Married?" Tauren felt a warm wash of pleasure run through her. She had known of his pursuit of the elusive widow, but she had always thought of Calder as immune to such domestication. She shook her head fondly. "It's high time someone took you in hand . . . Cassie's just the one for it."

As she spoke, Haldan exited the hatch and paused to assist someone behind him. Murdock, wrapped in her heavy gray cloak, emerged and took the sturdy vicar's arm, her face beaming girlish pleasure under his close attention. Something in their intimate contact made

489

Tauren's jaw drop, and she reached for Holt's arm, searching his face in astonishment.

"Them too?"

Holt nodded, a roguish twinkle in his eye and a wry curl to his mouth.

"Then, congratulations to you, Haldan, Mistress Murdock . . . er . . . Haldan." Tauren greeted them warmly.

"'Twas part his doing." Haldan nodded amicably at Holt. "He'd only take married folk to this new colony of his . . . and it was just the boost me own manly persuasion needed to make her come about."

"Come about?" Murdock glowed mischievously, seeming years younger. "What makes you think it wasn't me that gave Holt the idea in the first place?"

They all laughed, and in their shared joy, each felt and understood the common bond that would sustain them in the days ahead.

"What other surprises have you in store for me?" Tauren leaned back against Holt's broad chest and tilted her face up to his as he circled her waist again.

"Well, you've a wedding to witness this morn—"

"Wedding? Another? But, who—"

"Roxie and Ransom." Holt grinned, seeing in her brightening eyes the memory of how that started. "She wouldn't let Haldan speak the vows until you stood by her. So we let them come unwedded, but promised. She's been on nettles for three days."

"At least I had a hand in something!" Tauren giggled, snuggling back against her husband. "Are there still others?"

"Old Jerome, the cabinetmaker, and his wife; and Daniel Fahlen, the young smith, with his little wife.

There are three tenant farmers and their wives, and two of Calder's men and their new wives; then we've brought a slew of stores and livestock—and a few horses."

"We're well equipped and prudently manned." Calder spoke up proudly. "Each one has a skill or a trade . . . and nothin' left to run home to."

Tauren gazed mistily up at Holt. "Then old Jerome will have his stand of trees after all."

"Yea." His arms tightened about her. "He'll have his trees, and more."

"Ahoy below!" a familiar voice called from above and Tauren's head snapped up to search the ropes above them. Halfway up the main mast, Revan was clinging to a rope net, waving his free arm, red-faced with exertion and the pride of discovery.

"That's Revan!" Tauren pointed skyward, horrified. "Come down from there!" she shouted angrily, starting for the center deck. Holt held her back and she turned on him. "Let me go. Can't you see that's dangerous? He'll get himself killed."

"Of course it's a bit dangerous." Holt frowned bemusedly, pulling her away from the group, toward the railing. "That's what makes it fun."

"Fun!" she gasped. "Get him down from there or I'll break both your necks myself." How dare Holt be so casual about Revan's safety and her concern!

"Tauren." Holt drew her, protesting, against the rail and held her trapped in his arms as he looked down into her reddened face.

"If you care about him, you'll see to it he doesn't take such foolish risks," she charged.

"I *do* care for him, Tauren . . . like he was a bit of my

491

own. Can't you see that by now? But the lad must have some rein to explore, to risk, or he'll grow up a pampered, fearful weakling. We'll be on board this ship for weeks and he must learn his limits. It won't hurt him to learn to climb a rigging with the deck safely beneath him. Think, Tauren, would you have him always lolling about in his cabin or simpering behind your skirts? He'll need all the spirit and courage we can foster in him for the times ahead. What his destiny may require could destroy him if he is not strong enough to seize and conquer it."

Every word drilled its way into Tauren's heart. She sighed sharply, her rigid shoulders rounding as she leaned against his welcome hardness. "You're . . . right, I suppose. It's just that I've been responsible for him for so long it's hard to . . ."

"To share it with your husband?" Holt's eye twinkled mischievously.

"No— Well . . ." She squirmed under his sympathetic grin.

Holt laughed, that same, charming exuberant sound that always seemed to entrap her will and draw forth her acquiescence.

"You needn't fear, I'll see the whelp through to manhood safely. I'll protect him . . . from even you."

"M-me!" she sputtered.

"Yes, you."

He was enjoying this far too much to suit her and she loaded for a broadside when that grooved dimple in the lean surface of his cheek distracted her, pouring a familiar wave of heat into her limbs.

"It's good, then. Were it left to me, His Noble Grace might not live to see shore again," she mused tartly, then allowed the grin that had been lurking about her mouth to escape.

Holt nodded with the largess of the victor and turned her about to view the awesome spectacle of the sea, keeping his arm about her.

"Why didn't you tell me about the others last evening?" Tauren tilted her head to indicate Calder, Haldan, and Murdock, who now drifted away to seek their own company. "It would have made things much easier."

"So you say now," he chided, "but I'm not so sure. Besides, what we had to settle had naught to do with them—or with plans for a colony. I had to know you cared for me, Tauren, that you could accept and trust me . . . without arguments or evidence. If we're to have a life together, it cannot be on the vouchsafe of another's word. It must be between us alone."

She caught his hand and put its square palm to her cheek. Her eyes were liquid warmth. "You're probably right"—she sighed—"as usual."

He chuckled. "You're probably the only thing I've been consistently wrong about."

"Not always wrong. . . . You were right about the most important things."

"Oh?" He seemed genuinely surprised.

"I love you."

"Yes . . . I was right about that, wasn't I?" His face was smug with delight.

"That, and about the babe . . ." Her lashes fluttered as her face colored sweetly.

Holt raised one brow and grinned crookedly. "And about the babe," he affirmed in low, intimate tones, "I want her to be as beautiful and irresistible as you, and as reasonable as me. . . ."

Tauren's jaw dropped and she pushed against his embrace. But Holt's laughter boomed out across the deck, and he scooped her up into his arms, whirling her about and drawing her deep into the vortex of his love.

PASSIONATE ROMANCE BY PHOEBE CONN

CAPTIVE HEART (1569, $3.95)
The lovely slavegirl Celiese, secretly sent in her mistress's place to wed the much-feared Mylan, found not the cruel savage she expected but a magnificently handsome warrior. With the fire of his touch and his slow, wanton kisses he would take her to ecstasy's searing heights — and would forever possess her CAPTIVE HEART.

ECSTASY'S PARADISE (1460, $3.75)
Meeting the woman he was to escort to her future husband, sea captain Phillip Bradford was astounded. The Swedish beauty was the woman of his dreams, his fantasy come true. But how could he deliver her to another man's bed when he wanted her to warm his own?

SAVAGE FIRE (1397, $3.75)
Innocent, blonde Elizabeth, knowing it was wrong to meet the powerful Seneca warrior Rising Eagle, went to him anyway when the sky darkened. When he drew her into his arms and held her delicate mouth captive beneath his own, she knew they'd never separate — even though their two worlds would try to tear them apart!

LOVE'S ELUSIVE FLAME (1267, $3.75)
Enraptured by his ardent kisses and tantalizing caresses, golden-haired Fláme had found the man of her dreams in the handsome rogue Joaquin. But if he wanted her completely she would have to be his only woman — and he had always taken women whenever he wanted, and not one had ever refused him or pretended to try!